Ming knew s~~he was~~ .... heavy with full trim tabs and requiring climb power to reach the 4800 feet they would need to clear the hills between them and safety. They'd be visible now, a dark mass against the sky.

Then the temperature began to climb. Like it or not, they had to shut the engine down; and fast, before it froze up. A Khmer Rouge bullet had nicked an oil line; it was running out fast.

The pilot started a slow circle, trying to nurse a few more feet out of her over the foothills. Ming went back and took off the door, and was starting forward for the first box of gold when she hit. It wasn't real hard, more like a sloppy landing. The second shock, though, that was the bad one. Ming saw and heard the port wing go as the plane plowed into the trees.

Then, nothing . . .

KHMER GOLD

Hugh McCaffrey

IVY BOOKS • NEW YORK

Ivy Books
Published by Ballantine Books
Copyright © 1988 by Hugh McCaffrey

Library of Congress Catalog Card Number: 87-92146

ISBN-0-8041-0184-1

Manufactured in the United States of America

First Edition: July 1988

To my sister, Anne McCaffrey, who kicked me in the ass until I started to write; and my wife, Kit Ping, who kept me going.

The author is both amazed and gratified that actual events which occurred subsequent to the October 1978 first draft of this story, such as the Vietnamese invasion of Cambodia, tend to confirm the purely imaginary plot and change fiction to faction.

ACKNOWLEDGMENTS

My continuing thanks to the cheerful, friendly staffs of the Wahiawa Public Library and the U.S. Navy Pearl Harbor Library for helping me with my research work.

To M. Sgt. Sid Horsefall, U.S.A., Ret., and his charming wife, Krisana, who contributed nearly one hundred pounds of Thai newspapers, vital maps, and continuing technical editing.

To my daughter, Gwen, for typing semilegible drafts, and to my wife, Kitty, for her patience.

INTRODUCTION

UNTIL THE VIET CONG BEGAN USING THE NORTHEASTERN quarter of Cambodia as a sanctuary in the 1960s, it was a quiet, peaceful little backwater, principally known for Angkor Wat, the ruins of the capital of the ancient Khmer civilization. Sadly, but inevitably, Cambodia was dragged remorselessly into the Vietnam War, despite the best efforts of her politically agile Prince Sihanouk.

By the time the Americans and South Vietnamese invaded this sanctuary in 1970, it contained some three hundred thousand Viet Cong. The Cambodians were powerless to resist their unwelcome guests, so they tolerated them and wished they would go away. But the invasion dragged Cambodia, willy-nilly, into the war. From that point onward, the once peaceful and prosperous country was torn by the opposing forces, including a formerly minuscule "revolutionary" group that called itself the Khmer Rouge (Red Khmers).

Impotent in the 1960s, this group of dissidents was led by a dozen French-educated Communist intellectuals. Their fortunes changed radically when Sihanouk was deposed by a military coup and he retaliated by endorsing the Khmer Rouge in an effort to regain power. Sihanouk's popularity was so great that the Khmer Rouge grew, almost overnight, to a force of tens of thousands. Eagerly welcomed by the Viet Cong, they were trained, armed, and used to occupy and hold large areas of the countryside, thus relieving Viet Cong for duty in South Vietnam.

The graft and corruption of the Lon Nol regime, which usurped power from Sihanouk, is well known. When the regime crumbled and fled in April 1975, the Khmer Rouge unexpectedly found themselves in complete control of the little country; the victorious North Vietnamese had their hands full assimilating their own conquest.

The last months before the April collapse were highlighted by a massive exodus of the "fat cats" of the Lon Nol government and the hundreds of businesses, mostly foreign and mostly Chinese, which had made fortunes through graft and inflated wartime profits. The more cautious moved their profits out early in the form of gold and hard currencies. Others lingered, to squeeze a few final drops; in some cases, they lingered too long to escape by normal means. The final days were similar to those of the Chiang Kai-shek regime in China in 1949: the businessmen fled, mostly by air, using anything with wings. Some made it out, some didn't.

The Cambodian people's joy that the war was finally over was extremely short-lived. Within days, all inhabitants of the major cities and towns found themselves driven into the countryside by grim-faced, black-clad Khmer Rouge soldiers, who showed no mercy to the old, the sick, or anyone who straggled.

Two years after the Khmer Rouge took over, Cambodia was one vast refugee camp in which people died by the tens of thousands from disease, malnutrition, and the mindless brutality of their fellow Cambodians of the Khmer Rouge. All who could, fled to Thailand in the west or the lesser evil of Communist Vietnam to the east. It has been reliably estimated that for every one of the one hundred thousand who escaped, two or three died trying. As the genocide continued, more and more of the Khmer Rouge, themselves appalled at the carnage, also fled the country.

Nor were the Khmer Rouge leaders—the self-deserved Higher Authority ("Angkha Leou")—content with their internal butchery. They launched a campaign across their borders with Thailand and Vietnam, attacking defenseless villagers whose only crime was to live near the border. The

Thais and the Vietnamese reinforced their border guards, but the raids continued, often resulting in small bitter, pitched battles. Both countries absorbed mounting streams of refugees from the Khmer Rouge terror. Inevitably, some of them formed small resistance groups to overthrow the Angkha Leou. The resistance groups received increasing support from the Thais and the Vietnamese, mainly as a matter of expediency to help protect their border inhabitants. By late 1976, both borders were practically under siege by the unpredictable Khmer Rouge terror squads.

CHAPTER ONE

As he unconsciously scratched at it, Ming Tong's already prominent left ear was made more so by grease from the elderly C-47's port engine. He had long ago learned to associate the itch with impending disaster of one sort or another. His first jump as a member of the Thai Police Parachute Battalion over twenty years previous firmly cemented his conviction from childhood that an itching left ear spelled trouble. On that occasion his main chute had fouled its shroud lines into a classic "Mae West," and his landing, had it occurred on dry land, might have ended his career. Instead he splashed into shoulder-deep water off the sunbaked Hua Hin beach, and nearly drowned as the misshapen canopy collapsed on top of him.

Ming's face was anything but inscrutable as his long, greasy fingers automatically checked the cowling fasteners and he wearily descended to the scorching concrete of Phnom Penh Airfield.

He swore aloud in a mixture of his childhood Taejew dialect, schoolboy Thai, and the English he had been learning since his first contact with the Parachute Battalion's American advisors. As his Buddhist "silent voice" admonished him for the profane outburst, he lifted his hands, palms together, in a silent supplication to Lord Buddha to forgive him. Ming

1

knew that even the infinite patience of the Buddha himself
might well be tried by the huge accumulation of ominous
events that had shoved him into his present situation.

A week earlier, in the ornate study of his uncle Visarn, he
had felt confident that he could perform the complex task his
almost-father had asked of him. But that was a week ago.
Today was April 24, Buddhist Era 2016, anno Domini 1975.
Surveying the squat old Royal Cambodian Air Force Gooney
Bird a final time, Ming ignored the crump of Khmer Rouge
mortar shells falling on Cambodian army positions barely a
kilometer from where he stood. He could also hear, and occasionally see, the tracers from Communist 12.7-mm machine guns, which had all but closed Phnom Penh Airfield in
daylight for the past three days.

Nights aren't all that much better, Ming thought. Though
most of the overloaded escapee aircraft make it out through
the maze of tracers. They're getting an awful lot of practice.
I just hope it hasn't been enough to let them get us tonight.

By full dark, the effects of his bath at dusk had worn off as
he made a final check of the tie-downs that would keep the
olive-drab .50-caliber ammo boxes from shifting in flight. His
itching ear did nothing to quell the feeling that, given the
overload, the possibility of never getting airborne was at least
close to fifty-fifty.

Ming's pragmatism made him all but ignore the nature of
the ammo boxes' present contents: 2,540 kilograms of pure
gold—ten million U.S. dollar's worth—which he had personally loaded from his uncle's Phnom Penh warehouse. More
money than he would ever see again—if he would ever see
anything again, his itching ear added.

Two and a half tons! That was twice the normal 2,500-
pound load of a C-47. Adding the weight of the ammo boxes
themselves, closer to three times. After reinforcing the floor
with planks to keep it from buckling, Ming had stripped the
old bird of everything possible to cut down the weight. Even
at that, she was way over gross. Ming had stacked the gold
as far forward as he could and as high as he dared, but when
the pilots had figured the center of gravity, they had both

refused to try to fly it. So Ming had torn out the remaining radio gear and stacked some of the boxes in the radio cubicle and forward luggage area. Even so, the plane was tail-heavy as hell . . . but the pilots were willing to try after Ming agreed to double the original price.

The flight plan was simple. Direct to the 4,500-foot red laterite strip at Chantaburi, unload the gold onto Visarn's waiting trucks, dump in some gas, then fly into the big Royal Thai Air Force Base at Utapao, half an hour to the northwest, pretending to be refugees.

He and the Gooney Bird were as ready to go as they'd ever be. He turned toward the roadway, hoping to pick up the sound of a vehicle. He checked his watch. The pilots weren't late—yet. And he wouldn't have cause for worry if they were not on time, not with all the fighting and stray bullets. They weren't the best available; they were the only ones who could be trusted. His left ear continued to itch. Ming squatted comfortably to wait. He was used to waiting.

Suddenly a battered American army jeep swung around the hangar, swaying from the angle at which it had been wrenched around a ninety-degree turn. The jeep had barely braked to a lurching stop when two men propelled themselves from its interior. With gears grinding, the jeep backed and was swung around, before disappearing noisily into the night.

"You got it all set up right, Ming?" asked one of the pilots, but the other man was already climbing into the C-47. "Then let's get our asses out of this place," he said as he saw Ming nod.

Suspicious suddenly, Ming glanced in the direction of the jeep. He heard the faint rasp as gears were shifted into a higher speed.

"C'mon then!" And the pilot grabbed him urgently by the arm, almost pushing him into the entrance.

A sudden spurt of not too distant machine-gun fire added speed to Ming's entrance and ended his suspicions about the pilots' abruptness. They were already in place, running the checklist as he fastened the door.

From the moment the engines caught, coughed, caught

again, Ming's ear itched abominably and everything got worse in a hurry.

The tail-heavy C-47 used an awful lot of power as she creaked and groaned down the taxiway. As Ming walked forward, the pilots were arguing.

"We've got to use the overrun, Swarn," the older man was saying. "It adds an extra hundred meters to the runway. And we're going to need every goddamn millimeter to get this bird off."

"And the overrun gets us that much closer to those Commie rockets. Didja think of that?"

"I've more hours in these birds than you do."

"How many more hours do we both got?" Swarn asked in savage sarcasm, but he was busy following takeoff procedures.

Ming couldn't see that there was much choice. The Commies were within easy mortar and rocket range of the field, so even a normal takeoff or landing would be hairy. At that, they'd have to sweat out Khmer Rouge small arms and machine guns after they got off. With their load, there would be no way to climb fast enough to avoid it.

Despite his claim, the older pilot didn't have as many hours flying C-47's as Ming would have liked and both had spent most of their time in the right-hand seat. But they were the best Ming had been able to find of those he dared trust.

By the time the C-47 reached the overrun and they checked the engines, they were running up well—everything in the green. Ming stood behind the throttle pedestal, where he could see the instruments. The pilot stood on the brakes, opened the throttles, and then let her go. And off they went. Like a herd of turtles. She lurched forward and struggled down the runway. They'd used half of it before she hit sixty knots. The tail-wheel seemed glued to the concrete.

Finally, at eighty knots, the tail came up. But the end of the runway was coming up fast, too fast. At eighty-five, Ming was really sweating. Even in the dark they could see the outline of trees at the end of the runway. Beyond the trees, Communist tracers cut angry red arcs in the sky.

Ming's eyes ran an epileptic pattern over the instrument panel. Manifold pressure, oil pressure, cylinder-head temperature, and then the dreaded airspeed that stuttered and stammered as it struggled painfully past eighty-five, past ninety, and hung for an eternity at ninety-five. The white knuckles of the copilot's left hand were jammed tightly over the pilot's right on the throttles.

Ming's peripheral vision registered the tiny runway lights as they flashed by. Too fast, too fast. The runway was being eaten up while the devil controlling the airspeed indicator spelled out their imminent deaths in ghostly green. Like a robot, Ming continued his uncontrollable scanning. One second grateful that the engines were still in the green, the next second in agony as the airspeed hit ninety-five and seemed to stick. Then from the trees ahead came the red stabs of tracers. Always the peripheral flashes balefully recorded the exorbitant and spendthrift use of precious runway.

Suddenly the long-familiar smell—gasoline, oil, stale sweat, musty, mildewed leather—was gone. A new, frightening odor permeated the cockpit. Acrid, nauseating, and somehow more terrifying than the grim messages his eyes kept relaying to his reluctant mind. Through his own terror, Ming felt, rather than saw, the two pilots stiffen. Then Ming knew that the new smell was raw, uncontrolled fear and the certain knowledge that unless some incredible miracle occurred in another sixty seconds, they would all be reduced to formless lumps of flesh.

Then the miracle happened. The pilot gingerly pulled the yoke back and the lumbering plane staggered into the air a handful of feet. Then she sought the runway again. But the airspeed needle had jumped—to one hundred knots. Again, the pilot eased back on the yoke. The overloaded bird fought to gain her element, and the copilot's hand was a blur as he reached for the gear lever. Uncertainly, almost as if making up her mind, the plane hesitated, dipped a little. Then she gathered herself for one final effort. And flew! The altimeter quivered upward; slowly, agonizingly, upward.

Then there was nothing ahead, no trees, only wonderful, welcome black sky. But only for an instant. The air came

alive with sudden bright red streaks of tracers. The Khmer
Rouge sought to negate the miracle the ancient airplane had
wrought. The three men in the cockpit winced instinctively
as a graceful, deadly stream curved toward them.

Abruptly the tracers winked out. The altimeter read an incredible 300 feet, and airspeed was a comforting 115 knots.
A mechanic's grateful love for his engines broke Ming out of
his trance. Gently he reached for the pilot's hand, still maintaining a death grip on the throttles. Slowly the pilot relaxed
his grip and eased back. The copilot, motionless since his
instinctive move to raise the gear, also came alive and slowly
withdrew the flaps. The three exchanged glances and, almost
in unison, let out explosive sighs. Training, however dimly
remembered, took over, and by the time they had completed
checking the post-takeoff list, they were passing through 700
feet, airspeed 120.

With the power at normal climb, it took another fifteen
minutes to reach fifteen hundred feet. Ming was still worried
about the engines. They should have burned up from the extended demand for maximum power; half an hour later, when
they were close to three-thousand feet, he was breathing easier.

Ming knew she was being a bitch to fly, tail heavy with
full trim tabs and requiring climb power to reach the forty-
eight hundred feet they would need to clear the hills between
them and safety. They'd be visible now, a dark mass against
the sky.

Ming had just passed the map to the pilot when the needle
indicating oil pressure on the left engine began to jig downward. Then the temperature began to climb. The pilot looked
at Ming and read his instant agreement. Like it or not, they
had to shut the engine down; and fast, before it froze up.
Ming guessed a Khmer Rouge bullet had nicked an oil line;
it was running out fast.

By the time the pilot had feathered the left engine and
boosted the right engine as high as he dared, they were at
forty-one hundred feet, still seven hundred too low. Even

worse, the remaining engine was barely maintaining altitude. There was no way she could climb with her load.

Quickly they talked it over. They had nearly three hours' gas, about seventeen hundred pounds. They still needed about half of it. But the pilot was having trouble even maintaining altitude, and the engine was likely to burn up long before they could use enough gas to make a difference. So they had to dump some gold, or crash.

The pilot started a slow circle, trying to nurse a few more feet out of her over the foothills. Ming went back and took off the door. He had jammed it into the toilet compartment and was starting forward for the first box of gold when she hit. It wasn't real hard, more like a sloppy landing. The second shock was the bad one; Ming saw and heard the port wing go as the plane plowed into the trees.

CHAPTER TWO

Roused by the whining of his dog and the loudness of airplane sounds, Remrut woke. He was accustomed to seeing planes during the day from the ridge located between his two charcoal kilns. Occasionally these days he had seen many planes, mostly flying northwest, high enough to clear the hills but low enough not to be too visible. But this plane was not only very low and close, it sounded bad. He heard the first smack reverberating in the night air. He tensed and the dog howled as a second dramatic crash followed.

Remrut was at the door of his hut in time to see the violent surge of flame over the ridge tops. The concussion of the third detonation could be felt through the ground under his feet, and he clung to the door frame. No one in the plane could have survived. Then he remembered that sometimes men fell slowly from the sky by means of parachutes, surviving the death plunge of their planes. His wiry legs took him quickly to the clearing on the ridge, the little dog hard on his heels. He peered into the dark sky above. The burning mass lit up the forest and the swath cut by the crashing plane in the trees at the top of the next ridge. It had plunged deeply into the valley beyond the second ridge.

Remrut shrugged. He could do nothing now. Nor did he

think the fierce fire would burn itself out by dawn. He would certainly go and see.

He listened to the night noises for a long time, wondering if the aircraft had been pursued, but he heard nothing more than the usual night noises. Certainly no plane from northwest or southeast.

The lack of pursuit relieved his mind to some extent and he returned to his hut, resuming his rough bed. The little dog trembled against him and he soothed it with the soft words he had once used to comfort his children. The dog's spasms soon eased and it slept.

Remrut wished that he could relax as effortlessly, but the crash so close to his hut was a worrisome thing. He didn't wish "others" to intrude on his solitude. Others were anyone beyond the small village where he bought his few requirements and received rare letters. Perhaps the others, the bad people, were also responsible for the lack of news from his daughter. He had been anxious for some time. He had a son, too, but his daughter was his joy, though his wife had died of a massive hemorrhage giving birth to her. Probably because he had raised the child from perilous infancy, he had been closer to her than to his son. He had somehow managed to send both of them to the Teacher's College at Battembang. The son had gone into the army. After a few widely spaced letters over two years, Remrut hadn't heard anything. His daughter wrote regularly and had sent money, though he had often told her that he had few needs and she should keep her coins. She had insisted; she had a good job in the capital, Phnom Penh. He must take the money, if only to keep it safely for her. She wasn't a teacher; she worked for the *ferang*, the Americans. That was part of his concern. He hadn't had a letter from her for two months, and the news that filtered down to the little village distressed him. The "new people" from the jungle—"others," as far as Remrut was concerned—were supposed to have captured Phnom Penh.

Despite the many planes going northwest, a few returned in the direction of the capital, so Remrut allowed himself to doubt the news. The crash of the plane tonight so near to his hut replaced doubt with certainty.

The dog's feet twitched in some uneasy dream, and Remrut stroked the rough fur, seeking comfort for himself in that action. *Mai pen ari,* he thought, using the Thai phrase of resignation that had fallen so frequently from his wife's mouth. He would go and look tomorrow, and also watch the river road from the village. He could always go deeper into the hills. A charcoal maker was welcome anywhere.

After checking the kiln that he had fired the day before, Remrut started reluctantly on his way to the farther valley. It was strange, but only because he knew the silhouette of the ridge could he track the path of the plane. Some trees were missing their crowns, some had been broken, but if one didn't know the ridge so well, the changes would be hard to spot. Especially on foot. Remrut cast an anxious eye upward once he reached the first height. No planes in any direction. He grunted. That was good.

His little dog bounded ahead, delighting in the departure from the established routine. As Remrut began to climb the next height, the dog's barking took on a new note: the growling, short, snapping kind of a noise a dog makes when he's about to fight. Remrut hurried. He couldn't believe that the dog had found anything, but it was an animal that never made unnecessary noise. He saw the vultures first! Three great birds. Their obscenely naked heads were turned toward an object on the ground. Suddenly one of the hideous trio jumped clumsily, half opening its wings to keep balance. A handful of pebbles clattered to the bare ground to one side of the carrion bird.

Remrut rushed forward. The little dog, emboldened by re-inforcement, sprang forward, growling and snapping at the air, just out of range of the cruel beaks, moving subtly to face the creatures and to protect something on the ground. Something that managed to throw another stone at the waiting vultures.

Remrut gathered rocks as he ran, lobbing them expertly at the birds, sending the creatures bouncing awkwardly away before they unfolded their huge wings and forced their bodies into flight.

As Remrut reached the wounded man, he exclaimed in surprise. He had thought no one could have survived the crash. The wounded man must somehow have been thrown clear before the plane reached the next valley. Yes, there had been three separate impact sounds. The man groaned, struggling to rise to defend himself against a return of the vultures. He was badly hurt; blood had dried on his face and head. His left arm lay at an odd angle. Remrut felt the legs, his knowing fingers finding the swollen knee. How lucky this fellow was, to have fallen from a dying plane and survived a long night in the jungle.

Telling his dog to stay as guard, Remrut slithered down the slope to the stream that ran through the heart of the small valley. He scooped up fresh water in the battered cup fastened to his shoulder strap. He took off his shirt and doused it in the cool water, thinking how best to get the injured man to his hut. He could just get his ox cart around the ridge through the stream. He must also get some of the little pills his daughter had sent him—the white for pain, the yellow for fever. And he had that powder she had said would make wounds heal without proud flesh.

He returned to the man, raising his head to give him water. The man drank thirstily, then muttered something in Thai. Then he grabbed at Remrut's arm, his eyes staring from their sockets as he gabbled something that sounded to Remrut like Chinese. Then switched abruptly into Cambodian. Before Remrut could answer, the man's face twisted in a pained grimace and he fainted.

As well, thought Remrut, squeezing his shirt over the man's head to see the extent of the head injury. It had stopped bleeding, but it was very bad.

He ordered the dog to stay. It waved its tail like a plume, then sat at the injured man's head. Remrut trotted away to make his preparations. The man did not look Chinese, but he had neither the fine bones of the aristocratic Cambodian nor the flat features of a villager. No matter, the man was injured and needed help.

On his return trip, urging the oxen to their best pace, Remrut could see the vultures circling in the sky. The man must be conscious again; one small dog could not keep hungry carrion birds at bay for long.

Remrut left the oxen and cart by the stream, pausing long enough to fill his water pot. A stone bounced down the slope as he ascended. He was pleased at the man's defiance; he had a brave heart for one so gravely injured.

But when Remrut reached him, the man's eyes were closed. The little dog whined as if trying to communicate. Remrut gave him a small pat of approval and carefully lifted the man's head. He unstoppered the flask of potent home brew and cautiously poured a little of the liquid through the slack lips. The man stirred. Remrut grunted, knowing well how the drink burned the lips. The man swallowed and his eyes opened. The appeal was plain. Remrut tilted the flask and the man swallowed and gasped. His eyes did not focus, but he was aware that someone had come to his aid.

Now Remrut fumbled in his pack and carefully picked two small white pills from their box. He filled his cup with water. Convulsively, the man swallowed again. Good. The journey to the hut would be much easier if the man was unaware of pain. Gently Remrut washed the man's face. No, not Chinese. Not Cambodian. Probably a mixture. But a strong face, and a brave one, one to be trusted—if one were given to trusting men. Remrut seldom had.

The man's head slid to one side of Remrut's knees. The charcoal maker waited no longer. By the good arm, he hauled the man to his feet, supporting him away from the injured leg and arm. Remrut bent and slung the limp body over his shoulder.

By the time he had put the patient into his own bed, unhitched the oxen, and replaced the cart under its covering brush, he had still heard no plane noises. The absence of any airborne search was reassuring.

He turned his attention to the man's injuries.

* * *

The sun was at its highest before a groan signaled that the man was rousing. Remrut leaned forward so he could see the face. The eyes struggled to focus but could not. The man tried to raise his left arm, but Remrut gently restrained the movement.

"You are hurt. You must lie still," Remrut said in Cambodian, his own voice rusty with disuse. Then he repeated his words in Thai. The man stopped a second attempt to move his left arm. Moaning with pain, he turned his head toward Remrut. His eyes rolled. "You have cut your head. Lie still. It will pass."

The man licked dry lips. "Water!" The word was in Thai.

Remrut gently lifted the man's head, regretting that he had not thought to collect a hollow reed. Thirst was a more pressing matter than pain. The man drank, at first in a rush, then more slowly as if he realized he might choke. The old man refilled the cup. He also gave him two more of the white pills for pain. The man took the pills eagerly and swallowed the water. Closing his eyes, he lay breathing slowly and from the belly. Remrut approved. The man was not only brave, he had control over himself.

Assured that his patient was as comfortable as possible, Remrut took up the chores of his normal day. These, because he had one kiln working and was chopping wood for the second, kept him within listening distance of his hut. He also killed a chicken, plucked it, and set it to drain. The man would need a nourishing broth. Remrut found several suitable reeds to aid drinking without turning a sore head, the leaves he required to reduce the swelling of the knee, and more jugs of water to hang where they would cool. If the man developed fever, he would need much water. All during these tasks, Remrut kept one ear tuned to the sky, but no plane noise broke his work rhythm.

That night, as he tended his restless patient's needs, he turned over and over in his mind what to do about the plane. If the man had been thrown clear, other things might be strewn about the jungle. Sometimes these things were valuable. Probably useless to him, but of use in barter to those in the village. It might be wise to find out if anyone there had heard the crash. Considering the screen of mountains that lay between his hut and the village, Remrut doubted it. But a cautious inquiry of any unusual happenings might bring useful information. Then he would know whether or not he could, or should, offer whatever salvage he could find. The matter could wait. First he would have to see if he needed to inquire at all.

Remrut did not resent the care the man required. Such tasks are laid upon men from time to time, as the care of his infant daughter had been after her mother's death. One completed the cycle and one was free to pursue one's own wishes, as Remrut had until the plane crashed. He was worried about the injured man, for the man's eyes did not see Remrut. After each ministration, the man murmured thanks, usually in Thai, occasionally in a language Remrut could not understand. The head injury healed slowly and cleanly over the next few days, and the swollen knee reduced in size to purple and blue glory, though not yet to match the other knee. The arm bone had not been moved despite the unconscious attempts of the man to raise it. The leg and arm would be all right, Remrut decided. But the mind of the man had been damaged with the head. The unfocusing eyes told Remrut that. Ai! Perhaps the man would have been better dying with his plane.

To reach the crash valley did not take too much time for an experienced jungle walker. Remrut made his first trip on the third day after the crash, when he was positive that no planes were likely to come. And his first trip necessitated many more. No harm could be done by his actions. All would be safe until the man regained his head. If he did not, mai pen ari.

Although Remrut did not count days, he was aware that many passed before his patient looked at him with clear and understanding eyes.

"I am Remrut," the old man said by way of introduction, feeling awkward that he had not been able to perform such a courtesy before.

The man smiled and then the smile wavered. "My name is . . ." He cleared his throat, frowned, and opened his mouth again. "My name is . . ." He turned with a half-worried, half-angry expression.

"You fell hard from the sky. From a plane." Remrut used the ferang word his daughter had taught him. He gestured to the man's head. "You hurt head. Take time. Your name will come."

When he had first undressed and bathed the man, he had found a wallet and a passport. These he produced from his shoulder bag, where he had kept them safely by him all the time. He showed the passport to his patient, glad that the picture resembled him.

"Lim, Ming Tong," the man said, taking the passport from Remrut and staring at the picture.

"Your name is Lim Ming Tong. That is your picture." Remrut nodded his head, smiling broadly, encouraging his patient, who now must know what his name was.

But Ming slowly and cautiously shook his head.

"Look. There are other papers." Remrut pressed the wallet to Ming.

Every piece of paper, all the cards, were carefully studied by Ming but meant nothing to him. He could read the characters and the words, but they did not strike any familiar note in his aching head.

"Don't worry," Remrut assured him. "Your head still hurt?"

Ming had to agree.

"When head is calm, awareness of self will return." Remrut said that because he hoped it would be so. Then Ming opened the bank note side of the wallet, and Remrut gasped at the number of beautiful, multicolored engraved bills. Ai! But that was riches. To Remrut's surprise and embarrassment, Ming immediately thrust them all into the charcoal burner's gnarled hands. "You have saved my life."

"I have no need of money. No place to spend it," Remrut argued indignantly. He thought of the gold coins that his daughter had sent, carefully hidden. He had wealth enough. He needed no more.

But Ming was insistent, and finally, when the injured man became distressed because Remrut would accept no recompense, he did take one of the red ones. They were not large monies. He could take one with dignity.

"Where am I?" Ming asked after shuffling again through all his cards and papers.

"Cambodia. This"—and Remrut tapped the passport—"says you are a Thai citizen. Your plane was going toward Thailand."

"Thai!" Ming repeated the word as if trying to make it connect somehow.

"Soon. Soon," Remrut murmured, and then, seeing that lack of memory depressed Ming, he remembered the other object he had removed from Ming's body. Just in case "others" might come.

Ming took the heavy ring from the old man. He examined it closely. It had a tiny parachute on one side and the numerals 94 on the other. "Ninety-four?"

"Perhaps," Remrut suggested, "that is the year. My children, who went to the Teacher's College at Battembang, were given rings when they completed their studies. Ninety-four in the Buddhist calendar would be twenty years ago. What age does it say you have in your passport?"

"Forty-two," Ming said, frowning at the age.

"That is appropriate, I think. You are not a youth and have many old scars. There is other writing on the ring?"

"Yes. 'Special Weapons School Erawan Camp.' "

Remrut lifted his arms in awe. "You are soldier. And there is the parachute that helps men fall slowly from the sky. You have been a parachute soldier. My daughter told me of such things."

Ming let out a heavy, discouraged sigh. He put a hand to his head.

"It aches with much thinking? Do not think!" Remrut reached into his pouch and, to distract his patient, showed him the treasured picture of his daughter and told him of her success with her job in Phnom Penh. He did not care to say that his daughter worked for ferang, for some Thai do not like ferang, and he also did not wish to upset Ming. Soon it would be time to give him the pills that bring sleep. That would be good for Lim Ming Tong. Sleep was always good for the headache.

CHAPTER THREE

"LIM MING TONG." THE INJURED MAN REPEATED THE phrase in his mind endlessly, like a mantra, hoping that at some point the syllables would touch association in his mind. He flipped through the papers, seeing every place this Lim Ming Tong had been during the life of the passport. In and out of Thailand, Cambodia, Singapore, Hong Kong, but the dates of his entrances and exits made no more sense to him than his own name. The nations and cities had a familiar ring. He thought until his head ached, or until Remrut returned from his various tasks and prepared their food.

The old charcoal maker was an excellent nurse, starting Ming on chicken soup, some meat, gradually adding bigger bits of vegetables and more and more rice. He also insisted that Ming finish a bottle of pills: "sulfadiazine," the label said. Ming did not wish to deplete whatever small store of modern medicine the old man had, but Remrut smilingly showed him two more full bottles. So Ming complied.

The painkillers, either morphine or codeine, were gradually withdrawn as Ming's wounds healed. Why Ming knew the medicinal names was one of those anomalies he tried to puzzle through but finally accepted, as he accepted the fact that he could read several languages and recognized that

Remrut's Thai was rusty. Not that the man talked very much, but his silence was comfortable.

Gradually Ming became stronger. His left knee shrank to its normal size. The torn shoulder and arm muscles responded to his kneading and massage. His arm bone was healing and he could use his fingers. Remrut fashioned a crutch from a forked stick, and Ming was able to get to the outhouse by himself.

Each day Ming went a little farther after a trip to the outhouse, but sudden movements still gave him dizzy spells and hurt his head. Each evening, after their simple meal, Ming would ask Remrut how his day had gone. After the first few nights he knew as much about the theory of charcoal making as Remrut. The old man had two kilns. While one was cooking charcoal, he would rebuild and fill the other. He cut wood from the hills and hauled it down in his ox cart to the two streams on either side of the ridge. Downstream the creeks joined to form a much wider stream that ran all the way to Tonle Sap, a huge lake in the rains, but mostly a swamp in the dry. Just then, the two creeks were easily wadeable, but could rise to two or three meters in the rainy season. Then wood cutters much farther upstream than he was could float bamboo rafts down to where the streams joined to form the Pang River.

When one kiln had produced finished charcoal, Remrut would load his ox cart and bring it into the little village, a full day's trip away. Each batch took several trips.

As Ming's health and strength improved, so did his sense of humor. In these evenings, the little dog, whom Remrut called simply "dog," would sit between the two men, looking from one speaker to the other. During the days, sometimes it stayed with Ming, matching its quick steps to his as he hobbled about. Other times it went off, tail like a plume, trotting behind Remrut.

"I must go to the village. My charcoal is ready," Remrut said solemnly one evening.

Ming nodded with equal solemnity and asked, Was there any task he could perform while Remrut was gone?

"Do not stretch your strength."

In the morning Ming insisted on helping to load the finished charcoal and promised Remrut to rest while he was
gone.

No sooner did Remrut's figure and the ox cart disappear
down the trail than Ming realized that he might test his
strength. He knew where the airplane had crashed. That had
been the subject of so many evening discussions and Remrut's
patient detail. He supplied himself with a water flask and
rice, then set out at a slow and careful pace. He was pleased
to find that he only had to rest twice. Finding the charred,
pathetically small wreckage was easy. It wouldn't have filled
a ten-wheel truck. The thought came unbidden into his mind
and he struggled to hold on to the memory, but it escaped
him.

Looking over his shoulder, he could see the swath the plane
had cut in the heavy growth. He followed it and found the
outer half of the left wing and the tree that had sliced it off.
Still no recall. He knew he must have been aboard the plane
just before it crashed.

When Remrut returned that evening, he was clearly upset
by something. Ming had never seen him perturbed. His story
didn't make much sense either. Some soldiers, clad in black,
had come to the little village. They called themselves Khmer
Rouge. They said that they had been ordered by their commander to take an inventory of everything in the bare half-
dozen shops in the village. Nobody knew what it all meant,
but this had never happened before. Everyone was worried.

Soldiers or not, Remrut didn't like their sudden appearance, nor their brusque, impolite manner. He advised Ming
to exercise as much as possible, building his strength, but to
keep out of sight if anyone came by. Remrut's hut was literally the end of the line and a short way downstream from the
first of Remrut's beehive charcoal kilns. The second was in
the next valley; the hill, actually a finger ridge, separated
them from the place where the plane had crashed.

Ming was as worried by the strangers in the village as Remrut, though he reasoned it was unlikely they could be inves-

tigating a plane crash in the vicinity after such a long time. He began to test his strength, climbing up the near hill without stopping once. He was so encouraged that he climbed it twice that afternoon. Despite the exercise, his knee felt fine and his shoulder and upper arm moved freely, though his forearm was still splinted. But his head throbbed, and sudden movement brought on a flash of lights and dizziness.

The next two days, with his one good arm, Ming helped Remrut to load the near kiln. The far one, which Remrut had been unloading, was all but empty. The third day they filled the cart with the remaining charcoal. Even though it was already midmorning when they finished, Remrut took the load to the village.

He got back very late, even more agitated than the last time. The soldiers, many more than before, had returned. The villagers' fears, and Remrut's, had been justified. The rough, harsh-mannered Khmer Rouge had herded everyone together for a meeting. Their leader had harangued the anxious and confused villagers for over an hour. No one had understood what was said. Something about a new government that would get rid of all the politicians, and all the rich, greedy city people, by moving them out into the countryside to be farmers. Then the blow fell. An allotment of the despised fold was coming to the village. The villagers, and especially the shop owners, would have to supply the new arrivals, and house and feed the soldiers who were coming to make sure that the corrupt city people worked hard. Everyone had to contribute. The black-uniformed leader passed out lists to everyone: food, cloth, tools, seed, thatch, and bamboo were required. No one was exempt. Remrut was ordered to supply five loads of charcoal a week. When he protested that this was more than twice his normal output and would leave him no time to cut and cook more, the soldier angrily told him to shut up. He would have a lot of help when the corrupt city people arrived. Payment would "be taken care of later," a further agitating statement for the villagers.

Ming was alarmed, not only by the old man's fears, but by some unnameable signal emanating from the sleeping portion of his mind. The black-clad soldiers were danger for him as well, though why he could not dredge from his memory. He was almost fit, except for the dizzy spells. He would exercise longer and harder the next day.

"Khun Ming," said Remrut, his manner suddenly tentative and reluctant, "could I borrow two of your red bank notes?"

Instantly Ming dug for his wallet, handing the notes and proffering more, which Remrut refused with a gesture. The gaudy five hundreds were folded respectfully and tucked into Remrut's belt.

He was gone before daylight the next morning. He returned much earlier than Ming, busy with his exercising, had expected. In the cart Ming could see the reason for the old man's unexpected request for a loan; half a sack of rice, three big dried fish, a dozen brittle slices of dried meat, and several smaller parcels wrapped in banana leaves.

Remrut didn't mince words on his return. They were leaving! The imminent prospect of the harsh, demanding soldiers—who called themselves Khmer Rouge—was something Remrut wanted no part of. Other villagers were equally upset but hesitant to give up their homes and land. Not Remrut. Poor, barely literate, Remrut instinctively sensed that the soldiers spelled an end to his peaceful, plodding existence. So he didn't hesitate. As he told Ming while they packed his meager possessions into palm-leaf panniers under their food, people always needed charcoal. Everywhere! He would go someplace that did not have grim-faced soldiers. To Thailand, over the mountains. He had been there as a young man when all of his province of Battembang had been part of Thailand, not Cambodia.

"What learning I have was taught to me in Thai. It was my parents who spoke Cambodian," Remrut reminded Ming as they loaded the cart. "My wife, too, was Thai."

Ming nodded, murmuring encouragement to the old man in Thai. Remrut's anxieties were contagious. Since Ming knew that his passport made him a Thai citizen, he did not worry about himself. Perhaps he could somehow, despite his lack of memory, also be able to protect Remrut, who had so long protected him, once they reached Thailand. Nor could Ming think of a life without Remrut, who was his only human contact.

Well before sunrise they were on their way, panniers on the backs of the two oxen, the dog acting as rear guard, tail high. The first two days they made pretty good progress. The oxen toiled up and down the slopes slowly, but they kept going until full dark. As they entered the verges of the rain forest, the going got rougher. They had to hack their path more and more often. By the fourth or fifth day—Ming lost count—they were reduced to following a streambed. Then it, too, gave out. The last slope was covered with ten-foot-high elephant grass, difficult to cut and full of razor-edged leaves that crisscrossed their bare arms with bloody cuts.

They made a dry camp that night. The next day, after crossing the ridge at noon, they saw the welcome trees below them. They were almost to the trees when one of the oxen lost its footing and fell heavily. They could hear the leg snap. Ming almost cried at the expression on Remrut's face as he cut its throat. Even so, the old man grimly cut out the filet, such as it was, and the liver. That night he forced Ming to eat until he thought he would burst. Remrut ate only rice and a little salt fish. Ming hadn't the heart to try to get him to eat the meat. Nor would the dog touch it.

The next day they made good progress, striking a game trail about noon. Remrut was obviously heartened at this and told Ming that Thailand was only a day or so farther on. Ming had to accept the old man's word. In spite of the rough going, Ming felt a lot stronger than he had when they had started. His arm was useful now, the sling discarded, and his knee had ceased to buckle or catch. Even his headaches were less frequent. So were the bothersome dizzy spells.

At nightfall they camped by the stream the game trail had crisscrossed all day. While Ming gathered wood and built a fire, Remrut and the dog went on down the trail. Just looking, he told Ming, as he had done every night of the trip. This time he returned with a hurried stride and a worried expression. He stamped out Ming's fire and said that someone was camped below them. Remrut had smelled the smoke. Might be "bad people."

They ate a cold supper. While Ming slept, Remrut and his dog kept watch. It was still dark when Remrut gently shook Ming awake. Now Ming could also smell smoke. The old man's uneasiness affected him. Ming held the dog while Remrut went to take a closer look.

When he returned, his face told the story before his terse words.

"They are bad people. They have guns."

They retraced their steps and then cut left, over another ridge covered with maddening elephant grass. On the way down the farther slope, they lost the remaining ox with a broken hind leg. This time they both cried.

It took the rest of the day to rig two of the panniers as packs and get down to the tree line. They found another stream and followed it until a well-traveled game trail appeared. Three hours later they smelled smoke again.

Remrut crept silently forward to investigate; more bad people were camped close to the stream where the trail crossed it.

After a gloomy cold meal, Remrut led Ming off the trail to the bank of the stream. It was now easily four meters wide and nearly a meter deep. The current was strong. Remrut nodded in satisfaction and told Ming that after the bad people had gone to sleep, they would float down the stream until they were well beyond danger. As Ming didn't know whether or not he could swim, the idea didn't appeal to him, but there was no discounting the old man's urgency. It stifled his doubts.

After the moon rose, they launched themselves, dog under Remrut's arm, and Ming with a parcel of food on a string. They were lucky at first. As they came around a bend, they could hear loud snores and smell smoke. They lowered themselves deep in the water, pushing occasionally with their feet to keep in midstream as the current swept them soundlessly past the outpost.

An hour later they emerged from the stream, shaking and chattering with cold. It was narrowing rapidly and they could hear the ominous sounds of a waterfall ahead. Shivering in their wet clothing, they forced their way through the thick undergrowth as quietly as they could. When Remrut finally stopped, their arms were again bleeding from old and new cuts, but the effort had warmed them a little. Exhausted, chilled to the bone, they huddled together, the dog between them under the plastic wrapping taken from the food parcel.

After a fitful sleep, they awoke in the gray, misty predawn. The exposed skin on their arms, legs, and faces was a maze of crusted blood from cuts as well as red welts from insect bites they had never felt. After a few mouthfuls of salt fish and soggy rice, Remrut crept off through the brush. He returned almost at once, smiling wearily. The trail was only a few meters away. Gratefully, Ming forced his stiff muscles to follow. And there it was . . . a trail. A real walk-upright trail.

The streak of good fortune was short-lived. Half an hour down the trail, the dog raised its head to sniff the air, faced back along the trail, and growled low in its throat. They quickened their pace to a trot, stopping every few hundred meters to listen. The second time they heard a shout, faint but clear. Remrut increased the pace to a near lope. Ming was panting before the old man stopped again to listen.

The voices were louder. They ran as fast as the narrow, winding trail would let them until Ming gasped for a halt. Head down, he was fighting to pull air into his searing lungs; his head throbbed almost as painfully as his heart. Through the sweat that streamed down his face, he saw that the wiry old man was still breathing evenly if deeply. As Ming tried to hear over the pounding of his pulse, the old man's face suddenly lost its anxious look. Dragging Ming along, Remrut sprinted down the trail. Then Ming saw why. The stream, still bearing froth and bubbles from its plunge over the falls, gleamed dully a bare hundred meters away.

The water was waist-deep and moving swiftly. They plunged in, adding their own efforts to the current, half swimming, half wading. At Remrut's gesture, Ming stopped stroking and drifted. The voices were fainter. Ten minutes later, they slowed their forward motion again, listening. Then they heard the sound of the approaching rapids—too late. The banks on both sides were overhanging, undercut by the stream. Remrut grabbed hold of a half-submerged log, then pulled Ming on. Ming found an exposed root and tried to pull himself up so he could grab at a sapling. The root broke off in his hand. He fell back, starting a chain reaction that freed the trapped log, swinging it into the stream. Pushed by the current, the log was swept away, carrying the two men and the dog with it. It saved their lives.

As the swift current caught and spun the log end for end, they scrambled to the other end. For once the bedraggled little dog was afraid, crouching nervously on the log, tail between its legs, whining uncertainly. Then they were in the rapids. These had no falls, only a steep drop-through passage the river had cut in soft dolomite. But there were boulders, marked by little flags of white water or ominous roiled swellings. Their log, over half its girth submerged, was pushed to one side or another after nudging a boulder. Both men kicked and paddled with their arms to straighten it out after each encounter. Then a huge boulder divided the stream in front of them. Their log hit it a glancing blow, swinging broadside, too far for Ming and Remrut to correct.

Scrambling to change ends, Ming never saw the thick root that caught him squarely over his ear. When he came to, Remrut was holding the flask of the evil-smelling home brew to his lips. In spite of himself, he swallowed some. Then Remrut pulled it away as Ming coughed and cried out in pain. He put his hand to his head and felt a large lump with fingers that came away bloody.

Remrut cautioned him to silence as he stuffed the bottle in his waistband and heaved Ming up and over his shoulder. Ming's head exploded in the now familiar bright flashes.

He remembered coming to half consciousness several times, seeing the corded bandy calves and the slippers of old tire tread on Remrut's feet. Again, he remembered stumbling along with his arm around the old man's neck for ages before they stopped and he was allowed to sleep. The rest was a blur. He was alternately coldly shivering or burning hot. And Remrut was merciless, dragging him until his legs refused to move and carrying him again until they could.

Then Ming was sitting, back against a tree, and the sun was comfortably warm on his blood-caked legs. Out of nowhere, it seemed to Ming, a huge wheel, a truck wheel, was suddenly right in front of him. He was being lifted up. His limp legs bumped against a steep step. Then he felt the smooth wooden seat and a blanket being wrapped around him.

The warmth and steady roar of the engine made him sleep again. He woke to the sensation of being lifted, carried, and finally, something soft under his back.

Faces were bending over him. He tried to answer questions but couldn't make any words. People were doing painful things to him, which he couldn't stop. He welcomed the black wave.

When Ming regained consciousness, he felt much better, except when he tried to move his head. He was fed, examined, and then asked questions he couldn't answer. His wallet and passport, which he knew Remrut had wrapped in plastic and strapped to his body, were gone. He couldn't even remember the name he had so carefully learned.

The only name he could remember was Remrut, and no one, even the man in the white coat whom Ming identified as a doctor, knew the name. Two men from a logging truck had brought Ming to the hospital and then left. Neither of them had given a name.

CHAPTER FOUR

THE PROVINCIAL HOSPITAL'S DILEMMA OVER WHAT TO DO with their destitute amnesia case was solved as soon as Ming's Parachute Police ring was noticed. Within twenty-four hours, Ming was ensconced in a room in the modern Police Hospital in Bangkok. Fingerprints quickly proved his identity, and his mother was informed of his unexpected but welcome appearance. Unknown to the police, his uncle Visarn also rejoiced.

Considering that Visarn was still missing his ten million dollars' worth of gold bars, his warm reception of his nephew did him credit. Visarn's discreet chauffeur had collected Ming on his release from the Police Hospital, his head wound healing nicely. He was allowed a few hours with his tearful mother, whom he could not remember but had the courtesy to accept. Then he was driven to Visarn's office.

He also accepted Visarn as his uncle and dutifully recounted his rescue by the old charcoal maker. Their escape to Thailand brought continuing clucks of dismay and "wahs" from Visarn and lifted the old Chinese merchant's hopes. Until he learned that Ming had no recollection whatever of his former mission. Ming was also positive that there had been no ammo boxes strewn in the plane's crash path or amidst the blackened confusion of shattered aluminum that bore no resemblance to an airplane. Knowing that his nephew had to be telling the truth, Visarn was left with the unhappy conviction that the old charcoal maker must hold the key to his missing treasure.

Within days of his release from the Police Hospital, Ming began his search for the missing Remrut. He was conscious that he owed this uncle of his some great debt, though what it was, Ming was unsure. If Visarn needed to find a charcoal maker whom only Ming could identify, he was certainly willing to try. Starting from Cholburi, where Remrut had left him, Ming applied the same meticulous concentration that he had once used when repairing aircraft engines. His conscientious efforts brought no result.

Thais prefer charcoal to any other form of cooking fuel; so Ming's search was a needle-in-a-haystack proposition. Days grew into weeks, and then months, of interviewing charcoal burners in difficult back-hill sites. As the frustrating search continued, Ming was increasingly bothered by headaches, and then more and more frequent episodes of blurred vision and vertigo. After three months of searching, and increasing worry over the alarming bouts of illness, Ming returned to Bangkok and consulted the doctors at the Police Hospital. Their prognosis, after a variety of tests, was either almost invalid status or brain surgery to remove the bone fragments that they believed to be the cause of the headaches and the increasing attacks of vertigo.

When Ming informed his uncle, he was surprised to see his foster parent's features tighten. Then the wizened old man's entire body slumped momentarily, as if he had suddenly become unable to sit erect. The reaction was so fleeting that Ming wasn't sure if it had been his imagination or not. The next moment Visarn was insisting on an operation by one of Thailand's top surgeons in the modern Rama Hospital, Bangkok's newest and most expensive.

The operation was as lengthy and delicate as Ming's tough constitution made his recovery brief. His worst aftereffect was a gradually decreasing series of nightmares in which he relived the harrowing takeoff from Phnom Penh and the crash in the Cardamom Range. Physically, his resilient, well-conditioned physique and sturdy good health had him up and about within a week. Then, despite protests from both doctors and family, he informed his uncle that he intended to resume his search for Remrut.

The old Chinese merchant's response was what Ming sensed to be an almost perfunctory and, somehow, resigned protest. Recalling their last meeting prior to the operation, Ming broke the unwritten rule in the family.

"Uncle Sarn," he began hesitantly, "have I said something to offend? Or . . . is there some problem you have that I may help you with?"

Visarn was silent for a long interval during which Ming regretted his uncharacteristic boldness. Then, as the old man stroked his heavy jade paperweight, Ming noticed that the familiar huge diamond ring, which had dwarfed his uncle's finger as long as Ming could remember, was missing. The truth suddenly hit the younger man: his uncle, his beloved foster father, must be in serious financial difficulty. Nothing else could have forced him to part with the huge solitaire. With a sick feeling in the pit of his stomach, Ming jumped to the conclusion that the ring had gone to pay for his operation.

Visarn, old and with his back to the wall, was as perceptive as ever. "Yes, my nephew, my ring is gone. But only temporarily. Things have gone poorly with us these past months. The loss of the gold was bad, but the Americans' sudden departure has thrown the whole country into a bad situation. I have survived many such times. What I have done before, I can do again."

"Is there anything I can do to help, Uncle?"

"Find me a buyer," said Visarn, his words accompanied by a faint smile, "for that antimony mine we bought to cover our resmelting of the gold bars, and we will be able to come out of this crisis with ease."

Ming's puzzled look made the old man hurry to an explanation. "I guess that occurred while you were missing. Prior to the final American defeat, we planned to convert our holdings in both Cambodia and Vietnam into gold. No major currency is stable anymore. Gold is the only safe and liquid asset left. But you can well imagine what would happen if too much gold was suddenly put on the local market. The police would ask us questions. So we bought an antimony mine. Gold mines are too few and too expensive to consider. Antimony, on the other hand, produces some gold as a by-product—four or five percent—and a lesser amount of silver. The mine we bought had no smelter, so we purchased one, new. They are not inexpensive, but considering the amount of gold we planned to process . . .''

The mine, Ming learned, was located deep in the mountains of Chantaburi Province, some three hundred kilometers southeast of Bangkok. It could only be worked half the year—during the dry season. Without the illicit gold to resmelt, it ran at a loss. While the mine itself could be worked all year, the tortuous haul road down to the valley was impassable for six months. Even in the dry, big ten-wheelers could only make it about halfway; the rest was accomplished by long-bodied Land Rovers and Dodge Power Wagons.

Were it possible to operate the mine on a year-round basis and solve the transportation problem, the partially refined antimony crudum, selling at over eighteen hundred dollars a ton, would let them break even or show a slight profit. The by-product gold and silver, illicit and real, would guarantee a respectable profit. As affairs stood, the mine was losing money annually, and worse, the cash flow ceased completely in the rainy season.

"We indeed have a modern white elephant, my dear nephew," Visarn concluded with a grim twist of his thin lips.

The word "elephant" sparked a sudden thought in Ming's mind, which a second reflection killed. Thai elephants could haul huge teak logs that weighed two or three tons. But unlike their African cousins, they could not *carry* more than two hundred pounds without quickly and seriously injuring themselves. As the picture of elephants laden with crudum faded, Ming received a second inspiration. Knowing his uncle well, he tried to conceal his excitement as he asked to use the old man's ancient hand-cranked Facit calculator. Punching keys and turning the handle furiously, he cranked in one more multiplier and then grinned broadly.

"Uncle, it will work!"

"What will work, Ming?"

"A STOL airplane, Uncle, of the type called a Porter. The kind I worked on for my friend, Major Somboon. They can land in very small, rough places but carry at least five hundred kilograms safely. Look at my figures."

Visarn's expression turned to hope and enthusiasm as he cranked through the same figures Ming had used.

The final pull showed an indisputable "bottom line," as the Americans called it. It was a profit.

Within a week, Ming's idea was turning into reality. His erstwhile employer, former Police Major Somboon, once an Air America pilot and a fellow Parachute Battalion comrade, welcomed Ming back from his extended leave of absence to his job as Somboon's Air Services' chief and, frequently, only mechanic. The welcome was even warmer when Ming proposed the charter of Somboon's less-than-half-paid-for Porter Pilateus STOL workhorse.

A quick overflight of the rain-bound mine and the tiny truck stop hamlet of Ban Het on the new highway made all their spirits soar. The mine's tailings, properly graded and somewhat extended, would provide the nine hundred feet the Porter needed to take off with a load. Its steep incline would have dismayed anyone unfamiliar with STOL aircraft. But Somboon and Ming nodded approvingly as they circled the site. On downhill takeoff, the incline would add thrust to the Porter's own powerful engine. On uphill landing, it would provide a gravity brake to supplement the Porter's spoiler flaps and brakes.

Ban Het was even better. The hamlet had once been the laterite storage site of the construction company that had built the new road. Now it was stripped flat, except for an old construction shack at one side. The ground was well compacted by the hundreds of trucks that had loaded up from the huge pile. Somboon landed on the four-hundred-meter surface without flaps, and needed only a touch of brakes to bring the Porter to a stop.

The mine workers, whose annual unpaid vacation had been unexpectedly terminated, were shepherded back to their jobs. Rented trucks battled their way up the muddy old logging road. They only got up almost half of the winding, treacherous way before even winching the ponderous ten-wheelers became impossible. The final fifteen kilometers of dry-season jeep trail were covered on foot.

As Ming and his weary, muddy followers slogged the last few meters from the edge of the lush jungle to the cleared mine area, they saw the rusty smelter stack at the far end and the head-high mound of old tailings on which the landing strip was to be laid. To his right, Ming noticed a neat bungalow perched on a little rise that commanded a view of the whole pocket plateau, and below it, the rusty GI sheet roofs of the miners' dormitory and mess hall. The drab, unpainted wooden structures and the reddish GI roofing contrasted sharply with the deep green of the surrounding jungle, which seemed to be about to overwhelm the wound the miners had made.

Nearing the weedy tailing mound, Ming saw a sudden movement. A small, nondescript, but somehow familiar dog was poised on the crest of the rubble, tail high and beginning to wag. Ming took a few steps farther and the dog began a furious barking and rushed straight at him, tail streaming like a cavalry guidon.

As the dog's hurtling progress brought it closer, Ming gave a glad shout and amazed his companions by sprinting toward the little animal. A last leap brought the dog into his arms, its tail threatening to separate from its body and its tongue slathering Ming's face as he shouted. "Remrut! Khun Paw! Khun Paw, it's me, Ming. Lim Ming Tong!"

From the brushy undergrowth of the jungle verge, the old charcoal maker emerged. It took them the better part of an hour to communicate the bare facts of their lives since Remrut's sudden flight from the Provincial Hospital.

Still wiping tears of joy from his seamed, leathery face,

Remrut delivered an almost dispassionate account of his flight and his search for a safe place to hide.

After carrying Ming into the hospital, Remrut fled, fearing his accent would betray him as a foreigner.

Well outside Cholburi town, the sight of a charcoal kiln had given him the reassuring beginnings of a plan. The last of Ming's hundred-*baht* notes provided food and bus fare to a village where he was readily hired to work in a small three-oven charcoal business over a hundred kilometers south of Cholburi and well north of Chantaburi.

This proved only a temporary refuge; Remrut's simple country mind just wasn't equal to developing a passable cover story to use with his employer and fellow workers. But a chance remark by one of the latter solved his problem. During a lunch break, the employee spoke wistfully of an offer he had just received to work at an isolated mine, far up in the mountains. The pay was double what he was earning, but his wife had flatly refused to leave the valley, so he had turned down the offer.

Remrut waited only until he collected his week's wages before taking a bus to the mine's access road. He hitched a ride halfway up on an empty ore truck and then another ride on a battered four-wheel-drive Land-Rover the rest of the way. He was hired immediately and without question. When the mine began closing down for the rainy season, the supervisor had eagerly accepted Remrut's offer to stay on as combination watchman and charcoal maker. Safe in his made-to-order hideout, Remrut never left the mine, perfectly content to live there until it seemed safe to return to his hill home, something he felt was a long way in the future.

Then it was Ming's turn. When he showed the old man the dully gleaming metal plate that the doctors had used to replace the damaged skull bones, the charcoal maker fingered it in awe. Suddenly he averted his gaze. "I did a very bad thing," he said in a quavering, fearful tone, "to take your gold and hide it, without telling you."

Remrut recoiled as Ming jumped to his feet to embrace him.

"No, no, Khun Paw! You did the right thing!" Ming caught the old man and whirled him about. "You did exactly what I would have done if I had remembered anything. What you did was very, very wise."

Remrut's look of happy relief belied the sudden burst of tears that streamed, unheeded, down his sun-blackened face. "I am sure it is safe, my dear son. No one will ever think to look for all those boxes under the fire pits of my ovens. Oh my, they were heavy. My poor old oxen and I were very tired when we finally got the last of them down the trail." With a sheepish grin, he continued. "I dug the holes and buried the boxes during the nights while you were sleeping. I was afraid someone might find them and steal them. I wasn't really sure what to do about them, except to hide them first.

"Then, when you could talk, you said nothing about the boxes. I was very confused. But when I saw you couldn't even remember your name, and the bad people began to come close, all I could think to do was to get away from them. Whatever else happened, your possessions were safe." Remrut chuckled. "Do you not remember that you helped me load the kilns and make new charcoal? They are safe, my son. No one digs in old fire pits. They only scrape out the old ashes on the top of the ground. Your gold is safe."

CHAPTER FIVE

"YOUR GOLD IS SAFE!"

The four simple words repeated to Visarn by Ming a week later brought tears to the old man's eyes. He flew from behind the massive teak desk to embrace his grinning nephew.

Visarn beamed like some half-starved Buddha as Ming related his astonishing reunion with the old charcoal maker.

"But where is this man, Ming?" cried Visarn as his nephew concluded the account. "I must meet this honorable person who has saved not only my beloved nephew but my fortune as well."

Ming's face sobered slightly. "You must remember, Uncle, that Remrut is a country person. And, quite truly, he is also an illegal alien. He has no papers, no passport—"

Visarn was suddenly the forceful business tycoon again. "Papers! Papers! They are like rice and peppers, nephew. One buys them and sells them. Get me a snapshot for his ID card and he'll be a Thai citizen in twenty-four hours!" Less imperiously, he changed the subject as he resumed his seat behind the desk. "Now, Ming, about recovering the gold. From what you have told me, this may be more than a little difficult. As I remember, we have about twenty-five hundred kilograms, in twenty-kilogram bars."

"Two thousand five hundred forty kilograms, Uncle. One hundred twenty-seven bars."

After an hour-long discussion, which often bordered on the acrimonious, Visarn finally agreed that, despite his long experience and success at minor cross-border smuggling, two and a half tons of gold bars presented a unique problem that he was unable to solve by traditional methods.

"Well," he said finally, deftly throwing the onus to Ming, "if we can't get the gold out using the old methods, how do *you* suggest we do it?"

The challenge provoked a long silence from Ming, not because he didn't have an answer, but because he didn't quite know how to present it. Finally he began. "I know a man, Uncle, a ferang, who could do it if anyone could."

"A long-nose?" Visarn snorted. *"Wah!"* What can any long-nose teach us Chinese about smuggling?"

"Uncle, all long-noses aren't the same. The one I am thinking of is better at the kind of work we need than any Thai or Chinese."

"Does he have some great magic?" Visarn's scorn was massive. "Like one of our famous *maw suk dai see,* perhaps?"

"No, Uncle, not in that way, but I have worked with him for many years. I owe my life to him. He does work a kind of magic with airplanes, helicopters, radios, and many complex American secret things."

"Wah!" Visarn's exclamation was more temperate and he frowned, considering Ming's words of "magic" and "American secret things." "Tell me more about this long-nose magician of yours."

"Uncle, his name is Mark Jordan, a colonel of the Americans as a soldier, but now retired. Khun Mark is not like most long-noses." Ming spoke nervously, wondering if he had irrevocably overstepped the bounds of propriety. Ming had no choice but to continue. "Khun Mark can speak Thai and Lao and Hmung quite well. He even knows some Mandarin and our own Taejew dialect." Ming grew more confident. His uncle ought to be impressed by Mark Jordan's linguistic accomplishments, so rare in a ferang. "He looks like a *dai see,* a professor, but he has killed men with only his bare hands." Visarn's eyebrows raised slightly, and Ming wondered if he should have mentioned Khun Mark's martial prowess quite so soon. "He is, however, a quiet man. Yet when he speaks, you *have to* hear him. When everyone else is too tired to go on, Khun Mark can make them keep going. I don't know how or why, but when you see him, you *feel* things will go well just because he is there."

Visarn's third *"Wah!"* was slightly less skeptical, and he gestured for his nephew to continue.

"I have seen Khun Mark do things that everyone else scoffed at as being impossible, just as you do. . . ." Ming faltered, his enthusiasm overcoming discretion.

"Go on, nephew."

"Well, it's his mind, Uncle. He has a power to see solutions to situations that no one else can. Often he had to fight with his own superiors to get approval to proceed. But always his way would work!"

"And just how," Visarn began blandly, "Supposing I agree, do you propose to get this 'superman' to work for us without stealing all that gold from us poor ignorant people of the Middle Kingdom?"

"If he has not changed, Uncle, Colonel Mark just doesn't care about money or wealth." Ming stood straighter, prepared to counter the surprise that registered on Visarn's face at that claim, but the old man said nothing. "He is what the Americans call a workaholic—he is in love with work, and nothing can keep him from it."

For the first time, his uncle's uncompromising expression relaxed slightly. Seizing the opportunity, Ming rushed on. "In that way he is like you, Uncle. He thinks only of his work and the people who work with him."

Lim Ming Tong had never heard of applied psychology, but he had just earned an A for his effort. He waited patiently while his uncle considered not only the comparison but the references.

"Very well, my impudent nephew." A slight smile played

on Visarn's lips. "There is no doubt in my mind that you believe this long-nose can solve our problem. With these secret and magic American things. But there is a very great doubt in my mind that we can trust him not to steal it from us by a further use of his magic."

"Uncle, I would not be alive today if it were not for Colonel Mark's risking his life to save me. I have trusted him with my life. I think we can trust him with your gold."

CHAPTER SIX

MING SUDDENLY REALIZED THAT HE HAD NO REAL IDEA HOW to contact Colonel Mark Jordan. The man was retired from the army, or the CIA—Ming had never known exactly for whom his boss had really worked—but where did he now live? In the United States? An answer came unexpectedly when Ming went out to see his new charter pilot, Somboon.

The source was a young American army attaché, one of the bare handful of uniformed Americans remaining in Bangkok after the United States had abandoned Thailand. The air attaché and a group of other skydiving enthusiasts regularly chartered Somboon's Porter or his smaller Cessna for almost weekly jumps. A brief query to the American elicited an immediate response.

"No sweat, Major Somboon. I'll just twist the Pentagon's arm and have an answer in a day or so."

With Mark Jordan's Utah phone number in hand, Ming developed and discarded a dozen ways to approach his old boss. They all sounded too much like a grade-B spy thriller. Finally he settled for a simple—and for an Asian, direct—approach. He reached for the phone.

"Ming? Ming Tong? From the PARU?"

The genuine warmth in the surprised American's voice on the remarkably clear connection encouraged Ming.

40

"Khun Mark, *krop*—" Ming switched to Thai. "I and my family have a problem that we would like you to help us with. Are you working now?"

"Yes, Ming. Well, sort of, anyway." The American answered in the same language. "I'm trying to relearn my college training as a mining engineer, but from the very bottom. I'm running a drill in a mine."

"How wonderful for us, Khun Mark. Our problem here is with a mine my uncle owns in Thailand. It needs some good leader to make it profitable again."

"What kind of mine, Ming?"

"Antimony, Khun Mark. They call the ore stibnite. It is quite pure, almost eighty-five percent."

"Well, I'll be go to hell!" Mark lapsed into English. "When can I start?"

"You mean you'll come?"

"Damn well told, I'll come! I'm sick to death of this crap here. Hell, I'll work for rice if I have to, just to get back to Thailand. Give me, let's see . . . four days should do it. Give me a cable address and I'll send you my flight number and ETA."

Ming was more than a little stunned as he hung up. Not only was Mark Jordan a mining engineer, but he hadn't even mentioned money. He was ready to buy his own ticket to Bangkok from Utah! Ming took Mark's unfeigned delight at an opportunity to return to Thailand as a great compliment. Like many Americans who had worked with the tough little PARU men, Mark Jordan had a long-standing love affair with the lovely country and its ruggedly independent people.

Mark Jordan's arrival with a civilian U.S. passport that labeled him a mining consultant passed unnoticed except by a couple of former PARU officers working for Customs and Immigration at Don Muang Airport. They happily waved him past the long line of envious fellow passengers and into a tearfully warm bear hug from Ming outside the customs gate.

Several days later, however, his unbelievably rapid approval as a permanent foreign resident reached the desk of another of his former student *cum* comrades and caused a low whistle and much thought. This former comrade penciled a neat note before he returned to checking the other names from the Thai immigration Department.

Mark Jordan was back in his second home, Southeast Asia, and in his favorite country, Thailand. Even the still wary Visarn couldn't help but be impressed by the graying, slightly balding American. Mark hadn't gone to fat at fifty-seven, but his five-foot-ten-inch frame was easily ten kilograms heavier than when Ming had last seen him in 1971. What had changed not at all was the ever-present cigar rolling in the burly American's mouth. And when thinking about anything of importance, he still traced tiny circles with a finger in the vicinity of his emerging bald spot.

During the rapid-fire conversation in Mark's rusty Thai and "goddamn"-laden English, Ming noted his old boss's reticence about discussing what he had been doing the past five years.

At first Ming was silent about the gold affair, but talked freely and happily about the way his airlift of the antimony crudum was working. "I owe the whole idea to you, Khun Mark. Remember, it was you who first used the little birds to carry ammunition up to the Hmung in places where we couldn't send the choppers and didn't want to risk the big planes to enemy fire while they were dropping the ammo by parachute. So far, Somboon has done all the flying, and you would be proud of him. He's been able to make at least four or five trips a day, even with all the cloud cover, and sometimes he makes as many as eight or nine."

"Old Gary's the one who would be proud, Ming. He's the guy who trained Somboon and the others."

"I agree, Khun Mark. Gary was the best of them all. You remember how he got me the job as A and E mechanic with Air America after I came back from school in America? Oh, but he is a careful man, Khun Mark! It was over a year before he would trust me when I said a plane was ready to fly. Especially after an engine change."

"Now, about the mine, Ming." Mark deftly reverted to the original subject. "With the Porter working out so well, what is there for me to do? Seems like I'd just be a fifth wheel down there."

Ming paused several long moments before he spoke.

"Khun Mark, I'm not supposed to tell you anything until you have met my uncle, Khun Visarn, but"—and suddenly Ming threw his uncle's strict warning to the winds—"we have another kind of problem. It's sort of like the old days in Laos, but the mine is involved." Ming trailed off in embarrassed confusion as the big American turned to face him squarely, rolled his cigar slowly, and stared at him. "Oh, like that, eh, Ming!" he replied softly. "Well, well. Like the old days in Laos?" Mark's face twisted into a grin. "Well, Ming, you get good marks on security. I can wait till we see your uncle. Don't sweat it."

In Visarn's ornate study that evening, Mark's cigar and finger danced a lively duet as Visarn and Ming concluded their initially cautious, then increasingly frank briefing of the former CIA covert operations officer. Ming was amazed at how adroitly the American handled his almost truculent foster father.

Mark had greeted Visarn in accented, but quite understandable, polite Taejew, making an immediate dent in Visarn's skepticism. After that, Mark listened silently for the most part, but his occasional questions slowly eroded much of the old Chinese's distrust.

When they had answered Mark's final question about the situation in the area around Remrut's former home with gestures implying ignorance, Mark sat silently for over ten minutes. His cigar rolled slowly in time with his circling finger. "Seems to me you've got yourselves a real dilly of an operation here, Khun Visarn."

"He means a very difficult problem, Uncle."

"One thing is for damn sure. We don't know anywhere near *what* we have to before we can even think about the *how* of it." Turning to face Ming, Mark went on. "You know what I mean, Ming. And remember, we don't have the setup we did in Laos or Nam. No commo, no air, no files, damn near nothing but bare hands, and the brains the good Lord gave us. I won't say it can't be done on a shoestring, but Lord, man, it's not going to be a piece of cake. If we have the money to do it, we ought to try and set up some real simple information-gathering agents. Those refugee camps on the border between Thailand and Cambodia ought to have a bunch of people who can tell us a lot about how the Khmer Rouge work. And your friend Remrut can be real helpful with his local knowledge.''

Once he started talking, Mark completed his conversion of Visarn by the clear, logical outline of all the things that had to be accomplished before any actual plan could be developed.

During the ensuing week, Mark and Ming worked long hours collecting the simple but critically important basic tools without which no intelligence operation can even begin. By the seventh evening after his arrival, Mark's multipage yellow pad list of these had been crossed out with only a few exceptions. Two file drawers were already full of maps, newspaper clippings, photos, pertinent books, mostly in Thai, and a long list of names and addresses of former PARU officers and men.

A valuable contribution had come when Mark renewed an old friendship with a senior member of the small Joint U.S. Military Advisory Group. The JUSMAG officer had winked knowingly at Mark's story of his new mining job and cheerfully offered to provide the near-legendary operator with anything he could "beg, borrow, or steal."

"Son of a bitch is sure I'm still working for the Company, Ming. And I'm damn sure not going to do anything to make him think I'm not," was the American's comment when he opened a suitcase full of classified documents, studies, air photos, and overlays ranging from CONFIDENTIAL to a few TOP SECRET. To protect his source, Mark had insisted that the classifications be blanked out when the originals were Xeroxed.

Visarn's connections provided Collins single-sideband radios to link the man with his home in Bangkok. Ming recruited a pair of former PARU radiomen. Both were overjoyed to be working again for the famous Colonel Mark.

On the eighth day after his return to Bangkok, Mark and

Ming and the intelligence booty flew down to the mine for the first time. After an only mildly hairy descent through the heavy cloud cover that clung to the four- and five-thousand-foot peaks that surrounded the mine plateau on three sides, they first unloaded and stored their "treasures."

Then Mark inspected the sacks of refined antimony ready to be flown to the trucks waiting at Ban Het. The bulky ingots gleamed dully when he opened one of the double rice bags used to save weight but still make it easy to lash the load down for the fifteen-minute flight to the valley.

As Mark straightened from his examination, Ming was protesting to Somboon. "But, Khun Boon, *krop*, are you sure he can fly in this kind of weather?"

"Mai pen ari, Ming. Sure he can," the slender Thai major replied. "I'll check him out in the right-hand seat for the first two days. After that he'll be able to take over. Frankly, I can't afford to work down here all the time. I've got a new dusting contract to get started up-country in Lopburi." Somboon's confidence was misplaced. Three pilots, one bent prop, and a complete new landing gear later, Somboon admitted defeat.

"I am very, very sorry, Colonel Mark, krop. But those three are the best I know of that are available." Then, almost timidly, he suggested, "Could you get one of the old Air America pilots? Like Khun Gary? This would be easy flying for Khun Gary."

CHAPTER SEVEN

SEVERAL THOUSAND MILES TO THE EAST, GARY SONDERBERG grimaced as he picked up the microphone in the cockpit of a converted C-45 Beechcraft.

"Good morning, ladies and gentlemen," he said, forcing himself to sound genial. "Welcome aboard All-Hawaii Air Tours' Around-the-Islands flight. Our route today will take us over and around all the major islands and . . ."

Nine hours and twenty minutes later, Captain Gary Sonderberg climbed stiffly into his battered beetle and drove through the evening rush-hour traffic to his tiny studio apartment in Aiea.

And all for a lousy five hours' flight pay. Jesus, he thought, dragging on a cigarette, at this rate I'll be in a wheelchair before I can get that tree farm even started.

It was dark before he got home, seething with the obstacles that kept getting in the way of his modest dream. He had the land—that was what made all the delays and the lack of money to plant the first trees so frustrating. And he had tried. By God, how he had tried! The old VW stalled out and Gary cursed. Clogged fuel lines. Dirty petrol. Take him another morning's work, but the car had to be functional.

More from habit than hope, he flipped open his mailbox and removed its contents. Phone bill, two envelopes of junk mail, and then he was suddenly alert. "Thai stamps, by Christ!"

The return address was unfamiliar. Mark Jordan's neat handwriting was! Gary read the brief letter twice. Once in the dim light of the hall as he opened his door, again under the full glare of the overhead inside. He paused long enough to open a can of beer before he read it a third time.

He made one decision and two phone calls. He did not relax until he had listened to the RCA Cable Office clerk read back the message:

MARK JORDAN, WONGTRADE, BANGKOK, THAILAND, ETA 1435 17 AUGUST, THAI FLIGHT 601. GARY.

The broad smile under Gary's close-cropped, graying moustache was still slightly tinged with disbelief as he replaced the receiver. He raised the empty beer can in a toast. "Aloha, Hawaii Air Tours." And gave an exultant yell.

THAI International flight 601 broke through the rainy season overcast at five thousand feet and allowed Gary Sonderberg to watch the familiar pattern of straight lines of the centuries-old man-made *klongs*. The canals stretched for ninety miles north of Bangkok's Don Muang Airport, providing irrigation for the almost painfully green rice paddies and easy transport for their owners.

Gary winced at the near one hundred percent humidity and rippling heat shimmering from the baked concrete. His colorful sport shirt was already darkening with sweat as he exited the shuttle bus and entered the over-air-conditioned arrival area. A grinning immigration officer, whose name Gary tried desperately to remember, wearing the familiar gold ring and blue stone of the Royal Thai Police Air Resupply Unit, the PARU, led him past the milling confusion of newly arrived passengers.

"Just go on to the baggage area, Captain Gary," the officer said, "while I get your passport stamped. I'll meet you at customs."

Only minutes later Gary raised his hands in a deep *wai* of thanks to the ex–PARU officer. Then he was reaching for his former boss. Gary noted that Mark Jordan was grayer, balding, and definitely paunchier. But the strength in the grip of the former Special Forces officer and CIA operator was the same, as were his ever-present cigar and the penetrating gaze of his gray eyes.

Gary cocked his head in amusement as Mark scanned him from head to foot for a long moment. Gary recalled the times he had wondered why he bothered to keep fit. He had an appetite for beer and sweets, but as long as he kept flying, he checked those cravings and insured a lean body that would be ready to react on those sudden occasions when a pilot's life depended on complete coordination of body and mind. With over twelve thousand hours in his logbooks, Gary had no illusions about the truth of the old saw that flying was ninety-eight percent utter boredom and two percent sheer terror. The smooth, confident, almost feline grace of his movements was no pose; it was the outward mark of a man ready to react to any emergency.

By the time Gary and Mark had fought their way through Bangkok's snarled, bumper-to-bumper traffic and reached the small bungalow in Bangkapi, they had pretty well caught up on each other's activities since they had last met in late '71. Mark showed him the bedroom. It was similar to so many rented homes in which he had stayed that he felt instantly at home. The rattan furnishings, the inevitable brass and carved-teak stands in the living room, were of good quality and reasonably new. Certainly that part of Bangkapi was a good few marks above many previous accommodations. Joining Mark on the verandah and gratefully accepting the beaded glass of Singha beer, Gary stretched his five-eleven frame limb by limb. "Well, friend Mark, what sort of a mess has Mrs. Sonderberg's idiot son gotten himself into this time?"

"No mess, and it might just put a few saplings on that tree farm of yours."

Gary raised his glass.

"For you," Mark continued, "it's a real piece of cake.

Remember those postage stamp strips we used in Laos?''
Gary nodded. ''You've got a Porter, one of Bird's old ones
that Continental took over when they bought him out. We've
got her worked over good, zero-time for the most part. New
engine and a zero-timed spare. Your mechanic is an old Air
America type; you should remember him—Ming Tong? He's
also our boss's nephew, so no sweat on parts or taking good
care of your bird.''

Gary remembered Ming Tong; he smiled, nodded.

''Anyway, here's the deal. Guys we work for, a bunch of
local Chinese, have a mine. It's way down in Chantaburi,
about two hundred klicks southeast of here. We get around
eighty percent or better in antimony, plus a healthy amount
of gold and silver. They run enough to pay for most of the
operation. The antimony is all gravy.

''Trouble is, the damn mine is way to hell and gone up in
the hills. About four thousand feet, and it's a good thirty
klicks from the road. Which is new since your days. It runs
from Aranya Pratet on the Cambodian border all the way
down to Chantaburi town itself. In the dry season they can
get a ten-wheeler truck about halfway up the mine road. Use
Land-Rovers for the rest of the way. Rainy season. No way.''
Mark sliced his hands in a definite gesture. ''It's a rough
enough trip on foot.

''What they've done is build a strip up at the mine out of
the tailings, laterite. Not too bad, about nine hundred feet.
Runs uphill, a lot like the one we called the ski slope up at
Ban Na in Laos. But so far we haven't been able to find a
pilot besides Boon who can use the damn thing unless everything's almost perfect. Even then they won't take out a decent
load. After the last guy, we had to rebuild the damn landing
gear before we could fly her again.

''With you driving''—and Mark jabbed his cigar at Gary—
''we can make it work. What you do is fly loads of what they
call crudum, partially refined ore, down to the road. Takes
about ten to fifteen minutes each way. There's a little sort of
a truck stop, Ban Het, where we've got a pretty good strip.
Then the crudum is loaded on ten-wheelers and hauled to the

port at Klong Toey. And about once a week, there's enough gold and silver to make a run up here. We'll schedule that for Fridays. So you get to spend the weekends here in Bangkok. Nothing much to do at the mine on weekends. Ming can pull his maintenance checks. And you've got the whole city."

Gary grinned, gesturing back toward the bungalow. "This is pretty good. How bad is it at the mine?"

Mark chuckled. "Not bad there either. We've got a good bungalow, and a cook. Ah Lee. I'll be down there most of time now."

Still grinning, Gary nodded that he was reassured.

"Production is picking up. Guess you didn't know that I had a mining degree from Colorado?" Mark twirled his cigar, watching Gary's face through the smoke, pleased by the pilot's mild surprise. "Never used it until now. Done some heavy reading. Mostly it's been organization to make the mine into a going concern. Antimony, the kind we ship, is running around eighteen hundred bucks a ton. With the gold and silver as extras, it works out fine."

To Gary's surprise, it did. Not that he didn't trust Mark's word as far as a job was concerned, but Gary was not by nature an optimist. Murphy's Law had operated against him too often, and Murphy was *supposed* to be an optimist. However, even though the end of the rainy season was still several weeks away, Gary was able to make eight to ten trips a day, bringing out loads of six and seven hundred pounds each time. The Porter was a good bird. Things got even better after three weeks, when Mark Jordan, with a broad grin, produced an old U.S. Air Force portable beacon.

"Just don't ask where we got it, Gary," Mark said. "I passed the word and, well, you know how the Thais are. It just appeared! We also have another one for you down at Ban Het."

With beacons, Gary was able to fly in all but the heaviest overcasts. The pile of semirefined crudum began to shrink rapidly. Then the end of the rains allowed production to increase, so Gary was hard put to hold his own. It was still a great job despite the crude strip and tricky winds up in the hills. Mark never pushed. Several times he tried to talk Gary out of flying in marginal weather. But Gary, who was banking most of his eighteen-hundred-dollar-a-month salary, did his best to earn it. All his living expenses, even beer, were furnished. Ming Tong was keeping the needle-nosed Porter in perfect shape, and Gary didn't have to give the crudum a running commentary on the scenery. That was the part he had hated most about his job in Hawaii.

Gary first met the owners of the mine in January at their annual Chinese New Year's celebration in Bangkok. The principal owner was Visarn, whom he knew was Ming Tong's uncle. Like most Thai last names, Visarn's was long, and Gary never did know more than the first three syllables. Visarn put on a real spread for the three days of festivities. Not the least appreciated part was a bonus of a month's pay for Mark and Gary. The pilot noted the surprise and pleasure on the old Chinese's face when both Americans made the formal wai reverence of folded hands at his presentation of their checks.

Visarn had the ageless look of his Chinese ancestry. His thin face, with its bony cheekbones, bore lines of character and strife. Visarn was smiling at having caused such pleasure and receiving the courtesies of his own country, but Gary felt the man could be a formidable ally or enemy.

Then Visarn ushered them into his study and motioned them to be seated. Gary glanced around at the priceless objects on the wall and in the little lacquered cabinets. He noticed, too, the piece of jade at the side of the desk, which Visarn unconsciously stroked. Still smiling, Visarn inquired after their tastes in liquor and served them himself, a subtly more significant mark of his favor. Then he sat down behind the huge teak desk, which dwarfed his skinny five-foot-nothing frame. "Khun Mark and Khun Gary, we are very pleased with your work at the mine, as we have tried to show you." Visarn waved off their thanks and continued. "Now I would like to discuss a rather delicate matter in which I hope you will also be able to help us. First, however, I must request that whatever your feelings, you will never mention the matter outside this room.'' He paused, thin brows raised in question.

Gary and Mark exchanged glances, shrugged, and nodded assent.

''So. Now I shall reveal to you a story that only a very, very few people know. It is rather . . . how do you say?'' Visarn gestured with his thin-boned hands. ''Complicated? Yes, very complicated indeed.

''I believe both of you had left Thailand when this story began. It was early in April 1975. The Khmer Rouge, as the Communists call themselves in Cambodia, were on the out-skirts of the capital, Phnom Penh. As you may know, busi-ness was very good during the American days. My partners and I had extensive interests in the city. As we saw that the Americans were certain to pull out, we had grave fears. Grave fears! We began to convert our holdings into hard currency. Some, very hard. Gold, to be exact. Unfortunately, events moved much faster than we had anticipated. So much so that a large quantity of gold, in bars, remained in Phnom Penh when the Khmer Rouge began their final assault.'' Visarn reached out to stroke his jade, he went on equably. ''This called for rather extraordinary measures. To move this gold, amounting to some twenty-five hundred kilograms, about ten million dollars' worth at today's prices, was a problem. Over-land travel was far too uncertain as the Communists had con-trol over many roads. And frankly, the Cambodian army was completely unreliable. So we decided to move the gold out by air.''

Gary shot a glance at Mark, but his boss was just smoking and listening.

''Even this was difficult. Not only finding an airplane, but pilots whom we could trust. The Communists were then so close that the airfield could only be used at night. Even so, planes were often hit by Communist fire. But we had no other option.''

Visarn leaned forward and pushed a button on his desk. Ming Tong, smiling broadly, entered in response. He was dressed formally, as the New Year's festivities required, but clearly he had also expected the summons.

"Ming was our representative," Visarn said, extending his hand to his nephew, "on the plane we finally obtained. I will let him tell you what happened next."

Visarn picked up the jade and sat comfortably back in his chair, his fingers softly stroking the gem while Ming Tong spoke.

CHAPTER EIGHT

"KEERIST ALMIGHTY, MING, THAT'S GOT TO BE THE HAIRI-est deal I *ever* heard!" Gary ran his fingers through his shock of hair, gazing at his mechanic in near awe.

Despite having hung on to every word of Ming's harrowing experiences, the pilot's inborn pessimism had been triggered by the tale and what it might lead to. Occasional glances at Mark had done nothing to ease the feeling. Throughout the story, Mark had listened intently, but his reactions to the more alarming parts of the story seemed just a little forced, almost as if he had heard it all before.

That thought, still aborning, was forced away as Visarn, fingers templed, gave both Americans a searching look. The jade had been quietly replaced. "As you can appreciate, my friends, my partners and I are faced with a highly unusual problem, one that is beyond our own resources to solve. My nephew has told me of your extensive experience in Laos and Vietnam during the fighting here."

The old Chinese paused as he sought his next words, and Gary flashed a cocked-eyebrow look at his cigar-twirling friend. Here comes the pitch, Gary thought, sure's my name's Sonderberg. And I know already I'm not going to like it. Not one little bit.

"Can you think of a way to retrieve the gold from its burial place inside Cambodia? Discreetly, you understand."

With a dry smile, Gary gestured that Mark should answer.

"That's a pretty tall order, Khun Visarn. Two and a half tons of gold would take about fifty good-sized mules or horses. From what Ming told us about the border guards . . . well, seems damn near impossible to miss 'em at some point in that sort of trek." Mark paused to twirl his cigar, his finger seeking the thought spot. "I can't see any way we could possibly use a truck," he went on. "And there's no way we could get a big enough plane down anywhere in that terrain."

Gary let out his breath in relief. If Mark had known they were going to be asked to rescue gold, he'd have probably had some kind of answer ready.

"Honestly, Khun Visarn," Mark said after a short pause, "I haven't got any real bright ideas on how you could pull it off."

"But you would be willing to think about it, Khun Mark." The appealing tone of voice was reinforced by the wistful smile on Visarn's wrinkled face.

"Hell, yes, Khun Visarn. I'll think about it. And so will Gary, I'm sure. But right now, well, I have to tell you honestly, retrieval looks damn near imposssible."

Visarn steepled his fingers again. "My nephew Ming Tong has told me quite a bit about your exploits in Laos and Vietnam during the war, Khun Mark. He feels strongly that if anyone can solve our problem, it is you."

As Gary watched closely, hanging on to every word Mark said about time passing and methods changing and old ruses too familiar in this area, his feeling of unease returned again. Much as he liked and respected the graying ex-colonel, Gary's lifelong instincts to look at things from their worst side pushed at him: The whole exchange of information, and Mark's announcement of impossibilities could be for his benefit. A plane was going to be essential, and he, Gary Sonderberg, was a pilot. A good one. He had proved that to himself, and he had also proved it to Visarn. His hand touched the spot where that bonus check lay in his jacket. The carrot? No, damn it, Gary thought. Rough and tough as Mark is, he

wouldn't pull a trick like this on me! Why should he? The
nagging splinter of doubt made him miss some of Mark's
concluding remarks.

". . . So you see, Khun Visarn, this business would be a
completely different kind of operation from my war days. I'm
sure you can understand that."

"I can and I do," Visarn agreed with smiling affability.
His steepled fingers arched toward the two Americans. "But
I would still like you and Khun Gary to think it over well.
Take whatever time you may wish to do so. But please also
remember that my partners and I will pay all your expenses.
Within reason." He smiled faintly. "Plus doubling your present monthly salaries, of course, and also five percent of all
the gold you recover. That would come to roughly half a
million American dollars to divide between you. A nice cush-
ion for your old age, my friends."

Inside the bungalow Mark poured two nightcaps of Black
Label. "Well, want to go back to Hawaii, Gary?" He handed
the pilot one drink. "Or buy that damn tree farm of yours
for cold cash?"

"*If* we can get the stuff out and *if* he pays off."

"The first 'if' is the biggest one, Gary. I'm not too worried
about the second. He'd pay off, all right. So what about it? Are
you game? If we can come up with something halfway reasonable as a modus operandi?" Mark grinned around his cigar.

"Depends on what *you* call reasonable, Mark. Remember,
I've been on some of your 'reasonable' deals before and followed your moduses operandi. Some of them damn near cost
me my ass!"

"Modi is the plural, son. Hell, that was the old days, and
a completely different ball game, Gary. This one's pure
Sneaky Pete, not thud and blunder stuff."

Gary smiled despite his misgivings and then shrugged his
shoulders, not really meaning consent but not denying the
possibility.

"Okay, tiger," said Mark, "let me work on it. Now let's
get some sleep."

CHAPTER NINE

Just past six the next morning, Gary sat drinking his second cup of coffee while Mark splashed noisily in the Thai-style bathroom. Gary rose when a car honked outside their gate. As the garden boy let an ancient gray Mercedes Benz 180 enter, Gary went to stand at the front screen door and stiffened as he recognized one of the two Thais who got out.

Even in a neat gray business suit, Border Patrol Police Colonel Banchert was familiar. There was no mistaking the trim, erect figure, the thin-nosed face, and the Clark Gable mustache. The other man, in Thai police uniform, was a stranger.

Gary decided to take refuge in his All-Hawaii geniality. "Colonel Banchert, it's real good to see you again, sir. Come in; we're just having coffee. Mark's still in the *hongnam*."

"Captain Gary, it has been too long since we have met. This is Dr. Chamien."

Gary relaxed as the smiling colonel introduced his companion.

Banchert was head of the Border Patrol Police Special Intelligence Center. Very few people even knew it existed, much less its functions. Having worked with Colonel Banchert and some of his men in Laos, Gary did. A six A.M. visit by the head of a secret intelligence unit that specialized in anti-

57

Communist and antismuggling operations wasn't exactly ordinary. Especially when Gary and Mark had just been asked to smuggle gold from Cambodia!

Gary called Ah Sam, the Chinese cook and maid-of-all-work, to bring more coffee and cups, and gestured the two men to take seats. Mark joined them, and the three former allies indulged in some mutual catching up.

"I could reminisce all day with you, Khun Mark, Khun Gary," said the colonel, his tone the essence of regret. He turned to Gary. "Khun Gary, we have a problem. It's rather like that of your new employer, Nai Visarn."

"Is it?" Gary replied.

"Yes, rather like Visarn. Ours involves some wounded border patrolmen, not mining products."

Gary did not show the relief he felt, though he thought he noticed the slightest trace of emphasis on "mining products." After four years at M.I.T. and three more working with OSS in World War II, Banchert spoke flawless English; he was up to such fine nuances of speech.

"You see," Banchert went on, "we've had a rather bad day—actually a night—in Loei Province. One of our platoons got pretty badly shot up in a fight with the Communists. We have so far lost two of our three choppers. The third was badly damaged when it was hit and forced to make an emergency landing on the airstrip at Pha Rang."

"We sent in a Helio Courier to take the wounded men out. Unfortunately, that pilot made a poor landing. The Helio needs a new propeller before it can fly again, as well as some work on the landing gear.

"Major Chamien"—and Banchert waved a courteous hand at his companion—"has advised me that two of the wounded patrolmen and the chopper pilot are in critical condition. He believes he can save them, if Khun Gary, flying the Porter Khun Somboon is chartering to Visarn, can get him in there in time.

"I know you are easily the best Porter pilot in the country right now, Khun Gary. So I would like to ask you to do me the favor of flying Dr. Chamien into Pha Rang."

Gary didn't want to get involved in any way with Banchert, in the same way that he wouldn't want to get involved with any special police or intelligence services. Especially not with this Visarn thing in the offing. He wanted to ask why Banchert couldn't use one of his own pilots. Having helped train some of them, he knew at least two or three who could do the job. Unless they'd gotten themselves killed in the meantime. He was still trying to figure out a way to refuse gracefully when Banchert spoke again, his expression and manner sincere.

"To be honest, Gary, we do have a pilot who could make the flight, but he is down on the Malaysian border. We have a big operation going on to clean out some of the Communist terrorists. We haven't time to divert him here. And you are much the better pilot. The other reason I have come to you personally is because we have no STOL planes left in Bangkok. Somboon has offered us the Porter on the condition that *you* fly it."

Approached in this way, Gary had to agree, though he fumed as he dressed. Christ Almighty, with friends like Somboon, I'll be lucky to live till the end of my New Year break, much less get in on that deal Visarn's offering.

In half an hour, the three men were flown by chopper from the police headquarters pad to Don Muang, then by Caribou to Loei. The doctor and his gear, together with the new prop and gear parts for the Helio, were loaded into the waiting Porter.

Gary chalked another score up for the Thai colonel. Wily old bastard knew he had me over a barrel and set the damn Porter up even before he came to see me, he thought as he lifted the plane off Loei's field.

Thirty minutes later he reached the strip at Pha Rang, and saw why the Helio pilot had pranged the plane. Making a low pass over the little runway, he saw that it was on an exposed shoulder, about four thousand feet above sea level, with strong updrafts and occasional heavy gusts crossing it. He guessed the gusts were easily thirty knots. He got his wheels down and was rolling out before the first gust caught him. Being prepared for it, he avoided the fate of the Helio pilot, but only just!

While the parts for the damaged aircraft were being unloaded, Gary had the patrolmen place bamboo poles with strips of cloth along the little runway. The flags would indicate when the wind died. The hazard shouldn't affect him at all on his second trip in. He'd have to circle each time, though, watching the little flags until the gusts died, then bring the Porter in fast. In all, Gary made four trips, getting out all the badly wounded as well as a few less serious cases.

Back in Bangkok that same night, Colonel Banchert insisted on taking Gary and Mark to one of the best restaurants in Bangkok for special filets. During their dinner at the Fireside Grill, Colonel Banchert expanded on the problems of the ill-fated platoon.

The local Border Patrol commander hadn't known that he was up against a new group of regular North Vietnamese, instead of the less well-trained local recruits, who had only small cadres of North Vietnamese. The latter usually avoided a fight with the tough patrolmen, generally preferring to attack small, weakly held Provincial Police outposts. In this case, the Communists had deliberately leaked the information that they planned to raid such an outpost—and when. They had also leaked the location of the camp from which they would launch the attack. The Border Patrol Police commander had already pinpointed that camp from previous reports and infrared air photos, but he hadn't been able to risk an operation into such an obviously heavily defended area.

Now that he had the information that the majority of defenders would be taking part in a raid two days march from their base, a quick raid was feasible. So he planned a two-pronged operation. His major force of two platoons would set up an ambush near the town the Communists were going to raid. At the same time, he would use his choppers to put a third platoon down close to the purportedly lightly guarded base camp and clean that out.

The operation had looked good on paper. And it would have worked if the information had been correct. The Communists *had* left the base area in force. But most of them had doubled back. Only a handful came near their supposed target, and they were expecting the Thai ambush; so it failed.

Far worse, the platoon that was dropped in by chopper was hit by the larger group of North Vietnamese regulars just as the last of them got off the chopper. It was dark within half an hour. They were neatly trapped. The fight went on all night. By dawn, more than half the platoon was killed or wounded. With full daylight and air cover in the form of Huey gunships, the choppers tried to get the men out, but they lost half their wounded when the Communists shot down two of the choppers on the second trip. It had been a real nasty business.

As Banchert was telling them the grim story, Mark was in his thinking mode, his cigar rolling fast and finger twirling on the bald spot in time with the cigar. "You know, Colonel," said Mark, "unless the Viets have changed their spots— which I doubt—I'll bet you a stale fortune cookie to the price of this dinner, they're back in that same camp, busy congratulating themselves, right this minute!"

Mark's supposition obviously surprised Banchert, but he nodded urgently for Mark to go on.

"Out at the field today, I saw one of those C-47's we converted to flying minigun platforms—the ones we used to call Puff, the Magic Dragon. Why not crank that Puff up and go take a look? I'd bet anything you name they'll spot a bunch of warm bodies and probably some cooking fires. Those North Viets are tough hombres; but even they make mistakes. Especially after they figure they've given *you*''—the cigar pointed at Banchert and swung away to indicate Thailand in general—"a really bloody good lesson."

Mark had scarcely finished before Banchert was out of his chair and all but running to the phone. He was back in less than five minutes, wearing a pleased grin. He called for the bill, paid it, and apologized for deserting them—they must, of course, have liqueurs—but he wanted to go along on the Puff flight himself.

Early the next morning, Banchert phoned, sounding, as

Mark put it, like he'd just inherited a million dollars. Gary could have heard the jubilance in Banchert's voice even if his ear hadn't been at the receiver. Mark just smiled, nodded, and dragged at his cigar as he listened. His chuckle told Gary more than half the tale even before he summarized Banchert's report.

Puff had come in downwind, throttled low, and spotted three fires and a lot of bodies on the infrared scope. Then the pilot had cut loose with his six-thousand-round-a-minute miniguns and cut a swath through the heavy jungle like a tornado's path. When the Puff's guns finally ran out of ammo, RTAF planes dumped in napalm and rockets for good measure.

They had worked the area over again at dawn and followed up with a full company of Parachute Police. Not a shot was fired at them. The PARU boys had flushed three live Viets out of a cave full of ammunition. That was all. But they destroyed enough stored hardware, ammo, rice, canned stuff, and other supplies to equip a hundred men.

CHAPTER TEN

FOR OVER TWO WEEKS AFTER THE LOEI BUSINESS, MARK struggled to figure out a way to get Visarn's gold out of Cambodia, going through yellow legal pads like Kleenex. Night after night, Mark was plugging away until the early hours, but he still hadn't come up with anything either of them felt good about. On the third weekend, Mark got a fresh batch of air photos from his friend in JUSMAG Air section. The Thai air force had shot the entire border because the Khmer Rouge were increasing their raids into Thailand. After supper, Mark slammed down a handful of photos.

"Got something?"

"Wish to hell I did, Gary, but no, I don't. I just can't get around the goddamn weight. Two and a half tons, twenty-five hundred kilos—either way, it's just too damn much. No way you can take more than eight or nine hundred pounds in the Porter. Right?"

"Nine hundred would be tops, Mark, even with a good strip."

"That's the number I've been using. Which means at least seven trips. Never mind we stay well away from that village, Phum Krachap. No way can we go in more than a couple of times without causing a fuss. Just digging the gold up from under those kilns will be no mean trick! Not with people working them and the Khmer Rouge guards.'' Mark puffed on his cigar. ''Sarn, that Free Cambodian guy, says his people could take care of the guards all right, but then they'd have to haul ass quick. His men couldn't hold the area against even a couple of platoons of Khmer Rouge. And no way they could move the damn gold. It'd take over a hundred strong men just to carry it, and they'd need another hundred as escort.''

Drag, carry, or fly, Gary could see that one way or another, his services were going to be involved.

''No way we can spring a Caribou, Mark?'' he asked without much hope of a favorable reply.

''No way. At least, not without cutting the Thais in on the fact that we're smuggling gold into the country. And that's about as illegal as you can get! I tried that idea on Visarn. But he wasn't having any. Said the damn cops would grab the whole business. He'd rather leave it than lose it, for sure!'' Mark paused, puffed, grimaced. ''No, Gary, it's got to be the Porter. Some way, but I'm damned if I can figure out how.''

''How about all those people you told me about? The ones the Khmer Rouge have herded out from the big towns. More than fifteen thousand in the area, you said. Seems like we could get all the volunteers we'd need right there, on site.''

''Oh, they'd probably volunteer, every one of the poor devils. But Sarn says they're all either half-starved, sick, or both. Those black-pajama guys have the country so screwed up, most of their camps are on half rations and have been for months. They killed off hundreds on the marches from the towns—old people, kids, and anybody who got sick. They'd've been in bad enough shape when they got to the camps, but Khmer Rouge have been working their asses off ever since. When Sarn's guerrillas want to bring out some recruits, they have to smuggle food in and feed 'em for a couple of weeks before they're strong enough to make it to the hills.''

Gary picked up the photos Mark had thrown down. They were very clear. He could see Remrut's two kilns on the banks of their respective streams. ''Too bad those damn creeks and the river run east instead of coming our way," he said, laying the pictures down.

Mark looked at him in disgust. "Jesus Christ, Gary, we've got enough headaches without reversing the course of a bloody river! Let's go eat. I'm sick of sitting here spinning my wheels."

As he often did, the next day Gary let Mark fly the Porter from Don Muang until they got close to the mine. Under Gary's tutelage, Mark had become a better pilot than his nine-hundred-odd logged hours would indicate. But STOL landings were one thing on a reasonably long strip like Ban Het and completely different on the mine's tricky one. So Gary made all the landings and only let Mark take off from the mine when the wind wasn't a problem.

On the first trip that morning, they brought Ming Tong down. Mark wanted to have one more talk with the old man, Remrut, using Ming as an interpreter.

Hoping that the session would bear some results, Gary spent the rest of the day hauling crudum down the valley, at lunchtime grabbing a hasty sandwich between flights. When he quit that evening, he was really ready for the cold Singha beer that Ah Lee handed him the moment he walked into the door of the mine bungalow.

Gary grinned as he watched Mark, Ming, and Remrut poring over a sketch. Just as Gary entered, Mark leaned back and smiled in a way that meant the problem was licked. Mark gulped half his own beer and beamed at Gary.

"Between that crack of yours about changing the courses of creeks and Khun Remrut's knowledge of the area"—Remrut looked up at Mark at the mention of his name, and smiled shyly—"I think we got it, old buddy."

Gary smiled encouragingly at the old charcoal maker. The man would have made a great subject for a portrait painter. His leathery face was a maze of crow's-feet and, despite his rough life, laugh lines. He still had all his teeth, though a second look was required to be sure. They were black from the betel nut he chewed constantly. Remrut was perhaps five foot five and one-hundred-thirty-five pounds. There wasn't an ounce of fat on him; his hard, ropy muscles flexed and coiled as he moved. His hair was still jet-black and close-cropped, like a new recruit's. Right then, Remrut was obviously pleased with himself.

"Yessir, Gary, Khun Remrut has put the last pieces in place for us. See what you think of this. I'll go over it. Check me out, Ming, if I'm wrong anywhere.

"Remrut hid the gold in about equal portions under the fire pits of his two kilns." Mark pointed them out on the map and on the photos. "From all appearances, nobody's found it. The Khmer Rouge are using people from the camp outside Phum Krachap to make charcoal in them right now. See the smoke on the photo here?

"Now, here's where the two creeks join and flow nearly due east for about twenty miles till you come to the highway bridge on the road to Pursat. The road is paved, blacktop, from the north end of the bridge to Pursat . . . over fifty klicks.

"From these photos you can see the two creeks are running pretty full right now. Remrut says when they're that wide, they're over two meters deep and moving right along. Now, look up here!" Mark indicated the higher mountain area and some oblong shapes in two photos. "You can see piles of logs and bamboo poles cut and stacked along the creeks. Must be about seven or eight klicks upstream from the kilns.

"Remrut"—and Mark paused to smile gratefully at the charcoal maker—"says they tie these logs up into small rafts and float them down to where the creeks join to form the Pang River. Then they lash a whole bunch together into a really healthy-sized raft and float all the way down to Tonle Sap—here." Mark's finger jabbed at the large lake.

Remrut then pointed to the bridge at Pursat and spoke rapidly. Ming translated as the old man spoke. "Sometimes, Khun Mark, they only take the rafts as far as the bridge where the highway crosses and then load the wood on trucks. But most of them used to go all the way to Tonle Sap. Remrut says some families build a little shelter on the larger rafts and live on them all the way down. After they sell the raft, they take a bus back to the bridge, walk into the mountains, and build another raft. But Remrut says that was how it *used* to be done. Now he's not sure how they'll work it—with the 'bad people' around.'' Ming grinned as he finished Remrut's comment.

Mark twirled his cigar, studied the photo minutely again. "Well, Ming, from this photo, they're obviously continuing to cut and stack wood and bamboo. It seems pretty likely Khmer Rouge or not, they have to use the old system. Actually, it doesn't really make too much difference to us as long as there's plenty of wood or bamboo cut and stacked on the creeks.

"What is really crucial is the ox carts and animals we'd need. Is Remrut sure we can raft them down the river? It could get pretty hairy on a flimsy raft if oxen cut up bad afloat.''

Ming queried Remrut, who gave a long and obviously confident answer.

"No sweat, Remrut says, Khun Mark. They brew up some kind of weed, acts like a tranquilizer. As long as the oxen have grass and water, they don't make any trouble. Remrut *is* a little worried that Khmer Rouge might have killed off or taken away a lot of the animals, even though you can see many carts up here near the big clearing.''

Mark examined the relevant photo closely. "Good point, Ming. I can get Sarn to check on the livestock.''

By this time, Gary was staring at the other three as if they were crazy. Mark noticed his expression and laughed. "No, Gary, we're not planning to go into the lumber business or smuggle the gold out in the ox carts. We're just going to relocate it a bit.

"Look here, on the map. That first section of paved road at the bridge is straight as a string for five klicks. With that for a strip, you can haul a full load. Now look where the road turns east. Those X's of mine are other possible landing strips. They all look pretty good on the air photos. We'll get Sarn's people to check 'em out ground level. Now, where the Pang River swings way north and east, Remrut says the country's all pretty flat with nothing but scrub bush. We don't have photos, but from what Remrut says, there seem to be at least four pretty good areas, all close to the river.''

As Gary bent to examine the map, Mark slipped a piece of acetate overlay on it. "Here are the strips, Gary. I've numbered them. By playing hopscotch, like the numbers show, you'll have about thirty to thirty-five klicks between any two consecutive landings. How's that grab you?''

Gary studied the overlay a long while, and then, with obvious reluctance, replied. "Well, it *is* a real improvement over making a whole bunch of trips to the same place. But it's still an awful lot of trips. Coming in dead stick shouldn't be any real problem in flat terrain like that around the Pang River, but that Porter's going to make a hell of a racket on takeoff. I can see maybe a couple or three trips, but seven or eight? Mark, I just think we'd be taking the pitcher to the well too many times. And the pitcher is me!'' His thumb hit his breastbone emphatically.

Mark's grin was disconcerting, and the pilot braced himself for the rebuttal.

"I know it sounds a bit much, Gary. But I've got something else that I took out of the Viets' book of tricks. Otherwise I wouldn't even consider that many trips. Remember the deception bit the Viets pulled on Banchert's boys up in Loei? It got me thinking along the same lines.

"Actually, my plan is a series of deceptions.'' Mark paused to light another cigar. "First off, we use a little goodie that worked real well in Laos. We make a tape recording, stereo, of a couple of choppers coming in, landing, idling a while, and then taking off again. We set up a couple arrays of these small four-inch speakers, about a dozen of the little guys, all hooked together and facing each other about fifty feet apart. If you're in between them, with your eyes closed, you'd really swear there were choppers coming!

"When Sarn's teams take out the Khmer Rouge guards at Phum Krachap, they keep a couple alive as prisoners. They blindfold and bring 'em along the trail to the clearing where we have our sound effects set up. On the way, Sarn's guys will grunt and groan and complain about the heavy loads and all that so the prisoners can hear them. Up at the clearing, they tie 'em, park 'em where they get the full benefit of the 'Chopper Concerto.' '' Mark pulled on his cigar, thoroughly enjoying his recital. "By the time the prisoners can work loose, Sarn's people will be long gone down the creek by raft. No footprints. The Khmer Rouge guards should be convinced they all left with their 'heavy' loads on the choppers they heard.

"Meanwhile, the rest of Sarn's people have taken over the kilns, dug up the gold, and stashed it in the huts on the rafts and started going down to the bridge. The way I figure it, they'll make the bridge about dark, pull over, and tie up. All perfectly normal. But after dark, four loads, about seven-hundred pounds each, go up the road to where it meets the trails and on to the strips on the west side. The other rafts, with the remainder of the gold, just keep going to the next day. Tie up the second evening, wait until it's good and dark. Then use carts for the rest of the load!

"We time you in to pick up the first batch at the bridge during the 'Chopper Concerto.' You probably won't be able to hear it, but when you come back out, I think the odds are that if anyone has heard you, they'll figure you were one of those choppers."

Mark's multiple deceptions were impressive. If the misdirection worked, the Khmer Rouge ought to think that the operation had been strictly a one-shot affair. They would see the digging at the kilns; no effort would be made to hide that or the slain guards. The ones who 'escaped' after hearing the recordings would report that whatever had been dug up was lifted out by chopper.

"A few of Sarn's men will hang around a while," Mark said, as they rehashed the possible flaws in the scheme. "They should be able to tell us whether or not the Khmer Rouge bought the deal. Once we're sure of that, then you can start the hopscotch pickups."

Gary heaved a long sigh, shaking his head. There were too

many elements to coordinate; just one slipup, one hunk of misinformation, and the pitcher boy would buy it.

"Look, how's this grab you as extra insurance?" Mark asked, lighting yet another cigar. "You start a series of supply drops close to our pickup points, just as if you were supplying PARU or refugees. We let the Khmer Rouge pick up a few pounds of rice and stuff, but if they do see you, they'll think you're just on another supply round."

Some disquiet continued in Gary's mind, but he couldn't finger it. He wasn't worried as far as the Khmer Rouge went; at least, not until Sarn's men had ground-surveyed his hopscotch landing spots.

"Well, what *is* worrying you, Gary? Spit it out and let's chew it over. We've got a good plan, good men to carry through the details, the best plane for the job—"

"That's it, Mark. The Porter."

Mark took the cigar out of his mouth to stare at the pilot. "Now, what could be wrong with the goddamn plane? Ming keeps it ticking over like a dream."

"Have you forgotten that every plane authorized to fly in Thailand has an ELT set?"

Mark slapped his forehead, shoved the cigar in his mouth, and began his finger game. Ming slumped as his own elation faded.

The emergency landing transmitter sends out a signal that identifies the aircraft on the Thai air force radar as friendly and legal. If the pilot got in trouble or the plane actually crashed, the ELT would broadcast an emergency signal that would appear on radar scopes and alert operators.

"Mark, I know damn well that if I show up on a Thai radar screen without that ELT on, I'll have a bunch of trigger-happy F-5 jocks on my tail in no time at all. If I keep the damn ELT on, the Khmer Rouge can track me all the way in, mock supply drops or the real thing."

"Hold it." Mark began rummaging through the file of overlays. He pulled one out, examined it closely, and, with an air of triumph, placed it on the map.

"I had to put the screws on my buddy in JUSMAG for this

one, even if I didn't know then why we'd need it. It's always useful to know where the weaknesses are."

Gary saw the title, "Deficiencies in the Royal Thai Air Force Radar Coverage."

"Of course, he's convinced I'm still working for the CIA on some real hush-hush; so I got it." Mark was standing aside so Gary could inspect the filmy treasure. Certain areas of the map were now blanked out. One shielded the mountain range they were on. Gary quickly saw that he would be able to fly by two different routes without Thai radar picking him up, as long as he stayed under three thousand feet inside Thailand. The Thais would probably pick him up after he was over the Cambodian border, but that wasn't much of a problem because he'd drop down again after he cleared the Cardamon Range and disappeared. Coming back, he'd still be on the other side of the blank, and when he went off the screen in Cambodia, the Thais would figure he'd landed there.

"No sweat now, huh, Gary?"

"I'd like a test run. I'm not real sure about those Thai radar guys not spotting me in spite of this." Gary tapped the overlay.

"Like I said, no sweat, Gary. We set up a test run. My guy in the Air Section at Utapao is there to keep a close watch but not to alert the Thais while you're airborne. Okay?"

"What's with this Air Section buddy, Mark? You own him or something?"

"No." Mark twirled his cigar, relaxed and confident. "But we did work together on some spook jobs in Laos when I was with the CIA. The more I tell him this is just a personal favor, the more he's sure I'm still working on some real deep job for the Agency. Once you've been in the business, nobody'll ever believe you've really quit. From his point of view it all fits. Cambodia is what CIA calls a denied area. What's more logical than using a supposedly retired CIA guy to try and crack it under a commercial cover?"

"Okay, Mark, okay." Gary shook his head slowly. "I get my test run with your man overseeing, but that damn Thai radar still scares me. And another thing . . . say we can duck the radar; how do I find these damn strips?'' He tapped the hopscotch points. ''The first one should be pretty easy, I know; it's the only bridge for miles with a hard road on one side. What about the others?''

''Was wondering when you'd think about that.'' Mark's grin was broader as he pulled a schematic scale drawing out of an envelope and laid it down on the table. ''Here's our handy-dandy do-it-yourself locator beacon. It all fits inside one of my cigar boxes. Nickel cadmium batteries, good old USAF surplus stuff. Screw in an ordinary automobile radio antenna and you can pick it up twenty miles away at five-thousand feet.

''Each of Sarn's teams who leave the hopscotch loads will have one, set on a single fixed frequency. One frequency for each strip as a security measure. If you don't get the beacon signal on the right frequency for a particular strip, you come right home.

''Ming's getting them made up by one of his people. Ming will test them out somewhere around here when you're on a routine flight for the mine.''

''Ming?'' Gary glanced in surprise at the mechanic, who gave him a big smile back. ''What's he know about that kind of gear?''

''You didn't know, Gary?'' Mark affected dismay. ''Ming was cross-trained as both a radio *and* beacon operator when he was with the Parachute Battalion's Pathfinder Platoon. So we can use him for this job and keep it all in the family.'' Mark drew on his cigar, exhaling a wreath of smoke that obscured the satisfaction on his face.

Even if Mark had answers for every objection, Gary was not fully convinced that such a complicated scheme would work. Gary had run out of questions, but he was afraid he hadn't heard all the answers.

CHAPTER ELEVEN

Once Mark got Visarn's approval of the plan, he buried himself in developing a schedule. Then he wrote up detailed training courses for the reception teams, the initial raid to remove the gold from the kilns, how the raft crews were to operate, and the other bits and pieces that a complicated retrieval operation required.

As Gary read each of the elements and critiqued them from a pilot's viewpoint, his respect for Mark's ability grew. Meticulous to a gnat's eyeball himself—as far as aircraft were concerned—Gary found his lingering qualms disappearing as he read page after page of Mark's neat handwritten script.

The reception teams who would operate the beacon, mark the hopscotch strips with flares, move the gold from the temporary caches, and load it on the Porter were each to be trained separately. They were to be given the impression that they were to be used for a completely different purpose, such as sending out agents or retrieving wounded. Nothing would be mentioned about gold during their training. The reception teams would only learn the true nature of their mission a few hours before Gary was due—too late for any leakage of information. Each four-man team would be returned to Thailand after the pickup flight. Sarn had carefully chosen men whose families were already in Thailand, and thus hostages.

The tough little Free Cambodian leader took no chances when it came to security. Any breach by anyone involved in the operation would mean death for the offender and the immediate revocation of his family's Thai residence permits. All the men chosen had been sometime residents of the squalid refugee camps that housed over one hundred thousand refugees. Death would be nothing to the threat held over their families.

The men who posed the greatest risk were those who would carry the individual loads from the kilns by raft and ox cart and cache the gold near the landing strips. They would know that there was more than one load of the precious metal. Sarn suggested that, as soon as these men returned from their part of the operation, they be secluded at one of his numerous little camps in Thailand until the operation had ended.

A small temporary camp was built a few kilometers from the mine by the former Parachute Police troopers whom Mark and Ming recruited for the training job. None of them was told the real purpose of the drills. Being old hands from Laos and welcoming the well-paid jobs, they didn't ask questions. Like most Thais, they had no love for Cambodians in general, Khmer Rouge in particular. The other employees were told that the instructors were guards for the mine.

Ming and Gary repainted the Porter at the mine strip. Light gray they chose for the underside, dark blue for the rest. Ming told Somboon he'd gotten the paint free. Gary was a little surprised at Somboon's casual acceptance of the new design, which blotted out the original bright red of the tail and wing tips, but he didn't pay much attention at the time; he was too relieved by Somboon's indifference.

As the first teams completed their fitness training, they were given a live test down the valley, well within radar dead space. On the ground Ming and Mark would simulate being wounded men to be evacuated. Four teams had been trained and tested prior to the scheduled date for the first flight. As soon as each team passed its "exam," it was sent to isolated and well-guarded camps to wait.

Inside Cambodia, Sarn's men had been keeping a close

watch on the target area and the sprawling Khmer Rouge concentration camp. Fifteen thousand half-starved people there were driven into the fields every day by their Khmer Rouge liberators. Sarn's men counted 218 black-clad soldiers in the town and a dozen in the woodcutters' camp by the clearing. Fearing no threat from the cowed physical wrecks in the camp, the Khmer Rouge were pretty lax about security at the camp. There was even less at the kilns and woodcutters' camp.

Most of the soldiers kept a girl or a woman; the ability to give extra food and grant remission from grueling fieldwork gave them the widest choice of the females. As far as the wretched camp inmates were concerned, the woodcutting and charcoal details were a boon. To keep the Khmer Rouge in Phum Krachap supplied, the food rations for such work were doubled and then tripled to fulfill the increasingly more frequent requisitions of charcoal from Pursat, Battembang, and as far downriver as Tonle Sap Lake. The relatively good condition of the work gangs turned out to be both a blessing to Sarn's operation and a headache.

The woodcutter and charcoal gangs numbered nearly one hundred. There were another thirty to fifty ox cart drivers— the census varied from day to day as wood and charcoal were hauled to the camp a dozen kilometers away. To a man, they wanted to escape, but their families were held in the main camp.

Sarn and Mark discussed the problem while Gary listened. If Sarn's men recruited the woodcutters to make up the rafts that were to carry the gold from the kilns to the eight sites, his big manpower problem would be resolved and a lot of time saved. On the other hand, Sarn couldn't, and wouldn't, consider using them to help and then abandon them, and their families, to certain butchering by the Khmer Rouge.

The deciding factor came when Sarn's men reported that the families of men cutting wood or making charcoal were in far better condition than the average camp inmates. Husbands and fathers smuggled extra food to them on the daily stream of ox carts. The laxity of the Khmer Rouge camp guards also contributed. Further, it was reported that the black-clad soldiers had given up counting the number of people who died every day. They let their relatives bury them. No wood, of course, could be spared for proper cremation, so mass graves were dug outside the camp perimeter. Twenty, thirty, sometimes as many as forty, Sarn's report said, died in a twenty-four-hour period. Anyone who claimed to be too sick to work was forced to move into large huts. There they were given barely half the normal starvation rations and only what medicine or treatment friends or relatives could improvise from herbs and roots. The result was inevitably death. Burial took place in the early morning, before the dawn call to work.

The guards paid no attention to the daily predaylight burial parties unless the mourners were late getting back to work in the fields. If the previous day's death toll had been too high and burial incomplete by daylight, the gruesome job had to be finished after work in the dusk. This grim routine solved the problem of getting the families out of the camp: they would pose as corpses or burial parties in the twilight groups, and just keep going.

Mark and Gary had reservations about this ruse. Sarn insisted that it would work. They compromised with a trial run with a group of twenty women and young children. There were no babies to worry about; the few born in the camp soon succumbed to disease. The Khmer Rouge imposed a death penalty for sex among the inmates.

The trial group got out safely. Eighteen women and young children, escorted by Sarn's hand-picked men, reached the safety of the foothills without any reaction from the Khmer Rouge. Two more trips were needed to collect the families of the woodcutters and charcoal makers.

Getting such a large number of women and children safely across the border in Thailand was a different problem. Even with extra food, the long-abused ex–camp inmates made slow progress up the steep, thickly forested range of mountains. The trails that were passable were either mined or guarded by Khmer Rouge. When the black-clad patrols were small enough, Sarn's men would attack and wipe them out. Far more often, they had to rely on stealth and make long detours, as Ming and Remrut had done. They got one hundred seven women and children safely into Thailand, losing six to sickness and four to a Khmer Rouge mine field. But the family retrieval operation was considered a huge success.

But the ease with which an almost insurmountable hazard had been overcome bothered Gary. He kept his pessimism to himself, however, as he, Sarn, and Mark set firm dates for the first phase of the main operation, recovering and relocating the gold, and for Gary's first flight to the bridge strip at Pursat.

Once the families had been reported safely out of the Phum Krachap area, the raiding party—including the first reception team, with Remrut as guide—went in. A week later they were placed and ready. The Khmer Rouge guards at the kilns and the woodcutters' camp had been changed the previous week and, being on a monthly rotation, wouldn't be relieved for another three.

Gary, Mark, and Ming had tried to talk Remrut out of going along with the first group. To no avail. As the old man pointed out, he was the only person who knew exactly where the gold was buried. Since the bases of the kilns were over twenty feet in diameter, even a slight error in excavation could waste precious time. Remrut's brown eyes twinkled as he added a clincher. With him along, no one else need know exactly where the gold was, nor that it was gold to be dug instead of the weapons that the raiding team had been misled to expect. Thus no one could possibly break security, except Remrut himself. Then the old man waved his Buddhist amulet in front of the three dissuaders. Grinning, he slid open a panel at the back of the gold shell to reveal two white pills.

"Can kill rats, and me, too. No worry. I die quick." He flashed his blackened teeth in a sad smile as he handed Ming an envelope and added, "If I die, still can find. Next trip. I can draw map, too." His benign grin fell on Mark, who chortled at the unexpected allusion.

On the date set for the first gold pickup, Gary was nervous all afternoon. He tried to sleep but just lay there, his mind conjuring up an endless list of things that could go wrong—most of them fatally so, in obedience to Murphy's Law. Abruptly he got up. Much more talking to himself and he'd lose his nerve.

Mark and Ming were in the lounge when Gary joined them, drinking cup after cup of Ah Lee's good coffee and the Ovaltine he had taught the Chinese cook to prepare. He succeeded in making the other two men as miserable as he felt.

Finally it was 1820 hours. Buoyed by an absence of wind, Gary went meticulously through the preflight checklist and found everything in good order. Once in the air, the concentration required by flying took his mind off bizarre emergencies.

As planned, Gary kept well down in the valley south of Ban Het, swung east at the pass he'd picked out in the trial runs, and hugged the dark mass of the range until his watch told him elapsed flight time had brought him well inside Cambodia.

"Okay," he said aloud despite the fact that the noise in the Porter's cabin made it necessary to shout to be heard, "let's just see how good Uncle Sam's surplus beacons are."

He poured on the fuel up to nine thousand feet, forced himself to stop thinking as he cut the switch and feathered the prop. He flicked on the little beacon receiver, unconsciously holding his breath a moment. To his relief, he heard the signal right away. It was a bit to his left, so he corrected his glide.

At 0200 he saw the blinking recognition signal, answered, and took a deep breath as little spots of light outlined the road.

He amazed himself by greasing the Porter down. She rolled to within twenty meters of the bridge. Grinning faces peered in at Gary and then the Porter was pushed the rest of the way and swung around as the team had been trained to do.

It didn't take fifteen minutes to load the gold in its sooty, smoke-smelling ammo boxes. He tied them down himself, grunting as he knotted the tie-downs. Murphy hadn't yet put in an appearance.

Just as he was about to close the door, someone tugged at his ankle. He stared down at the runty, burdened figure.

Remrut! Something was wrong, Gary thought wildly. Bad wrong. Remrut was supposed to have hauled ass for Thailand as soon as the gold had been unearthed. The old man knew too damn much to stay a minute longer than necessary. Yet there he was, a full day's hard walking from the kilns and more than five from safety!

All that flashed through Gary's mind as he stared down at the old charcoal maker. Then, in the dim, moonless dark, Gary realized that Remrut was carrying someone in his muscular arms. In the faint light from the runway flares, it looked like a child.

"Khun Gary, my *lukesow*," Remrut said in an exhausted, entreating tone. "She too sick. Close to die. You can take?"

Christ Almighty! Remrut had a daughter? Gary looked down the cabin of the Porter, and his mind whirled in a lightning computation. Remrut's daughter was small; couldn't weigh more than seventy or eighty pounds. But he had already nearly a ton in gold and ammo boxes. Even with all the runway in the world, there's a limit to what an aircraft can lift. He was already asking the limit from the Porter. Another eighty pounds of sick girl would guarantee the bird would never make it.

The two men stood, eyes locked, for what seemed an age. Remrut's expression was one Gary would never forget. His face pleaded far more eloquently than any words he could have chosen. Then the girl moaned. Gary scrubbed from his mind all the mental pictures of what happens when a pilot tries to break the laws of aerodynamics.

Then he held out his arms and took the limp body. With Remrut's eager assistance, he eased her into the right-hand seat. Seventy pounds, he guessed, eighty at the most. He strapped her in.

He turned, pulled the fire extinguisher from its bracket. Nine pounds? Beacon receiver! Five more? Ten ammo boxes? Another thirty! The discarded items disappeared as he worked. While Remrut stacked loose gold bars on the cockpit floor under his daughter's feet, Gary dipped the wing tanks. Three gallons out of each would save thirty-six pounds, but Gary had damn well better hit Ban Het on the nose! And Murphy, stay the hell out of the way!

After he'd drained the tanks, he started to climb in, but Remrut stopped him and led him to the rear door. The old man opened it, released the rear tie-down strap, and lifted out an ammo box. "I carry. Just like Ming. Can do," he said, grinning up at Gary.

"Good man, Khun Remrut!" Gary slapped the old man's muscled shoulder. Fifty-odd pounds less to carry might be crucial.

Gary paused just a moment before he closed the rear door, visualizing a shifting shadow, an old charcoal maker lugging an incriminating load through hostile jungle to save a girl who might die despite all their efforts. But Gary felt lighter in heart as he fired the Porter up. She caught first try. He checked his map as he began taxiing.

Gary held her down until she flew herself off. She must have used two thousand meters before she did. Despite the overload, she climbed pretty well. There was overcast at about four thousand over the gap that had been selected for the return trip. Gary took her all the way up to eight thousand in tight circles, then headed west and flew time and distance to what he hoped was the Ban Het valley. With his gas reserve nonexistent, he'd better be right. He was staking two lives on his skill, and the pressure began to get to him.

He was really sweating—hearing Mark's voice, "No sweat, Gary," in his ears—as he chopped power and began spiraling down through the overcast. Then he cursed himself up and down the air lanes for jettisoning the beacon receiver at Pursat. And gave a bark of laughter as he suddenly realized he didn't need the bloody thing! The old air force beacons at Ban Het would bring him in.

Gary felt a complete fool for his moment of panic after he tuned his ADF and heard first Ban Het and then the mine. He was still calling himself seventeen kinds of a fool when he cut the Porter's whining engine in front of the little shack where Mark and Ming stood waiting.

When their flashlights revealed someone in the Porter's right-hand seat, the incredulous shouts and expressions revived Gary's sense of humor. Mark and Ming were pointing and gargling unintelligible questions while Gary sat there smiling, mightily pleased. Sliding the window open, Gary jerked his thumb at the now conscious, dazed passenger. "Don't worry about her. She was on 'space available,' and since I didn't have a cojock—"

"Space available!" Mark exploded so that his cigar shot out of his mouth to the ground. "You idiot! Who is she? What the hell are you pulling? You're not on All-Hawaii Air Tours picking up rich passengers! We had this planned to the last pound and second. How the hell could you?"

There was a lot more along the same lines as Gary unbuckled the girl's safety harness and eased her over the seats to the Porter's left door. Ignoring Mark's angry questions and Ming's head shaking, Gary gathered the frightened girl into his arms and carried her to the shack. Setting her down in the only chair, he turned around, ready to explain. But the anger on Mark's face triggered a reaction in Gary. He began to laugh, and he laughed until the tears flowed down his cheeks.

The poor girl sat, trembling like a frightened deer, until Gary's outbursts subsided enough for him to notice her. Her big scared eyes were darting back and forth between the men, then settling with more frequency on the half-filled glass of coffee on the plywood table. Her intensity stopped Gary's outburst of nervous relief. Ignoring Mark, Gary quickly mixed a fresh glass of Ovaltine, dumped in a big glob of gooey condensed milk, and handed it to the girl.

The way she gulped it down effectively silenced Mark's tirade. As he made more Ovaltine, Ming found cold fried rice and began to feed it to her in between sips of the fortified drink. Gary had barely recounted what had happened at Pursat when the poor girl vomited everything right at Mark.

"Damn it all, Gary, why didn't you warn us she was

starved? Too much food too quick. Look, you and Ming unload about half the gold while I get her cleaned up. We'll
take her with us up to the mine.''

As Gary and Mark and the space-available daughter of
Remrut flew off to the mine, Ming dug deep in his toolbox
and took out a small package wrapped in plastic. Inside was
a flat oblong of extremely thin paper. Unlike normal pads,
this one was glued on all four sides. Using his Swiss Army
knife's small blade, Ming gently slit a corner to free the top
sheet. His sensitive fingers guided the knife blade around the
edges until the translucent sheet came free.

Across the top in red print was the Thai word for ''send''
and a serial number. The rest of the sheet was filled with
rows of five-digit numbers. After a cautious look outside the
shack, Ming wrote a short message in English on the numbered page, making sure each letter was directly above a
numeral. Then, with a small plastic card taped to the back
of the pad, he computed each letter/number pair and wrote
the result on a clean piece of lined notepaper.

After rechecking his work, he lit a match to the numbered
page. When it was consumed, he ground the ashes into dust
with his foot. Adding two more five-digit groups to the bottom of the message, he folded it carefully and put it in his
wallet. He rewrapped the message pad and put it back in his
toolbox.

As he waited for Gary to return from the mine to collect
the remaining half of the gold, he smoked and drank coffee,
relaxing completely after the hours of uncertainty and the
day's surprises.

When Gary came, he and Ming made short work of re-
loading the ammo boxes. Ming knew how tired the pilot must
be and tried to load faster. They were both relieved when the
Porter set down again at the mine. The mine foreman took
over the unloading. The gold would be resmelted into bars
of a shape and size that matched Visarn's legitimate antimo-
nial efforts.

Mark was waiting for them in the mine bungalow, just
starting a breakfast.

"How's Space Available?" Gary asked, his voice flat with exhaustion.

"Ah Lee's fed her some Chinese stuff, mixed with soup. She's in bed and asleep now. Breakfast?"

Gary shook his head and tried not to reel down the corridor to his room. He dropped fully clothed onto his bed, asleep in seconds.

Ming joined Mark for a quick meal. Throughout it, both men were quiet.

"I'm for a little shut-eye, too, Ming," said Mark, rising from the table. "What about you?"

"The Porter first," Ming said with a slight smile, and left the bungalow.

While the gold was being unloaded, Ming fussed with the Porter's engine. When no one was in sight on the plateau, he walked casually down to the thatched guard shack near the mine's entrance gate. He handed the message in a sealed envelope to an off-duty guard and told him to take it to the radioman at the training site.

His duties accomplished, Ming took a quick dip-bath and went to bed.

CHAPTER TWELVE

UP IN BANGKOK, AS MING WAS FALLING ASLEEP, COLONEL (Special Grade) Banchert Paireenantri, M.I.T class of 1949, emerged from a weekly session with his boss, the secretary of the Thai National Security Council. As usual, Banchert was neatly attired in a well-tailored dove-gray suit, white shirt, and subdued tie. His battered attaché case contrasted sharply with its owner's dress. But it would be impossible, locally, to replace the case's complicated inner features, developed by the American experts. Nor did he wish to ask his present contact in the American embassy for a replacement. Banchert's relationship with both CIA and the American Dangerous Drugs Bangkok unit had been deteriorating for quite a while.

So had his country's relations with the American government, in the time since the Communists had occupied Laos and Cambodia. As Colonel Banchert had long predicted, the victorious North Vietnamese were not content to merely assimilate these new conquests. Having destroyed and mismanaged their own resources, they needed Thailand's agricultural wealth and her far more developed industries. The North Vietnamese threat was causing Thai officials increasing concern, as Banchert well knew.

At least once a week he heard these fears expressed by the

secretary he had just left. The fracas up in Loei Province was only a sample of what was to come. The Khmer Rouge, especially its brutal teenage conscripts, were stepping up their raids inside Thailand. The mass of refugees who had escaped the genocide were arriving in Thailand, starving and destitute. Most were genuine; a few were Khmer Rouge agents. Another problem for Colonel Banchert and his hundred-odd men.

Banchert snorted in discouragement as he took off his coat before settling back into his old Benz. He told his driver-bodyguard to take him to "the house."

As the enervating heat of Bangkok poured in the open windows, he loosened his tie. He really ought to get an air conditioner, he mused, or a new car with one already installed. But the special operations group's budget was already stretched. His continuing pleas for more operating funds were rarely successful. Grudgingly, he admitted that the very nature of his little group and its endeavors was a major factor; Banchert's group never appeared on any organizational chart. Legally speaking, it did not exist.

Banchert and his group were officially assigned to various units of the sixty-thousand-man Thai Police Department, and received their monthly pay from that source. But their parent unit's records showed them to be on merely temporary duty at police headquarters, Bangkok. Banchert's irrepressible sense of humor made him smile at the euphemism—"temporary duty." Like most of his group, he had been on temporary duty for well over a dozen years. His smile grew wistful when he recalled the early years. Then they had worked hand in glove with Americans like Mark Jordan in Laos, and occasionally deeper inside enemy territory. Money had never been a problem in those days. But now, the Americans were long gone and his group's budget had to be secretly skimmed from budgets of other Thai government departments, which contested every *satang*.

On the other hand, Banchert groused to himself, the government was far too openhanded when it came to adding new missions that he was somehow supposed to run on his already skimpy funds.

Today had been a perfect example. The prime minister, the secretary said, wanted an increased effort to reduce the Khmer Rouge's depredations along the hundreds of kilometers of common border. Banchert was to increase his intelligence flow to the Border Patrol Police. But Banchert's question as to how he could do this without additional funds was answered with a shrug. "We're trying, Banchert, but it takes time. You'll have to get along somehow on what you've got for now."

As the Benz approached the two-house compound at the end of a narrow, tree-lined *soi* and the gate opened, Banchert's mood was beyond glum. The paint was peeling from the weather-beaten wooden house, another reminder of something for which his budget, private or professional, couldn't provide. The casually dressed gate opener and his counterpart, lounging in a battered rattan chair on the shady front porch, both stiffened slightly as Banchert emerged from the car and entered the house. Even the squeaking of the unoiled hinges and the shrill ring of the alarm as the heavy front door opened did not please him today, as they usually did.

He sat down at his tidy desk in a windowless office and one of his men appeared from the door on the right, placed a sectional folder in front of him, and then withdrew. Banchert leafed through the folder quickly at first. Then his fingers slowed and he withdrew two single sheets of paper. As he scanned, his sudden smile showed an abrupt change of mood. Pressing one of a bank of buttons on the side of his desk kneehole, he reread the sheets more slowly. His deputy, Major Prasong, entered from the left-hand door.

"Ah, Prasong," said Banchert, waving the man to a seat. "This report on LeFrere sounds like we may be finally getting somewhere. What's your opinion?"

The slightly paunchy major blinked behind his thick glasses, a mannerism that had caused Banchert to mentally nickname him "the Owl." "I'd say LeFrere is going to try something big this time," said Prasong, "just as you suspected."

Banchert said nothing. Prasong tended to conservatism and hadn't an ounce of intuition despite his years of dealing with "special problems."

"As you can see from our team's report," Prasong continued, leaning forward in his chair and touching the relevant sheet, "LeFrere was very busy yesterday. First that meeting with Carlotti at the airport transit lounge. Then the telex to Singapore about the *Alameda*, and finally the meeting with Charn Nol's man, Seng Long, in the Dusitanee Coffee Shop. It all fits your theory nicely, sir."

"Very nicely, Prasong. Tell our men on the tap and surveillance teams they've done a good job, but to be even more alert from now on." Banchert permitted himself a small smile. "We can all thank the Lord Buddha that we had sense enough to let LeFrere run free while we kept the tap on his phone." Banchert added with a derisive chuckle, "One would assume that Commander Charn Nol has the same money problems we do, Prasong, if he had to go into the heroin-smuggling business. Looks like Pol Pot's moneyless economy, of which he is so proud, isn't working. With just a little more luck, Prasong, the Khmer Rouge may contrive to solve some of *our* monetary difficulties." The irony brought a small smile to the Owl's face as well. "Now," Banchert went on briskly, "keep everybody on this very closely. Use anyone you need. And bring me Charn Nol's file and the one on his Bangkok organization."

Being eminently pragmatic, as well as a skilled professional intelligence officer, Banchert was never completely candid with his boss, the secretary, where money was concerned. He justified his reticence on the basis that neither he nor his men would ever receive any formal public recognition for their numerous successes. For their inevitable failures, they were roundly and loudly abused—if not publicly, at least privately—by the U.S. National Security Council. The NSC was quick to blame, but never praised.

In what an American would have termed "the good old days," the CIA had been more than generous with cash bonuses. Failures, as long as they had not been through incompetence, were accepted philosophically. Recently, however, Banchert had been forced to find other ways to compensate them for their arduous and often dangerous work.

The only official funds that he could use were the amounts

he could extract for per diem, and this pittance was rapidly eaten up by inflation. Unofficially there were a number of sources, time-honored, but more than slightly illegal. Captured foreign agents were relieved of cash and valuables prior to being turned over to regular police units for prosecution. Some Soviet-sponsored agents had also had healthy bank accounts, which they had sooner or later agreed to withdraw in cash under the watchful eyes of Banchert's men. But far and away the most lucrative sources of Banchert's secret unofficial funds were the drug smugglers he was able to apprehend.

Although the official reward was twenty-five percent of the street value of the intercepted contraband, that percentage went through many hands—diminishing each time—before it reached the actual captors. However, if drug smugglers were caught at the time of transaction, the cash tide flowed in the right direction. Ideally, the exchange of cash for drugs was allowed to proceed. When the person or persons receiving the cash were a reasonable distance from the site of the transaction, both supplier and receiver were apprehended secretly. The drugs were duly turned in, intact; Banchert was vehement about that, as two of his men had been dismayed to learn. But the cash was something else. The recipients were in no position to complain; their freedom was worth it.

Banchert scrupulously divided half of such unofficial windfalls among his men. The other half went to supplement the group's operational funds. Combining paternalism and prudent regard for security, Colonel Banchert dictated precisely how his men used their bonus money.

He "laundered" it first in an accepted fashion, via several friendly lottery ticket sellers. The bimonthly government lottery tickets bore only numbers; no names were involved. A winning ticket had only to be presented at the Lottery Office on Rajdamnern Avenue. The winning numbers, the top prize being one million baht, were printed in all newspapers. The majority of winners, especially those outside Bangkok, much preferred their local ticket seller's immediate cash payment—at a slight discount on the face value, of course—to a long trip to the Lottery Bureau. Thus marketing winning tickets was a profitable sideline for all ticket sellers. People with uncomfortable and inexplicable amounts of cash were quite happy to pay five percent of the total to purchase a "winning ticket," thus neatly covering the real, usually illicit source of their cash. Lottery winnings had the added advantage of being tax-free.

After "lottery laundering," Banchert's men were free to invest their "bonuses" in carefully screened, solid investments like real estate or government bonds. No wild spending sprees were permitted, nor was anything else that might draw attention to a police corporal, or even an officer, who had "won" a big lottery prize. The use of lottery laundering was too well known and widely practiced, officially and unofficially, to risk speculation from any other group on the extraordinary "luck" possessed by Banchert's men.

Too much a realist to waste time speculating on how big a drug "buy" LeFrere seemed to be setting up with the Khmer Rouge, Banchert turned to the second piece of paper. He nodded in silent approval as he read Ming's brief report that Gary's first gold pickup had been successful. He frowned over the girl's rescue. An unnecessary risk, he thought, but mai pen ari, never mind. It was what one expected of Americans. All told, it was plain that his old teacher and comrade, Mark Jordan, had lost none of his old skills. Now all Banchert had to do was wait.

He indulged himself in a moment of anticipatory calculation. He'd already half decided that twenty percent of the gold's value would be a reasonable price for his official silence. Visarn wouldn't really have any choice. Twenty percent of ten million dollars came to twenty million baht—almost twice as much as his annual budget from the satang-squeezing Thai NSC.

With no regard for the incongruity, Banchert reminded himself to stop by the *wat* on his way home, to offer thanks for the first safe gold pickup flight and a prayer for the success of the ones to follow.

CHAPTER THIRTEEN

WHILE COLONEL BANCHERT GLOATED SECRETLY UP IN BANG-kok, Gary and Mark sweated out the return of Sarn's raiding party and, especially, the old charcoal maker, Remrut.

When Gary woke from a restless, out-of-phase sleep in the early afternoon after his first gold trip, he found Mark sitting at the dining room table in what Gary referred to as his "deep thought configuration." Rolling the well-chewed cigar from one side of his mouth to the other, his left hand described the rough circle around his bald patch while his right scribbled furiously on the yellow legal pad.

"*Now* what kind of crazy scheme are you cooking up so I can get my ass shot off, Mark?"

Half covering the writing pad with one arm, Mark looked up at the pilot with a sheepish expression. "Ah, no schemes, Gary. Just a list of stuff I want you and Ming to pick up tomorrow in Bangkok for Remrut's kid, Pranee. She's in rough shape. She'll need a lot of vitamins and that kind of stuff." Mark puffed vigorously on his cigar. "Ah Lee is making up a list, too. All sorts of Chinese herbs and roots. Ah Lee claims her medicine is better than anything ferang." Mark chuckled. "Could be. I figure we cover all bases on this one."

"How is the girl? I never got a real look at her last night."

Gary stretched his long frame, yawning until he cracked his jaw joint. "She doesn't weigh as much as a bag of cement."

"She's sick, but Ah Lee says she can't find anything really wrong except, of course, starvation." Mark's gesture was one of acceptance of such an uncommon diagnosis. "I took her temperature—ninety-nine. But that was right after Ah Lee had given her a hot bath. And boy, you should see her lap up the soup Ah Lee concocts every time she wakes up. I figure we ought to get her some real milk, some of those filets from the Kangaroo Market. You know, Gary, high protein to build her strength up."

The next morning Mark presented a list that filled a whole page; Gary's reaction was a low whistle and an eyebrow cocked at his boss. "I'm flying a Porter, not a damn C-47, Mark," he said. "Sure you haven't forgotten some little thing?"

An atypical flush spread across the older man's face, and Gary muttered something about *couldn't Mark take a razzing,* then climbed quickly into the Porter beside Ming and took off for Bangkok.

At Don Muang Airport, Gary taxied the Porter over to the big Thai air force hangar that Somboon shared with the Air Force Flying Club. Visarn himself was there to meet them. After seeing Gary's grin and thumbs-up signal, the old man had smiled, but he said nothing until they were in his gleaming Benz.

"Your flight was productive?" Visarn asked.

Gary just pointed at the gate toward which the Benz was smoothly gliding; only when they were past it and on the public road did he open his leather pilot's bag. Visarn looked inside and sighed with relief as he saw the sample gold bar nestling among the neatly folded world aeronautical charts.

Visarn's smile was matched by Gary's when the pilot saw the checks Visarn handed him. Ten thousand dollars each for himself and Mark. And that didn't include the three grand the Chinese merchant has begun to pay them every month.

Though Gary answered Visarn's brief questions on the ride

to Bangkapi, his normally cautious thoughts were nine thousand miles away, near the California-Oregon border. No longer would he have to squeeze every paycheck to keep up the payments on his three-hundred acres. Hell, he thought, just the ten and a half percent that the Hong Kong and Shanghai Bank was paying on his time deposits would take care of the monthly payments. With another ten grand for each of the remaining trips . . . and then his half of the five percent of the ten million . . . Gary's pessimistic nature reasserted itself after a moment of roseate dreams.

Be just my luck to get clobbered on the last damn trip. Stop daydreaming, Gary. You've a long way to go with your head on straight—all the time!

The next day, with Ah Sam's help, Gary acquired from various stores the items on Mark's generous list. A cheerful taxi driver assisted them in carrying the plastic shopping bags into the bungalow. The driver's grin widened as he pocketed a generous twenty-baht tip and agreed to transport Gary to the airport the next morning.

At Don Muang, Ming and one of the Thai air force mechanics helped Gary stow the boxes into which he had packed the shopping for easier handling. Somboon arrived to remind Gary that the Porter had a three-hundred-hour maintenance check coming up in forty-seven hours. Quick calculation showed Gary that this meant he could only make two gold runs in addition to the regular crudum hauls.

"You got anything I can use while you're doing the three-hundred-hour, Somboon?"

"I just bought a Dornier, DO-28, Khun Gary. But I need that for my charter taxi work. It won't hold as much as the Porter. Besides, it's all repainted and fixed up inside. Do you have to have another plane?"

Gary sympathized with Somboon's concern, but the thought of having a Dornier, with twin engines to replace the needle-nosed Porter's single one, made him ruthless.

"Sorry, 'Boon, but they're really going like hell down at the mine. I can't afford to lose a week while the Porter's out of service. I can make sure we keep the Dornier clean. Okay?''

Landing back at the mine, Gary yelled exultantly for Mark, to tell him the good news.

"That Dornier will be a damn sight better for those two short strips, Mark," he said, brimming with enthusiasm. "I sure like the idea of having two engines for a change.''

"Yeah, yeah, that would be great," Mark responded absentmindedly as he opened the Porter's rear door. As he saw the bundles and boxes, his smile became genuine. "Yeah, good deal, Gary. Real good deal. We'll switch the schedule a bit and take those two hairy pickups with the Dornier. You did get everything on the list, didn't you?" He started to unload the Porter, peering into each bag as he carried it to the Land-Rover.

"Yeah, yeah," Gary replied, but his irony passed Mark unnoticed.

"Pranee's doing real well, Gary. Eating like a horse. Correction, make that two horses. With this stuff, we'll have her healthy and hearty in no time. C'mon! Think you'll see a change in her in just two days.''

Gary's space available passenger was sitting in one of the old rattan chairs in the living room when, laden with shopping bags, they came in. It was Gary's first good look at her.

The effects of her long starvation were evident. She had deep hollows under her broad, high cheekbones. Three days had not removed the dark circles from beneath eyes that seemed to dart about like a frightened animal's. The deep brown eyes were out of proportion to her small, tip-tilted nose and far too dark in her pale, nearly white face. Her hands also showed the effects of her ordeal, and her small bones stood out, fleshless, stretching at the skin as she lifted both hands to clasp Gary's in an amazingly strong grip.

"You are the man to whom I owe my life." Her low, tremulous voice held a tone that flushed the pilot's face.

"I can never thank you a right way," she said in lilting English, "but every day of my life the Lord Buddha will hear my prayers for you. When my father told me you were a good man, I was too afraid to believe. Now I know. He was telling the truth.''

Just then Mark arrived with a glass of fresh milk. ''Here you are, honey. Drink this,'' said Mark, watching the level of the liquid as he passed the glass to her.

Gary noticed the burly man's unusually gentle tone. Well, I'll be go to hell, thought Gary. She's witched him! The old bastard's fallen for a pair of big brown eyes.

While Mark gently spoon-fed the girl a bowl of filet-based stew, Gary ate his own sandwich, waiting with amused resignation until Mark and Ah Lee had put the girl back to bed, Mark closing the door very quietly behind him.

''If you're through playing nursemaid,'' Gary said, ''how about filling me in on some minor details—like how're Sarn's boys and Remrut doing?''

Mark glared but refused to be baited. ''Last word we got, they should be across the border by tomorrow night. I guess they're doing okay.''

''What about the guys Sarn was leaving behind to see the Khmer Rouge reaction to the raid?''

''Too early to tell for sure, Gary. Only report Sarn has from them is that they had to haul ass up into the jungle. The whole area was crawling with black-clads, so they figured to be scarce awhile.''

Two days later, landing at Ban Het on his third trip, Gary was taxiing the Porter to the old construction shack when he saw Remrut. The prop was still slowing down when Gary answered Remrut's silent query with an upraised thumb. Once out of the plane, Gary received a powerful bear hug from the normally undemonstrative old man.

''Christ Almighty, Remrut, you'll bust my ribs!''

Gary was still protesting when Remrut released him. The old man's face had resumed its solemn expression as he carefully unwrapped a *pakima* that covered the gold bar he had removed from the plane six days before.

''Here, Khun Gary, like I tell you. No trouble!''

"Neither is Pranee, Remrut! Just wait till you see her."

Two more men came out of the shack and Gary greeted Sarn with enthusiasm and met the leader of the raiding party. During the short flight back up to the mine, Remrut barraged Gary with questions about his daughter that Gary couldn't understand; he repeated to Remrut that he would see for himself "how good Pranee is."

In the bungalow, father and daughter had a tearfully joyful reunion, both talking at once through their tears. After a few moments, Mark approached them, frowning paternally.

"C'mon, Pranee, such excitement is bad for you. You go rest; bring your father with you." Mark directed Ah Lee to escort Pranee and Remrut into the bedroom. As soon as Mark turned back to Sarn and the other guerrilla, he dropped into his familiar mode. "Let's hear all about it now, Sarn," he said, lighting up a cigar and gesturing to the others to be seated.

The leader of the Free Cambodians and his lieutenant were exultant. They'd had only slight difficulty evading most of the Khmer Rouge border guards. The one outpost they hadn't been able to avoid, they had wiped out in a dawn attack. This had yielded an unexpected bonus. Among the documents they had taken from the dead was a sketch of the locations of other Khmer Rouge outposts and mine fields. The sketch covered a ground distance of almost thirty kilometers. With this, Sarn realized that he and his men could avoid most of the previous hazards of infiltrating and exfiltrating reception teams.

Both men thought that the gold recovery flights could be stepped up now that the hubbub caused by the initial raid had died down. The disposition of Khmer Rouge outposts and mine fields had been the crucial piece of missing information. The one point still in doubt was whether or not the Khmer Rouge had been taken in by Mark's "Chopper Concerto."

Three days after Remrut's return and Sarn's report, the surveillance team transmitted welcome news. They had returned cautiously to a ridge above the woodcutters' camp, where chopping had resumed. Though far more Khmer Rouge guards were in evidence at the woodcutters' site and at the one charcoal kiln the watchers could observe, there was no other sign of unusual Khmer Rouge activity.

So Sarn dispatched two teams by separate routes. When they also reported that their gold caches were undisturbed and that there were no signs of Khmer Rouge activity in the countryside, Gary made two pickup trips in one week.

"It's too goddamn easy, Mark," he told his boss after the second one. "It's getting to me. These flights are milk runs! It's weird."

"Gary, for Christ's sake!" Mark puffed on his cigar with disgust. "So the plan's working! What's wrong with that? We've pulled out damn near nine hundred kilos in only three trips. That's thirty grand for your farm; not counting your half of the five percent of the total value of the stuff."

"Cherry picking!" Gary countered.

"Okay, okay. These were the easiest ones. But the plan *is* working. Next week, with the Dornier, we get those two little guys. They're only about a hundred sixty kilos." Mark broke out in a hearty laugh. "Listen to me! *Only* a hundred sixty kilos. Kilos of pure gold, Gary, old buddy."

Gary refused to be cheered, pacing and running his fingers through his hair. "Yeah, but you aren't hauling those pure gold kilos. They feel *cold* to me! You know what I mean?" Unable to articulate his feeling, Gary held up his right hand, his fingers closed. "Look, Mark, can we give it a rest for a while? I think we're taking this pitcher to the well too damn often."

Mark regarded him for a long moment. "Okay, tiger. We'll shut down for two weeks. Then, if nothing looks amiss, we'll run the two little guys"—and he smiled at Gary cajolingly—"with the Dornier. Deal?"

"I need some air," Gary mumbled, and strode out of the shack.

Mark sat staring after him, cigar clenched in his teeth. As he reviewed the conversation, memories from the past came forcefully to mind.

Remember that North Vietnamese ambush, Mark? You

should. That long, jagged scar on your left shoulder came from refusing to listen to your own vague uneasiness.

You know Gary Sonderberg's got more guts than any airplane driver you ever met. It's not that he's scared. He's got one of those weird half premonitions. Honor it. After all, he's survived eight years' war time and as many thousand hours of really hairy flying.

Mark was still wrestling with himself when Gary strode back in, smiled his usual half-sardonic grin, and said, "Great idea that, Mark, standing down. But the goddamn moon isn't going to cooperate. I can hack a quarter, or even close to half moon, but more than that would be framing myself for target practice." He let out a deep breath. "Set up the next flight right away. I'll go as soon as the teams are in position. Same deal. Two nights in a row. G'night now!"

Gary was walking to his room before Mark could think of anything appropriate to say. He told himself he should be happy that the moon's phase changed Gary's mind. Strangely, he wasn't. Hunches were hunches! However, Gary was a pessimist and had been putting in some stiff flying time.

Mark ripped the wrapper off a fresh cigar and, reaching for his yellow legal pad, began penciling the messages that would set up the next two gold pickups. He made a dozen mistakes in barely five lines, threw down the pencil, and gulped half his beer. This is a kids' game. But even as the thought came, part of him vehemently denied it.

With a savage bite on his unlit cigar, Mark flipped the pad to a fresh sheet and began again.

Six nights later, he sat with another unlit cigar in the little shack at Ban Het. It was already well after two in the morning. Ming was reading a luridly covered Thai paperback, but also sneaking quick looks at his watch every time he turned a page. Mark didn't even pretend. Gary was late.

Both of the small, barely adequate pickup sites were much closer to the border than the earlier ones had been. With the captured Khmer Rouge outpost map, Sarn's two teams had reached their positions in only four days. Last night's pickup had been uneventful, except for Gary's bitter complaints about an anthill that he had nearly hit on landing and about trees at the upwind end of the field, neither of which had been included in the report.

Tonight, barring ants and trees, should have taken no longer. But it had. Gary should have been back by two, and it was now two-forty.

At three Mark and Ming went outside to listen. Neither heard the distant *thrum* of an airplane. Back inside, they gave up all pretense of confident waiting and bent over the tattered map.

"He still has almost two hours' gas, Khun Mark," Ming said after a few quick calculations. "Maybe he hit clouds, or . . ."

Three-thirty came and passed. By four, both men were pacing in front of the shack, stopping every few feet to listen. At ten past the hour, Ming suddenly halted and cupped his hands over his outsize ears.

"Listen!" And Ming pointed north.

"What the hell?" Mark also caught the faint drone. "Damn it, that's a single-engine plane. And Gary's supposed to cross down south and come *up* the valley."

Within a minute Mark was glad to be wrong. It was the Dornier, but flying on one engine. As it came closer, they could make out the motionless right prop in the rosy gray predawn light.

Gary made a respectable two-bounce landing and then taxied, only slightly erratically, over to them.

As the good prop wheezed to a halt, Mark and Ming crowded together to open the door. Gary managed a feeble thumbs-up and a faint shadow of his familiar sardonic smile.

"Sure glad *that's* over!"

Fatigue was written in his movements as he slowly climbed out.

"You're a very lucky man, and a good pilot," Ming said as he stared at the remains of the second prop.

"Yeah, I sorta figured that's the way it'd look," said Gary. He ran his hand over one tip, which was twisted out of line for at least four inches. The other tip was much the same. "I need some coffee."

He turned on his heel and walked to the shack, but it was Mark who poured Gary a cup, lacing it with brandy. Gary took several long, quick sips, then lit a cigarette. His hands trembled. He regarded them, puzzled, as if they belonged to someone else.

"I think I scared the living daylights out of myself on that one," he said. Then he chuckled more in relief than amusement. "And was she ever a bitch to fly! In case I forget, you guys be sure to tell Somboon that that baby will not, repeat not, maintain altitude on one engine with nine-hundred pounds in her!"

"What did you run into, a goose?" Mark asked with an attempt at humor.

"You won't believe it!" Gary shook his head as he looked with widened eyes at his boss. "I hit a goddamn deer on takeoff! A buck at that. Damn thing must've been paralyzed by my lights. My tail was already up. Too late to abort. And no way to miss without taking on another anthill. So I figured the deer would be softer. It was, but not by much. When I hit, I damn near lost her. Only thing saved me was I got her off the ground for a couple of feet. On the third bounce, I got her off completely, even if I couldn't pull to the right, and I got some altitude.

"I cleared those damn trees, but even throttled-down, the vibration was something fierce. I near decided to bring her back down and take my chances on the ground!" Gary emptied his cup and waved it in a grateful toast. "Well, I stooged around, jockeying the RPMs and the pitch, and finally got her to climb. I knew I couldn't get her to forty-five hundred, to go the way I'd planned. So I headed north. Got lucky a couple times. Some thermals helped me up to about three thousand. But that was all she'd go. Had to shut the bad engine down. Too much vibration and it was overheating really bad.

"I stayed as close to the hills as I could, 'cause I was pretty damn sure I wouldn't make it all the way. I was losing twenty to thirty feet a minute with the good engine way up. Then *it* started to heat. Jesus, I was scared!

"I took a chance and fired up the bad one. Got back up to three thousand and shut it down again. I kept doing that every ten or fifteen minutes. Finally I reached that big gap, about eighty klicks south of Aranya. I was right tempted to just go on in there and land, but the wind decided me. It was from northeast and picking up. So . . . here I am." Gary laughed. "What're we going to tell poor old Somboon?"

CHAPTER FOURTEEN

GARY DIDN'T HAVE TO EXPLAIN THE DAMAGED PROP TO MAjor Somboon. The Thai was on a week-long charter to Chiengmai when Gary flew the Dornier back to Bangkok after he and Ming had replaced the twisted propeller. Somboon's new chief mechanic clucked in sympathy at Ming's blatant lie.

Gary flew back to the mine the next morning in the Porter, fresh from its three-hundred-hour check. Then he, Mark, and Ming indulged in some happy calculations.

"A hair under twenty-three hundred kilos out, Gary." Mark punctuated his statement with bobbing cigar. "Only three more sites and twenty-two-hundred-odd kilos to go."

"Yeah, but they're the heaviest ones," Gary said. He jabbed at the pencil-marked map. "That four-hundred-fifty-kilo lot there is really asking one hell of a lot, even from the Porter."

"But look at the runway you've got," Mark countered. "Damn near twelve hundred feet of road, instead of rice paddy—or anthills and deer."

"It could be Don Muang or Honolulu's reef runway, and it'd still be a lot for the Porter to lift."

Mark ignored him, sauntering off to join Pranee in her room.

* * *

Two days into the new moon, Gary took off for the next pickup, having selected the heaviest load for the first; he liked to get through the worst when he was freshest. Once in the air, he reversed his normal route by flying north first and then heading east to cross the Cardamom Range at a new gap that he had originally discarded as being too close to Aranya Pratet, the Thai border town. This route might convince any watching Khmer Rouge operator that he was enroute to Surin, another Thai border town. Once through the gap, Gary followed the steeply sloping terrain, well below the shoulders of the valley. As he emerged from its walls, he flipped on his radar detector and made a beeline for the pickup site.

He picked up the faint beacon signal with no trouble, cut the Porter's powerful engine to a whisper, and brought her down on the old road as if he'd been practicing on Don Muang. The grinning reception team had the charred ammo boxes ready, and loading took no time at all. Gary was smiling broadly as he urged the near overload down the old dirt road and coaxed the Porter into the air.

He put the needle-nosed plane into a shallow climb that would bring him to the six thousand feet he needed to recross the Cardamoms. When the Porter passed four thousand, Gary began to whistle tunelessly and gave the instrument panel an affectionate pat. As he peered out the opposite window, a sudden brilliant and sickeningly familiar stream of red balls half blinded him. He felt the Porter shudder as machine-gun bullets ripped through the left wing, behind him!

"Keerist Almighty," he shouted. "Two of 'em. I'm boxed! Cold turkey!"

Gary's thousands of hours of experience had included other grim tastes of the "two percent of sheer terror" of flight. These meshed the veteran pilot's mind and body into superb coordination. The little plane flipped into a steep dive. Before his angry words had died, the Porter was approaching her redline speed. Pilot and plane fused into a single organism, seeking survival like a frightened animal. Using the airplane's unique capabilities, Gary turned it almost inside itself by applying the Beta-gear, reverse thrust, and spoiler flaps. The Beta-gear brought the Porter down to less than flying speed. Gary cranked furiously at the flap controls and avoided the two enemy planes. T-28 trainers, they were, armed with .30-caliber machine guns in each wing.

Gary stole a moment to wipe the sweat that bathed his face. He knew the T-28 well, and his wild aerobatics were buying time, but they were also costing him the one thing that he needed most: altitude.

Grunting with relief as a pursuer sent a long burst of angry red tracers into the air on Gary's left, he calculated that his pursuers might run out of ammunition if he could just "borrow" a few thousand feet of altitude.

No way, no way in hell, another part of his mind told him. Sixteen hundred feet left and . . .

Then he saw the starlight glittering where a stream exited the mouth of a steep-shouldered valley. Gary threw into a wing-straining turn and dove for the mouth of the valley.

"If you don't get too narrow up by the waterfall, you beautiful valley, you're just about to save my ass."

Coordinating his skills and the Porter's capabilities, Gary just made it past the right- and left-hand shelter of the steep, rocky shoulders. One of the T-28s fired a long burst that half blinded the sweating pilot and put two more holes in his left wing.

Unmindful of a raw neck, chafed from constant straining to see in all directions at once, Gary made out the dim shapes of his pursuers and felt a real glimmer of hope. They were behind him, but the lower one was effectively masking the higher, rearmost from firing. Even better, with the throttle to the wall, he was holding his distance. Still, he had to pay attention to the narrowing valley and its steeply rising shoulders.

"Where the hell *is* that waterfall?" He stared into the gloom ahead, begging for the faint moonlight to aid him.

He flung a glance behind and saw that the T-28 was doing what it should have done well before, diving steeply to gain airspeed and bring the Porter into range. A wave of panic shook Gary's concentration.

But the T-28 was too late. Gary shouted a loud ''Hallelujah'' as he saw the white blur of the waterfall, all two hundred gloriously high feet of it. Cautiously he eased the Porter to the right as he put his right hand on the Beta-gear knob, focusing all his efforts on judging the exact moment to use it.

The shock as the Beta-gear brought the Porter to a near stall made the lower T-28's burst of fire harmless and, Gary knew, blinded the pilot to the proximity of the waterfall.

Slamming on power with all the flaps he dared use, Gary was brushing treetops with his wheels as he completed his 180-degree turn. A sudden bright glare and a barely heard roar told him the story: the T-28 pilot had seen the waterfall too late.

Building his own airspeed as he fled back down the little valley, Gary searched anxiously for the second T-28. Halfway to the mouth, he swung right, to the south, and nursed the laboring Porter over a small dip and down into the next valley. Still no sign of the second plane. The adjoining valley was one that he had used on previous flights. Well before it ended in the tangled Cardamom hills, Gary saw the clouds that he so desperately needed to reach.

Afterward, Gary had no recollection of the rest of that flight; mind, body, and airplane must have done what had to be done. Gary did remember his landing at Ban Het. Safe on the Thai side of the border, reaction set in. For the first time since he had used the generous Ban Het strip, Gary had to use the full power of the Beta-gear to get all three wheels on the ground at the same time. Barely avoiding a ground loop at the far end of the runway, Gary wrenched the still moving plane away from the trees and taxied rapidly to the little shack where Mark and Ming had been pacing anxiously.

Fatigue made Gary fumble releasing his harness and opening the door. Then he stumbled to the ground. Mark, cigar motionless for once, stood silently with Ming as Gary gave the Porter a half-affectionate, half-angry pat. "You're a good bird, baby, but you've seen the last of me!"

The declaration broke the spell on the other two. Ming played his flashlight over the holes in both wings, murmuring as he saw fuel dripping from the right-wing tank. Mark barely glanced at the damage; his nose had already told him that fuel was leaking. Though there had been a number of times when Gary had brought back bullet holes courtesy of the VC in Laos, Mark had never seen him like this.

Gary began shambling toward the shack. He angrily refused Mark's arm and hauled himself past the doorway, making for the bottle of Hennessy on the rough table. Two deep gulps seemed to have no effect. He ruined a cigarette trying to get it out of the crumpled pack with his trembling fingers. He sucked deeply on the lighted one that Ming proffered. Then he took another deep pull at the Hennessy.

"I mean it, Mark," he said, his voice a snarl. "That's all! All, forever and never! No more birds for Gary. No goddamn way!" Another puff with shaking hands. "They were waiting, Mark. The bastards were waiting for me!"

CHAPTER FIFTEEN

MARK AND MING LAID GARY ON A MATTRESS IN THE BACK of the Land-Rover before lugging the heavy ammo boxes from the Porter and adding them to the load. It was after noon when Mark arrived at the mine, turned the gold bars over to the smelter foreman, and carried the still unconscious pilot into his room.

Pranee was dismayed at Mark's seemingly callousness. "No big problem, Pranee. He'll sleep it off, and outside of a helluva hangover, he'll be fine."

She was still absorbing this aspect of the man who had nursed her so tenderly when Mark, in brief, bitter sentences, told her the real cause of Gary's unusual condition. Then, while she helped Ah Lee with a belated breakfast, Mark began trying to analyze the information Gary had given him.

It seemed obvious the operation had been penetrated. But *how*, and *by whom*? Scrawling occasionally on his legal pad, and chewing on his cigar, Mark went over the story Gary had told him several times before he scowled fiercely and scrawled, "Why after pickup?"

To Mark, attacking Gary well after he had picked up the gold seemed irrational, even foolish. Why not hit him as soon as the plane had landed? Or while the reception team was loading the gold? That way they'd get gold, pilot, airplane, and the reception team. By letting Gary take off, they risked missing the opportunity to capture alive a knowledgeable prisoner, and failing to secure the gold. Shooting Gary down meant searching for the wreck in thick rain forest, at best.

Mark scribbled, "Protect informant in team?" stared at it for several minutes, and then crossed it out. No way, he told himself; nobody on the team knew which route Gary would take on his return trip to Thailand. He had selected a dozen different routes. Only Mark and he knew which he planned to use on a given night; and even then, weather or mechanical problems might change that. No, damn it, the team's clean. I can't prove it, but I'm sure they're clean.

A sudden thought made his finger stop twirling. Radar! Gary had said nothing about seeing anything on his radar detector. But suppose it hadn't been turned on? Nope, Gary's too damn meticulous for that. Malfunction, then? Mark's pencil printed in big letters, "Check radar detector!!"

For another half hour Mark's mind dredged up increasingly unlikely possibilities, but he dismissed them all. It *had to* be the damn radar detector. Too damn incredible to put it down to the two Khmer Rouge pilots, obviously inexperienced, just stumbling into Gary with only faint moon and starlight to help them.

Despite his fatigue, Mark's inner turmoil let him slumber only fitfully. He woke before the pilot, to find it was well after dark. When Gary finally emerged from his room, grunted an obviously painful greeting, and disappeared into the bathroom, Mark could empathize. Brandy hangovers were something he preferred never to experience again!

In the primitive bathroom, Gary's first fumbling efforts were to try to relieve the painful parching of his throat, mouth, and tongue. Water, stinging Listerine, more water, more Listerine, toothpaste—nothing helped. Aspirin for his throbbing head, a dip-bath in the chilly water from the Shanghai jar, and he had exhausted the bathroom's possibilities.

Outside in the big room, Mark wordlessly handed him a glass of tomato juice, liberally spiked with lip-searing Thai Siricha Sauce, while Pranee hovered nearby with a cup of steaming coffee. Mumbling his thanks, Gary drained the juice in two gulps, exclaimed as he felt the bite of the Siricha Sauce, and burned his lips with the hot coffee.

While Mark smiled and Pranee stared, Gary slammed the coffee cup down, wheeled, and took a beaded bottle of Singha beer from the refrigerator. "Hair of the dog, Mark. Nothing else works for sour apples!"

They were all silent as Gary emptied his first glass of beer, lit a cigarette, and grimaced at its taste. Then he looked Mark in the eye. "What I said last night still goes. That wasn't the brandy talking. You'll have to get yourself a new idiot. I've had the course!"

Mark just grunted and relit his ever-present cigar.

"I mean it. I may not be too bright about some things, but I'm not completely stupid. Those guys are on to me! Us, I mean. Next time they won't miss. Better tell Visarn to forget about the rest of his gold—no way anybody can get in there now and get back out in one piece."

Mark waited quietly until the lean, handsome pilot ran down. Then he asked, very softly: "You *did* have your radar detector on . . . ?"

Startled, Gary thought for a brief instant. "I know I did. About the only time I even took my eyes off it was landing."

"When did you check it out last?"

Gary paused, rumpled his shock of hair, then said, "Must have been right after takeoff on the last trip down here. I check it and my emergency landing transmitter with the Don Muang tower. And I know both the ELT and my transponder were off last night. And the transponder works, otherwise the Thais would have been all over me for not having it on during the flight down here. He paused. "No, it won't wash. That detector was on, and the transponder and the ELT were off. I don't make mistakes like that!"

The next morning, they loaded Gary's gear aboard the Porter. Ming had put a temporary patch on the broken hydraulic line, so they could use the flaps and spoilers. He had sealed off the bullet-punctured wing tank, saying it should be replaced.

Gary insisted Mark fly. As they passed three thousand feet, Mark said, "Just for the hell of it, try that radar detector."

Gary flipped the switch to ON, and they saw the tiny green light appear over the switch. "Not that, Mark, I—"

Both men jumped as the radio clamored. "Four Niner Zulu, what is the nature of your emergency?"

Both men sat speechless for a long interval until the worried voice repeated.

"Utapao tower calling Four Niner Zulu. What is wrong? Come in, Four Niner Zulu!"

Mechanically, Gary took the microphone and answered. "Utapao, this is Four Niner Zulu. We have no emergency."

There was a distinct pause after they heard the Utapao operator press his transmit switch, then, "Four Niner Zulu, Your ELT is transmitting on the emergency frequency. If you do not have an emergency, you are violating regulations by testing it without telling us first. Please turn it off, or I will have to report you."

Gary's fingers confirmed what his eyes told him. "Utapao, Four Niner Zulu. My ELT is not, repeat not, in the on position. I think it may be malfunctioning if you are receiving a signal."

Gary had barely finished when Mark shouted, pointing at the still glowing green radar detector light. "Look! They have us on radar, but it's not red! It's green!"

Gary's finger beat Mark's to the radar detector switch. He was about to speak into the mike when they heard the radio again. "Four Niner Zulu, Utapao. Very good. Your ELT is no longer transmitting. Please have it attended to when you get to Bangkok."

Gary's fright and anger slowed his normally skillful fingers as he removed the offending instrument's access plate. He compared the actual wires with the little diagram on the plate.

"Those bastards! They shorted the son of a bitch to the ELT! Look, Mark. The black wire!"

Minutes later, Gary again erupted as he checked the wiring in the ELT.

"No wonder they found me. Christ on a crutch! When I

turned on the radar detector, it not only didn't work, but it switched on the goddamn ELT! A blind man could've found me!''

CHAPTER SIXTEEN

AFTER SOME DISCUSSION, GARY AGREED TO SEVER THE SAB-oteur's wire where it and others ran through a clamp, but to leave it still attached to the switches, so that a casual check would not reveal it was no longer working. Mark would tell only Visarn.

The frail Chinese was standing with Somboon when they taxied up to the hangar. As they got out of the plane, he strode forward and quietly spoke. "I have explained to Khun Somboon that one of the mine security guards accidentally hit the airplane when his gun went off. I thought it better that way."

Both Americans agreed, and said nothing more about the subject until they were on the road into Bangkok. Then Visarn spoke again. "I deeply regret what happened, Khun Gary. And I understand from Colonel Mark that you do not wish to continue. I cannot blame you in the least."

Gary was taken aback by the old Chinese's words. Then Visarn surprised him even more by handing him an envelope.

"Inside, you will find a check for the most recent flights, another for this month's salary and a month's bonus, and also a promissory note for your share of the five percent of the gold recovered so far. I regret that I cannot pay you for that in cash at this time. But you see, Khun Gary, we cannot

convert the gold too rapidly. It must appear to have come
from our own mine. Otherwise the Thai government . . ."

The old man spread his hands in a universal gesture. Gary's
heart sank a bit at Visarn's words, but he soon recovered and
thanked the old man effusively. He understood the problem.

After dropping the pilot off at the bungalow, Mark left with
Visarn. Gary telephoned and got reservations on a flight to
Honolulu the next morning. Then, over a beer, he took out
his pocket calculator and an envelope containing his Hong
Kong and Shanghai Bank statements. In a small notebook he
entered the twenty thousand dollars for the two trips, and the
four thousand dollars for salary. Adding them to the totals in
his checking account and time-deposit statements, he read
the total from the little computer:

One hundred forty thousand dollars in round figures. Picking up the legal-looking promissory note, he shook his head.
No way in the world I could ever force Visarn to pay it—not
if I want to stay out of a Thai pokey! They take a damn dim
view of any kind of smuggling. Not to mention busting a
whole raft of Thai civil air regulations. Forget it!

Glumly, Gary dug a large file folder out of his worn pilot's
bag and studied the neat budget he had spent so long putting
together for his tree farm. The bottom line was almost exactly
double the amount he actually had in cash. Gary went over
his neat notations twice before he slapped down his pen.

The pain of having to give up again, at least temporarily,
his long-cherished dream nagged at Gary incessantly as he
went down to pick up his ticket, purchase traveler's checks,
and toy with the tender filet he'd ordered at the Fireside Grill.

No matter how he tried, his mind kept returning to the
bitter facts. At age forty-four, Gary had no illusions about
his marketability as a pilot. Airlines were delighted with the
more than twelve thousand hours in his logbook, but his age
turned them cold. That left little freight and commuter out-
fits, like the one he'd left to come to fly for Visarn. Work his
ass off for far less than one half what Visarn had paid him,
and pay over half of that for food and a crummy apartment,

plus . . . Gary slapped his hand to his forehead. Goddamn taxes! I forgot the goddamn taxes!

Ignoring the food before him, Gary scribbled furiously on the ticket envelope. He'd only been out of the United States eleven months. To qualify for the twenty-five-thousand-dollar IRS deduction for overseas residence, he needed exactly eighteen months. Otherwise—. He gulped as he estimated what he'd have to pay as an "unmarried" with no significant deductions. All he had was the unimproved land of his farm. Deducting the interest on his mortgage wouldn't even dent his income.

Gary resisted the answer that suddenly replaced the nagging anguish. But back at the bungalow, he faced it, rationalizing to himself. Two more trips, Gary, two more trips. The only reason they got you was that damn jimmied radar detector. That's another twenty grand, and at least a couple months' salary.

Then, if you play it right, you can keep on flying the crudum until you've got your eighteen months in, and spread it over two years to boot. And with Mark around, Visarn won't dare not give us the five percent.

When Mark arrived an hour later, Gary, grinning sheepishly, completely surprised him. "If you've put an ad in the paper for a new jock, cancel it! I just hope I live to spend my take!"

CHAPTER SEVENTEEN

MARK AND HIS NEWLY DETERMINED PILOT SPENT THE NEXT four days in frequently heated arguments while they waited for the Porter's new gas tank to be installed. Gary was vehement in demanding that Sarn's Free Cambodians knock out the Khmer Rouge radar sets, or at least their power source, but Mark thought it would be impossible to be sure all available sets were knocked out, even if Sarn's guerrillas could get close enough to the ones they knew of.

"Hell," Mark insisted, "they're probably using those air force sets mounted in six-by vans, with a generator towed behind. Even if Sarn's guys take out the ones at likely places like Battembang, Pursat, and Khemerat, the Rouge could bring replacements in from Phnom Penh in a few hours. Knocking out their radar will just alert them we're going to go back in."

Gary was equally opposed to Mark's plan—using a decoy plane with its ELT turned on, to draw the Khmer Rouge away from the real flight.

"Goddamn it," Gary countered, "you're a pretty decent pilot for the hours you've got. But you're still no great shakes on instruments, or aerobatics at night at low altitude. One little mistake, like not believing your instruments, and you'll either get shot down or run into a hard cloud!"

114

The two argued until they got back to the mine, where, as he helped Mark unload a small mountain of boxes and packages from fashionable Bangkok women's stores and boutiques, Gary's dry sense of humor returned.

Gary had cocked a quizzical eyebrow when Mark pocketed a thousand dollars' worth of red Thai hundred-baht notes at the money changer, but he made no comment. He'd repeated the reaction when Mark returned with purchases from Design Thai, Thai Daimaru, and other expensive shops. Mark's only reaction had been an annoyed mutter.

In the bungalow's spacious living room, Pranee gaped at the mass of packages while Ah Lee clapped her work-worn hands in delight.

"Pranee honey, c'mon, open them," Mark said. "It's Christmas in April."

Pranee's reaction surprised Gary. As she tentatively opened a package wrapped in Design Thai's colorful paper and then shyly held up the beautiful Thai silk dress, the look on her still thin face was one of sadness and pain. After a few seconds, she dropped the dress in a heap, covered her face with her hands, and burst into bitter sobbing.

Mark and Gary watched, dumbfounded. Ah Lee was beside the distraught girl in seconds, stroking her hair and talking to her in rapid Thai that neither man could follow. Pranee lifted up her tear stained face and answered the elderly Chinese in a burst of equally rapid angry words. Then, almost defiantly, she pushed Ah Lee's obvious protests aside, looked steadily at each man in turn, and almost shouted, "This is all wrong! I do not deserve such fine things. I am not as you think. I am dirty and unclean!"

Then she continued in a lower tone, her voice trembling at times. "I am not ungrateful for all you have done. But it is all wrong. My father and I were hoping to leave before you came back, but—"

Pranee shushed Mark's startled reply with her tiny hand. "Yes, leave. But now I must tell you the truth about what happened to me—back there."

Though Gary was even more reluctant than Mark, Pranee's

huge, hypnotic eyes again held him against his will. After one look at Mark's face, Gary wanted to run from the room, but the intensity of the girl's tortured eyes held him like a cobra holds its prey.

After completing Teacher's College, Pranee told them, she had gone to Phnom Penh to find a job in the fall of 1973. Her relative fluency in both English and French made that easy. Within a few months, however, the American military buildup increased and she was recruited at triple her former salary by an American major. Her new employer, she quickly learned, was an intelligence officer.

Her new boss, Major Bradburn, learned almost as quickly that the shy, petite girl was his best translator, hands down. After a fast security check, he began assigning her to secret material—taped interrogations, intercepted radio messages, captured documents.

As the pace of the war increased, and the Khmer Rouge and Viet Cong pushed closer to Phnom Penh, she began putting in longer days. She didn't mind. Her work had convinced her that, bad as the corrupt Lon Nol government might be, a Communist victory would be far worse.

But in early March 1975, it was obvious that the outcome was only a matter of time. Major Bradburn called her into his office and stunned her by saying he wanted to fly her out of Cambodia to Thailand, where she could resume her work with another American intelligence unit; Pranee knew too much to be allowed to fall into enemy hands. For her own safety, as well as for security reasons, it was necessary that she go.

Pranee, though shocked by the suddenness, had to agree. She knew she was already on Communist "wanted lists," as were all Cambodians who worked for the Americans. Her only request, that her father be allowed to accompany her to Thailand, was quickly answered. One of Major Bradburn's units was in Battembang, close to where her father's little charcoal business was located.

The next day Pranee loaded her meager belongings into a

jeep driven by an officer from the Battembang unit. They never got there.

"We were only a few kilometers from Pursat when it happened. It was all over so fast. One second we were driving along; the next we were in the rice field. The American was dead, bleeding from a dozen bullets. I felt so sorry for him; he was a nice man."

Pranee told how her sorrow for the dead American turned to envy as the exultant Khmer Rouge ambushers raped her until she lost consciousness. When she came to, they were gone. She tried to crawl away from the burning jeep but passed out again. When she regained consciousness she was in another jeep, being held by a huge, dirty, bearded ferang wearing foul-smelling green fatigues. Too frightened and hurt to move, Pranee feigned unconsciousness when the jeep stopped. The bearded man carried her into a building, out of the broiling sun.

Inside, she was surprised to hear the voices of women, foreigners speaking English. The bearded man laid her on a bed. "She's had a pretty bad time of it, from the looks, Sister. Here, you'll need this for buying medicine and stuff."

Then he left. All Pranee ever saw was his dusty, sweat-stained back as he strode away.

The English and American nuns who ran the little mission school got a doctor the next day. Under their care, Pranee recovered physically, but had continuing terrible nightmares. As therapy, the nuns pushed her into helping with the younger children. Soon she was starting to teach again.

But it was only for a few weeks. They had heard unbelievable stories of how the savage Khmer Rouge were evacuating all major cities and large towns, but the little mission wasn't in a town; it was twenty kilometers from Pursat, an hour's walk from the main road—so they felt safe. That was an illusion. A motley band of black-clad soldiers arrived one morning. Within hours all the foreign nuns had been raped into unconsciousness or screaming insanity. With the rest of the Cambodian women and children, Pranee was forced to

watch as their bleeding, naked bodies were thrown into the
burning mission.

Paralyzed with fear and shock, she found herself being
herded roughly into a waiting truck. When it was full of the
girls and younger women, it drove off. After a terrifying trip
in the wildly careening truck, they arrived in Battembang.
Their relief at stopping was short-lived.

In minutes it was clear that they were new recruits for a
Khmer Rouge brothel. Bitterly, Pranee's voice rose. "I didn't
have to go with the others." An officer looked over the trembling, weeping girls and women at length before grabbing
Pranee by the arm and half dragging her to his quarters.

She had a choice, he told her with a grating laugh. She
could stay with him or go with the others to the soldiers'
quarters. She stayed.

It wasn't good, but it was far better than the alternative.
The only faintly redeeming part was finding that her "pro-
tector" had a thirst for alcohol that far exceeded his sexual
appetite. As often as she could, she traded the food he brought
home for whiskey, wine, or beer. She spiked the beer with
straight alcohol as long as she could find any. The rest of the
time she endured.

Then her fortunes changed again. It was the cold season—
Pranee had long ceased keeping track of time—and the Khmer
Rouge officer came home unexpectedly, in midmorning, in a
towering rage. Between blows, she finally grasped that he had
just come from the hospital. He had "woman's disease"—
VD! Naturally, it was her fault!

What followed—grim semistarvation in one "resettlement
camp" after another—was, to Pranee, preferable to her former role of unwilling mistress. But the grueling days, trying
to clear new fields with bare hands and crude wooden tools,
wore her down.

She had resigned herself to dying when the Khmer Rouge,
in one of their frequent, illogical forced migrations, moved
the people in her camp outside Battembang to another one
close to her former home. Although the long days of march-
ing on scanty food killed off many of the weaker prisoners,

Pranee sustained herself with the faint hope of finding her father. With his help, they might escape, somehow.

Her hopes died soon after she arrived in the new camp. From some of the woodcutters and men who worked at her father's and other charcoal kilns, she found out Remrut had long since fled.

Pranee sank into apathy for several months. She didn't die, mainly because the Khmer Rouge, frightened by the rising death rate and pathetic crop yields, increased the food rations dramatically. So Pranee was still alive when Sarn Nol's Free Cambodians began secret recruitment among the ox cart drivers and wood and charcoal workers. Pranee befriended several of them in hopes they might take her with them in their often planned but seldom attempted efforts to escape over the mountains to Thailand. Her hope kept her from complete despair, but only just. Then, out of nowhere, came the chance of escape.

Again her hopes were smashed. She had an attack of malaria. Delirious, she was left behind when Sarn's men took the families of the woodcutters and cart drivers from the death camp at Phum Krachap. But they had not forgotten her; when Remrut arrived with Sarn's raiders, they told him.

Pranee's voice faded as she finished her story. She lifted her hands. "Now you know the truth about me. I cannot stay here longer. It is not right."

Her head lifted defiantly as she started to rise. Tears welling up in her eyes, Pranee took only one step before Mark had her in his arms. Holding her closely, he only nodded as Gary, halfway to the door, threw over his shoulder, "Takeoff as soon as you're ready, Mark."

Pranee clung to Mark like a frightened child during the flight to Bangkok. It was nearly three in the afternoon when their taxi disgorged them at Bangkok Samaritan Hospital.

With Pranee in his arms, the burly American followed Gary's blocking-back drive through the crowded lobby to the emergency room. Waving off the wad of red baht notes Mark tried to give him, Gary returned to the lobby and plunked down a neat ten-thousand-baht package with the Bank of

America's wrapper still in place. By the time he'd bullied his way through startled admissions clerks, Pranee had finished with lab tests and X-rays. She and Mark were in the office of a tolerant Canadian, who gave her a detailed examination and, at Mark's insistence, wrote prescriptions that, he smilingly said, "will cure anything she may have in the way of VD, and a lot of other things she probably doesn't have. But they won't hurt her. Come back tomorrow afternoon and we'll go over her test results and X-rays."

Back at the Bangkapi bungalow, Mark stuffed the still dazed girl with initial doses of the medicines, forced her to try and eat a huge sirloin steak and then ordered her to bed.

Then he mixed himself a tall glass of Scotch and ice, replaced his tattered cigar with a fresh one, and looked at the silent pilot. "Old and beat-up as I am, Gary, I'd sure like to work over some of those bastards!"

The intensity of his tone caused Gary to cock an eyebrow before nodding. Then the familiar telltale finger twirling and cigar rolling told Gary there was no need for conversation. Mark's brooding silence and unconscious finger motions were nothing new. But the amount of Scotch the big man silently consumed was. He had emptied the bottle before he stood up and stretched. "I'm hungry. How about you?"

Despite the steady flow of Scotch during a meal he barely touched, Mark gave no clue to the amount he had imbibed—until they got out of the cab and he simply collapsed on the bungalow's porch.

As he struggled to lift Mark and get him to the living-room couch, Gary's grunts woke Pranee, who insisted on helping put Mark in his bed, where she had been. There they undressed his unprotesting form to underwear, covered him with a sheet, and left.

Pranee made coffee while she argued with Gary about who would sleep on the couch. After finally agreeing to take Gary's room, she fixed him with her compelling eyes. "Khun Gary? You are Mark's good friend for a long time."

"About twelve years, off and on, Pranee. Why?"

"I want to learn about him. Everything you know." She

hurried on. "I cannot make him happy until I know why he is many times sad. I see sadness, and I think he also is lonely. It is in his eyes and his face. He tries to hide it, but I know it is there."

Gary squirmed for a long moment before he replied. "You might be right, Pranee. Never gave it much thought, to tell the truth. Mark's always been sort of a loner—since I've known him, anyway. Course, he's always been the boss man, too. That's part of it, for damn sure. It gets pretty rough when you have to make decisions that can get people killed. And Mark's had his share of 'em.

"Don't really know too much about his personal life, like family and all that. I know he had a pretty rough divorce, a while before I first met him up in Laos. He's got a couple of sisters. He never says anything much about them. And his ex-wife didn't do much of a job with their two kids. The boy took off to Canada in the late sixties, to duck the draft. Mark locked himself in his room and stayed drunk for three days when he heard about it. But he never said anything. And nobody wanted to ask.

"He gets damn few letters from anyone, as far as I've seen out here. And I can't remember him sending anything much but a few Christmas cards."

Gary threw up his hands as he stopped. But Pranee wasn't satisfied. "Has he no woman, or girlfriend?"

"Mark's not what you'd call a real ladies' man. Actually, Pranee, he's what we call a workaholic—it means a guy who's too interested in his work to have time for much else. He's not much for nightclubs and bars—you know, the ones with girls and all that."

Pranee's smile brightened as she softly patted Gary's hand. "Khun Gary, I thank you for this, very, very much. You are a good man and a good friend to Mark. Already you saved my life. Now you have done a more important thing.

"I have thought that Mark is a lonely man. Now I am sure I am right. He has been lonely and sad for too long. I will change that! It is not right! He is too good a man to be unhappy. I, Pranee, will *make* him happy. All my life will

be to make him happy, in any way I can. I am glad he does
not go often with the bar girls, but even if he does, I will not
care if it makes him happy. Once I used to think they were
very bad, very low-type girls. Now, now I know better. I
have been like them, and sick, too. But even so, Mark does
not look down on me. He would be right to look down—I
am no better than they. But I *will* be better, for him. I will
be everything he wants. If I cannot make him happy myself,
I will find girls who can! But always I will be there to take
care of him.''

A week later they all flew back down to the mine. Gary
attacked the large backlog of crudum that had built up, while
Mark spent a long day with the foreman.

After his last flight, Gary arrived at the bungalow to inter-
rupt a loud argument between Mark and Pranee. She was
sitting on the couch with her legs tucked under her, wearing
a frilly housecoat Mark had bought her on his shopping spree.
She wore a half-amused, half-tolerant smile as the burly ex-
colonel paced up and down, chewing savagely on a tattered
cigar. When he saw Gary, he stopped in midstride.

''Gary, damn it, *you* explain to her. Maybe she'll listen to
you!''

''Explain what?''

''Tell her she can't just move into my room like this. It's
just not right, or . . . or anything.''

Pranee smiled sweetly. When Mark subsided, she said,
''Why must we wait for some silly piece of paper? That is
stupid. I love Khun Mark, and I know he loves me. I am
happy to be his wife. A piece of silly paper will not make
me love him any more.''

It took a while, but every time Mark started off with a new
''But, Pranee . . .'' she had an answer. Eventually Mark gave
up, and in. Gary thought, Damn fool is more *embarrassed*
than he is anything else. . . .

CHAPTER EIGHTEEN

MARK WAS A CHANGED MAN AS HE AND GARY FINALLY SET-
tled on a compromise plan for the remaining gold pickups.
Using Visarn's "connections" and Mark's cash, Pranee became a Thai citizen on the same day she and Mark were
quietly married by a cooperative Thai *Nai Amphur* in Bangkok.

On the same weekend, the two Americans broached their
plan to the old Chinese merchant. Mark had agreed, finally,
that his pilot's skills were unequal to the task of the decoy
flights. Gary had suggested trying to recruit former Major
Somboon. Having trained Somboon on covert intrusion flights
during the war, Gary felt Somboon was the best available
choice. "Look, those Police Air Reinforcement Unit pilots
are good, but so is Somboon. Even if your old buddy General
Pranet would close his eyes, it'd be awfully risky for Visarn.
A cop is a cop."

Visarn's reaction was as Gary had predicted. So was egg-
bald Somboon's. As Visarn made the proposal, Mark and
Gary saw the Thai pilot was putting two and two together as
he listened. But when Mark took over and explained the reason they needed a decoy, Somboon's face tightened in anger.

"I cannot believe one of my mechanics is a Communist!

They were with me in the PARU, in Laos, and I know them for too many years, Khun Mark.''

''I know, 'Boon. But somebody got at that Porter while you were doing the three-hundred-hour. And remember, you were on that charter to Chiang Mai part of the time.''

Somboon's anger ebbed as Mark unfolded the decoy plan.

''It shouldn't be too tough, 'Boon. You file for a flight to Surin with a stop at Aranya Pratet. You have some real cargo for the gold merchants in Aranya. Visarn will set that up. At Aranya you fake engine trouble till it's time to start. You'll take off half an hour before Gary.

''With the overcast we're getting from the monsoon buildup, you should have plenty of good cloud cover around four thousand. As soon as you're over the border, kick on your ELT. Stay in the clouds and just inside the border till you get opposite Surin. Don't take any chances. Stay in the clouds.

''We'll give you some rice and medicine to drop so's it will look right—same thing Gary used to do. After you dump the stuff, cut the ELT, and when you're sure you're over Surin, switch your transponder on so you don't get the Thai Air Force on your ass on the way back to Don Muang.''

On the flight back down to the mine, Gary chuckled as he said, ''Old Somboon must be at least half-Chinese himself! I thought he'd blown the deal when he told Visarn his price. A brand new shiny Porter, FOB Don Muang! Christ, Mark, 'Boon'll have himself a real operation in no time.''

The first flight was scheduled for the first of the new moon. As promised, Somboon radioed a weather forecast the night before, and Mark confirmed the flight for the next night. Even Gary, the inveterate pessimist, went to sleep easily. But just as the predawn sky began to lighten, all their careful planning was rudely shattered.

Even to the initiated, the slamming thud and deadly whine of metal fragments from a hand grenade are frightening. So is the chattering, staccato bark of an M-16 automatic rifle. The closer the sounds, the more ominous. A combination of the two woke Mark and Gary. Half-forgotten instinct ruled their first waking seconds—their bodies hit the floors of their bedrooms, and each cursed as he realized frantic pawing for nonexistent weapons was futile.

Belatedly, Mark remembered his new bride. But she was gone. He crawled to the hall, saw the bathroom door closed, and shouted, ''Pranee, get down on the floor, and stay there till I tell you it's safe.''

Mark and Gary exchanged worried looks as the firing abruptly ceased.

''What the hell?'' Gary wondered. ''Sounded like it was at the gate, and up behind the crusher, too.''

Mark had no chance to answer; black-clad figures with rifles poured into the bungalow from front and rear. Mark and Gary rose slowly to their feet, hands raised. Ah Lee, weeping and trembling, was herded after them.

In the half light, Mark stiffened as one of the grim-faced riflemen kicked open the bathroom door. When he found it empty, Mark exchanged a worried glance with Gary. Then a somber, lean figure strode into the room, looking at them closely.

''Radio?'' the lean man wanted to know.

Mark gestured with his right hand toward the rear of the room. The grim figure spoke rapidly in what Mark and Gary recognized as Cambodian. Another black-clad figure came in from the porch and sat down as he studied the old surplus American army AN/GRC-9. Then, with a brief answer to the apparent leader, he took out a notebook, turned the set on, and began tuning it.

By the growing light, Mark could see the mine workers and their families being herded by other black-clad riflemen into a group in front of the bungalow. He counted over two dozen outside, plus six more and their leader in the living room. Mark and Gary searched the group outside for Pranee and Ming, but saw neither. Both silently prayed this meant that they had somehow escaped.

During the next hour their captors ignored them. Ah Lee was put to work preparing food while the radio operator sent and received messages. The answers apparently pleased the leader. Then there was a chorus of dismay from the huddled group of mine workers. Ten more of the raiders, whom Mark and Gary had decided must be Khmer Rouge, were escorting four of the ex–border patrolmen who had been at the training site.

Mark swore to himself when he saw that two of the green-uniformed patrolmen were half carrying Ming. Ming had a bloody rag tied around his head. He seemed only half-conscious as the patrolmen stopped in front of the bungalow and lowered him to the ground.

Gary froze in fear as Mark strode over to the wall and lifted down the blue and white first aid kit, pointing to Ming. "That man's hurt. I'm going to take care of him."

For a tense few seconds, while their guards' hands tightened on their rifles, Gary read murder in their faces. Mark ignored them, fixing his glare on the leader. Then the leader shrugged and barked an order to his men.

Mark examined briefly the ragged gash on the side of the mechanic's head. Then, with one of the patrolmen helping, they carried in Ming and laid him on the couch. The Khmer Rouge watched closely as Mark's stubby fingers cleaned the still bleeding wound and bandaged it. Finished, Mark favored the Khmer Rouge leader with a curt "Thanks."

After the raiders had taken turns eating, the leader pulled a map from his pack and motioned Mark and Gary to join him at the table.

Seated, they saw the map covered most of the Thai-Cambodian border. They had barely registered this dismaying fact when the thin-faced Khmer Rouge leader snapped, "You will pick gold where?"

The two Americans' stomachs lurched in unison. As they sat, trying to think, the Khmer Rouge added menacingly, "You show now. No show, I kill him first"—he jerked his finger at Ming's unconscious body—"then others."

Mark's mind whirled as he sought a way out. If he showed the Khmer Rouge leader the pickup site, he was condemning the reception team to sure death. If he didn't . . . The lean, almost handsome face opposite him gave him the heart-breaking answer. There were over fifty mine workers, in addition to Ming and the four surviving patrolmen. A Hobson's choice—five of Sarn Nol's men or more than one hundred here.

Hating himself, Mark jabbed his finger at the pickup site as Gary sighed in sympathy.

"Good. Now"—he turned to Gary—"your airplane is ready?"

The unexpectedness of the question caught the pilot off guard. He thought furiously, but finally shrugged. "Have to preflight it. Where do you want to go?"

"Good," said the Khmer leader. "We go later. Now sleep."

Half an hour before Gary had been scheduled to take off for the pickup, which the Khmer Rouge leader obviously had known about, he was led down to the plane. When Gary saw the impossibly heavy stacks of resmelted gold bars in the plane, he looked at them in the flashlight beam for a few seconds before forcing a rough laugh.

"You want to die in a hurry, huh? You want to fly it like that? Go ahead. I'll stay here and watch."

When the reduced load had been tied down to the now grimly resigned pilot's satisfaction, he preflighted the Porter as slowly as he could. Pranee had apparently escaped, so there was at least a faint hope that she might have reached help.

Finally, he could delay no longer. The Khmer Rouge leader, whose name the Americans learned was Charn, shoved him toward the cockpit and climbed in the right-hand seat. He laid his rifle against his door and pointed a .45 automatic at Gary. "Now go, or . . ."

As soon as Gary settled onto his first leg, he began trying frantically to think of a way out of his predicament. But everything he thought of seemed like certain suicide. Reviewing all he had learned since the Khmer Rouge had taken over the mine, the only faint bright spot was that Charn didn't know much about airplanes. Gary tried as hard as he could, but he

couldn't think of a way to use this to his advantage. Charn
obviously knew enough to strap on his safety harness, so wild
aerobatics weren't the answer. Charn was holding the black
.45 automatic in his right hand, away from the pilot.

Gary was still vainly trying to figure out an answer when
they crossed the Cardamom Range and he started to switch
on his radar detector. Charn surprised him by reaching to
stop him with his free left hand.

"No need. No planes tonight."

The pilot was still trying to force his mind to accept the
implications of Charn's curt words when his receiver picked
up the beacon's signal, and then a quick signal from the strip.
After he landed, his body slumped in hopeless defeat. There
was no way out.

At the end of the strip Gary saw a cluster of black-clad
figures. Charn removed his last desperate hope by forcing
him out of the cockpit. He shouted orders to the waiting men.
They laid their weapons down and began to unload the gold
bars.

Standing where Charn had shoved him, by the Porter's needle nose, Gary ducked in fear as Charn and an unseen companion suddenly opened fire on the men who had unloaded
the plane!

It was slaughter. Paralyzed, Gary watched the second man
stoop to check each of the bodies. Then he began walking
toward the plane. The man was barely six feet away when
Charn's M-16 spat out a short burst and the man crumpled to
the ground. "Now we load the gold!" Charn said after
checking him.

In a trance, Gary started toward the pile of bars the dead
men had just unloaded. Charn stopped him with a harsh
laugh.

"Not them. They not gold. Over there, real gold."

Seeing Gary's disbelief, the Khmer Rouge leader waved
him to the pile, scratched one of the dully gleaming bars with
his knife, and then flashed his light on it. "Chinese too very
smart. I, Charn, more smart!"

As he carried the real gold in the charred metal ammo

boxes, Gary noticed two well-wrapped cartons lying beside the pile. They were about the size of beer cartons. After he finished with the gold bars—which, despite his protests, Charn made him remove from the ammo boxes—he was told to load the cartons. Each weighed barely ten pounds. When they had been lashed down on top of the gold bars, Charn nodded approval and ordered the thoroughly confused pilot back into the plane.

Airborne again, Charn flashed the first smile Gary had seen on his normally grim face. "Now we go here. You can land on sand near water, no?"

As Gary saw where the Khmer Rouge's finger pointed on a duplicate of his own WAC chart, he nodded as his mind tried to take in this newest surprise. He knew the area, about halfway between the Thai towns of Rayong and Chantaburi. There was a several-kilometer-long stretch of white sand beach. Screened from the land side by mangrove swamp and coconut plantations, it was a perfect site for a smuggling rendezvous.

Gary tried to get high enough so they would be picked up by Thai air force radar. His captor didn't notice at first. When he did, he dug the .45 in Gary's side. When the beach came in sight, they were at barely eight hundred feet. Gary's assumption that Charn was planning to transfer his cargo seemed to be confirmed by the dim shape of a Thai fishing *tankay* anchored close to the shore, and the flashing of a light from the beach.

Charn blinked an answer with his own flashlight and then pointed down. As the Porter slowed to a stop on the firm, wet sand, Charn again surprised him.

"You guard me," he said, handing the pilot the M-16 rifle. "I no trust these."

Gary stood anxiously outside, trying to calculate his chances of emptying the M-16 at Charn and the group of men approaching the still-idling Porter. He was weighing the idea when a figure emerged from the group of smugglers. "Good timing," he said in American English. "Bring it over here, so we can check it."

Charn opened the rear door, tossed the two cartons away from the plane, and stood watching as Gary heard the men who retrieved the boxes exclaim in Thai at their lightness.

The English speaker quickly slit a corner of each box and removed small, clear plastic bags of white powder. Heroin, sure as my name's Sonderberg, Gary thought. My God, first gold, and now heroin. This Charn's really something else!

Satisfied with the results of his testing, the kneeling man called out. "Okay, Mike. Bring it down."

Another man appeared carrying an attaché case. Gary saw Charn flash his light on the contents as the newcomer opened it. The man closed it again and handed it to Charn, who took it in his left hand, his right held close to his automatic. The Khmer Rouge leader spoke something so softly, Gary couldn't hear it, but the man called Mike laughed. "Take all you got," he answered. "Same deal. We'll be waiting to hear."

Walking crabwise, never taking his eyes off the two men, Charn kept clear of the idling prop. "I get in first, then we go fast," he said softly.

Gary's shoulders tightened, half in anticipation of a burst of gunfire from the ground, but none came. As he cleaned up the Porter and began a slow turn to the east, toward Cambodia, Charn stopped him with a wolfish grimace. "No. Other way. We go Singapore!"

For the first time that long day, Gary felt a surge of hope. Charn was planning to escape himself. That meant Gary's previously grim estimate of his chances of surviving might be wrong. But he kept his face straight as he pointed to the fuel guage. "No can, Charn. We'd be lucky to reach the west side of the gulf."

As they argued in the plane's cockpit, Gary took a chance. While he jabbed at the outspread map, he used his left hand to flick the ELT switch to EMERGENCY. Charn showed no sign of noticing the movement.

After Gary informed him of the distance the Porter could possibly travel on the remaining fuel, Charn studied the map's scale and measured off distances with his free hand. He only grunted when Gary insisted that to make even Nakorn Srithammerat on the far shore, he would have to get the Porter up to its most fuel-efficient altitude. Praying silently, Gary increased power and began a steady climb. Charn's eyes roved from compass to map and back.

As the minutes ticked by, Gary began to worry that his ELT signal wasn't working. He switched on the radio and chanced Charn's reaction. "Need the weather forecast. Head winds this time of year."

Again Charn only grunted. At five thousand feet it was almost full daylight. Gary's initial brief optimism that his ELT emergency signal would alert the Thai air force was ebbing fast. He was working out another plan: to dive out of the Porter as soon as it slowed down on landing. He might get a couple of broken bones, he reasoned, but they'd heal. Charn couldn't shoot him once he got clear. And if he did it right . . .

Gary's scheme ended as a burst of tracers blazed past the Porter's nose. Then the radio came to life. "Four Niner Zulu. Turn to eighty degrees at once or we will shoot you down!"

Gary ignored Charn's angry shout and thumbed his mike. "Don't shoot! We'll be good!"

CHAPTER NINETEEN

POLICE COLONEL (SPECIAL GRADE) BANCHERT'S COOK AND maid of all work, long familiar with his moods, correctly concluded the colonel was in an especially good mood—he'd ordered a ferang-style breakfast of bacon and eggs instead of his usual thick rice soup, *khow thom*.

Dressed unusually in his green field uniform, Colonel Banchert ate with delight as he went over his careful plans for the day. By this time tomorrow, give or take an hour or two, his increasingly critical American contacts in the CIA and the Bangkok Dangerous Drugs detachment would be forced to admit he had been right. More important, his boss in the National Security Council would almost have to submit his name for promotion to major general.

By late afternoon, everything was going exactly as he had planned. Four hours before the Khmer Rouge leader forced Gary to take off from the mine, Colonel Banchert tightened his seat belt as the awkward-looking C-123 began its approach to Chantaburi's dusty airfield—barely ten kilometers to the south. Unaware of the Khmer Rouge raid, he watched the tough, heavily armed police paratroopers trot down the lowered ramp and load into waiting trucks.

Two more planeloads were already in their assigned locations, farther south. Some were already on Ko Kut Island, whose location and sheltered coves had long since made it a favorite smuggling rendezvous. Others were aboard the Thai Water Police's two fastest patrol boats as backup.

Thai Air Force F-5 jet fighters were standing by at Utapao Air Base, while four T-28's waited at Chantaburi for spotter or air support missions.

Banchert's lethal little task force was complemented by a fleet of seven fishing tankays that would track the scruffy Panamanian-flag *Alameda*'s course from Bangkok Bar to the rendezvous. Banchert's men on board would radio the four-thousand-ton old freighter's course and speed along her expected route to Ko Kut Island. The first report was handed to him as he landed at Chantaburi—course southeast, speed eleven knots.

During the ride from the dusty field to the Chantaburi Police Station, Banchert reviewed the combination of patient police investigative work and the strokes of what he cheerfully admitted to himself had been sheer luck. The latter he accepted with the mental note from his college studies at MIT—something about good luck coming to those who were prepared to exploit it.

For example, it was pure luck that an experienced smuggler like LeFrere had talked so freely on the telephone. But had Banchert not had his phone tapped for weary, unproductive months, the conversations between LeFrere and his Cambodian contacts, as well as the *Alameda*'s Bangkok agents, would never have been recorded.

The Cambodian connection had led to using Sarn La's Free Cambodians to keep a close watch on Battembang and Khemerat airfields, either of which Banchert felt could be used as the takeoff point for a flight to drop the drug shipment to the *Alameda* out in the gulf. In that he had been wrong: Sarn La's team at Khemerak had reported only days ago that two beer-case-sized cartons, under unusually heavy guard, had arrived by plane from Phnom Penh, but had been immediately turned over to Khmer Rouge Commander Charn Nol, who had loaded the two cartons in his jeep and, accompanied by two truckloads of Khmer Rouge soldiers, driven north.

Banchert had been puzzled by that but finally decided that the Cambodians feared being spotted on Thai radar, so had decided to transfer the drug shipment overland or by sea. Only two days earlier Banchert had received a second report from a Sarn La agent on the Khemerat waterfront about the hurried day and night work on the engine of a fast-looking former American sport-fishing boat, newly arrived from Sihanoukville. This was enough to convince him that the transfer would be by sea. Since Khemerat was barely forty-five kilometers from Ko Kut Island, everything fit together nicely.

Now, with the *Alameda* under way and on a course in the general direction of Ko Kut Island, Banchert felt his confidence was fully justified.

At ten o'clock the *Alameda* was still on course, doing almost thirteen knots. The next fishing-boat report was due in about an hour, and the *Alameda*'s present speed would bring her to the vicinity of Ko Kut about four A.M.

Banchert wrote a short message to his patrol boats and ambush party, informing them everything was proceeding as anticipated. But as he entered the radio room, his own operator finished decoding a message from his deputy in Bangkok, Major Prasong. Banchert read it with a sinking feeling in his stomach. LeFrere and an unidentified ferang companion had driven south from Bangkok at ten that morning. The surveillance team's radio had quit on them, and they hadn't dared stop on the long drive to Rayong for fear of losing the speeding car. LeFrere had driven directly to the waterfront in Rayong, boarded a waiting water-ski boat, and disappeared downriver toward the gulf before the team could locate another craft. While one of the team relayed the news to Major Prasong, the other had spent a fruitless two hours searching for LeFrere's boat!

The only encouraging part of the message was that LeFrere and his companion had been empty-handed when they boarded the speedboat. Banchert strode quickly to the map. If the *Alameda* was still on course, she should be ten miles off Rayong in thirty minutes.

Banchert used all his willpower to force himself to sit and

wait quietly, but his men noted his taut expression and the rapid filling of his ashtray with half-smoked cigarettes.

When the next report from the fishing boats arrived, twenty minutes late, Banchert's self-control began to crack. The *Alameda* had, incredibly, altered course to southwest, away from shore and Ko Kut Island. Even more mystifying was a sharp drop in her speed, which was now barely six knots.

The map merely confirmed what the colonel's racing mind had already told him. The rusty old freighter wouldn't come close to Ko Kut on her present course, regardless of her reduced speed. What was she up to? The frustrated colonel couldn't fit the new information into any reasonable picture. After the first news of LeFrere's unexpected trip to Rayong, Banchert had half convinced himself it was an attempt to decoy surveillance into thinking the transfer would be made near Rayong. But the sudden change of course and slackened speed of the *Alameda* blew that theory. LeFrere clearly didn't have any money with him—why had he gone empty-handed? Except for the strange change by the *Alameda*, the decoy theory held water. Could she be just waiting for a rendezvous later on? Or would the pickup still be at Ko Kut the following night? And where was the drug shipment? Had something gone wrong on the Cambodian side? Banchert paced the little office he had borrowed, his mind whirling with questions he couldn't answer.

Banchert began walking slowly toward the radio room, formulating a message to his ambush forces, but his train of thought was broken by a loud commotion from the front of the ancient wooden police station. Annoyed, he strode angrily to quell it. As he opened the door he heard a fragment of a woman's sobbing words—''Khmer Rouge, I tell you . . .''

Banchert quickened his steps. Several policemen were trying to restrain a disheveled woman. As Banchert approached she screamed wildly at him. ''You've got to listen! Help me! It's true. The Khmer Rouge have attacked the mine and killed the guards!''

It took Banchert less than five minutes to get the bare bones of Pranee's semicoherent story. It drove his own problems from his mind.

The Police Paratroopers' commander, hastily summoned, studied the sketch Pranee had drawn of the mine and the clearing. The trail Pranee had used wasn't on the map, but she solved that by accompanying the troopers to guide them to it. While a paratroop medic treated Pranee's torn feet and scratched face and arms, Banchert and the troopers' commander worked up a plan to retake the mine. Based on what Pranee had seen and heard, they decided to use roughly the same tactics—attack from the uphill side, and from the direction of the clearing.

The troopers and Pranee were just leaving the station in their trucks when Banchert was called to the station's voice radio. One of Banchert's inviolable rules was that his unit never use the easily monitorable police voice circuits. But his sudden flash of anger evaporated as Major Prasong double-talked his message. Prasong had just received a message from "tonight's friends." Their "housekeeper" had been abducted by "guess who." The others had been unable to "phone in" until they reached a "quiet spot." After receiving this news, Prasong had tried to contact "our local messenger service," but they were inexplicably "not at home."

Banchert's trained mind sorted out his deputy's double-talk and tried to make sense of it. The "housekeeper's abduction" meant the Khmer Rouge had somehow discovered his presence near the gold cache, before the reception team had arrived. Though Mark was completely unaware of it, Banchert had been closely following the entire affair via his own contacts with Sarn's men, and also from his other agent, Ming. As soon as he had learned of the recovery operation from Ming, he had decided to let it alone, at least temporarily. While it was illegal on any number of counts, breaking it up before it had barely begun seemed wasting a literally golden opportunity. But once some, or all, of the gold had been moved into Thailand, all sorts of interesting possibilities would arise. Especially as a means of greatly supplementing his department's tiny budget. Ever a realist, Banchert knew precious little of the official reward for seizing smuggled contraband, especially gold, would trickle down to his unit if he made an *official* capture. However, properly implemented, his actions might allow him to finance a number of important operations his superiors insisted he undertake, but refused to provide the funds for.

The Khmer Rouge attack on the mine, which accounted for Prasong's report that their ''local messenger service was not at home,'' meant the end of Visarn's operation. Banchert's Khmer Rouge counterpart, Commander Charn, obviously knew all about it. The raid, however, was disturbing. It seemed clear that Charn intended to take over the mine and then bring the gold back into Cambodia. Banchert was impressed by the audacity of the idea. But how did Charn plan to transport the gold from the mine? There should be well over nineteen hundred kilograms there. At, say, thirty kilograms per man, Charn would need at least sixty-odd men to carry it, and as many more to protect them should they run into a Thai border patrol. From Pranee's account, he couldn't even guess how many Khmer Rouge had attacked the mine. But if Charn had sent one hundred or so men, the two forty-man PARU platoons might be heading for trouble!

Negative messages from the two fishing boats nearest the *Alameda*'s last known position decided him to recall two other PARU platoons from the patrol boats waiting at Trad. That done, he returned to plans to capture the drug shipment.

The minutes crawled by as Banchert tried to fit together the scanty information. A report from the paratroopers that they were starting up the mountain trails to the mine, and the briefing of the two reinforcement platoons airlifted in from Trad, helped his spirits slightly. Then another confusing element was added to the muddled picture. Narong, the PARU commander, reported hearing the distinctive whine of a Porter aircraft taking off from the mine's strip, and Wing Commander Rangsan, at Utapao airbase, confirmed an unidentified aircraft heading south from the same vicinity! Asking his air force friend to keep him informed of the plane's progress, Banchert hurried to the map. He had clearly underestimated

Charn Nol! The Khmer Rouge leader had no intention of trying to carry the gold back on foot; he was flying it back!

When Utapao reported the plane was on a heading that would take it to the area of the pickup site the Khmer Rouge had just captured, Banchert was sure that Gary or Mark was flying the Porter at gunpoint! His admiration for the two Americans was genuine and of long standing, but he could not let the Khmer Rouge fly the gold back to Cambodia! In another hour or so it would be returning for another load. He would have to order the air force to shoot it down, and one of his friends with it!

Banchert decided to fly to Utapao in one of the T-28's. During the short flight he consoled himself that the fighters might be able to make the Porter land, instead of being shot down.

As he climbed into Commander Rangsan's waiting jeep, Banchert got another shock. "That plane, or at least one like it, came back on our screen about ten minutes ago, old friend. But it's not heading back to the mine area, as you told me it would. It's going almost due east, well south of a course to the mine."

Banchert watched the tiny speck move steadily toward the gulf. He took a quick look at the map before he could force his thoughts into words. "They're *flying* the stuff to the *Alameda*!"

As Banchert hastily explained his sudden inspiration to the air force officer, the radar screen confirmed his hunch. The plane had lost altitude rapidly. Now it was within a few kilometers of the coastline.

Banchert snapped his fingers as a new thought struck him. The Cambodians weren't going to *drop* the drugs to the *Alameda*. They were going to make the transfer right on the beach!

It made sense. The buyer, LeFrere, would want to inspect the drugs before paying. But the Cambodians would want to be paid at the same time. Nobody trusted anybody, Banchert knew well.

Alerted by Wing Commander Rangsan, the F-5's were already screaming shrilly as Banchert watched the speck disappear from the radar screen.

"I'm sorry about your friend being the pilot, Banchert. I've told my pilots to make every effort to force them to land, but . . ."

Banchert nodded glumly as they stared at the radar screen. Banchert's professional mind forced him to admire the complex scheme. Had it not been for Pranee, and whoever was flying the Porter high enough to be picked up on radar, Charn would have retrieved several million dollars' worth of gold, and sold his drugs for several million more! All in a single operation! Enemy or not, Charn Nol was a brilliant officer.

This train of thought was interrupted as the plane again appeared on the radar screen, climbing rapidly. The last of the F-5's thundered into the night as both men exclaimed and looked at each other. The speck on the radar screen was swinging to the west!

Banchert merely nodded when his friend said, "My boys have them on their own radar now. They'll do their best."

CHAPTER TWENTY

GARY WAS AFRAID TO LOOK AT HIS CAPTOR AS HE BANKED steeply and steadied on his eighty-degree course to Utapao Air Base. He was half expecting the grim-faced Khmer Rouge commander to shoot him. With the Porter on course in a shallow glide to increase her airspeed, Gary flinched away from his captor as he saw him start to move. Charn's short, bitter laugh ended the tension as he finished opening his window and calmly threw out his automatic and then his rifle.

"I no want die. It is break Thai law have gun."

Charn's face wore an expression Gary decided was part self-derision, part resignation. Through his own wave of relief, the pilot was surprised to find he was feeling almost sorry for his ex-captor.

After landing, Gary was surrounded by jeeploads of Thai Air Police, who led him to a low concrete building. After his brief interest in his ex-captor's reactions, his mind had been busy with his next problem. What to tell the Thais? He was still spinning his mental wheels when a familiar figure emerged and welcomed him with an astonishingly strong bear hug! It was Colonel Banchert!

"Thank God for small favors," Gary muttered. "I might just get out of this mess with a whole skin!"

The broad smiles and pats on his arms and back from a

wing commander and two other Thai air force officers were
equally astonishing, but heartening. Amid the hubbub of in-
troductions and words of, amazingly, congratulation, Gary
suddenly stiffened and almost shouted, "Colonel Banchert!
The mine. The Khmer Rouge—"

"Not to worry, Khun Gary. The PARU took care of that
half an hour ago. Everyone is safe, except . . ." The colonel's face lost its smile as he paused before adding, "Except
poor Ming. He and Mark tried to escape while you were
taking off with Charn Nol. A guard they hadn't seen ran at
them shooting. Ming deliberately ran right at him. Mark got
into the jungle okay, because of Ming."

Gary's expression of sorrow was interrupted by Wing Commander Rangsan. "I'm sorry, Banchert, Captain Gary, but
the smugglers—will Captain Gary help us?"

Ten minutes later, from the rear seat of Wing Commander
Rangsan's swooping jet trainer, Gary tapped Rangsan's shoulder and pointed down at the spot where he had landed with
Charn. "I saw them heading almost due west as I climbed
out, Commander. It was a normal-looking tankay. Hull was
a dark color."

As they swung east and climbed steeply, Gary saw over a
dozen tankays heading generally west. He shook his head in
frustration; any of them could have been the one he had only
half seen in the darkness.

Gary's dismay was short-lived. The radio's metallic distor-
tion couldn't mask the exultant tone of the Thai F-5 pilot who
announced sighting *"rua yai, si damm"* and *"tankay wing
layo layo!"* A big black boat and a tankay traveling fast.

The two were on opposite courses; the tankay's smuggler's
outboards raised high rooster tails behind her. On her deck,
Gary saw figures rigging a net with two familiar cartons in
it. He came close to blacking out as Rangsan zoomed up after
his wave-top pass. His vision was still foggy as an F-5's guns
raised a line of splashes halfway between the rapidly closing
smuggler's boat and the black freighter.

Neither craft slowed or changed course. While Gary shook

his head at this display of sheer madness, Wing Commander
Rangsan spoke the words that turned his eager pilots loose.

Remembering his own encounter with the same F-5's only
an hour previously, Gary winced as he saw the accuracy of
their fire. They screamed down in line astern, lined up so
their guns and rockets could hit both the tankay and the old
freighter in one pass.

The two were barely fifty meters apart when the first F-5
pilot let go with his guns and streaking rockets. The second
and third were only seconds behind him.

Even before the third F-5 fired, all Gary could see were
angry orange flashes in the billowing black smoke. The final
two F-5's concentrated on the dimly visible freighter. The
tankay had simply disappeared.

Before Wing Commander Rangsan could stop them, the
first two F-5's made another attack. This time they hit the
blazing, smoke-shrouded freighter amidships. Before the third
F-5 could fire, the freighter exploded and split in two. The
second plane's rockets must have hit a boiler, Gary realized.
The two sections sank in minutes. The blazing bow and stern
sections raised brief steam clouds as they sank. All that was
left was an oil slick littered with debris, and two or three
objects that looked like bodies.

Gary had thought his years in Vietnam and Laos had inured
him to sudden, violent death. But somehow he was nauseated
by the combination of the sparkling blue sea, fat lazy clouds
lit by the just risen sun, and the widening, wreckage-strewn
oil slick.

To try to clear his mind of the still vivid pictures, Gary
returned to his own problems. His reception by Colonel
Banchert and the Thai air force officers had been a welcome
surprise. Obviously, he couldn't be in any really serious trouble with the Thais. But he knew he still had some explaining
to do. The gold bars in the Porter, for instance. How the hell
to explain them? Could he possibly get away with playing
dumb as to their real origin? If he did, and some of the paratroopers who had recaptured the mine found out about what
had happened . . . Gary squirmed in his harness.

When he climbed out of the jet, Gary had decided to at least try to play dumb about the gold, and hope for the best. But his inborn pessimism was still arguing his decision when he followed Wing Commander Rangsan into his headquarters.

More to test the water than anything else, Gary held up a protesting hand when the smiling Colonel offered him a beer. "Not if they'll let me take the Porter back down to the mine today, Colonel. Thanks anyway."

Banchert's cluck of approval encouraged the pilot. If they'd allow him to fly, things mustn't be real serious, he mused. They weren't.

Aside from writing out a brief statement in his neat script, and a short session with Thai TV and newspaper photographers, at which Banchert cautioned him against answering any questions, Gary was able to stay out of the limelight.

His "hijacker," Commander Charn Nol, handcuffed and leg-chained, was led out by guards with drawn guns. He gave the pilot a long, hard look as he was forced to pose behind him, but said nothing. Colonel Banchert posed endlessly with the attaché case full of American money—five million dollars' worth, he said.

Oddly, but very comfortingly, not a word was said about the gold bars. Poor old Visarn! Gary thought. He'll never see that load, or any part of it. And, he added, since old Banchert's keeping quiet about it, Mark and I may be home and dry, in spite of everything!

After a sumptuous lunch, Gary flew the quietly ebullient Thai intelligence officer down to the mine. Gary's pessimism suffered yet another defeat when Banchert made no mention of the gold during the brief flight.

Mark forced a brief smile on his drawn features as he greeted the pilot. "Damn glad to see you in one piece, tiger!" was all he said. But his look and handshake told Gary the depth of his feelings.

For the next few hours, before Colonel Banchert, suddenly sober-faced and serious, insisted they all fly to Bangkok with him, Gary heard various versions of what had gone on at the mine after he had taken off.

Mark's own terse account left out a great many details his triumphant former students in the Parachute Police filled in with mingled awe and pride.

Though still woozy from his head wound, Ming had insisted on accompanying Mark on his attempt to escape while their single guard's attention was distracted by Gary's takeoff. Ming had further distracted the guard's attention, enabling Mark to fell him with a brass candlestick. Before they could catch his falling body, it and his rifle had fallen out the door onto the porch.

They had no chance to get the rifle. The guard's fall had been seen, and a shout, followed by shots, made them head for the jungle behind the bungalow.

They were halfway to the shelter of the trees when another guard appeared in front of them, to their left. Ming had seen him first. Shouting to Mark to keep going, the former paratrooper had run straight at the Khmer Rouge soldier. The guard's fire cut him down, but the diversion let Mark escape.

Mark's version of the next few hours was brief and curt. "I got away clean—thanks to Ming. They milled around awhile, shot up a bunch of shadows where I'd gone into the jungle, but they didn't try to follow me. I waited until they quieted down a bit, then I decided to take a look around to see where their sentries were before I hightailed it for help. Well, I got lucky. I was down near the gate, behind the guard shack, and I found a machete." Mark shrugged. "After that I decided to even things up a bit before I took off. Except that guy Charn, and a couple of others, they were all punk kids. They had a lot to learn about pulling guard in the jungle at night. I taught a few before I headed for Ban Het." A savage expression punctuated Mark's words.

"Ran into Major Makorn's scouts a few klicks down the road. Surprised the hell out of them, too. Told Makorn he better give 'em some extra night work. The rest was a breeze. They hadn't begun to relieve the guys I'd taken out, so it was a turkey shoot. We didn't lose a man."

From Major Makorn and other old-timers he recognized, Gary learned that the ex–Special Forces colonel had taught seven Khmer Rouge sentries his silent, deadly lesson. As a result, the PARU platoons found most of the Khmer Rouge asleep. What could have been a bloody battle had been averted by Mark's deadly "lessons."

The unexpected and puzzling insistence by Colonel Banchert that they fly the same evening to Bangkok was a cause for concern to Pranee and the two Americans. Banchert's uneasy manner, most unlike his normal self, and vague answers that his superiors felt it safer and better for them all to stay in Bangkok for the time being, did nothing to help things. Gary's pessimism grew rapidly as a result of Banchert's inexplicably sudden change in attitude.

It deepened into real alarm when Banchert told Gary to land on the military side of the field. As they taxied behind an air force "Follow-Me" vehicle, Banchert suddenly launched into a defensive explanation. "I, uh, our people feel you will be safer staying out here in one of the air force's guest houses. It's for your own protection. Some of the members of the smuggling ring are still at large."

A great deal of the plausibility of Banchert's words vanished when they saw their belongings from the Bangkapi house neatly stacked in the air force house. Ah Sam was also there, looking extremely worried.

Mark's voice was harsh as he turned to the clearly uncomfortable Thai officer. "Goddamn it, Banchert! What the hell is going on? Are we prisoners? If we are, say so. But for Christ's sake, cut out this Sneaky Pete stuff. We're all big boys."

Banchert's halting, placating answer was interrupted by the arrival of a subordinate in civilian dress who handed him a bulky manila envelope. Banchert hurriedly checked the contents before flashing a wan smile. "My friends, I beg you to believe that I have absolutely no say in this matter. I protested as strongly as I could."

His listeners hung on to his words, suddenly tense, as he patted the envelopes and said, "My superiors have ordered me to give you these tickets; your passports are all stamped. They feel it is vitally important that you leave Thailand immediately. Your flight will leave at midnight, Pan Am, flight one. I'm terribly sorry, but this drug business is causing a great deal of trouble. There are already many foreign reporters asking questions that we prefer not to answer. Now I must leave you to go to police headquarters. The air force will get you to the plane. And, oh, yes, I personally promise to forward whatever money you are owed by Khun Visarn.''

After Banchert's hurried departure, Mark opened one of the Pan Am tickets, did a classic double take, and said, ''Hey, look here. First class, no less! And they're round-trip—Bangkok–New York–Bangkok. What the hell is that supposed to mean?''

CHAPTER TWENTY-ONE

AFTER LEAVING THE TWO AMERICANS AND THE PETITE HEROINE of the previous day's encounter with the Khmer Rouge raiders, Colonel Banchert drove to police headquarters through the maddening late-afternoon traffic. He finally pulled into his reserved parking space shortly after seven. His usually unshakable composure was for once rudely broken when two burly uniformed policemen, accompanied by an officer he recognized as the aide of Police Lieutenant General Sarong, accosted him as he stepped out of the car. Without a word he was frisked and his .38 special deftly removed from its shoulder holster. His surprise at this incredible affront was so complete that he had no chance to resist.

Minutes later he found himself in the office of the bearlike deputy director of *Santiban*, the Thai Criminal Investigation Department. Lieutenant General Sarong was widely known, feared, and at the same time held in contempt by almost all members of the Thai Police Department. Big by any standards, the hulking, shaven-pated Sarong looked more like a born criminal than most of the actual criminals his department dealt with. Violently xenophobic to the point of paranoia, he included all the western-trained Thais as almost equal partners in what he often stated was the disastrous decline of Thai culture and morals that exposure to the ferangs had vis-

ited upon his country. Despite this fanatical obsession, he
was not a stupid man. Rather, he was gifted with that sixth
sense that marks the successful police officer, and from the
very early days of his career in the Crime Suppression Branch,
his record had been brilliant. This, plus his fortuitous ability
to know when to switch sides in the ever-changing Thai power
group's internal battles, had combined to bring him to his
present position.

Banchert was still struggling to regain his composure when
the hulking general spat in gutter Thai, "So, ferang-lover.
Now you prove again how right I am. You and your so secret
little group thought you could get away with anything. Didn't
you!"

At this, the grim-faced general rose to his feet, and his
voice rose with his body. Despite his shock, Banchert was
able to concentrate on the contorted face and the engorged
veins in the older man's neck and make a mental bet as to
how long it would be before one of them burst. The bull-like
figure continued his tirade in a voice so choked with anger
that Banchert, despite his concern, could only understand bits
and pieces. The "crime" he was apparently being accused
of still lay buried in the torrent of invective. Finally, just as
Banchert felt sure the distended veins in the face before him
would burst, the tirade ceased as if switched off, though the
neck and facial veins still remained engorged. Sinking to his
chair behind the cluttered desk, General Sarong lowered his
voice to a whispered rasp. "We know you have hidden the
heroin, Banchert. It will give me very great pleasure to strip
this information from you. Very great pleasure indeed."

Reaching in a drawer, the general removed a small glassine
bag that he threw contemptuously on the desk. "You thought
to fool us again with flour. Well, you may have fooled the
others, but not me. Where are you hiding the heroin you took
from the Cambodian?"

Despite the menacing face now regarding him in cruel triumph, Banchert had recovered from his initial surprise. He
looked the big man in the eye, and answered in a calm, controlled voice. "You know perfectly well where the heroin is,

General. It went to the bottom of the gulf when the air force destroyed the two boats.''

"Crap, Colonel. Pure crap. The heroin was never on either boat.''

"Then, sir, why did the smugglers not surrender when the air force planes gave them the chance?''

For the first time Banchert noticed a hint of uncertainty as the enraged general again rose and bellowed. "That is beside the point! I don't know or care. They were smugglers, and we're well rid of them. What concerns me is the heroin. Where are you hiding it, Banchert?''

Banchert was feeling more sure of himself now that he knew the reason for his sudden arrest. "The heroin was destroyed with the smugglers and their boats, sir. I'm sure the gun cameras of the air force planes will confirm this; the Water Police report is very clear that no one or no cargo remained on the surface.''

The livid face again threatened to explode as the newly enraged general jumped to his feet at these words, and then suddenly subsided. The contorted face relaxed into what Banchert mentally called a look of cunning evil—reminiscent of Sydney Greenstreet at his best—as the general pushed a button on his desk and said to two entering guards, "Take him away. Remember, no contact with anyone!''

Banchert shrugged off the policeman's grasp and marched stiffly out of the office. In the hall, as the aide led the way and the two policemen followed closely behind, Banchert's eyes searched the area for a familiar face. He saw none. Outside, he was hurried into a VW van that screeched out of the parking lot preceded by a pair of waiting squad cars, lights flashing and sirens wailing. Despite the seriousness of his plight, Banchert smiled ruefully as he told himself that General Sarong's xenophobia was unable to cope with the American police TV shows.

Colonel Banchert had barely left the small bungalow within the sprawling air force base where Gary, Mark, and Pranee were being sequestered when two unmarked vans drove up and disgorged a dozen uniformed policemen. They quickly

disarmed Banchert's two plainclothesmen and surrounded the
house. For the next hours, they ignored the questions Gary
and Mark threw at them as they slowly and methodically
searched the house and its contents, including the baggage of
the three now badly frightened detainees. When the silent
searchers began to slit the seams of Mark's suitcase with a
razor, he overcame his worry and protested. A violent shove
and a quickly drawn gun made him subside and watch in
anger as the suitcases were expertly reduced to scraps. The
apparent leader of the search team slammed the last remnant
to the floor wordlessly, and then, without even a glance at the
two Americans and the terrified Pranee, waved his team out.
They were replaced by a grim-faced member of the group
outside, who placed a chair in the doorway and sat with drawn
pistol.

"Now, what was all that about?" Mark asked.

"Beats the hell out of me. You got any ideas, Pranee?"

She raised her tear-streaked face from Mark's shoulder and
shook her head silently, but her eyes clearly revealed how
frightened she was.

"Well, something's really changed," Gary said. "I can't
figure Banchert pulling anything like this. It just isn't his
style. Besides, why should he? He knows we haven't anything
hidden. It must be some other part of the police force. Those
guys, and this one, are cops, for sure. I don't like it, Mark.
Do you think maybe there's been a coup?"

Mark answered by picking up the small transistor he had
bought for Pranee. After an inquiring glance at their guard,
he turned it on. A quarter of an hour of close listening settled
the question. All stations were broadcasting a completely normal collection of music, news, and commercials.

"Well, it's not a coup." Gary and Pranee nodded their
agreement. "If it's not a coup," Mark continued, "then
maybe Banchert's gotten into some kind of trouble with his
own people. But how? Hell, after all he's done in the last
couple of days, they should be hanging a medal on him."

Another half hour of sporadic conversation brought them
no closer to an answer. Still worried and puzzled, they helped

Pranee prepare supper, and had the slight satisfaction of seeing their guard unbend enough to accept a cup of coffee—though he waved his gun menacingly when Mark tried to follow this up with a request to use the telephone. Finally they went to bed, but none slept easily or well.

In the murky world of intelligence, be it domestic or foreign, there is a common tendency among the various elements of almost every nation's intelligence and security services to waste considerable time, talent, and money penetrating each other. This detracts from the overall effort against the nation's real enemies. But in most countries, no chief of a given intelligence agency feels at all secure unless he knows what his fellow chiefs are up to. This syndrome extends even to the more advanced countries such as the Soviet Union. There, the KGB spies on the entire country—while at the same time spying on themselves.

Thailand is no different, though the entire intelligence community would fit nicely into a small provincial office of the KGB. Colonel Banchert's setup was no exception to this rule. In his present circumstances, he was confined to the bedroom of a house he knew to be close to the Chao Phya River, because of the snarling of the long-tailed passenger ferries; he derived considerable comfort from the knowledge that at least one of General Sarong's men, who also reported secretly to Banchert, would soon learn of his arrest and inform Banchert's own group. When this news was relayed to Banchert's immediate superiors in the National Security Council, his release *should* be a matter of hours, at the most. Despite his annoyance at General Sarong's crudeness, and a fleeting concern for Mark, Gary, and Pranee, Banchert's inborn Asian patience enabled him to sleep soundly while the two Americans and the Cambodian girl tossed and turned.

The next morning, after a scanty bowl of rice soup, Banchert had trouble keeping a straight face while two of Sarong's men fingerprinted and photographed him. Now his already firm belief in early release was confirmed. He had men in both the fingerprint section and the photo lab. Both were independent entities, serving the entire police department.

His release came shortly after noon, in the person of his longtime mentor, the minister of the interior, who angrily dismissed Banchert's guards and drove him directly to the offices of the National Security Council. En route he listened to Banchert's account of his arrest and interview with the CID chief. Inside the NSC secretary's office, Banchert had the pleasure of listening to both sides of the brief telephone exchange, which reduced the initially belligerent General Sarong to "Yes, sir" and "No, sir" replies.

This done, the chief relaxed, and abruptly opened a new subject as he said, "Forget the old fool, Banchert. We have far more important matters. The Khmer Rouge are causing both us and the cabinet a great deal of concern. That raid you so neatly smashed is only one of several serious incidents that have occurred in the last forty-eight hours. These raids are no longer just nuisances. We have got to find a way, short of all-out-war, to stop them.

"I have promised the prime minister a plan, within the next two weeks, to counter these raids and protect our people in the border areas. Can you do it?"

Banchert was surprised by the urgency in his chief's tone and expression. He quickly marshaled his thoughts. "With the resources I now have, sir, I doubt it will be possible to do more than react. We need much more hard intelligence on what the Khmer Rouge are planning, and how strong they really are. This will take time and money. Time to recruit, train, and dispatch additional agents, and money to pay them and purchase more radios, equipment, and so on. I will also need more men on the border, and all of the companies of the parachute battalion in close support. Right now we're spread far too thinly to even begin to stop them."

"Write up what you need. I'll see you get it this time, Banchert. But I also need some plan, however basic, to show to the cabinet. It doesn't have to be hard and fast, or in great detail. But I need something, and quickly, quickly!"

Banchert nodded. "I would also like to ask your permission, sir, to uh . . . retain the two American advisors."

"Americans? Who? The two that were involved in that heroin business?"

"Yes, sir. They knew nothing about that part. They were only working there. Former Colonel Mark Jordan is the best operations officer CIA ever sent out here. The pilot, Captain Sonderberg, is also a very good man. I will need them to help me."

"All right, Banchert. If you say so. But keep them out of sight as much as possible. I've enough trouble with that old fart Sarong as it is. Use my car to get back to your office, and get your plan to me as soon as possible. Two weeks at the very latest."

When Banchert arrived at the air force bungalow, Mark, Pranee, and Gary showered him with questions, which he smilingly brushed aside. "All a terribly embarrassing mistake, my friends. Please forgive. But in spite of all this unfortunate confusion, I must also ask your help for at least several weeks, possibly months. I, we, have a big problem. Khun Mark, Khun Gary, I must have your help, both of you."

An hour later, all four sat in the living room of the bungalow in Bangkapi while Colonel Banchert outlined his problem, and an accompanying proposal to Mark and Gary to work with him in solving it.

After a quick exchange of glances, Mark and Gary both agreed to listen. Banchert smiled as he said, "I would be very happy to have you with me. This is going to be a truly difficult operation. I need your help. Now that you both know the problem, I would like to let you think about it for a short time, and then give me your ideas. I have seen from the gold operation that neither of you have lost your old skills. Now, happily, we can work much more closely, though I'm afraid you will have to move from here. My chief can handle General Sarong, but it is better not to attract any more attention than necessary.

"I have a small house down at Pattaya, near the beach, that should be both comfortable and convenient. Tomorrow I will send a car to bring you down. It and the driver will remain there at your service. He will also serve as your radio operator and bodyguard, which is what he used to be before he was wounded in Laos. His name is Viboon.''

"What about Charn Nol?" Mark asked.

"He is safe, and I plan to begin interrogating him tomorrow.''

"Ever think of trying to double him, Colonel?"

"Double him, Mark? Do you think it would be possible?"

"Don't know. But it should be worth a try. After all, he bugged out on his own people. Why? Might be interesting to find out, eh?''

Banchert was silent for a full minute before he answered. "You may well be right, Khun Mark. If so, it could be very, very useful. You see, I have a vague sort of plan. It would involve a great deal of work and a lot of luck. Fantastic luck! I would like to try and emulate the strategy of one of our former rulers, King Mongut. Setting our enemies to fighting among each other. I think, if you and I can work it out, it will solve our present difficulties. I have even thought of a good name for it, 'Indian Movie.'

Mark's face broke into a broad grin. "You mean where the hero gets into an impossible situation and the director just cuts, and then shows him starting off on a new adventure?''

"Precisely, my friend. If we could get the Khmer Rouge fighting with, say, the Lao? Or the Vietnamese . . . ?"

"I get it, Banchert. But it'll take a hell of a lot of doing to get two Communist countries fighting each other.''

"Granted, my friend. But . . . you do see the possibilities?''

"Sure do. Let me sleep on it.''

CHAPTER TWENTY-TWO

THE MORNING AFTER COLONEL BANCHERT, MARK, GARY, and Pranee were arrested by General Sarong's men, the programs on all of Thailand's radio and TV stations were interrupted by special bulletins. These announced the largest-ever capture, by the CID and police, of a heroin shipment, plus the five million U.S. dollars the smugglers had paid for it. TV viewers were treated to close-up shots of grim-faced CID plainclothes officers holding up glassine bags of white powder and neat stacks of U.S. hundred dollar bills, which the spokesman told them came to five million dollars.

Then the camera switched to a slim figure clad in the all too familiar "black pajama" uniform of the Khmer Rouge. He was handcuffed to two grinning border patrolmen with drawn pistols, who stood on either side. This, the announcer said, was the Khmer Rouge leader, Colonel Charn Nol, who had been caught red-handed with the money after delivering the heroin to "an international syndicate." The heroin itself had also been captured and even now was en route to Bangkok under heavy guard. The four members of the international smuggling syndicate had fought it out with the border police, and all had regrettably been killed.

This brief news bulletin was monitored inside Cambodia, and the details quickly relayed to senior members of the mysterious Angkha Leou, the Khmer Rouge's all but invisible politburo. After their initial shock wore off, the "Angkha," as it was called, issued a number of angry orders, two of which were relayed to their chief secret agent in Thailand, Sart La.

The news was equally distressing to a short, swarthy man who was registered at the Dusitanee Hotel as Mr. Anson Grey. Grey cursed fluently in a combination of English and Italian before hurrying down to the hotel's vaulted lobby, where he made two quick phone calls from the public pay phone. Then he called for a taxi, which took him right past police headquarters on the way to Siam Inter-Continental Hotel. He walked directly to a room in the left wing. After a knock and a guarded, low-voiced reply to the occupant's challenge, he was admitted.

All the morning papers in Thai, Chinese, and English, and the newscasts on TV and radio, devoted considerable space and time to a rehash of the morning's story. The only new detail consisted of shots of the only surviving smuggler, Charn Nol, blindfolded and head down, still clad in black "pajamas," being led from a police helicopter to a waiting squad car at Don Muang Airport. A police spokesman said Charn Nol was to be held initially at border police headquarters for preliminary interrogation.

Both Mr. Anson Grey and Sart La listened attentively to the TV newscast. Grey had it translated for him by a flashily dressed young Thai man, and in turn, Grey translated the gist into Italian for the benefit of the third occupant of the Siam Inter-Continental Hotel room. Sart La and his companion, Num Din, needed no translation; both spoke fluent, if uneducated, Thai, with up-country accents. When the two attentive Cambodian listeners heard that Charn Nol was to be held at border police headquarters, they grunted in satisfaction. So did Grey and his Italian-speaking companion.

Border police headquarters in Bangkok is located on the broad, heavily traveled Paholyotin Road. It is a major link to Don Muang Airport, some twenty kilometers to the north. It occupies a large, sprawling compound dominated by a three-story mildewed stucco building in the center. A wide drive-way enters from Paholyotin and sweeps in front of the main building. On the left, the entering driveway forks and contin-ues on behind the building to a motor pool and parking area. The rear of the compound is marked by a decrepit wooden fence. Beyond it are rice paddies, an orchard of evil-smelling, but highly prized, grapefruit-sized durian fruit, and small clusters of stilted wooden houses in which the farmers live.

The modest two-cell holding "jail" is located directly be-hind the main building. A covered walkway leads to its only entrance. The building itself is relatively new and constructed of concrete hollow block. There are no windows. Inside, in addition to the two cells, which have steel doors with foot-square grilled openings, there are two soundproofed interro-gation rooms, two small offices, and a guardroom with a dozen bunks. The outside of the building is well lit at night by a series of floodlights that paint a ten-meter swath of brightly illuminated bare grass and attract insects by the thou-sands.

On the first night of Charn Nol's incarceration, the casual observer would have detected no change in the normal rou-tine. A border patrolman, AR-16 slung over his shoulder, leaned against the wall just outside the single door. Inside, at the desk in the entry corridor, a corporal sat reading a copy of the evening *Thai Rat* newspaper. It might have been possible for a very keen observer to note some subtle differ-ences, but this would have required a close vantage point. The two separate groups who were now making their final plans, well away from the peaceful scene, were denied this.

About two kilometers away from the headquarters, Sart La and Num Din sat in a noodle shop and toyed with their glasses of *oleang*, the sticky sweet local iced coffee. After the last of many seemingly casual glances at his cheap watch, Sart La rose and left the shop, followed closely by his companion. Outside, they carefully unlocked their Japanese motorcycles. Sart La's was larger and more than twice as powerful. Gun-ning their motors, the two rode into the almost deserted street in the sultry darkness and made their way at a moderate pace up Paholyotin Road toward border police headquarters.

After a final glance at his watch under a bright street lamp, Sart La increased his speed slightly, and both turned together into the border police driveway until they reached the fork. There they suddenly switched off their lights and gunned their vehicles in a straight line for the brightly lit building in the rear. Engines roaring, they crossed the empty parking area. Just where the concrete stopped and the grass began, both men were suddenly swept from their seats. Their roaring cycles continued onward a dozen feet before overturning!

That was the last thing either of them would ever know. The thin, almost unbreakable airplane control wire that had been jerked taut in front of them was head-high on the shorter Num Din. It broke his neck. Sart La's unsuspecting throat hit the wire. The thin cable tore through flesh and muscles to the bone. It snapped clean, and left his head hanging by a few shreds of bloody skin and muscle.

Two black-clad patrolmen moved to silence the still-muttering motorcycles, while two others examined the lifeless bodies briefly before dragging them back into the shadows of the motor pool. At a sudden command from the shadows, the two who had turned off the cycles' motors broke off their examination of the machines and sprinted a few meters before diving headlong into an invisible ditch. The warning had been just barely in time. A tremendous blast slammed at their ears. Fragments of the smaller motorcycle made sharp zinging sounds as they flew in all directions.

The shaken patrolmen rose from the ditch and the shelter of the grease pit inside the motor pool building, surveying the damage to the surrounding buildings. They were still too deafened to hear a gray Benz, parked a hundred meters up the street, suddenly pull out and accelerate rapidly as it disappeared toward the airport.

In a small farmhouse behind the headquarters, three Thai men, dressed in dark clothing, also heard the blast and saw the bright orange flash through the trees. After a silent exchange of glances, they replaced three .22-caliber pistols with silencers still attached in a canvas flight bag, and walked stealthily along the narrow path to the road, where they entered a waiting taxi and departed as quietly as they had come.

CHAPTER TWENTY-THREE

AN ELDERLY THAI BORDER POLICE H-34 SIKORSKY CHOPPER lifted slowly into the air above Utapao Air Base, on the east coast of the Gulf of Thailand. Gaining altitude, it turned gradually until it was on a course slightly west of north. Inside the noisy cabin, two green-uniformed border patrolmen flicked on the safeties of their AR-16's, laid them on the stained canvas seat, and lit cigarettes in obvious relief. Across from them, Police Major Prasong abandoned his stern expression. Reaching into his pocket, he took out a key, which he used to remove the handcuffs from the fourth passenger. He left the leg irons as they were. Then, with a slight smile, he handed the prisoner, who was clad in a faded blue Thai air force work uniform, a pack of American cigarettes and the lighter that had been taken from him four days previously. The prisoner's thin, finely boned face looked with only faint curiosity at the donor. He opened the pack with a polite nod, and lit his first cigarette since his capture. The stocky, moon-faced police major smiled briefly in return and appeared about to try to shout something over the roar and vibration of the motor. Then, with a gesture of futility, he moved to a seat across from the prisoner.

The removal of his handcuffs and the gift of the cigarettes surprised the lean, wiry prisoner far more than he had shown his captors. Ever since he had emerged at Utapao Air Base from the Porter Pilatius airplane in which he had tried to make his escape, the Thais had been uniformly grim-faced and, while not brutal, certainly not overly gentle. His tiny, almost airless cell had been miserably uncomfortable during the heat of the day. His meals, eaten under the watchful eyes of two guards, had been plain and barely adequate. At night he had been chilled, clad as he was in nothing but a pair of thin shorts, but his pride made him keep from asking for any covering. This was also the first time in the four days that his hands had been free of the cuffs.

With the long-ingrained philosophy of all veteran guerrillas, he accepted his improved treatment gratefully, but without any great feelings one way or the other. He behaved, rather, as if a long drenching rain had suddenly stopped; he accepted the fact without mental comment. It had happened. So be it. Then his thoughts turned again to the odd, and seemingly irrational, chain of events that had led to the last-minute failure of his carefully laid plans. As he reviewed each step he had taken, he found himself forced to admit that fate really had little to do with it. His mistake, which despite this unexpectedly improved treatment by his captors, might yet prove to be a fatal one, had been in not making sure of the range of the little airplane he had successfully captured.

With all the things that could have gone wrong, it was embarrassing to have slipped up on such a detail. Then, and not for the first time, it occurred to him that the pilot, the American, had lied to him. After all, the fuel gauge had still indicated almost half-full. If he had forced him to head south, the Thai air force planes might never have spotted them. For a minute he toyed with the idea of asking the suddenly friendly Thai major, but then discarded it as being to no useful purpose.

Going back even further, he smiled to himself as he thought of the reaction that the seemingly all-powerful Angkha Leou must be suffering. They had neatly set him up to sell the heroin for them, taking all the risks involved. And then, when he dutifully handed over the four million American dollars, (which the Thais had apparently raised to five million), the squad at the tiny landing site would have done to him what he had done first: gunned them down. He felt a moment's regret that he had been forced to kill his onetime faithful follower, Sergeant Nam. But Nam would have stayed against him, too, if he, Charn, had not learned of the plot himself, and then hastily dangled the huge amount of money and escape from Cambodia as an inducement.

Charn Nol's train of thought was interrupted as the chopper's roaring engine slowed appreciably. His stomach and ears told him it was descending. He peered out the stained, heat-crazed window and—to his surprise—saw nothing but blue water. The ancient whirlybird slowed, hovered a moment, and then landed in a swirl of fine sand. As the engine subsided to a mutter, Major Prasong unlocked the leg irons and motioned him to the now open door. Charn shaded his eyes against the bright, painful glare as he emerged to find himself on a small sandy beach. Then Major Prasong took him gently by the elbow, and they ducked as they moved away from the slowly revolving rotor's dropping reach. As soon as they were clear, the pilot gunned the engine. They were momentarily blinded by the blast of sand-filled air.

Dropping his hands, which had been shielding his eyes, Charn followed the major up a steep, rocky trail. The two policemen followed, rifles now casually slung. At the top of the path, a bare hundred meters from the little beach, Charn saw he was on a tiny island. Looking around, he saw the faint, hazy outline of shoreline to the east. To the west lay another, much larger, island, which seemed completely bare of habitation. To the north and south there was nothing but whitecapped ocean. The path led into a welcome clump of shade trees, in the center of which was a gleaming white stucco bungalow. Two more green-clad policemen, one a sergeant, rose and saluted as the major came into view. On the porch, Prasong pointed inside. "The toilet is the second door on the left, if you need to use it. Then we will have some food out here."

More to gain a moment to think over this turn of events

than from any real need, Charn went into the gleaming tiled bathroom and gratefully washed his face and hands to remove the sand. He did so automatically while his mind attacked this sudden change in typical logical fashion. The harsh-to-gentle "treatment" was an old and often successful method of "softening up" prisoners before, as well as during, interrogation. So this must be a prelude to the ordeal he had been expecting ever since his capture.

The long delay had puzzled him. Now it was obviously over. Even now, he was uncertain what, if anything, he would tell his captors. He was fully aware that, like anyone else, he could be broken, one way or another. He himself had done it to others, or ordered it done, too many times to have any illusions. Nor was he greatly concerned at the thought. Without really consciously thinking about it, he knew he might just be able to trade information for eventual freedom. He smiled ruefully at his reflection in the mirror. Charn, you've really come down in the world. Five days ago you had four million American dollars in cash, and more than three hundred kilograms of gold. Now you're probably going to have to settle for dubious freedom; exile, really.

Out on the porch, shaded by the overhanging roof, one of the patrolmen was adding two more dishes of appetizing food to the five already on the large wooden table at which Major Prasong was seated. Seeing Charn, he waved him to a seat. "Sit down, uh . . . is it Colonel Charn?"

"Thank you. No, we still have no ranks. I was officially called Commander of the Western Border. Charn will be quite fine."

He helped himself generously to the best food he had seen in longer than he cared to remember. "This is very kind of you, Major Prasong. I will say quite truthfully, I have not had such a wide and delicious variety in quite some time. Our, or should I now say *their*, food supply has not yet recovered from the two 'migrations,' and I seriously doubt it ever will."

As he ate, Charn told himself that his volunteered information would hopefully be understood by the expressionless

major as an indication of his, Charn's willingness to "trade."
If it was, the major gave no visible sign until after they had
finished eating and lit cigarettes.

"We are sorry that your first days had to be rather difficult
ones. Colonel Banchert asked me to tell you that there was a
good reason. You see, some of your countrymen are showing
an intense interest in your whereabouts."

As Charn's eyebrows indicated his interest, and at the same
time an unspoken question, Prasong continued. "Yes, a very
intense interest. And one which I fear, as the Americans now
print on their cigarettes, could 'be injurious to your health.'
The man we used to impersonate you while you remained in
that uncomfortable air force cell nearly lost his life in our
Bangkok headquarters cell. Fortunately, Colonel Banchert was
expecting such an attempt. We, uh, caught the two men before they could set a large charge of plastic explosives against
the wall."

"You caught them, then?"

Major Prasong's owlish grimace amused Charn. "In a way,
yes. You may have known them—Sart La and Num Din?"

Charn pursed his lips in a soundless whistle. "Well, I am
indeed grateful to Colonel Banchert. I do know them both,
and you are fortunate to have been on guard. They are very
old hands. They don't usually fail."

"Well, you can understand our precautions now. It also
took a little while to obtain the use of this island. I rather
doubt your former friends will be able to locate you here,
and, well . . ."

"And I am not likely to try to swim away, either?" Charn
finished the sentence with his first real smile.

"Well, yes," said the major, now also smiling. He rose.
"You are quite free to come and go. There will be someone
with you, of course. But other than that, you can do as you
wish. I expect Colonel Banchert will be down soon, tomorrow probably."

Charn replied in the same almost bantering tone. "I shall
look forward to thanking him in person for his excellent
care."

* * *

While the former Khmer Rouge western border commander pondered his unusual treatment, the man who had arranged it all sat in his Spartan office in the large suburb of Bangkapi, the eastern, mainly residential, part of sprawling Bangkok. This office was known to only a very few members of the Thai government outside of Colonel Banchert's own small group of highly trained officers and men. It actually consisted of two formerly rather luxurious villas of a type popular with the foreign community, due to their spacious, well-fenced compounds, verdant gardens, and cool, high-ceilinged rooms. Occupying adjacent corner lots, they were almost completely hidden from the adjoining lanes by luxuriant masses of purple-blossomed bougainvillea, which wreathed the high block walls and strained to lift themselves ever higher. Inside, the compounds were connected by a well-worn path and an all but invisible telephone line. A profusion of lofty coconut palms, mango trees, and three venerable banyans shaded the two houses from all but the noonday sun. In the shade of the front porticos of both houses, "garden boys" lounged, apparently engrossed in their newspapers. Both wore the loose, flowing *gankeng chin*, Chinese pajama pants; faded sport shirts; and cheap wide-brimmed straw hats. One would have to look very closely to see the .38 Cobra each wore in a shoulder holster. Very few people who were not supposed to ever had. Of those few who had, none ever talked about it.

Inside the air-conditioned houses, the furnishings were for the most part inexpensive rattan or plain wooden desks. Four-drawer combination-lock filing cabinets took up wall space in all the rooms except Colonel Banchert's. His room had only one two-drawer type, behind the huge polished teak desk which dominated the twenty-foot-square room. Almost every inch of the walls was covered with pictures, maps, and the various degrees, certificates, and framed letters that Banchert had accumulated in over thirty years of service.

The desk, behind which he now sat, was, in contrast to the cluttered walls, almost bare. Under the plate glass on the top was a copy of the most recent *National Geographic* map of

Southeast Asia. Three polished teak trays, marked "In" and "Out" and "Hold," lay side by side on one corner. Only the Hold box contained anything: two thick manila file folders. A third lay opened in front of the intent commander of the Thai Border Police Special Intelligence Branch, or SIB, as it was referred to, very guardedly, by those outsiders who had occasion to deal with it or its commander.

Banchert was wearing a pair of casual slacks and a white shirt with the tie loosened. Since he had discarded his coat, his shoulder holster was quite noticeable even though the white leather blended well with his shirt. Banchert was rather tall for a Thai, and slim. Even in civilian dress his long years of military service showed themselves in his erect posture. His thin face was smooth-shaven except for a pencil-thin mustache. His nose was both thin and straight, revealing that his ancestry included perhaps a touch of royalty dating back to the days when Thai kings had scores of wives and concubines. The alert black eyes behind his thin gold-rimmed glasses had a remarkable way of changing from quiet to amused to a hard glitter, depending on his thoughts or the impression he wished to impart. Despite his responsibilities and his long and often dangerous career, he looked a good fifteen years younger than his actual age of fifty-three.

Reading the file caused his face to assume an unusual expression of humorous doubt. The file contained every scrap of information his branch had been able to collect about his new prisoner. For the past two years, since Charn Nol had taken charge of the Cambodian forces in the western part of that tortured country, they had been opposite numbers in the shadowy game of intelligence and counterintelligence, not to mention an increasing amount of bloody paramilitary activity. To make use of the growing group of Free Cambodians who had ranged themselves about the former deputy chief of the Royal Cambodian Army, Sarn La, Banchert had been trading radios, medical supplies, and an increasing amount of small arms and ammunition. In return, he was receiving a substantial amount of raw information from inside the newest "bamboo curtain" that the incredibly ruthless Khmer Rouge had erected along the hundreds of kilometers of border they shared with Thailand.

Recently, the Khmer Rouge had become more aggressive, and now frequently raided Thai villages across the border. This had required a considerable reinforcement of the thinly spread Thai Border Patrol.

The raids were brutal and merciless. They killed like animals. No inhabitant was willingly spared, and precious few survived. Their merciless objective appeared to be nothing less than making the Thai side of their border, for a depth of ten or more kilometers, too dangerous to inhabit. Banchert felt they were trying to create a *cordon sanitaire* that would effectively keep their own helpless, starving inhabitants in, and all others out.

Rising with a quick grace, Banchert strode to a large-scale map of the common border and studied the assortment of multicolored pins, each with a tiny flag indicating the date of a particular incident. The black-headed pins, which far outnumbered all the others combined, showed where Thai villages had been abandoned, either through fear of, or actual annihilation by, Khmer Rouge raids. Scattered along the long red line of the border were a bare three dozen green-headed pins, which marked border patrol unit locations.

On the Cambodian side were a host of red pins, closely rivaling in number the black ones on the Thai side. These were the latest-known locations of the Khmer Rouge forces. Below the map there was a small box containing a number of bright yellow pins. These were only rarely put in their places, for special meetings. They would then represent Sarn La's Free Cambodian "assets." These locations were listed in a tightly bound and sealed file in Banchert's safe, to which only he and his deputy, Major Prasong, knew the combination.

After studying the pin locations intently for several minutes, Banchert snapped off the light over the map and drew the green curtains that hid it from view. Seated again, he lifted one of three black telephones and spoke briefly. Almost instantly one of the two doors that flanked his desk in the windowless room opened, and a slightly graying, stocky man, also clad in casual street dress, entered and stopped in front of the huge desk with a slight stiffening of his body and a hint of a bow.

"Ruang, here's Charn's file. I won't be taking it with me." Ruang's eyebrows lifted slightly as he took the proffered file, but he remained silent.

"Yes, I think we will go ahead with our project. What did we call it? 'Indian Movie'? Well, I think we'll just use that name. After all, even I agree it will take a whole succession of miracles to pull it off. Let's hope we can do it like the Indian film directors."

"You really think Charn Nol will switch over to our side, sir?"

"I think he may. If he doesn't, well . . . Then we'll have to drop the whole thing and try to think of something else. We have *got* to do something to stop these raids! Everybody from the prime minister on down is pressing on us harder every day. They'd like to put in army troops; but then we would have to run the risk of an open war.

"With Laos completely under the Vietnamese, they would certainly increase their attacks all through the northeast. That would be disastrous. We haven't the men or the money to fight along the whole eastern border at once. Not for any length of time, anyway. That's why we have to try to use King Mongut's strategy. Get our enemies fighting, or at least threatening, each other. When I was in school in America, they had a slang saying, "Let's you and him fight." Well, if we can get the Vietnamese and the Khmer Rouge busy worrying about each other, then we can relax a little. It would also give the Russians and the Chinese another thing for them to go after each other about, and concentrate less on us."

"It would be a wonderful thing, sir. But I still don't understand why you think Charn will cooperate with us. After all, sir, he's been our biggest problem!"

"Which is precisely why he could be such a great asset, if he will work with us. I think we have a chance now. Something made him try to leave. I think he somehow got in conflict with the Angkha top people. Even then, if we hadn't been lucky, he'd be in Singapore now with that load of gold and the money from the heroin. As it is, we have both the gold and the money, which our minister has told me we can use to finance Indian Movie. If I can recruit Charn . . . One thing I am counting on is the fact that he *is* a really brilliant officer. We also know he is proud of his successes. If we can turn that pride around, into anger at the Angkha, his former bosses, we will have the best possible weapon.''

''We all wish you good luck, sir. One thing, anyway—he seems to speak Thai well enough so you won't have to use an interpreter.''

With that, the bland-faced colonel put on his jacket, adjusted his tie, and walked out of the compound until he found a small three-wheeled minicab to take him out to busy Sukumvit Road. There he quickly took a taxi to border police headquarters and boarded the venerable waiting H-34.

Charn Nol and Major Prasong enjoyed the riot of color as the sun set through the banked clouds, and then moved inside and silently shared a second ice-cold bottle of Singha beer before eating. Neither of them was in a conversational mood. The dinner was as delicious as the lunch had been, and when it was over, they smoked in silence until Charn said, ''If you will excuse me, Major, I would like to go to bed early.'' Then, with a hint of a smile, he added, ''I will leave my door open, if you don't mind. I am a very light sleeper. With it open, your men can check on me without waking me.''

Major Prasong smiled at the sally and nodded.

Before going to bed, Charn reveled in his second bath of the day. Then, wearing the new T-shirt and gangkeng chin that had been laid out on the bed, he lay down and tried to sleep. It took a long time before he finally slept. His thoughts were flowing in what, for him, was an unusual turmoil. The Thais were acting completely different from what he had anticipated. Prasong's relaxed, polite, almost friendly manner seemed simply too good to be true. The very comfortable house, new clothing, the excellent food, and the whole attitude of his captors went far beyond the "carrot and stick" approach.

After the lunch he had expected to see the "stick." But instead, after a nap, Prasong had invited him to go swimming, and then, even more surprisingly, one of the patrolmen had driven a water-ski boat while both Prasong and the sergeant had taken turns helping teach him how to water-ski! This had been the reason for his silence at the evening meal. In the long years of his service, first with the Viet Cong and later the Khmer Rouge, he had never heard of an enemy acting like this.

So far, outside of the now understandable days in the air force base cell, there had been nothing but carrots. The stick was completely absent! At length, the puzzled captive decided that Colonel Banchert was withholding the stick until he could personally administer it. Relieved to have found an answer, Charn Nol fell into a dreamless sleep.

The following afternoon, after more waterskiing and two more excellent meals, the *whuk whuk* of a helicopter announced the arrival of Colonel Banchert. Charn and Prasong stood at the top of the path as the colonel, in civilian sport clothing, came rapidly and seemingly effortlessly up the steep trail. As Prasong stiffened and bowed slightly, Charn, on impulse, brought his hands up in front of his face, palms together, and made a respectful wai, which the now smiling colonel returned, equally respectfully.

Leading the way to the bungalow, Colonel Banchert called for cold beer and returned the salute of the patrolman with a casual wave. Seated at the outdoor table, he poured glasses for all three of them, lifted his to Charn, and drained a good half in obvious enjoyment. He turned to face Charn, who sat across from him wearing a slightly bemused expression. "Commander Charn, I am sorry it has taken me so long to get here. But, as you have probably read in the newspapers and seen on TV, I have been rather busy up in Bangkok. I trust that Prasong has made you comfortable?"

"I have been treated extremely well. The food, all this, it is not quite what—"

"What I might have expected had I been your prisoner, Commander Charn?" The smiling Thai finished the sentence for the suddenly disconcerted former Khmer Rouge commander.

Charn ventured a tight smile as he answered. "That puts it a bit bluntly, Colonel. But, I'm afraid, quite correctly."

"I quite understand. Fortunately, my superiors give me a lot of latitude, which I gather differs somewhat from the Angkha. To be quite frank, Commander Charn, we are all very happy to have you . . . how shall I say it? Out of action? You have been a very formidable opponent."

With this the smiling Thai sipped his beer while Charn thought furiously. What is this all about? Can this really be the same Colonel Banchert I've been battling all these months? What is he up to?

Then Charn answered, with the trace of a smile. "I should probably say the same, Colonel. Your successes were giving us an awful lot of trouble, and as you know, the Angkha are not sympathetic to failure. I, too, am quite content to be here."

"Good. Now, let me tell you a few of the things that have been going on up in Bangkok. Major Prasong *did* tell you why we brought you here? Good. I am frankly quite pleased with myself for handling it this way. There seem to be a great number of people interested in your future. Mostly negatively. Which is what I would like to discuss."

At this, Charn felt a reflexive tightening of his muscles, and Major Prasong started to get up from his chair. Then, seeing no change in Colonel Banchert's bland and still smiling expression, Charn, characteristically, came to a decision. He would play along with the game and "trade" some small bits. From Banchert's reactions he could then decide his next steps, if any.

So he said, "I see no reason for Major Prasong to leave us, Colonel. Unless you wish him to?"

At this, and a glance at his smiling chief, Prasong sat down again, and Banchert said, "Prasong told you about Sart and Num's attempt to blow you and my nice new jail to bits. Well,

after that, we announced that you were being moved to an
undisclosed location to await your trial. It will be held tomorrow, and as you might imagine, you will be found guilty
and sentenced to death. But more of that later.''

Charn again stiffened slightly and hunched forward at this
casually delivered account of his death sentence. Despite his
still all but expressionless countenance, he felt a cold shiver
and the beginning of a dull sinking feeling in his stomach.
His mind sped in a jumble of confused thoughts as he tried
to fathom the real meaning behind the smiling colonel's
words.

''As I was saying, all sorts of people seemed very anxious
indeed to find out exactly where you were being held.''
Banchert's expression turned sober as he continued. ''Even
one of my most trusted sergeants, I'm sorry to say, displayed
a very suspicious interest. It—''

Charn had a sudden thought and acted on it as he raised a
hand and interrupted. ''That would almost have to be Sergeant Boopan.'' The sudden flashing change on Banchert's
face told Charn his sudden inspiration had been right, so he
added, rapidly, ''Don't be too hard on him, Colonel. You
see, we are holding his wife, mother, and three children!''

''But they are all dead. They were killed in one of your
raids last year.''

''No, Colonel. The bodies found in the burnt house were
those of other villagers. We gave your sergeant proof that his
family was still alive and well. The price for keeping them
that way was to 'cooperate.' Actually, his information was
such that we dared not use most of it. I was afraid to, because
it would soon indicate to you that we had someone within
your group. If you haven't taken any action as yet, might I
suggest that you do not. Sergeant Boopan's information is
very highly regarded by the Angkha. He could prove very
useful should you wish to play a disinformation game.''

Now Banchert was tensely hanging on to Charn's words,
and having great difficulty in repressing a sudden elation!
Charn sensed this, so he played his next card. ''You might
also want to use one of the air force security officers at Don

Muang. Lieutenant Narang's wife is Cambodian. We also have her family—parents and younger sister—as control there. He was the source of the information that enabled us to almost shoot down your airplane. If Angkha hadn't killed off all the best of the old air force pilots, I think we would have succeeded.''

With considerably greater inward assurance, Charn saw that his frank and open revelations had had the effect he hoped for. Banchert's smile was still there, but now it was a little strained. And he also noted the quick exchange of glances between the colonel and Prasong. Quickly Charn continued. "If you wish to have Major Prasong act on this right away . . . ?''

Banchert relaxed, visible, and at his nod, Prasong left them. Then Banchert's face relaxed a bit more. "That information may save the life of my man who is standing in for you up at Camp Erawan, in Lopburi," Banchert said earnestly. "Lieutenant Narang is in charge of the outer security precautions. My own men and some from the army parachute battalion have the interior responsibility.''

At this Charn sat up quickly. "Then you'd better have Major Prasong send another message, Colonel! Lieutenant Damrong is a member of that unit, and he is a dedicated Communist!''

Prasong quickly reappeared at Banchert's call. Charn repeated his startling statement and amplified it. "Damrong is really half-Vietnamese, on his father's side. When he was very young, about ten or eleven, his father was the leader of a Viet Minh group who were very active in Laos. Your police arrested him on their side of the Mekong, at Mukdahan. Then they turned him over to the French. He was shot. The mother dropped the father's name and moved to Korat. She remarried a Thai man. The boy was recruited a few years later, and trained at Dien Bien Phu, and later Hanoi.'' With a disarming and rueful smile, Charn gestured with his hands. "He's the only dedicated Communist among all the agents we have. Your Thai people don't seem to be very susceptible to the ideological approach. But Lieutenant Damrong is, of course, half-Vietnamese. He is also very dangerous. We have had quite a bit of trouble restraining him from useless violence.''

As Prasong again reentered the bungalow, Banchert refilled their glasses. Charn found that he was actually enjoying the situation. His sense of humor, long suppressed under the grim conditions of his guerrilla days, and even more by the unbelievably harsh strictures of the new regime, impishly provoked him. Another, more logical part of his brain amazingly agreed that what he was doing was somehow the best way to handle his delicate situation. So he continued what soon became an amazingly casual ''give and take'' conversation. He sensed that his erstwhile opponent was enjoying the little game at least equally as much. The game, by mutual, unspoken consent, developed into a format in which one or the other would mention an agent or an operation that had failed. The response would be an explanation from the other side as to why and how it had been detected. From the outset, each man had had considerable respect for the other's ability. As they compared notes, almost like old friends, this respect increased rapidly. To both men's growing but unspoken surprise, something that almost bordered on friendship was growing between them.

Charn's information occasioned several more brief departures by Major Prasong. On the other hand, as Colonel Banchert informed him how the Thais had detected Khmer Rouge operations, Charn's own grimaces obviously pleased the Thai colonel. After over three hours of this back-and-forth trading of secrets, Charn, almost without thinking, ventured a thought that had been worming its way to his conscious mind. ''You know, Colonel, it's really a shame we were on opposite sides. Had fate put us on the same team, I, for one, would hate to have been our opponents.''

It took all Banchert's willpower to keep his face from betraying him as the former Khmer Rouge himself flatly stated the proposal that Banchert had been racking his brain for a way to introduce!

For a long minute, Banchert was silent as he willed his face to assume a studious expression, which he then changed to a smile as he said, "I must agree completely, Commander Charn. I hadn't thought of it, but what you say is indeed quite true."

Charn's senses were suddenly intensely alert. Long experience and intuition that he could not explain, even to himself, suddenly told him he had unwittingly hit on something of critical importance. He rapidly reviewed his offhand remark, and added to it the tiny but vital reaction he had noted. Then he, also, had trouble masking his excitement as he realized that Banchert had taken his remark as a probe. He turned his inward attention to consideration of the near certainty that the Thai, for some reason, might consider him as a partner, rather than an unusually fortuitous source of information. Well, he thought, why not? At best, his present prospects were rather dismal. After he had divulged all he knew, however slowly, he would, hopefully, be freed. He knew he would then have to put a long distance between himself and the vengeful Angkha. Then another grim thought hit him. The smugglers who had lost their money, heroin, and several men were a worldwide organization. They, also, would be after him for vengeance. Not a pleasant prospect. His information, once given to the Thais, would possibly also be welcomed by the CIA, though they would probably be only a slight additional and very temporary customer.

Like ice in the sun, his information was of fleeting value. If the pensive Thai facing him had a way by which Charn could be reasonably certain of a longer term, call it "partnership," with all the security this meant, his future might indeed be less than dismal. With his usual acuity, Charn added up the pros and cons. Then, with a smile, he forced his voice to remain casual as he declared, "It would certainly be a very unusual situation, Colonel. But the possibilities are really quite intriguing."

Banchert, now convinced they were both thinking in the same way, answered equally casually. "Very intriguing, Commander Charn. Shall we explore some of them together?"

"I am quite agreeable, sir."

Banchert barely repressed a sigh of relief. The effort was noted by Charn, who visibly relaxed, only to be suddenly startled as the still-smiling Thai said, ''Well, in that case, we'd better get on with details of your execution!''

Noting the obvious reaction, he hastened to add, ''I should have said the filming of your *apparent* execution. We can't have you alive, you know. From what I've seen so far, and especially from what you have just told me, the sooner Charn Nol is executed, the better off his, uh, ghost, will be!''

CHAPTER TWENTY-FOUR

Charn Nol's "execution" by firing squad at an undisclosed location was a prime-time television special. The slim Khmer Rouge commander was clearly recognizable as he stood, unblindfolded, tied to a post. His final words, a defiant party-line diatribe directed to his captors in his native language, were duly recorded. Then the bullets from his executioners's machine gun slammed the slim figure back momentarily before it collapsed. The spurting blood on the white shirt spread rapidly as Colonel Banchert himself, grim-faced, delivered the coup de grace with a pistol.

Seated again around the table on the island bungalow's porch, Banchert and a now completely relaxed Charn Nol watched the latter's execution on TV.

"You know, Charn, you might have a future as an actor. That was a very realistic performance!"

"Thank you, Colonel. But I think I would rather not have to go through that again. It was a bit too realistic for my liking."

"Well, I feel certain we have achieved the desired effect. Thanks to this"—he pointed to the TV set—"you are now thoroughly dead. However, I think we should still continue to take precautions. If you agree, I think you should remain

here on the island for the next several weeks, while we de-
velop a new identity and change your appearance a bit.''

"Whatever you say, Colonel. Frankly, I like it here very
much.''

"Good. I do, too. I think it might be a good idea to use
this as our headquarters for as long as possible. Now, you're
probably wondering about what form the new partnership of
Charn and Banchert will take.'' The colonel hesitated before
he continued. ''It's a very aptly named project. We've chris-
tened it 'Indian Movie,' *papayon khek*.''

Charn's intent face relaxed at the joke.

"It is a rather ambitious affair. My American counterparts
would probably call it a 'pipe dream.' '' Noticing the look
on Charn's face, he quickly added, ''No. The CIA are the
last people I want to know anything about Indian Movie. Or,
for that matter, the fact that you are still alive and working
with me.

"You see, my idea is borrowed directly from our history.
King Mongut, the father of King Chulalongkorn, was probably the first to employ the idea. Back in the last century,
when all the major European powers, and the Americans to
a lesser extent, were seizing colonies right and left, King
Mongut managed to play them off against each other very
adroitly. If, say, the French were threatening us, he would
alert the British, who would only be too happy to put the
French in their place as a means of furthering their own ends.
Then, when they in turn became a problem, King Mongut
would approach the Dutch or the Germans, and the British
would back off. It was really amazing how he was able to
balk the major powers by this tactic. As a result, Thailand is
the only country in Asia that was never a colony!

"I now believe, with your help, we can emulate King Mongut, here in the present century. What I want to do is to
provoke enough trouble between your country, Cambodia,
and the Vietnamese, or the Laos, so that they will be fully
occupied with each other, and thus leave Thailand alone!''

Charn's face reflected both admiration and astonishment at
the audacity of the plan. Again he congratulated himself on

his spur-of-the-moment decision to place his life and future in the Thai officer's hands. The idea was so outrageously daring, it immediately caught his fancy. So he leaned forward eagerly as he said, "That is a real challenge, Colonel. I like it! I like it very much! I also think it may have a very good chance of succeeding, with only one or two small miracles. When do we start?"

Banchert was pleasantly surprised by Charn's eager, almost boyish enthusiasm as he answered, "Right away, if you wish. I have made some rough notes on what I believe should be the first steps. But first I would like you to think about it for as long as you like. Then give me your own ideas. I think the best way for us to work, and get the maximum advantage from our partnership, is to attack each problem independently at first. Then discuss our ideas. If they differ greatly, we can try to work out an agreement on which way we should go. Does that sound logical to you?"

"I like it. I agree. It will help us to avoid making mistakes. I will tell you very frankly, Colonel Banchert, for myself, I will do my best to make your plan work. So when I disagree, as it is certain that I will, remember it will not be my pride, but my desire to see Indian Movie succeed, that makes me do so.

"I would like to take a day or so to think about this. If I may have a map of the Vietnam-Cambodian border provinces, I will try to give you everything I can remember about both the Khmer Rouge and the Vietnamese situation. Unfortunately, I have been somewhat out of touch with the Eastern Command for the past two years, but I believe I have a way to remedy that."

"I have a good map with me. And also an overlay showing what we already know about the area and the various dispositions on both sides. Please feel free to make any comments you please about their accuracy.

"Now, unfortunately, I will have to leave you for a few days. But when I return, I will bring all the latest information we have, and we can go over it together.

"The chopper that will pick me up will bring in several

more of my men, for guard duty. I will have to bring Prasong
with me, but he will be replaced by one of my brightest
operations officers, Lieutenant Samruay. He planned some of
the operations you have since told me were quite successful.
He speaks Cambodian quite well. I hope you and he will get
along. He's a very intelligent lad, though occasionally a bit
too outspoken for some of his former senior officers' liking.
Personally, I find this quite refreshing, and I have encouraged
him."

"I like that myself. Unfortunately, the Angkha didn't. I
was often hard put to protect the one or two similar ones I
had. If he is as you say, I see no problem working with him.

"At the risk of being told it's none of my business, Colonel, do you really think the extra guards are a good idea? It
seems they will only attract attention."

"Hmmm? You may be right about that, Charn. I was only
thinking of your safety. But since you're already dead and
gone . . . No! I am sure you're correct. We'll cancel that and
I'll just leave the four who are here. They should be sufficient
to keep the odd fisherman or tourist from Pattaya away. I will
have it given out that the navy and we are using this as an
antismuggling headquarters. That way the fisherman will give
us a very wide berth, since most of them engage in it from
time to time."

The colonel rose with a muttered apology and went into
the house. He quickly returned with a surprise. He carried a
Russian AK-47 automatic rifle, a Colt .45 automatic, and
several loaded clips of ammunition for each, which he handed
to the amazed Cambodian with the words, "In case my guards
should somehow slip up, you might like to have these
around?"

Charn accepted the proffered weapons with a tumult of
inner emotions. He knew Banchert realized that it would be
no real problem for him to make his escape with these weapons. But the thought never went beyond the realization. He
had already been firmly sold on their odd partnership. Now,
by this gesture, Charn recognized the final proof of the smiling Colonel's trust in him. Suddenly unable to speak, he ac-

cepted the weapons wordlessly and then, like the well-trained soldier he was, quickly made sure both were unloaded before putting them down on the table.

CHAPTER TWENTY-FIVE

LIEUTENANT SAMRUAY'S INITIAL MISGIVINGS ABOUT WORK-
ing directly with, and actually for, a once feared and often
deadly enemy, was swept away within days, replaced by a
sincere and growing respect for Charn's professional ability
and his surprisingly affable personality. Charn himself worked
twelve or more hours a day, his only real breaks being half-
hour swims in the early morning and late afternoon. The
results of his work amounted to a thick master file and three
dozen smaller ones. There were also two acetate overlays
crammed with colored grease pencil notations and indicators.

There was an initial snag due to the written language problem. Charn could only write Thai very slowly and imper-
fectly. Samruay's ability to read written Cambodian was no
better. A message to Colonel Banchert outlining the problem
resulted in the arrival of two typists. Both were fluent in Cambodian. One was an elderly former schoolteacher named
Boonliang. The second, Pranee, was introduced as the widow
of a border patrol officer who had been killed in action during
a Khmer Rouge raid slightly over a year previously. She had
also been a schoolteacher and could read, write, and speak
Cambodian with native fluency. Despite her grave and sober
mien, and the less than becoming policewoman's uniform,
she was a very attractive girl. Knowing her history, Charn

went out of his way to show her every consideration. Despite her calm, impersonal manner, he could sense the bitterness she held in check under her businesslike facade. This bothered him more than he liked to admit. His uneasiness grew as the days passed. So did his respect for her quick mind and ability to grasp the intricate subtleties of the intelligence business and their already complicated plans.

During the first week she was working with him, there was only one occasion when her face and manner lost their impersonality. This came while Charn was dictating biographic information on key members of the Khmer Rouge. In calm, even tones, he added a final sentence to the biography of the commander of the eastern border region, Smarn Ton, whom he described as the most dangerous, from Indian Movie's point of view, of the top echelon of the Angkha Leou. The sentence was: "He should be eliminated as soon as possible."

Charn noticed, but ignored, the sudden sharp intake of her breath and the slight break in the tempo of her typing. Other than that, Pranee might have been a well-programmed robot as far as Charn could tell. His increasing frustration led him to attempt a number of casual nonbusiness sallies, all of which the pert widow either ignored completely or at best answered with flat, expressionless questions as to whether he wanted that included in her typescript. Her veiled hostility, for he decided that this was what it was, was partially balanced by his increasingly smooth relationship with Lieutenant Samruay and the elderly Boonliang.

By the time Colonel Banchert next visited the island headquarters, two weeks after Charn had started work, he was genuinely impressed by both the quantity and quality of the mass of information Charn and his little team had assembled, organized, and carefully filed in manila folders. Where possible, it was displayed visually on the crowded acetate overlays. Charn felt his face flush with pride and pleasure as the colonel studied the overlays and praised his work.

"Amazing, Charn. I would never have believed anyone could accomplish even half this much in such a short time.

Now, I'm more than ever convinced Indian Movie can succeed!''

"Your people have done most of it, Colonel. They did nearly all of the real work. All I've done is talk."

With the temerity Banchert was already familiar with, Lieutenant Samruay interrupted his seniors. "Commander Charn is too modest, Colonel. Without his ability to organize, and then teach us how, we would have been lost."

"Well, not to argue. It's a splendid job by all of you."

"Now, if you will join me in a Singha, I'd like to hear your ideas on what comes next."

Banchert was mildly surprised when Charn urged that both Pranee and Boonliang join the little session. "It will be very useful if both Khun Nai Pranee and Khun Boonliang can sit with us, Colonel. That way we can save a lot of explanation later on. Also, I know both of them will be able to help us. If you have no objections, of course."

Though he said nothing, Banchert noted the use of the familiar "Khun" for Boonliang and the formal "Khun Nai" for Pranee. Outside, Pranee declined the beer and drank tea instead.

"Our first problem, Colonel," Charn began, "is to fill in a great number of gaps in our information about our target area and the enemy personnel, especially the more senior ones." The four Thais noticed the slight stress on the word "enemy" but made no comment.

"You see, many of the enemy leaders are very poorly educated, and while they were quite good at small-scale guerrilla operations, they have little or no experience in its opposite: counterguerrilla operations. I think this can be very useful.

"Another equally important requirement is collection of as many official documents as possible. The lack of any really strict administrative organization among the Khmer Rouge military makes our job easier. But there are an increasing number of official documents being used: written orders, passes, individual IDs, and so on. I assume, Colonel, that you have some competent forgers? Good. They will be of vital importance. I suggest they start practicing with such recent enemy documents as you already have. Also, would you please instruct Sarn La to concentrate on obtaining both completed documents and, if possible, blank ones, for our future use.

"Since the enemy is not used to much paperwork, I believe wastebaskets will be a very good source for these. Security on such things is very poor by any standards. Khun Nai Pranee and Lieutenant Samruay have prepared lists of our major requirements in these two areas. Oh, yes, we will also need a number of enemy uniforms, as well as the contents of their pockets, wallets, and any small personal items.

"We have made a list of our potential personnel assets in the eastern border area. As you can see, these include the two men that Sarn La has been able to place, plus the non-Cambodians. At the moment, the non-Cambodians seem to be our best bet. The problem with all of them, the Vietnamese Hoa Hao, Cao Dai, old Chinese Special Forces, and the former South Vietnamese army groups, will be to get them to do what we want them to—without telling them too much."

"I don't see too much of a problem there, Khun Charn," Banchert said, "if we can supply them with what they need. The ones over on the Vietnamese side have already been making occasional small attacks on the Vietnamese along the border. They have tried to give the impression that they were Khmer Rouge. I'm not sure just how successful they have been, but for them, it's a matter of self-preservation. I think this will be a very good place to put some of your documents. They can 'accidentally' drop a few here and there, or place them on their own dead. They are already using captured Khmer Rouge uniforms, when they can get them."

The meeting continued through lunch. After lunch they discussed the most difficult of all their problems: how to get men and supplies into the two areas they had selected.

The northern one was centered in the tangled jungle and three- to four-thousand-foot mountains of the Trois Frontiers, where the borders of Laos, Cambodia, and Vietnam meet. Here the terrain favored the guerrilla, regardless of ideological persuasion. So did the large expanse of the Bolovens Plateau to the west. Here, inside Laos, Kha tribesmen still resisted, as did their Montegnard cousins to the east in Vietnam. Except for minor infiltration overland, all supply to this area would have to be by air—from nearby Thai fields. Given the inability of the Pathet Lao Communists to control much beyond the major towns, even with massive help from the Vietnamese, these overflights presented relatively little risk.

The second area, the famous ''Parrot's Beak,'' was an area Charn knew well. A maze of rice paddies, swamps, twisting streams, and few roads, it had been a sanctuary for the Viet Cong, Khmer Rouge, and large formations of North Vietnamese regular troops. Even the last-gasp efforts by American and ARVN troops had only temporarily disrupted the huge Viet Cong base area. Once men or supplies were on the ground, the Khmer Rouge would have similar problems tracking down the recipients. Charn was very optimistic about the area, but also agreed it would be very difficult to get supplies in. Then he snapped his fingers. ''The old caches, of course. Colonel, I think we may be able to cut our supply problems down a great deal if we can dig up even a tenth of all the old caches of ammunition and weapons my own men put there! Sometimes it used to seem as if all we did was bury things, and dig more tunnels.'' He continued with a smile. ''Are the Americans still taking pictures with their planes?''

''Yes, Charn; as far as I know, they still make a couple of runs every month.''

''Good. If you can get me copies of their recent pictures of the eastern border area, on both sides, I think I can probably pinpoint a number of our old caches. With all the weapons and equipment we captured from the Lon Nol army people, I doubt if any of the Khmer Rouge have bothered to dig up the old caches.''

''They will be a big help. The big problem still remains. We must also get men, radios, and medical supplies into the area. That will be a really difficult problem, I'm afraid.''

The little group sat in silence.

''What if we tried sending such things *up* the Mekong,''

Pranee ventured, "and then the branches that lead into that area? From all I have learned from the commander, their security is much less tight for boats going up the river."

The four men sat for a moment, and then, as each thought about the girl's words, they began to smile. Charn, with a look of gratitude and respect, said, "Of course! She's absolutely right. Boats going upriver are seldom bothered, unless they have a big load of fish or two. Perfect, Pranee. That's the answer. And from what I've seen, you, Colonel, have an oversupply of both Cambodian and Vietnamese boats of all sizes. The ones the refugees come on. We may have to do some work on them to make sure they're seaworthy and the engines are in good shape. Add a compartment or two for *our* cargo. Oh, yes, we'll need some up-to-date samples of boat registration and permits."

That evening after dinner, Charn and Banchert sat together on the verandah and reviewed the results of the lengthy meeting. When they came to the subject of immediate operations by their limited assets already in Cambodia, Charn spoke up. "I think if Sarn's men concentrate entirely on getting documents and observing the pattern of the security forces in the area for the next month or so, that's about all we can really expect. We don't want them taking any unnecessary chances."

"I *would* like to see if they can do a little simple sabotage on Khmer Rouge vehicles. That is one of their weakest points. Jungle guerrillas don't get much experience in maintaining motor vehicles. Sand in the engine oil, or sugar in the fuel tanks, tire valves pierced where they join the tube, water drained from the radiators—that sort of thing is usually relatively easy to do, and every truck or car we can disable makes it just that much harder for them to control the area.

"Remember, Colonel, they have *no* replacements, few spare parts; fuel is getting short, too. Also, they killed off a great many of the trained mechanics, and the rest are hiding any kind of knowledge they have for fear of the same thing."

"I'll tell Sarn to see what his people can do along those lines. How are you getting along with your staff here?"

"They're really very well qualified, Colonel. I am impressed with the standards of your group. They are good workers. As I said before, they have contributed the majority of the effort. Samruay is very acute, and the girl, Pranee, is really wonderful! She's gotten everything filed so she can find it in seconds. If I had those two on my staff . . . well, you'd really have had a lot of trouble! Unfortunately, the Angkha has killed off most of our better-educated people, and the rest are all trying to hide any education or talent, for fear of the same thing.

"Frankly, Colonel, I'm very glad I was still in the hospital when the first and second migrations were going on. I'm not sure I wouldn't have come across your border then, rather than take part in *that* business." Charn grimaced in disgust as he uttered the final words.

CHAPTER TWENTY-SIX

TWO WEEKS AFTER CHARN NOL FLED FROM CAMBODIA, ONLY to be captured and then "executed" by the Thais, Smarn Ton replaced him as commander of the western border region. Smarn Ton was a complete and unwelcome change for the still stunned men of Charn Nol's former headquarters group at Battembang.

Big for a Cambodian, his once heavily muscled body had gone noticeably to fat, especially in the face and neck. His broad face, with its flat nose and thick lips, which were usually curled in a petulant snarl, had developed sagging dewlaps under puffy jowls. His close-shaven head now gave way to a roll of fat at the neck, making it seem wider than his head. In contrast to his bulk, his voice was shrill and seemed to have only two tones—petulant impatience and sly venomousness. Those in the Battembang headquarters who knew him, or of him, licked suddenly dry lips as he entered the main building.

The sight of the man who followed compounded their fears. Pol Pet, lean to emaciation, with a handsome face, was the opposite of the hulking Smarn, whose nickname "the Butcher," had been earned by his deadly ruthlessness long before the April 1975 bloodbath. Only a few at the Battembang headquarters even recognized Pol Pet. But those who did knew the handsome, sardonic face hid a ruthless, twisted brain. It was rumored even the most senior of the Angkha Leou feared him.

Neither of the two did anything to contradict their fearsome reputations. For two days after they arrived, the members of the headquarters group, and a number of subordinate commanders, were subjected to merciless grilling, often accompanied by sudden clouts from Smarn, the Butcher, if they hesitated in answering.

The morning of the third day, the entire old complement was ordered to line up in single rank in front of the main building. As they stood at stiff attention, Smarn walked slowly down the rank and, seemingly at random, ordered ten of them to step forward. Then he signaled to a waiting squad of men he had brought with him, and swung to face the ten he had selected. He shouted in his shrill, penetrating voice, now loaded with menace, "As an example to the rest of you, Angkha Leou has decided to show all the penalty for treason." He pointed with a fat finger at the already frightened ten. "You will see tomorrow how the Angkha deals with traitors, and those who aid them. Take them away! The rest of you go back to your duties. See that I have no cause for complaint, or we will have another lesson."

Stunned by what they knew was their death sentence, the ten men barely felt the vicious prods of their guards' rifles as they were herded behind the main building into the small, weather-beaten shack that served as the guardhouse.

As the door was slammed and bolted behind them, they looked at each other in disbelief. The biggest man in the group, a stocky, powerfully built Strike Force sergeant, Rangin, instinctively turned to the senior among them, Lam In, who had been the operations officer and deputy to Charn Nol.

"What is this all about?" Rangin asked in a hushed voice. "How can the Butcher do this to us? We have done nothing to deserve being called traitors and . . ." Rangin's voice trailed off into silence; he was unable to voice the words all of them knew should follow.

"I don't know, Rangin. Obviously the Angkha mean to kill

us as some crazy revenge for Charn Nol's desertion. The Butcher will be only too happy to do it.''

"I know him too well to doubt it," the big sergeant muttered.

For several long minutes the little group stood in silence until Nar Rang, thin, wiry, and the oldest of the group, spat and sneered at them. "Well, I for one will not wait like a stupid water buffalo to be slaughtered. Tonight I shall escape. Who'll go with me?"

Suddenly roused from his initial apathy, Lam In faced the speaker. "How will you, or any of us, escape?" Lam In demanded. "They will guard us closely. We have no weapons. We can't fight with our bare hands."

With a sly smile, the little man slipped his hand behind him and palmed a tiny black .25-caliber automatic. With the other he drew a slim six-inch knife from his boot.

"These will give us the start. Those smart-asses from Phnom Penh will supply the rest. Then we take the 'ready truck.' We take the Butcher's jeep, too. None of the other trucks or jeeps have any gas in them. You know that. We drive to Sisophon, duck the guards there, or kill them if we have to. Then to the border at Aranya and Thailand. I know that area well. We leave the truck about a kilometer from a town south of the main road, walk to the river, and swim across. I have relatives on the Thai side."

The others' hopes rose as the tough little man spoke, but Lam In, now roused from his shock, broke in. "The radio, Nar Rang. They will radio ahead if we don't smash it also."

"Easy, Lam In. One grenade will be enough. Now, who's with me?"

The hours passed slowly as the ten condemned men sweltered in their windowless prison. They rehearsed their desperate plan again and again, but only Nar Rang and his physical opposite, Rangin, seemed to have much faith they could pull it off and reach Thailand and freedom. Lam In said little, but his mind worked feverishly to find flaws and ways to correct them.

By the time two of their guards grudgingly allowed the cooks to bring them a scanty meal and a bucket of water, Lam In still had reservations about the plan's success, though he felt it would be far better to die trying than simply to wait for certain death in the morning. As the two cooks were leaving, one of them tripped in the half-dark room and fell heavily against Nar Rang, who cursed him for a clumsy fool and continued his diatribe until one of the guards silenced him with a jab of his AK-47.

Again in darkness, they heard the bolts slam home. Finger over his lips, Nar Rang led Lam In to a crack in the wall that admitted a ray of light. Eyes dancing, he unfolded a tiny scrap of paper and read it with a smile. Lam In smiled, too, as he read the note.

TONIGHT WHEN GUARDS CHANGE SECOND TIME. BE READY.

"See, Lam In!" The bandy-legged Nar Rang was dancing with suppressed glee. "That was Chumporn, my nephew. Even the Angkha cannot make him forget the time I stole medicine for his malaria. It saved his life when others died."

For the first time, Lam In's practical, experienced brain found a real basis for hope. With even a little help from the outside, their prospects improved immensely. Even if all Nar Rang's nephew did was knock out the guards on the prison door, it would be enough to tip the odds. Lam In went over a new set of actions based on their being able to get out of the prison without making any noise.

Adding in the rifles of the two guards was another big boost. After mentally adding and subtracting the new elements from the original plan, he outlined the details to Nar Rang and Rangin, who quickly began to brief the others on their parts.

The sun finally set, though their prison remained stifling. Just before dark, they were brought plain rice and more water, and a second note was passed.

HAVE TWO TRUCKS READY. BUTCHER IN TOWN. FAM-
ILIES READY.

The new information raised their hopes to a fever pitch. With the Butcher away, his men would undoubtedly slack off at least a little. Lam In reviewed his plan a last time, and then went over it again with Nar Rang and Rangin.

"I will take my three men and smash the radio. Rangin, you must take your team with Nar Rang's, first to kill the rest of the guards from Phnom Penh. Then blow or burn the generators. Get all the grenades you can. We may need them on the way out. If we can't bluff past the control points at Sisophon, we may have to fight our way past."

The ten men clustered in their assigned groups near the door as they heard the two guards greet their relief. Then the single floodlight that had illuminated the front of their prison went out! They heard thuds and one stifled cry. The bolts rattled, and they poured out and saw the grim smile on Chumporn's face.

Behind him four others were scooping up the guards' rifles and ammunition. Rangin and Nar Rang took two and ran silently toward the barracks. Lam In and one of his team took the other two and sprinted to the radio room on the first floor of the main building.

It was lit by a single bulb hanging from the ceiling. Lam In burst in the door and smashed the butt of his rifle into the Butcher's radioman's head before he could rise from his seat. Lam In's own operator rose from the cot on which he had been sleeping and begged to accompany them. Lam In surveyed the room. "Get all the message books and code books. We'll take them all with us. That should help with the Thais. Now, the little generator. Smash it, and then pour all the spare gas around the room. When you hear the trucks start, light it and come out front."

Taking two men with him, Lam In ran to his office and saw the body of the Butcher's guard on the floor with two more of the Strike Force standing over him. Using a flashlight from his desk, he opened the huge old safe and scanned the pile of file folders. Selecting over half, he jammed them in a knapsack, shut the safe, and spun the dial. As he straightened, he heard the roar of the truck engines, and the crump of grenades. The last of the lights in the compound went out with the explosions.

Outside, he swung toward the approaching trucks. Behind them he saw the generator shed blazing. Behind him, the radio room on the far corner was also alight. The flames were spreading rapidly as the tinder-dry wood caught quickly and spread up to the second floor.

Nar Rang and Rangin, with Chumporn behind them, reported everyone loaded. The two ancient American six-by-sixes were crammed full with thirty-odd women and children, plus ninety-four men from the garrison. As Lam In swung up to the cab of the lead truck, they lurched forward and slowly gathered speed. Behind them the flames were now climbing and spreading all over the buildings. There was no sign of pursuit, though the fire would soon be visible in Battembang town, ten flat kilometers behind them.

On the outskirts of Sisophon they cleared the first of the two roadblocks without incident. All the women and children were huddled on the floor, shielded by the men. Lam In jumped from the cab, holding the flashlight to his face so he would be recognized, and shouted, "Alert! The Thais are attacking north of Aranya. Tell the ones following us we will take the new road to the north."

Without a backward glance, he jumped back on the truck and waved the driver on. The same ploy was working equally well at the second checkpoint on the far side of the town until one of the children suddenly let out a frightened cry. The two guards had barely begun to react when they were cut to bits by a dozen rifles. The little convoy again sped toward the Thai border—and freedom.

Where the road forked, Nar Rang waved the driver to the left, southern road. It was barely a road. A streak of endless ruts and potholes covered with a deep film of fine, acrid dust. The old trucks creaked in protest as they bounced and swayed, jolting their human cargo into tangled heaps of screaming children and swearing soldiers. Within minutes Lam In heard and felt a rear spring go. Forced to slow their pace, Lam In pounded the dashboard in frustration. He knew the deep groaning of the engines in second gear could be heard for kilometers.

Their noisy, jolting trek continued for nearly an hour before Nar Rang pointed out a dim line of trees ahead, shouting, "We stop at those trees. There's a trail going around the village and on to the river. There may be guards in the village."

The silence after they stopped was a welcome shock to the ears. As they loaded, Lam In told Nar Rang to lead the women and children to the river and across. He gave him a dozen men as point guard. Then he sent Rangin with more to set up a flank screen between the trail and the still silent village.

After deploying the remaining men as rear guard, Lam In helped booby-trap the trucks with hand grenades in cabs and under their hoods. Anyone opening either would pull free the straightened safety pin. Five seconds later the grenade would explode. After booby-trapping, they hacked brush to try and hide the trucks from being seen from the road.

Then they waited, ears straining to catch the first sounds of the pursuit the shooting in Sisophon must have aroused. Thirty minutes went by. Still nothing. Lam In decided to wait another fifteen, to give the women and children time to get across the river. But it was barely ten minutes before they heard the sound of laboring motors, and then faint flashes as headlights lurched up out of dips. Lam In offered a prayer their hasty camouflage would work. It was answered in the form of the billowing clouds the trucks raised. The wind blew it ahead of them, almost obscuring the trucks.

After the three trucks had passed, Lam In signaled his men to start down the trail. Their fast trot brought them up to Rangin as the trucks' engines died.

"All the women and children should be across by now. I have an ambush set up halfway to the village. Nar Rang is crossing with his men now; he'll cover us if we need it. Take your men over now, sir. We'll cover the rear."

Lam In sent his men on, but stayed with Rangin. When the last of them passed, he and the big sergeant followed. They could just make out the dim smooth patch that was the river when they heard the slam of grenades and a furious burst of automatic fire. Crouching as they ran, with bullets snapping overhead, they reached the tangled debris at the high-water line.

Two men, carrying a third, emerged from the trees. Two more followed close behind, one with a leg wound, hopping as his comrade supported him.

"Help them, Lam In. I'll bring the rest with me. Only eight more."

Lam In dashed to the rear two, handed his rifle to the unwounded man, and slung the other over his shoulder. The river was only thigh-deep in the middle, but the muddy bottom clung to his feet as he staggered toward the far bank. His heart pounded and his legs felt like lead.

Hands pulled him up and his load was gone. His rifle was thrust into his hands as he turned back and saw Rangin and five others splash into the water on the far side. His own men on both sides of him began returning the enemy fire that showed yellowish stabs in the gloom and raised jets of water around the last of the rear guard.

Rangin reached midstream a meter behind his men. Then he stopped, swung around, and fired a long burst at dim figures rushing toward the riverbank. As he started to run again, he seemed to stumble, and dropped his rifle. Lam In threw his down and plunged into the river, half swimming, half running.

He reached the struggling sergeant with bullets splashing all around him. Grabbing Rangin's arm, he dragged him toward shore. A dozen hands helped them up the bank while the rest increased the volume of fire. By the time Lam In got to the top of the riverbank, the enemy fire had stopped entirely.

He followed the men carrying the wounded sergeant another twenty meters, into the shelter of high brush. With his flashlight he examined the wounded man. His heart sank as he saw the bloody froth and heard the sickening gasp and wheeze of a torn lung. The look of helpless anger in the medic's eyes as he taped a second compress over a third bullet hole confirmed Lam In's fears. He wiped Rangin's mouth and laid his finger on his lips.

"Just lie still, old friend. Don't try to talk. We'll have a doctor soon."

Rangin raised a calloused hand and grasped Lam In's in response. Lam In winced as the grip tightened and then abruptly relaxed.

Lam In knew without looking through blurring eyes. His men laid a stretcher down beside the sergeant's body. He shook his head slowly, and crossed Rangin's arms over his torn chest. Only then did he realize he could see without the light.

Lam In mentally tallied the cost of their escape as he followed the stretcher toward the village. Nar Rang had taken the women, children, and the main body on ahead. Three men had died on the far side of the river. Now Rangin. One of the three stretcher cases ahead of him had a stomach wound. Maybe the Thais could save him. That left an amazing one hundred and fifteen souls who had made it safely. Four, possibly five, lives to save over a hundred. A lot luckier than he'd expected!

Within half an hour they were in the village. One of Nar Rang's excited relatives was the village chief, the *puyaiban*. He had already sent his son on a Honda to fetch the border police and a doctor. When Lam In arrived with his wounded, the villager's festive mood was dampened for a moment.

Nar Rang handed him a glass of steaming coffee and took his rifle. "My cousin, the puyaiban, said it's better to have all our weapons and ammunition piled up in front of his houses before the Thai police get here."

Between sips of the coffee, Lam In checked the list of names Nar Rang was also preparing for the Thais.

It was ready when the green-uniformed Thai Border Police lieutenant arrived in a Land-Rover, followed by a truckload of patrolmen.

Under their watchful eyes, Lam In's men loaded their weapons and ammunition into the truck. A Thai sergeant grunted approval as he checked the last item of the list.

Lam In had handed the polite, but slightly hostile lieutenant the list of his people, and then asked about getting his wounded to the hospital. He was both relieved and grateful when another unsmiling Thai used his Land-Rover to take them away. Then the lieutenant questioned Lam In. "You say you came from the headquarters at Battembang? Why?"

The lieutenant listened attentively, with a detached manner, until Lam In remembered the code books and his files. As he emptied the half-full rice bag onto the ground, he said, "We brought all the radio room code books and schedules, and those are my files from our Operations Section. As far as I could tell when we left, the whole headquarters at Battembang is burned down, so no one there can tell if anything is missing or not. Please consider these documents as a little present for letting us come here to safety."

As he sampled the pile of documents, the lieutenant exceeded Lam In's expectations. As two of his men gathered them up, he beamed at his former enemy. "I am sure my commander will take this very nice present into account. I will bring them to him myself!" Then, more quietly, he added, "You will have to be held in our police compound for a few days, since you are . . . or were soldiers. I will send your women and children with you, though we usually put civilians in another camp. In your case, I am sure my commander will agree!"

CHAPTER TWENTY-SEVEN

THE MORNING AFTER LAM IN AND HIS GROUP FOUGHT THEIR way to freedom, Charn Nol was busy studying the new air photos Banchert had sent him. He had positively identified nine of his old cache sites and was plotting them on an overlay when he heard a chopper approaching the island headquarters.

He followed Lieutenant Samruay down the steep path and, at the beach, saw the bespectacled, pudgy figure of Major Prasong emerge from the ancient H-34.

"Commander Charn, we have exciting news for you! Your entire old headquarters group from Battembang escaped to Thailand last night! The leader's name is Lam In. He says he was your deputy?"

Charn's face lit with pleasure. "Lam In? Here? That's wonderful news, Major. What happened?"

As the Thai major related his sketchy account, Charn's face ran a wide gamut of emotions. When Smarn, the Butcher, was mentioned, the look on Charn's face made the major falter. In all his forty-six years, he had never seen a look of naked hatred like the one that twisted Charn's face. He was all but unrecognizable.

As Prasong continued, the former Khmer Rouge commander's face began to relax—until he told of the death of Sergeant Rangin. Then it twisted in grief, mixed with sudden anger.

"Colonel Banchert would like you to come to Bangkok," Prasong ended by saying. "Now. With me."

Three hours later, wearing a shoulder-length "hippie" wig, wide-rimmed opaque sunglasses, a garish sport shirt, and blue jeans, Charn Nol followed the chubby major into the smaller of the two houses in Colonel Banchert's innocent-looking compound. Inside, Banchert greeted him warmly. "I felt it so important for you to be here to help me that the risk is worth it. Frankly, in that disguise, I doubt even your family would recognize you!"

Charn grimaced as he took off the outsize sunglasses and, at Banchert's nod, removed the long-haired wig. "I know my own mother wouldn't recognize me in this! And I agree, I can be useful when you interrogate my old people. Have you talked to Lam In yet? Where are he and the others?"

Banchert laughed and held up a hand in protest. "No, I haven't seen any of them yet. We moved them to a safer place: the police recruit barracks at Rangsit, near the airport. I wanted to talk with you before I saw any of them."

"Have you any idea how they are feeling, what their attitude is?"

"Mainly relieved at being safe, I gather. Though I think a bit surprised at the 'guest' treatment I ordered for them. As you know, Lam In brought out the code books and signal plans, plus his own files. He told our border police officers they were 'presents.' They certainly are welcome ones! Even better, they thought to burn down the whole Battembang headquarters complex. If he's correct, no one will even know there are any documents missing. That was a brilliant idea!"

Charn smiled at the praise for his former deputy.

"That is typical of him, Colonel. He's often a slow starter, but once he does get going, I have trouble keeping up." He quickly added, "Those codes and signal plans should be most useful to you, Colonel—provided they don't change them. I can help you with them because I set up all the agent operator's safety signals. Only my old operator and I know them;

they are not written down anywhere, as you can understand. If he doesn't give them to you, I can talk to him and . . .''

As Charn broke off, Banchert looked at him quizzically for a moment before comprehension came. "Oh, yes. Quite right, Charn. That does present a bit of a problem, does it not? Mustn't forget you are dead and buried.''

Both men considered the problem in silence.

"I'd rather leave the decision to you, Charn,'' Banchert said. "After all, you can estimate the danger better than I can, and it's *your life* we are talking about.''

Charn's reply was hesitant. "I do trust Lam In, Colonel, completely. And I don't think either he or any of my old men would willingly betray me. But, well . . .''

His voice trailed off as Banchert nodded his understanding. But he remained silent, letting Charn think.

After a long silence, Charn put his inner debate into words. "I have been trying to weigh the risks against the benefits. *If* I reveal I am alive, I know there will be a great deal of information my men can give us, once I jog their memories. That would be almost impossible for anyone else. No matter how much my old people want to help, it would be terribly difficult to give your interrogators the necessary background. You know what I mean?'' Charn Nol spread his hands expressively.

"What about just Lam In?'' Banchert asked.

Charn's tone was positive. "That may be the best—for now, anyway. No one could make Lam In talk, not even the Butcher!''

Like his deputy, Banchert was shocked at the loathing and raw hatred as Charn spat the name between clenched teeth. He waited for the former enemy commander's face to relax. "I am glad to hear that. And I think the risk is next to nothing. Shall I have Lam In brought here right away?''

Charn's smile was his answer. Banchert made a quick phone call. Charn's face lit up as he had a sudden thought. "You know, Colonel, it just occurred to me Lam In may have brought us another answer to our Indian Movie problems. Men.''

"Men? You mean you think some of them would be willing to go back?" Banchert's tone mirrored his surprise.

"Yes, I do. If poor Rangin hadn't been killed, I know he would have." Forcing the sudden sadness from his face, Charn continued. "You see, Colonel, my men are all old-timers. All of us were really shocked at the Angkha's crazy orders, and especially the way all the new recruits have acted. They are unbelievable! We were all almost sick at some of the things we heard about them. Animals, that's what they are, animals! We used to laugh at them, dressed up like real guerrillas, waving their guns; we called them 'the children.' "

Charn's thin face tightened. "They are children in body, but they are vicious animals with little discipline and not a drop of humanity left. The main reason I and my men were assigned to Battembang was because the new ones are too poorly trained and too unreliable. Once I saw how they acted, I refused to use any of them on the border if I could possibly avoid it. Frankly, Colonel, I was beginning to consider defecting with all my men. But as you know, things moved too fast. No, I really believe most of my old men would volunteer to go back again. Especially if they got a chance at the Butcher!"

Banchert's face wore a thin smile as he thought of the idea. "It would certainly solve a lot of our problems if they would, Charn."

"I am almost certain they could, and would. We were Khmer Rouge long before these new ones. None of us had any great respect for the Angkha to begin with. And after they began their insane migrations, none at all. They became too powerful, too quickly. Then it was too late.

"Most of us joined the Khmer Rouge because of King Sihanouk. In those days we believed he could save us from war. We went to the jungle because our king, whom we then still believed in, urged us to. Now we know he is a powerless puppet. More likely, an actual prisoner. Those crazy dreamers in the Angkha were never any real use in the jungle. All they could do was talk, and write reams of high-sounding

words. Now, somehow, they're in control. We did the real
fighting. . . .'' Charn's voice trailed off into silence. He continued with a visible effort.

"So, Colonel, I think you will find that most of my old
men feel much as I do. Indian Movie will not only benefit
your country. It may also be the saving of what's left of
mine.''

"Well,'' Banchert said, "I am certainly willing to give
your idea a try. If even a dozen or so are willing, it would be
a real boost for us.

"Let's go over to the other house and have lunch,'' the
dapper Thai said, rising. "We can discuss how our little talk
with your old deputy, Lam In, should go.''

Banchert watched the play of emotions on Charn Nol's face
as his former deputy and old comrade was led into the adjoining room. They stood together, watching through the one-
way glass, as Banchert's sergeant pointed Lam In to one of
the tired rattan chairs and left. "Would you like to see him
alone first?'' the Thai colonel said.

"No, it's going to be enough of a shock as it is. Let's go.''

Banchert opened the door. "I am Colonel Banchert, Thai
Border Police,'' he said with a friendly smile. "I have what
I hope will be a welcome, if startling, surprise for you, Lam
In.''

The look of disbelief and then sudden joy on Lam In's face
was all the proof Banchert needed to confirm the soundness
of his decision to let the recent defector learn his former chief
was still alive. It took the dazed man several stammering
"but''s before Charn, with a look of genuine affection, lifted
the kneeling Lam In to his feet.

"Television is very advanced here, my old friend. So are
the special effects men. It is me, all right.'' Then, suddenly
serious, he looked his comrade in the eye. "But you must
not breathe a word of this. Not to anyone. You understand?''

"Of course, Charn. Whatever you say, as always. But what
is this all about?''

"A long story,'' Banchert interrupted. "I'll let your old

commander explain it all to you in your own language. See you later.''

After the Thai left, Lam In turned to Charn Nol with an eloquent plea in his eyes. Charn smiled as he answered. ''Yes, old friend. I have gone to work for, and with, our old 'enemy.' But we, and I hope you also, are enemies no more. After I explain things, I hope you will join us.

''Now, about my sudden, uh, disappearance. When I got to Khemerat to set up the cover for that damn heroin shipment the Angkha insisted on making, one of our old people at the airpost warned me. He came to see me at night, and told me how the Angkha were planning to dispose of me as soon as I returned with the money. So, I changed the plan completely. Told them a story that I had learned the Thai navy was aware of the rendezvous on the island, and were planning to ambush us.

''Then I took a company from the garrison. We went overland to the mine in Thailand. We surprised them completely. I forced the American pilot to fly me to the landing strip, after I found out where it was. We loaded both the heroin and the gold. Sergeant Nam and I killed the Angkha's 'executioners.' I had to kill Nam myself. I was sorry, a little, about that. But he had betrayed me, too. So . . .

''Everything went fine. We landed on the beach and made the exchange. I even had the American pilot guarding me while I did it. I thought I was really going to pull it off. But I had forgotten about the gas. The plane never would have made it to Malaysia, much less Singapore. Also, the Thais were much quicker and better organized than I thought they were. They sent up jet fighters and forced us to land at Utapao.

''Things really looked bad then. I was almost certain they were going to shoot me for the heroin business, not to mention the raid on the mine. But, as you will soon learn, Colonel Banchert is a very professional officer. He let me worry for about a week. Then, before I really knew it, I was volunteering to work with him!''

''Work with him, Charn? But . . . well, I mean, why?''

Charn's face turned grave. "I am working with him on a very daring plan, old friend. When you hear it, you will understand my reasons, and get a very good idea of just how brilliant our former enemy really is. We call it 'Indian Movie' . . ."

When Charn finished his summary of the Indian Movie project, Lam In sat back and thought. Then Charn saw the swarthy deputy's face lose some of its intentness as a slow smile spread over it. Charn waited silently until Lam In spoke.

"Elder Brother, you may have to change the name of the project."

"Oh? Why?"

"Because I don't think it's going to be as 'impossible' as you think! There is already more skirmishing going on along the eastern border than you may know about. Lart Ap went to Kampong Cham to see his family just before you, uh . . . before you left. He got back the day before the Butcher arrived. He said the Butcher had been doing the same thing to the Parrot's Beak area that we were doing to Thais over here. Raids, kidnapping of whole villages, planting mines and booby traps on trails inside their border.

"While Lart Ap was there, he talked to men from two big new groups that Angkha had sent up from the south, and another one from the north. None of them were very happy with their new assignments, because they were to go across to Tay Ninh and start attacking the Vietnamese. They are mostly northerners over there, and you know yourself how tough they are! Our men were very worried, and couldn't see how they could last very long over on the Vietnamese side of the border."

Charn had been nodding in agreement as his deputy spoke. He was only too familiar with the strict control the Viet Cong had exercised over the civilian population even while the Americans were still in Vietnam. Now it would be even tighter, particularly for any Khmer Rouge who might try to operate in the area.

"I agree with everything you've said about the Viets,"

Charn said. "But how is this going to help Indian Movie? I would think it would make it more difficult."

Lam In suddenly smiled. "Only for the Khmer Rouge who try to carry out the Angkha's plans. But I am certain that even now there are many of those groups who want no part of that form of suicide!"

"Oh, I see! You think we could win them over to our side?"

"I'm sure of it, Charn. What's more, I have an idea how we might be able to go even further. It will depend whether or not we can kill the Butcher."

Charn's face again twisted into a grim and frightening mask as he looked at Lam In, who knew the reason.

"Yes, Elder Brother. We must eliminate the Butcher. You see, he's been doing just what the old Lon Nol regime commanders did: creating units on paper so he can claim more food, gas, and other supplies. A man from the northern unit that Lart Ap talked to said he knew of at least three groups that the Butcher made up out of thin air, plus a group headquarters. The man told Lart Ap that everyone in his unit had to sign two names on the reports every month. Now do you see?"

The smile on Charn's face was, if anything, more terrifying than his expression when Lam In had first mentioned the Butcher.

"We will get the Butcher, my friend! I guarantee you that!"

Charn's face relaxed. "But the rest is as you say, a wonderful stroke of luck. I think it's time to talk to Colonel Banchert about this."

"Do you really trust him, Elder Brother?"

Charn barely paused. "Yes. Amazingly, perhaps, to you. But yes, I do trust him. And not only because our aims at the moment are the same, but because he is a real professional. I've never met anyone of his ability before! I'm also convinced that, with a reasonable regime in Cambodia, we have nothing to fear from the Thais. They have enough problems as it is. All they really want is to be left alone. If Indian Movie works, as it now looks like it can, they will be able to concentrate on their other problems, and we, in turn, on trying to rebuild what's left of Cambodia.''

As Lam In listened to Charn, he caught the slightest hint of a wink, which he quickly understood.

That same evening, over a multicourse Chinese dinner that Lam In attacked with obvious relish, he elaborated on the plan he had conceived that afternoon during his long talk with Charn. When he finished outlining it, the Thai colonel sat bemused for fully five minutes. The two former Khmer Rouge officers watched silently. Then Banchert seemed to relax slightly. A faint smile replaced his look of concentration.

''A very interesting idea. But I can think of some problems as well. For example, even with the Butcher out of the way, who will replace him as commander of these nonexistent groups? And how can we then make them real units?''

''The first is the easiest, Colonel,'' Lam In replied, after a glance at Charn. ''A child could imitate the Butcher's signature; it's really illegible. We write an order transferring the three groups and the little headquarters to a new commander. Our man. The orders also go to the three real units the Butcher sent down to begin the attacks inside Vietnam, putting them under control of the new commander. The Angkha *will* receive their copies, eventually. . . .

''Even then, I doubt very much they will raise any question. You see, it takes a long time for paperwork to be forwarded, and often there isn't any at all till long after.

''We aren't really the army the Angkha would like to believe. We're more like a large number of loosely connected units, each fairly independent. The reason is the lack of educated people, and especially staff officers. We have almost none who are any good at paperwork. So what little paperwork there is, is mostly after the fact. Hardly anyone pays much attention to it unless it comes directly from one of the highest of the Angkha.

''As Charn can confirm, we used to write our own orders most of the time. The top Angkha would tell us to do something. We'd write our own orders from what they said. Often we never did receive anything from them in writing. You just have no idea how confused things really are. That's why the Butcher, who isn't very bright at anything but killing, is able to work his little graft.''

''All right. I can see how that might work,'' Banchert said. ''Now, what about Pol Pet? He will know the Butcher is dead. Won't he appoint a new eastern border area commander? How can you get around him?''

Charn waved his hand at Lam In and interrupted. ''The new area commander has already been appointed—Sutep Im. He doesn't know the area. He was with our people who pushed west past Angkor Wat in the early seventies. He stayed there until a few months ago. He's not badly educated, but he's not a real fighter. For one thing, he's older than most of us, about sixty. And he's got a big family now. What's most important, he doesn't know either Lam In or myself, by sight. Now, if we 'execute' Lam In, like you 'executed' me . . . ?''

''I see. But it still seems very risky. Suppose someone recognizes you, Lam In. Then what?''

The broad face wrinkled in a tight grin as Lam In wordlessly drew his finger across his throat. ''It will either be a very quick recruitment or . . .''

Banchert nodded his understanding. ''I see. Now, how do you propose to infiltrate your men, assuming that some of them will volunteer to go with you?''

''Through Laos,'' Charn answered. ''Down the Mekong until they are a few kilometers inside the border. Then they and the headquarters unit become one of the Butcher's paper groups. They can go openly the rest of the way, and report as the orders we invent tell them to. They just pick a former village that is now deserted—there are plenty of them—and move in. No one will really think a thing about it. Believe me, it's true!

''When we first got to Battembang, it took months for us to find out just what groups were in our area! I'm sure the eastern border area is at least as bad, and probably worse. Remember, the Butcher was there for over two years. I doubt if he even knows the actual numbers or their locations.''

As Lam In had predicted, all of the former Khmer Rouge

volunteered to go back into Cambodia and fight against the Angkha.

Lam In gave them precious few details. He confined himself to saying they had a choice between a crowded, miserable existence in one of the makeshift refugee camps or becoming legal residents of Thailand if they agreed to go back to help bring down the hated Angkha Leou. Even though he had been quite confident of most of them, the almost violent enthusiasm they showed at the thought of dealing what he had called a major blow at the cruel regime surprised him.

"I'm very glad to hear it, Lam In," Banchert said when he was told of the men's reactions. "It makes me feel even more confident that your plan will work. The more I think about it, the more I have the feeling that your men are not an exception. All that is needed is a spark, an idea. And most important, a leader. Now, the next thing is the Butcher. He is our first target. Until he is dead, our plan is just a plan."

Charn hesitated before saying, "I'm not really sure, Colonel. If he was still in the old headquarters, I would say we could pull a night raid with excellent chances of success. But now that he seems to be spending most of his time in the town itself, there's a big difference. I think we have to get him out of Battembang town, with as small an escort as possible, then hit him. Knowing him, he's not going to leave the town unless we give him a really good reason. Frankly, I haven't been able to think of any."

"How would he react if we tempted him with about three hundred kilos of gold?"

"Gold? Even fifty kilos would make him go anywhere in the country! But I don't see how we could arrange it."

Banchert smiled broadly. "I'm afraid this may come as a bit of a shock, Khun Charn, but there is one more load of gold from that crashed airplane still waiting to be brought out!"

Charn's expression broadened Banchert's smile as he continued. "Yes, my friend. The shipment you thought was the last was indeed supposed to be the last. But the Americans gave you its location instead of the one they were to pick up that night. That way they saved Sarn's men from being captured. The gold is still where it was, about eighty kilometers south of Pursat.''

Unfolding a map, Banchert pointed to a tiny X as the two Cambodians looked on. They exchanged glances.

"The location is ideal," Charn said. "And you certainly fooled me. I was certain that the one I went to was the last of them. Well, this should make it easy. Now we can use your Sergeant Boopan, and the air force officer, Lieutenant Narang, very nicely indeed. We'll just feed the Butcher a few clues first. Then, after we get him thinking hard about all that gold, we send him the final clue: the actual location and time of the supposed pickup. I would bet every milligram of it that he'll get down there just as fast as he can. And we'll be there to meet him!"

The expression on Charn's face made both Banchert and Lam In wince inwardly.

To strengthen the Butcher's trust in the two Thai agents' reports, Banchert allowed each to learn of a planned supply drop and a raid. Both were carried out in a very halfhearted manner. The pilot of the small plane did drop two bundles of clothing and medical supplies, which the Butcher's men seized. The plane itself stayed far too high for them to try and bring it down. The raid was similar. A platoon of border patrolmen moved into a position close to a deserted section of the border east of Aranya Pratet on schedule. Just before the scheduled time of the "raid," they "lost" the element of surprise when one of them fired a short burst from his AR-16. As a result, the whole unit turned back.

The next morning, Colonel Banchert did a very competent imitation of an angry man, and gave Sergeant Boopan a blistering message to send to the platoon leader.

Unknown to either of the spies, the dead drops were under constant surveillance. So also was the radio operator who transmitted the messages. With the code books Lam In had brought with him, they decoded the messages as fast as they were sent, and also the replies. These provided another cheering piece of information: the Butcher was still using the old codes.

Now they could begin the buildup for the trap. Narang, the air force security officer, was personally briefed by Major Prasong on setting up a special guard on Somboon Air Charter's Porter Pilatens, which had been used previously to pick up gold at the tiny landing sites. Sergeant Boopan was briefed on his part in the as yet undated operation by Banchert himself. This was to lead a surveillance team down to a small field south of Chantaburi, and act as the advance party for the team that would unload the gold from the plane and bring it by civilian truck to the headquarters in Bangkok.

Meanwhile, Lam In, his men, and their families were taken by truck far to the southwest of Bangkok and installed in a village under border patrol control that already had a good fifty families of Sarn La's Free Cambodians in residence.

Once the families were settled in, the men were driven south to a jungle training base west of Hua Hin. There, in green Thai uniforms, they underwent a tough ten days of refresher training at a site far from any prying eyes.

They were given two days rest before being loaded onto border patrol planes and flown to Chantaburi, close to the Cambodian border. There Colonel Banchert and Charn gave a thorough final briefing. Then they loaded into trucks and drove south and east to the very end of a logging road, barely ten kilometers from the mountainous border.

In Bangkok, Charn was still inwardly fuming at Banchert's refusal to allow him to lead the group. They followed the progress of Lam In and his eighty men toward the site of the trap. On the fourth night, a brief message announced their arrival at the destination and readiness to move into position when ordered.

Both Charn and Banchert were greatly relieved. Lam In had gone beyond the original plan. Once inside the border, they had traveled openly, and even deliberately stopped one night with one of the new replacement groups the Butcher had ordered into the area. Lam In's audacity had paid off very well, according to his terse reports. The radio had been cached outside the town.

With Lam In in position, Banchert "fed" the final clues as to the location and time of the drop. To make it as realistic as possible, he sent the unsuspecting Sergeant Pramun down to the supposed landing site outside Chantaburi. For added spice, Banchert informed him that the plan would also bring out a very important Khmer Rouge defector, who was to be brought to Bangkok in Banchert's own car. Pramun would drive it down himself. As in the previous case, messages were sent within hours after the Khmer Rouge's two Thai spies received this information.

At Don Muang Airport, the day before the operation, Gary climbed into the cockpit of the familiar Pilateus and headed slightly east of south.

Late the same evening, a brief message from one of the Free Cambodian agents in Battembang told them that the Butcher, and two trucks carrying between twenty and thirty men, had hurriedly left Battembang town at dusk. The next afternoon, they got word from Pursat that the Butcher had swallowed their bait. Neither Banchert nor Charn had much appetite as they nibbled at the food brought to them on trays in Banchert's office.

Over five hundred kilometers from their two superiors, Lam In and his men were also anxious. But only for the sun to set, so they could spring their trap!

The Butcher had brought twenty-two men with him. Late in the morning, they had watched as he and two others reconnoitered the area of the strip, noting where brush had been cleared by Lam In's men. Watching through binoculars, Lam In and Nar Rang smiled grimly to themselves as they watched the Butcher point out where he wanted to put men. Each position had been plotted carefully on the sketch Lam In had made for briefing his men and assigning their targets.

Now it was fully dark. Lam In could hear trucks in the distance. Their sound grew louder rapidly, then stopped abruptly. At a whispered command, Lam In's men disappeared like shadows into the darkness. He, his radio operator, and two men waited a tense half hour. Then the operator turned on the little radio beacon. Barely ten minutes later they heard the faint drone of the plane. As Lam In and the radio operator watched, the other two men sprang to their feet, each carrying two small cans half-full of gasoline-soaked sand. A minute later the first of the four landing markers flickered its message skyward, followed swiftly by the other three. The plane was much closer, but still invisible until its red and green navigation lights blinked on and off twice. It was answered by a long and short flash from one of the flare lighters. They heard the engine die to a whisper; then the plane was almost on top of them, with only the faint glitter from the windmilling propeller, and the soft whistle of the slipstream to betray its approach.

Just as Lam In was able to make out its shape, the motor roared into life. With a loud snarl, the plane turned and banked away from the strip, almost over Lam In's head. The noise drowned out the first spatter of firing, and he barely heard the dozen grenades that exploded in the midst of the Butcher's main group. There were only three more short bursts before a flashlight blinked twice, then three times, from the end of the strip, where the Butcher had been waiting in ambush.

Breathing heavily from his run to the end of the strip, Lam In was met by a jubilant Nar Rang, flashing his light on a bulky object he held in his other hand. It was the Butcher's head, twisted in a death mask of hate and fear, still dripping blood.

Lam In felt a great urge to smash his rifle butt into the grisly remnant. Restraining himself, he listened to his men's reports. Not a single one of the Butcher's men was alive; only one of Lam In's men had been wounded, by a bullet in the thigh. He told his radio operator to turn on the beacon again. They relit the field with six flares in the shape of a T. After receiving the correct recognition signal, the little STOL plane whispered in for the second time and rolled to the end of the runway.

The gold bars were swiftly loaded in and tied down. Then,

after completing a hastily written message, Lam In ordered the wounded man into the plane, and Gary gunned it off the field and out of sight to the west. As the plane disappeared, the radio operator sent off a brief coded signal to inform Banchert and Charn of the success of their mission. Then they went quickly to the trucks in which the Butcher and his men had arrived, and drove several kilometers before they pulled off the road to set up the radio.

CHAPTER TWENTY-EIGHT

AIRBORNE WITH HIS LOAD OF GOLD BARS AND A GRINNING ex–Khmer Rouge soldier who was ignoring his leg wound, Gary hugged the rising terrain until he was over the border, then activated the ELT and the radio. "Base, this is Four Niner Zulu."

Mark, who had been monitoring the special frequency with growing unease, answered immediately. "Four Niner Zulu, this is base."

"Base, I have the goodies and one Purple Tree, medium rare."

"Purple Tree?" Mark had almost forgotten the old code they used in Laos. A Purple Tree meant a wounded man; the severity of the wound, moderate, was indicated by "medium rare."

"Roger; anyone we know?"

"Negative, base. My ETA is 1845 Zulu. Four Niner out."

At Don Muang, Gary taxied the Porter to the small hangar where Mark, a police doctor, and several of Banchert's men were waiting to unload the gold bars. "Piece of cake, Mark. From what I gathered, they wiped out the whole bunch, quick and dirty. This guy is the only one of ours that got hit. Sure felt good knowing there were a whole bunch of our guys down there, for a change."

* * *

The next morning, back at Pattaya, Gary and Mark were
up after barely four hours sleep. They were rehearsing the
results of the previous night's flight when Banchert's car drove
up. Banchert was accompanied by a shorter, slimmer man
attired in bizarre fashion. He was obviously an Asian, but his
attire was pure hippie. Red gold hat topped his shoulder-
length hair; oversize sunglasses hid half his face; strings of
beads dangled from his neck over a wildly colorful sport shirt
that hung to the knees of his faded blue jeans. Gary and Mark
gaped at the apparition, who contrasted so sharply with the
nattily dressed Thai.

Inside, after an "okay" from Banchert, his hippie friend
removed glasses, hat, and then a wig, revealing fine-boned
features, even white teeth, and piercing eyes, surmounted by
closely cropped black hair. The sudden transformation kept
the two Americans speechless.

"Khun Mark, Khun Gary," Banchert said, "I think the
time has come for you and Commander Charn Nol to become, shall we say, reacquainted? On rather a different basis
than your first meetings?"

As Banchert spoke, recognition dawned on both Americans. Both struggled to erase their initial scowls and replace
them, which made Charn Nol smile. A typical cultural reversal of western and Asian forms of greeting broke the tension. Mark and Gary automatically raised their hands, palms
facing, in the Thai wai, while Charn Nol extended his hand;
then, each seeing the other, they reversed, and wound up
laughing and relaxed.

Banchert took immediate advantage of the moment to
launch into a summary of the situation, and his reasons for
suddenly unveiling the former Khmer Rouge, whom both
Gary and Mark had believed dead.

His audience was still listening intently when the gravel-
showering arrival of a police Land-Rover interrupted Banchert. Pranee bounced out and ran up the steps, waving an
envelope at them. She made a hasty wai to Banchert and
Charn Nol, then flung her tiny body into Mark's powerful

embrace. Gary and Banchert both noted Charn's reaction, which husband and wife missed. The wiry Cambodian's face changed in rapid succession from anticipation, to surprise, and then sadness in a split second. He regained his normal composure as Pranee disengaged herself from Mark's embrace.

"Listen, all of you. I have great news from Lam In. He has a new plan, and wants your approval as soon as possible."

Lam In's plan was audacity itself. Pranee made a quick sight translation that left all of them speechless for a long interval. The plan, as outlined in the terse radio message, stemmed from Lam In's study of the crumpled, bloodstained documents his men had found in the Butcher's uniform pockets.

Lam In had examined them while his men were stopped for a hasty meal, an hour's drive from the ambush site. What triggered his inspiration was an order to the Butcher from the Angkha Leou, dated only five days previously. It directed the Butcher to send three of Charn Nol's former border garrison groups—roughly three hundred men—to the eastern border region he had formerly commanded. They were to come under the direct control of the fictitious headquarters group the Butcher had invented to pad his requests for food, gas, and other supplies. The three equally nonexistent garrison groups the corrupt Butcher had also invented were to move to the western, Battembang area, replacing the "unreliable" former Charn Nol units.

The order, signed by Pol Pet himself, made it clear that the Angkha had no inkling the Butcher's creations didn't exist. Lam In's fertile brain had quickly seen the opportunity to use the legitimate order from the Angkha to move into the Indian Movie target area immediately and openly. The document itself provided a perfect sample of the Angkha's current format and Pol Pet's signature, for future use by Colonel Banchert's skilled forger. The only obstacle Lam In could see was the necessity to recruit the leaders of the three garrison groups into the Indian Movie operation.

He knew two of the three, Lart Om and Mun Sin, very well. They had been comrades for many years. He felt sure of Lart Om. Mun Sin might present a problem. He was a stolid, relatively unimaginative type, but tough and courageous. Lam In felt it might take Charn Nol to convince Mun Sin to join them. The third commander, Lop Garn, would also be a task for Charn. Lam In was confident about him if Charn could talk to him.

Lam In had had a message to Charn half written when a chilling thought exploded in his brain. The Butcher and his men. Their bodies were still lying where they had fallen. As soon as they were discovered and identified, the precious order from the Angkha would be worse than useless! Lam In gathered his surprised men and they returned to the ambush site, with barely an hour of darkness left. Lam In gave his puzzled men quick orders.

"Get all the bodies stripped and into the trucks. Keep the uniforms and the weapons in separate bundles in the second truck. We must erase all traces of the ambush. As soon as it's light, pick up all the empty shells, clips, and anything else that might indicate there was a fight here."

The truck with the stripped bodies returned to the woods, and the second followed shortly after dawn. The bodies were dumped in a hastily dug mass grave and camouflaged. Empty cartridge cases, clips, and other telltale bits were buried with them.

While this was being completed, Lam In finished his message and sent it off, before moving boldly and openly north toward Lart Om's garrison.

As Lam In and his men drove north, the recipients of his message reread the final two requests, which would require fast action on their part—presuming they agreed to the daring plan.

TO COVER BUTCHER AND GROUP'S DEATH, WE CAN PUT SAME NUMBER MEN FROM CAMP IN UNIFORMS TO ESCAPE TO THAILAND. IF YOU PUBLICIZE DEFECTION BY

BUTCHER AND MEN, WE CLEAR TO USE ANGKHA OR-
DERS.

  REQUEST PLANE RETURN SITE BRAVO TO COPY DOC-
UMENTS AND BRING IN FUEL PUMPS, INJECTORS, AND
TIRES FOR GMC TRUCKS NEEDED FOR TRAVEL EAST.

"Well, Mark," Banchert asked, "what do you think?"

"Got to give the guy credit, Banchert, it's some plan. You
should be able to handle the phony defection okay. It's the
transportation that I'm worried about. Obviously those trucks
he's got are in pretty sad shape. Even with legitimate orders,
they can't move fast enough without trucks for my liking.
The longer they're on the road, the more chance somebody'll
get wise. I think that's their greatest risk, after they get over
the recruitment of the three guys he needs."

"Frankly, I like the idea. It gets a whole bunch of people
on the ground, where we need them, in a hurry. But I think
Commander Charn is a lot better qualified than I am to say
yea or nay—it's his country."

Banchert turned expectantly to Charn. "What are your
thoughts, my friend?"

"Well, Colonel, I think Colonel Mark has put it quite correctly. Lam In is very good at planning and carrying out
schemes that seem very risky in the beginning. In this case,
the lack of organization and communications will work in
favor of the plan. Often there are no written orders at all; this
has caused a lot of problems in the past. But with a written
order from someone as high as Pol Pet, I doubt anyone would
dare question them. As Colonel Mark said, the sooner they
get in place, the better. Once they are there, down in the
Parrot's Beak area, we can move very rapidly. The chances
of discovery are far less.

"As far as the group leaders go, I feel sure of Lart Om,
and almost so of Mun Sin. Lop Garn may be a problem. I
know he is ambitious, and his pride was hurt when I chose
Lam In over him as my deputy. But it's certainly worth trying.
If he won't join us"—Charn shrugged—"we'll have to make
sure he is rendered harmless. Nar Rang came from his group,

and I believe the men would follow him, with Lop Garn, uh, removed.''

The seemingly innocuous words about Lop Garn were not lost on Banchert and the others. ''Render harmless'' and ''removed'' were Charn's euphemisms for killing; his expression and tone of voice made this very clear.

Banchert then asked Gary his views.

''I've just been trying to figure how many truck tires you can cram into a Porter—never had that problem before. The other spare parts are no sweat. I just hope he's got a couple of decent mechanics to install them. Getting them all over to Parrot's Beak this way sure makes for a lot fewer overflights. That suits me just fine!''

Pranee shook her head at Banchert's glance in her direction. ''I'm also in general agreement,'' she said, ''but I would like to suggest we bring out Lam In, overnight, and go over this with him in detail. It seems too good an opportunity to risk failing because of moving too fast.''

Seeing unspoken agreement, Banchert nodded. ''Good. I'll work out a reply with Charn. If Gary is agreeable, we can bring in a load of tires and parts tomorrow, and bring Lam In out.''

CHAPTER TWENTY-NINE

LAM IN RECEIVED THE COMPOSITE MESSAGE ON HIS NOON radio contact. They reached Site Bravo by four, and dropped off one truck and half the men to secure it, while Lam In took the rest toward Lart Om's unit in Phum Tasanh. As Lam In had expected, they hadn't seen a soul all day. The dozen small villages and the dry, weed-grown fields were equally deserted.

Playing safe, Lam In stopped the truck about four kilometers from Lart Om's headquarters. He took Nar Rang and three men with him to reconnoiter on foot.

Their luck held. Using binoculars, Lam In surveyed the little village. He recognized several of the men, and then saw Lart Om himself, still apparently using the same house Lam In remembered from previous trips. Everything looked normal, but Lam In decided to wait until full dark.

He led his men to within fifty meters of Lart Om's house, reminding himself to chide Lart Om about his poor security.

"Nar Rang, you and the men stay here until I signal. I want to make sure he's alone before I go on. I don't expect any trouble, but if there is, get back to the others and get down to Site Bravo as fast as you can. Don't try to come after me. Understand?"

Lam In covered the remaining distance quickly. At the half-open door he rapped gently and heard the familiar voice say, "Come in." Grinning broadly, he walked inside. Lart Om's pudgy body bounced from the chair with surprising agility when Lam In entered. Then his round, smooth features convulsed in a classic double take when he recognized his former comrade and leader. His delight reassured Lam In, as the owlish Lart Om grasped both arms and struggled for words.

"Lam In," he almost shouted, then with a worried look, peered out the door before closing it and continuing in a lower tone. "But how can this be? You are supposed to be dead; killed by the Thais, like poor Charn Nol. Tell me, please. What's going on?"

The two friends talked for a long time. Lart Om swore bitterly, his normal placid face enraged when Lam In told him of the Butcher's death sentence and their subsequent escape. Sure of Lart Om now, Lam In told him of ambushing the hated Butcher and all his men. This brought another outburst.

"So the Butcher is dead, finally. Wonderful news."

Then Lam In brought Lart Om to his feet when he told him that Charn Nol was not only alive and well, but would fly in the following night. The pudgy man's joy was all Lam In needed to proceed with enlisting Lart Om to the project.

"You know, I like it," Lart Om said. "I really think it will work. Especially with you and Charn Nol to lead us. I'm sure the story about the Butcher padding his strength is true. And those Angkha crazies are getting worse all the time. The nonsense they send down is unbelievable. I don't know what I'd do if I had one of those hellish camps to run; probably go over to the Thais. I couldn't stomach it. It's bad enough having to run them down and turn them back. My men feel the same way. So a lot of them are getting away, and I wouldn't be surprised if some of the other group commanders, like Mun Sin, are doing the same thing. Let the poor devils go. They'll only starve in the camps; if those bloodthirsty kids they use to guard them don't kill them first."

Lam In was surprised and pleased at the normally quiet Lart Om's outburst. The mention of Mun Sin also gave him the opening he had been seeking. "How is Mun Sin? Still as grouchy as ever?"

"Much worse these days. You know, I never thought he really cared about anything but himself and his own men. You know how he was about them, always protecting them. Well, we were together when we heard about Charn Nol going over. You know, Lam In, he was really happy! I'd never seen him like that.

"But when we heard the Thais had shot him, executed him, Mun Sin almost went crazy. He was all set to attack Thailand single-handedly! I can't wait to see his face when we tell him Charn's coming here."

At midnight Lam In told Nar Rang to go back to their camp and bring the men in at daylight. Then the two men, talked out temporarily, went to sleep.

Nar Rang and his men had covered less than half the four kilometers back to the bivouac when they heard a truck approaching. They took cover until the truck had roared past and the acrid dust began to thin. The truck's canvas had been tied down, concealing its contents. Nar Rang stood watching, vaguely uneasy. From past experience, before his escape to Thailand, he knew how dangerous Free Cambodians had made night travel by single vehicles. So this truck must have been on a really urgent mission. Had the Khmer Rouge somehow learned about their ambush of the Butcher?

He heard the truck slow, and then stop. What should he do? For that matter, what could he do? Nar Rang's men stood quietly, waiting for him to decide. Unused to making decisions without orders to base them on, Nar Rang vacillated. Suddenly all four froze at the sound of firing from the village.

Nar Rang's indecision vanished with the sound. Now he was on familiar ground. He led his men at a dead run toward the sound. Lam In, second only to Charn Nol in the wizened sergeant's devoted loyalty, was in the village. The whos and whys of the unusual situation were unimportant; danger to Lam In was.

Breathing heavily from their run, they dropped to the ground a bare hundred meters from the village. Nar Rang forced his lungs and hands to obey as he shakily focused the binoculars on the area illuminated by the truck's headlights. He groaned involuntarily at what he saw. Still watching, he whispered hoarsely to his three men. "Something's wrong. They're holding Lart Om's men like they were prisoners. Oh, no! There's Lart Om and Lam In, with their hands up!"

Nar Rang tried to count the men who were roughly herding Lart Om's men into a building. At least thirty, he thought, maybe more. He had to get help.

With unsteady hands, Nar Rang handed the binoculars to one of his men. "Wait here, and watch. I'm going to get the others."

The simple commands had been automatic. But as he got far enough away to begin running, Nar Rang's mind recoiled at the responsibility that lay ahead. He was almost nauseated by sudden stabs of fear. Not fear of personal danger—fear of his inadequacy to give the right orders.

Before, through all the long years, there had always been someone to give him orders—now there was no one. What orders should he give? What would Charn Nol do? Or Lam In?

Nar Rang's feet raised little spurts of dust as he abandoned caution and followed the rutted road. What would Charn Nol do first? He forced his overtaxed brain to try and remember the dozens of times he had listened to orders for ambushes, raids, other missions. This would be a raid. But what orders should he give? Should he attack from the front? From the rear? Or more than one direction? Frantically, he searched his memory for answers. A flash of fear made him sob. Scout the enemy first. He relaxed slightly as he heard Charn Nol's familiar voice in his mind. *Never attack until you know where the enemy positions are—all of them!*

A spark of confidence drove some of his fear back. First find where the enemy was. Good. He'd done it too many times himself to make a mistake there. But then what? Again Charn Nol's voice in his mind: *Attack where the enemy is weak, where he won't expect you.*

Bit by bit, as Nar Rang's tiring muscles forced his body

onward, more and more surges of memory forced his fears from his whirling brain. He was so intent on his thoughts, the sudden challenge of the outpost guard frightened him.

Between gulps of air, Nar Rang alerted the two men before he began sprinting toward the rest of his men. His pounding pulse deafened him so that he didn't hear the oncoming noise of trucks until too late.

Then headlights shone in his eyes and he made a leap for cover. He groaned as he tripped over a ridge of caked mud and fell hard. Half-dazed and nearly exhausted, he struggled to get up as the truck lurched to a stop and pinned him in its headlights!

Lam In was sound asleep when the truck screeched to a halt. He and Lart Om were still groping for their rifles when half a dozen men burst into the room and overpowered them.

Furious at being surprised, and then tightly held while his arms were bound, his anger turned to despair when he recognized Pol Pet's voice behind the blinding flashlight.

The Angkha's handsome face was contorted in rage as a pressure lantern illuminated the room. Lam In tried to keep his fear from his face as Pol Pet's shrill screams of almost incoherent rage filled the little room. "Traitor! Spy! Murderer! You will pay for your crimes many times before you die!"

When Lam In refused to even acknowledge the enraged man's shouted demand to admit his crimes and reply to his interrogator's stream of questions, the emaciated Angkha security chief smashed his bony fists into Lam In's face. He felt his nose break before the half-crazed Angkha suddenly cried out himself, nursing one hand in the other. Dancing in pain, Pol Pet ordered the eager pair of guards, barely teenagers, to continue the beating.

Before he lost consciousness, Lam In felt his cheekbone split from a blow by a rifle butt. Two sudden shocks as pails of water were thrown in his bleeding face brought him to half consciousness. He was tied to a chair. Pol Pet's angry shouts, delivered inches from his face, barely registered. Summoning his remaining strength, he spat bloody mucus and fragments of his teeth into the malevolent Angkha's face.

Pol Pet recoiled with a shriek of rage. Pawing at his face, he screamed, "You will pay for that! Oh, how I will make you pay!"

Helplessly, Lam In heard the enraged Angkha order the guards to free one of his hands and hold it in front of him on the table.

"Now you will tell me where Charn Nol and your gang of traitors are!"

Lam In drew courage from the words. His men, at least, were still safe. Again he spat out a glob of blood and bits of teeth, which splattered the snarling, ratlike face. Pol Pet stepped back, wiped his face, and grabbed Lam In's left hand. With an incoherent shout, he tore at the little finger, bending it back till it snapped. Lam In screamed in agony. The scream galvanized the berserk Pol Pet, who continued wordless shouts as he bent and broke the ring finger and then the middle finger in rapid succession. Lam In passed out when the second finger broke. Pol Pet dashed water over his rapidly swelling face, but Lam In just lay slumped in the chair, held by his bonds.

Before the stunned Nar Rang could regain his feet, the lead truck had stopped only feet away. Out of the glare of the headlights came the burly figure of Mun Sin, rifle held ready. Then the rifle dropped and Nar Rang felt the big man's strong grip on his shoulders.

"I know you; you're one of the headquarters people!" The painful grip tightened as Mun Sin growled, "What are you doing here? You're one of the ones who escaped with Lam In. Answer me!"

Nar Rang tried to explain, but his initial attempts, mixed up as they were, confused his bearlike questioner. Then one of Mun Sin's sergeants interrupted him.

"Mun Sin, the men here say Pol Pet, from the Angkha, has disarmed all of Lart Om's men, and they have Lam In, too."

The words brought Mun Sin upright. He let go of Nar Rang. "Is this true? Lam In is alive?"

"Yes, Mun Sin, but now Pol Pet has him. We must get him away from Pol Pet and his men . . . about thirty of them. I watched them. They took Lart Om's men's weapons away and put them in the warehouse."

It took only a few more minutes for the hulking guerrilla to extract the information he needed from Nar Rang. As the little sergeant listened, Mun Sin gave orders to the combined groups.

Then they loaded into their trucks and drove toward the village, headlights on and motors roaring.

In the first truck, Nar Rang sat squeezed against the door by Mun Sin's bulk. The plan was simplicity itself. Mun Sin, with Nar Rang to lead, would use all the men in the first truck to rescue Lart Om and Lam In from the house. The other trucks would stop at intervals behind them, and shoot down everyone in sight who carried a weapon. Like most simple plans, Mun Sin's worked.

Pol Pet's men were mostly clustered around the truck they had come in. Mun Sin's convoy brought them to their feet, surprised, but not alarmed. Pinned by the truck's headlights, they never had a chance when Mun Sin's group opened up at point-blank range. Up front, Nar Rang cut down two men in front of the house, then was shoved aside as Mun Sin threw his shoulder at the door and tore it loose from its hinges. Another guard went down under his rifle butt. Nar Rang shot him where he lay.

There was a hoarse cry of rage from Mun Sin, followed immediately by a long burst of fire. Inside, Nar Rang saw the bedroom door hanging by one hinge. As he entered, he caught a flicker of movement behind it. His quick burst of fire was a split second faster than Pol Pet's. It slammed the Angkha security chief against the wall. His pistol shot tore harmlessly into the wood floor. He was dead before his body slumped to the floor.

Two more bodies lay across the bed. Automatically, Nar Rang checked them quickly before turning to see the burly

Mun Sin cutting a rope that held a figure to the chair. Looking over his shoulder, Nar Rang cried out and then felt his stomach retch when he saw the face! Wildly, he searched the rest of the little house, then ran outside, looking for a target to destroy.

But the brief fight was over. Pol Pet's men, as a dying one told them, had been expecting nothing. Nar Rang dragged the medic away from the dying man and hurried him into the bedroom.

Mun Sin's big hands were clumsily trying to wipe Lam In's almost unrecognizable face with a wet cloth. Even the combat-hardened medic swallowed bile as he examined his commander's horrible wounds. The maimed man moaned in pain. He gave him a morphine Syrette. All three were looking helplessly at Lam In's maimed hand when Lart Om, supported by two of his men, appeared.

His face was almost as swollen and distorted as Lam In's, but he was still conscious. He groaned as he saw his friend's grotesquely misshapen face. His men lowered him to the other bed. The medic examined him and then began to sponge off the blood.

"Must go to the landing place," he muttered. "Send Lam In to doctor." Then he lost consciousness as the relieved medic began to stitch a bone-deep gash in his scalp.

Mun Sin turned to Nar Rang. "You know about this airplane? Is it really coming tonight?"

"Yes, Mun Sin. Lam In left half our men down there to guard the place. It's about an hour's drive from here. Lart Om is right. We must send both of them to Thailand on the airplane."

The sergeant's words broke the big man's preoccupation with his wounded friends. While they were being cared for by the medic, he took command again.

Outside, he and Nar Rang were briefing their men organized there when one of Mun Sin's sergeants told him Pol Pet's driver was still alive, though badly wounded.

The man had two bullets in his abdomen. He gladly traded

all he knew for a shot of morphine. His information solved the puzzle of Pol Pet's strange actions.

One of the Butcher's men had escaped the ambush. Stricken with a sudden attack of dysentery, he had remained with the trucks. When he heard the shooting, he hid, then ran away. He'd been walking up the Pursat road when Pol Pet, en route to inspect the Butcher's booty, had found him. He told Pol Pet about the ambush, and a scrap of conversation he had overheard while hiding from Lam In's men when they took over the Butcher's trucks. He had overheard the names Lam In, Lart Om, and a reference to Phum Tasanh.

Enraged at the man's story of the ambush, Pol Pet had jumped to the conclusion that both of Charn Nol's former officers had been responsible. Taking a truckload of men from Pursat, and sending word, without explanation, to Mun Sin to hurry to Phum Tasanh, Pol Pet had arrived first.

On the ride to Site Bravo, Nar Rang answered a flood of eager questions from Mun Sin. His delight at the news his old commander and comrade, Charn Nol, was not only alive, but coming tonight on the airplane, overshadowed his worry for the two wounded men. Even though Nar Rang could only answer a few of the torrent of other questions, the combination of the Butcher's death and Charn Nol's miraculous resurrection had the usually enigmatic man laughing and clapping his hands.

After Gary ghosted the Porter down on the flare-lit strip, Mun Sin rushed to the plane. His rib-cracking bear hug as Charn Nol emerged told his old friend all he needed. Their mutual happiness was dimmed as Lam In and Lart Om were brought, still unconscious, and loaded on board. Charn Nol recoiled as his flashlight revealed Lam In's face and mangled hand, and then Lart Om's swollen features and bandaged head.

As Mun Sin's only casualty, a leg wound, was helped into the plane, Charn Nol held a hurried conversation with Mun Sin, Nar Rang, and Lart Om's sergeant deputy. Long before Gary tapped his arm to signal he was ready to take off, Charn knew he could count on the burly Mun Sin, as well as Lart Om's deputy and all their men.

"Now, Mun Sin, you will be in command until I return. I will be back, that I promise. But I must also keep my word to our friends who have made all this possible. Work as fast as you can on the trucks, with the parts and tires we brought. Tomorrow or the next day, more will come in. Send out a list of the parts you need for your trucks and Lart Om's. Do the same as Lam In did with the Butcher and his men: keep the uniforms and bury the bodies. I'll arrange things on the other side. Good luck, old friend!"

Over the border again, Gary reactivated his ELT and radio. "Base, Four Niner Zulu with four Purple Trees, two medium, one well done."

Gary heard Mark's mike click on, and then a hesitant, "Roger, Four Niner. Want to go to Alpha?"

"Negative, base. They'll keep. ETA 1910 Zulu, out."

CHAPTER THIRTY

BANCHERT AND MARK HAD A DOCTOR AND AMBULANCE waiting when Gary taxied up to the small, dimly lit hangar. Charn Nol helped them and the medics get Mun Sin's wounded man out. Then they gently eased Lart Om and Lam In onto stretchers and into the ambulance. Charn Nol sat holding Lam In's good hand in both of his, in silent misery. The others followed in Banchert's old Benz.

Inside the hospital, all four felt their stomachs roil as the young doctor uncovered Lam In's hand. It was three times its normal size. The broken fingers looked like obscene purple sausages, stuck at random into a shapeless reddish lump. The doctor shook his head, shrugging helplessly.

"This is beyond my ability, Colonel. We must get a specialist quickly; otherwise he will lose his hand. I will take the first X rays now, to save time."

Banchert was dialing within seconds. From his unusual vehemence Gary knew he was venting his anger and grief in a completely uncharacteristic loss of control.

By the time he came back to the little emergency room, the doctor had finished stitching the gashes in Lart Om's face and head.

"This one has a possible concussion, but otherwise I'm quite sure he'll be up and around in short order."

It was almost noon before the hastily summoned team of surgeons completed their operation on Lam In's maimed hand and unrecognizable face. Their report was guardedly optimistic. In time, Lam In would probably regain partial use of his fingers. A second operation would be necessary—after the gross swelling had subsided. There would also have to be additional plastic surgery to restore his face. His eyes were still an unknown, though they appeared to be only superficially bruised. Bridgework would have to replace the missing teeth. The doctor's eyes were eloquent with questions.

"In case you had any doubts about our country's enemies," Banchert muttered, "this is an example."

After the doctor's prognosis, they visited Lart Om, whose face was only slightly less puffy, but who was awake and disturbed at being kept in bed. They reassured him that once the doctors agreed his concussion was no longer a threat, he would be able to rejoin his men.

Mark and Gary napped on the ride down to Pattaya, but Charn Nol and Banchert spent the whole trip in conversation. At the bungalow, they gulped down coffee and then big breakfasts Pranee had prepared. After they had eaten, she showed them a message from Mun Sin.

He was ready to proceed with the fake defection, adding Pol Pet and his men to the Butcher and his group. From his base at Phum O Choar, he controlled a sizable section of the border; so there would be no problem getting the weakened former camp inmates across the border. They would wear the Khmer Rouge uniforms, and carry the meager personal papers of the dead soldiers. On arrival, they would all say their leaders, Pol Pet and the Butcher, had been killed by a Khmer Rouge border outpost platoon.

This heartening news was considerably dampened by the long list of truck spare parts and tires, and an inventory of the available fuel and lubricant supplies Mun Sin controlled. Aside from the spares and tires, at least three loads for the Porter, they lacked a third of the diesel fuel needed to make the seven-hundred-kilometer trip by the route Mark and Charn had planned. Nonetheless, Banchert ordered all the items Mun

Sin listed, and Gary got to work trying to figure out how to get them all in.

Mark was pleasantly surprised to see that Colonel Banchert had decided to let Charn Nol go in to replace his wounded deputy. After the initial shock of meeting him again, Mark had been increasingly impressed with the ex-enemy's abilities and intelligence. He also admired his courage, especially after having seen what the vengeful Angkha, Pol Pet, had done to Lam In. With the administrative work under way, Mark, Charn, and Banchert sat down to discuss the implementation of the first phase of Indian Movie.

"Well, Charn," Banchert said, with a trace of a smile, "it seems that you will get your wish. I think Mark will agree; no one but you can possibly replace Lam In. But I am still concerned that Pol Pet may have told the Angkha, or someone else, about the Butcher."

The wiry former Khmer Rouge commander's face wore a grim smile. "I think we should go ahead, Colonel. There *is* still a chance, as you say. Personally, I doubt it. So far none of the radio intercepts indicate any unusual activity. This is good. After you break the story of Pol Pet and the Butcher defecting, we should be able to confirm my feeling. Also, don't forget, Mun Sin has reported nothing out of the ordinary. So, gentlemen, I would like to go in as soon as possible. There will be a lot of organizing to do, and even if the Angkha aren't on to us, we still must hurry."

Banchert looked inquiringly at Mark.

"Makes good sense for him to get in there and try to speed things up," Mark said. "In a way"—he shot a quick glance at his wife"—I sort of envy you, Charn."

Charn and Banchert looked at him in surprise. Pranee glared.

"Yeah, I *almost* do. But I'm a bit old for helling all over the lot. That was fine when I was young, like with Patton in War Two. What I'm really trying to say is, it would be a real change to go charging across Cambodia like an armored column, hell-bent for election. Charn, you want to remember that. When in doubt, pour on the gas and bull your way through. By the time the other guy recovers, you'll be long gone."

"Thank you, Colonel Mark, I'll remember that, and many, many other things I have learned from you. Personally, I am glad you will be here to call on for advice. I know we will need it."

Banchert beamed contentedly at this exchange. "I don't want to get into a discussion of tactics, but please, Charn, don't take any unnecessary risks on the way over. Without you, Indian Movie is just that, a real impossibility, or series of them.

"Now, gentlemen, would we be tempting fate if we spent some time on our plans for the second phase of Indian Movie? No? Okay, Mark has done a great deal of work on this with my people. Over the past weeks, they have put together as accurate an appraisal of our potential allies in the eastern Cambodian border area as possible. Once Charn is in place, I'm sure he will be able to add to it. However, based on what we have now, there seem to be four potential groups. The most numerous, and probably the most effective, are the Vietnamese sects, the Cao Dai and Hoa Hao. Mark worked closely with both of them during his service in the war, an added plus for us. We have a radio link to each of the sects, but it is not secure. We must give them new codes and radios that use the 'squirt system.' Sending messages by hand-keying takes too long and is too dangerous.

"There is also a small new group, claiming to be the survivors of a Taiwan Special Forces detachment. They are an unknown factor. Might even be a Vietnamese provocation. But they do have a radio, and we are continuing contact. So far the information they are sending us appears accurate.

"Finally, our newest potential asset is a group of Vietnamese Special Forces men, considerably farther north, up where Cambodia, Laos, and Vietnam meet. With them, thanks again to Mark, we seem on firmer ground. Three of their people are former officers Mark knew well. The courier they sent out overland through Laos claims they have nearly one hundred men. We feel quite sure of them, because we have con-

siderable information from other sources tending to confirm
what their courier told us. We gave him one of the new radios
and code systems. We should hear from them any day now
. . . if he made it back.

"So, friend Charn, your first job, after you get into position, will be to make contact with the three southern groups—
Cao Dai, Hoa Hao, and the Chinese—and assess them."

Charn nodded and expressed his surprise at the potential
help the groups represented. His eyes twinkled. "This is quite
an about-face. Me, a former Communist guerrilla, working
with three groups of former enemy, supported and advised
by yet two more former enemies! Unbelievable! But oddly,
I'm really looking forward to it!

"One thing, Khun Mark. These new radios—I don't understand why they are so much better."

"Well," Mark said, "the old system meant the operator
had to key out his coded message by hand. This meant he
had to be on the air quite a while; he could be picked up
more easily. The new system uses a sort of tape recorder;
you punch out the message on tape first, then after contact is
made, the tape is played into the transmitter, very fast. A
message that might take an operator ten minutes by hand is
sent in seconds by the tape. The receiving end records it with
its tape at the same speed. Then they just slow it down and
copy it. To an enemy intercept monitor, it sounds like static,
a short squealing noise—very difficult to record, and impossible to locate by direction finders. The code itself, even if
they record it and find the right tape speed, cannot be broken
without a computer. So the new system prevents the enemy
from finding the location of the set, or the contents of the
message."

The rest of the day and early evening flew by in last-minute
preparations. Up at Don Muang, Lart Om was waiting impatiently. The doctors had released him. No concussion had
been found. He and Charn squirmed into empty spaces among
the load of truck tires and Gary took off, using a lot of runway in the process.

Mark, Pranee, and Banchert walked to the little hangar

office to wait. Inside, Mark felt a sudden stab of fear and grabbed Banchert by the shoulder. "Christ—what about those Khmer Rouge agents? Lieutenant Narang and your sergeant, Boopan?"

Banchert regarded the balding American in mock pain. "Khun Mark. I am surprised at your lack of faith in me. But you may rest easy. Narang is busy guarding a decoy plane, down at Chantaburi. Sergeant Boopan is with him, waiting for Somboon to bring out two very important defectors."

"Important defectors? Ohh, I see. Now, that is really beautiful, Banchert. My sincere apologies. Important defectors, eh—like maybe Pol Pet and the Butcher?"

"They weren't told any names—just two important ones. Somboon will return empty, and say they decided to come out overland—due to some mixup."

The admiration in Mark's voice made Banchert feel very good inside, but he simply smiled. "Beautiful, Banchert, simply beautiful," Mark said. "Thank God you're on our side!"

Gary returned just before four A.M. "Another milk run, Mark. It's too damn easy! I'm afraid I'm gonna take this pitcher to the well once too often. Oh, yeah, there's a couple sacks of documents and stuff they forgot last trip, and a letter from the big guy, Mun Sin. We don't communicate too well, but he sure strikes me as a pretty rugged type. Gung ho as all hell."

Pranee translated the short note from Mun Sin.

"Friends, So far we have no trouble, except the trucks. My only mechanic was killed in the fighting with Pol Pet's men. Lart Om's is only good for tires and small things. We need good mechanics badly. I will tell Charn."

After their first decent sleep in days, Mark, Pranee, and Banchert woke in the fading twilight to read a long radio message from Charn Nol. It had good news and bad news. The good news was the lack of any discernible reaction by either the Angkha or other Khmer Rouge units. Mun Sin had sent in his usual weekly truckload of firewood and charcoal to Pursat. It returned with four precious drums of fuel, several cans of motor oil, and two reasonably good tires, thanks to some discreet bribery by Mun Sin's deputy. Everything in Pursat seemed normal. The commander had asked the whereabouts of Pol Pet and the men he had taken from the garrison. Mun Sin's deputy, Pan Ti, replied they hadn't appeared at his area as yet. The answer seemed satisfactory, which lent strong credence to the belief that Pol Pet had not told anyone about the Butcher being ambushed.

The bad news was just that. Charn Nol said he simply had to have some trained mechanics. His men had tried to change the fuel pump and injectors on one truck. After a full day and night, they still couldn't even start it.

"Goddamn it!" Mark's big fist hit the table a sharp blow, startling Pranee into spilling her coffee. "Talk about want of a damn nail! After all this, to get stuck because they can't get those damn fool trucks running. Banchert! We've got to do something. Got any mechanics in those refugee camps?"

Banchert considered the idea for a moment, then shook his head regretfully. "There probably *are* some, Mark. But the camps are also full of Khmer Rouge agents as well. We've found a good number already. I'd be afraid to risk it."

"How about Thais? Christ, there must be dozens of good diesel men looking for work now that construction's about dead."

"That's a possibility, Mark. I'll call General Pranet, the PARU commander."

"Hell, yes, Banchert; should have thought of him myself."

"I'll be greatly exceeding my authority, you know, Mark. I have strictest orders not to involve any Thai citizen in this— as you can well understand. But I agree, we have to give Charn help, and quickly."

General Pranet, the doughty little PARU general, whom Mark had first known as a captain twenty years previously, brushed Banchert's misgivings aside. "Mechanics? How many do you want? A platoon?"

They settled for four, one of whom spoke good Cambodian. The senior, Sergeant Dechar, was also an old friend from Mark's Thai days. He quickly noted Gary's concern at

yet another landing, and offered to jump in with their tools
in leg-bags, at any altitude Gary wanted. This hit Gary's
pride, and he quickly vetoed the idea, agreeing to make one
more landing. Though Mark shared Gary's concern, he was
relieved when he agreed to land. They had already sent Somboon in the previous night to drop more tires, which free-fall
couldn't hurt.

Despite Gary's forebodings, the trip in and back was uneventful. This might well have been partially due to Banchert's press release of the "defection" of Pol Pet, the
Butcher, and more than sixty Khmer Rouge soldiers. Radio
Phnom Penh, the Angkha's station, was pouring out pure vit-
riol about Thailand's "interference in Cambodian affairs,"
making dire threats to any Thai so involved. But there were
no names mentioned. This pleased Banchert's group no end.
It meant the Angkha had "bought" the false story planted
with their two penetration agents, Lieutenant Narong and
Sergeant Boopan. Apparently they couldn't bring themselves
to believe the Thai news release yet.

But the furor forced Charn Nol into moving prematurely.
The whole western Cambodian border area was in an uproar.
Battembang and Phnom Penh were frantically querying all
units, trying to locate the missing Angkha member and their
western border commander.

Lart Om and Mun Sin sent in reports that they had received
orders from the Butcher to move east, but several days previously. Lart Om reported Pol Pet had stopped briefly, and
then driven south without saying where he was going.

These reports seemed to satisfy the Khmer Rouge, at least
temporarily. But Charn Nol knew he was running out of time,
so he moved the night after Gary had brought in Dechar and
his three mechanics. He had to tow two of the old GMC's,
but got well beyond Pursat before stopping just off the main
road in a deserted village. He was still over 150 kilometers
from Phnom Penh, but well south and east of where the
Khmer Rouge were still searching for their missing leaders.

While his men slept in shifts, the PARU mechanics labored
all day on the balky trucks. About noon, Charn Nol's high-

way roadblock bore fruit. A senior officer from Phnom Penh and two men in a jeep were completely surprised. Their information caused Charn Nol to abandon his plan to give the almost deserted capital a wide berth to the south. Most of the Khmer Rouge troops had moved from their Phnom Penh stations to set up blocks or to drive west on the road he had planned to use. In his message announcing the change in route, he reminded Mark of his own words at their final meeting. "We are pouring on the gas and bulling through."

The Khmer Rouge reaction, much more extensive than any of the anxious group back in Thailand had foreseen, worried them all. Banchert was especially concerned about the four Thai PARU mechanics, driving ever deeper into Cambodia with Charn Nol. Their capture could cause a major incident—precisely what Colonel Banchert had been expressly forbidden to risk. Should this happen, he would be the scapegoat, and among other things, his xenophobic enemy, the CID chief, would move in for the kill he had so recently been denied. "If it starts to go wrong," he reminded Mark and Gary, "General Pranet has agreed to get you three out to Malaysia. General Sarong would show you no mercy. He knows you are working with me."

Gary frowned. "How about you, Banchert?"

The Thai colonel's grim expression reflected a tight-lipped attempt at a smile as he wordlessly drew a finger across his throat.

That afternoon, General Pranet arrived with Gary in one of his Caribou aircraft. Gary had agreed to give four PARU pilots a refresher in flying "intruder missions." The tough paratrooper's optimism removed some of the gloom.

"Banchert, have you no faith in my men? After all these years, you should know them better. I'm sure they are having a wonderful time. It is much better they go all the way. How would you feel if the trucks broke down, and they were not there to fix them? You would lose all you have gained. We'll get them out; don't worry about that.

"Gary is working with my pilots, and when the time comes, they will be ready. Remember, Elder Brother, I have two

C-123's in addition to my two Caribous. If we have to, we can rig one of the 123's for a snatch pickup; we won't have to land to get them out. Not to worry so much, Elder Brother; things are going well.''

Radio Phnom Penh also helped to dispel the remaining gloom when it broadcast a demand that the Thai government hand back the two traitors, Pol Pet and Commander Smarn, for trial in Cambodia. They promised unnamed retribution if the two were not returned to Cambodian custody within the next forty-eight hours.

General Pranet and Colonel Banchert conferred and sent a string of orders, moving reserves to key border locations, as well as putting all PARU units on red alert. Then Banchert went to brief the full National Security Council.

His initial fears were groundless. To a man, his superiors were highly pleased at his successes, their only disappointment being the unfortunate deaths of the two Khmer Rouge senior officials. Banchert, with his boss's full approval, neglected to mention the deception as being such.

His report that Project Indian Movie was proceeding well occasioned further endorsement of his work. Even though his sketchy report left out most of the details, the news that there would soon be a sizable force in place on the Cambodian-Vietnamese border, ready to begin provocative attacks on both sides, was roundly applauded. Then Banchert's boss surprised him.

''You gentlemen understand, of course, that it will be necessary for us to send clandestine supply flights to support our efforts?''

The question sobered the group, but only temporarily. After a few questions about overland and sea resupply, which Banchert fielded skillfully, the prime minister himself gave approval, subject to his personal review of each proposed flight, in advance. This was far more than Banchert had dared hope for, so he returned to Pattaya in an ebullient mood.

His new optimism infected the others as they plunged into the task of detailed operational planning. Mark contributed another critical element when he returned from a visit with his air force friend. At his request, the high-altitude USAF recon flight had taken infrared photos over the reported locations of the various anti-Communist guerrilla groups. These provided strong confirmation of their radioed reports. Each had lit fires, as instructed, on the night of the flight. Interpretation left no doubt that there were a fair number of men in and around the respective locations.

Other photos confirmed a strip in the Vietnamese Special Forces area that Gary believed would take a half-loaded Caribou. There were several usable strips down in the Parrot's Beak, but both the sect leaders and the Chinese doubted their ability to secure them long enough to permit a landing.

At the same time, the group in Pattaya had been eagerly following Charn Nol's rapid progress. His change of route had proven wise. The column of trucks sped through the outskirts of Phnom Penh on near empty streets, and then down the west bank of the Mekong River to the bridge at Prek Khasay.

Continuing to use Mark's "bull through" tactics, they sped past the sleepy guards on the bridge, and finally stopped halfway to Svay Rieng, the Butcher's old headquarters. That was their final obstacle before taking up the positions in the Parrot's Beak itself. There was no feasible way to bypass Svay Rieng. Even had there been, they had to report in to the area commander in any case.

Charn Nol knew him by reputation only. An older man by a dozen years, he was known as a tenacious fighter, but poorly educated and fond of women and liquor—despite the puritanical preachings of the Angkha Leou. Lart Om and Mun Sin made the initial approach, carrying the order signed by Pol Pet. They drove straight into town in one truck, with thirty men crammed in the back, ready to fight their way out if necessary. Charn Nol and the rest of the men stopped several kilometers out of town, where Charn Nol waited impatiently with his ear glued to the short-range radio on which Lart Om was reporting their progress.

The two group leaders' entry went all but unnoticed. At the headquarters, a single sentry stood up and directed them to a restaurant down the street. There they found the corpulent area commander, Thom Pan, eating a big bowl of noodles and washing it down with a bottle of red wine. When they reported, he belched loudly, then cocked his head suspiciously. He reread the battered order, and then amazed the two nervous men by throwing back his head and laughing uproariously, pounding the table with one hand.

When he finally recovered enough to talk, still chuckling, they were stunned by his words. "Why, that crazy fool—did he think I wasn't on to his game within days after I got here? He may have fooled the Angkha *gentlemen* with his phony groups, but not me, not Thom Pan. And now he's trying to cover it up, is he. Not that it makes any difference, now that he's gone over to the Thais."

Mun Sin nudged Lart Om quickly and they both pretended not to understand. Mun Sin took the lead. "I don't understand, Commander Thom. We were both given our orders by Commander Smarn in person, just a few days ago."

"Well, you'll never receive another from that maniac. Ugh! We're well off rid of him. You obviously haven't heard the news. Smarn, the Butcher, and that little rat, Pol Pet, have gone over to the Thais. Good riddance, I say. Took their men, almost sixty, I hear, with them."

After another fit of laughter, he invited the two to join him, and shouted for more food and a bottle of wine for each. Nar Rang, standing respectfully beside the truck, used the little radio to report briefly to Charn Nol. He ordered his men to get back in the trucks and enter the town, while he and the four PARU crouched in the back of their truck, hidden by men on all sides.

After the impromptu meal, Thom Pan asked some brief questions about the number of men, weapons, and vehicles, and then completed their relief. "Well, Butcher or no, you're here. And we can use you. As a matter of fact, I think you may as well go ahead and occupy the positions down along the border, where Smarn said his phony groups were. I'm spread too thin, far too thin for my liking—thanks to not having all the groups that damn Butcher claimed he had. Now

I can pull back the group I had down there and put them over in Phum Prasar.

"We'll locate your headquarters in Phum Chiphu. Give me your map. Okay, here's Phum Chiphu. You'll be responsible for everything south of the big canal, up here, down to Kampong Rau. You got that, Mun Sin. You're commander as of now. You can always trust a big man; that's my motto.

"You'll have to keep outposts at Kampong Rau, Chantren, and on the three roads up here, to the east. They all cross the border. I'll send one of my men with you. He'll have my group show you around and then move back here.

"I'm really glad to see you. We've been having trouble with some bunches from the other side. Don't know if the Vietnamese put them up to it or not. Damn Butcher never took any prisoners, and so far we haven't had a chance. After you get settled in, we'll talk more about that."

CHAPTER THIRTY-ONE

To CHARN NOL AND DARK-FEATURED, HAWK-NOSED DE-char, crouched down in the back of the sweltering canvas-covered truck, the waiting seemed endless and ominous. Nar Rang's reports, passed on to Charn Nol, insisted that all was well. But he still fretted as the sun beat down and the stench of diesel, rank human bodies, and the residue of hundreds of former cargos made them both nauseated. Finally the truck engine coughed to life, and the men crowded back in to resume the trip. After another quarter hour of misery, the truck slowed to a halt. Pudgy Lart Om was helped over the tailgate, and the truck moved on.

Charn Nol forgot his acute discomfort as the owlish group leader recounted their strange meeting with the area commander, Thom Pan. Charn Nol listened with growing wonder and increasing optimism. Buddha must indeed be watching over them to send them a lax, stomach-oriented oddity like Thom Pan. By the time he had pumped his subordinate dry of information, the truck was again slowing. They turned off to the left as the men in the rear announced they had reached Phum Chiphu. Then they followed this with excited comments about great numbers of trucks, tanks, and guns, big guns. After the truck stopped, the majority of the men dismounted. Charn Nol peered over the tailgate and drew in welcome semiclean air. Beside him, Dechar's sharply hooked nose flared as he saw the maze of vehicles that filled a compound easily three times the size of a football field. Gold-capped molars flashed as he tugged at Charn Nol's arm.

"Look, Commander," he exclaimed. "No more worry for spare parts now. See, over there, the old sign? This was an American storage and maintenance yard. We can fix your trucks very good now."

Lart Om returned and told them it was safe to come out. The small detachment was accompanying Mun Sin and his group to effect the relief of the old troops. They found the headquarters building, the old town hall. It was a pigsty. Rather than try to clean it, Charn Nol selected another of the deserted buildings, across the square, and they moved in. Charn Nol set up in a second-floor room where he would be out of sight of any visitors. Dechar and his three mechanics begged to explore the huge vehicle park; Charn Nol approved with a warning to hide if any strangers showed up. Charn Nol wrote a hasty message that was sent as soon as his operator had strung his antenna out of sight, under the eaves in the back of the house.

By the time Mun Sin returned, after five, the new headquarters was well organized, a defense plan completed, and sentries posted—with brand-new M-16's from the old American supply center. Mun Sin's dusty, sweat-streaked face wore a rare smile as he reported. There had been no problems in relieving the scattered outposts of the former unit. They were only too happy to leave their isolated and, according to them, dangerous positions. Lart Om soon had Mun Sin's dispositions on the overlay, and the three happy leaders composed a message giving this information to Banchert, so he could initiate plans to contact the two Vietnamese sects and the Chinese group.

Back in Thailand, Banchert's little group in Pattaya were equally as elated at the unexpectedly easy acceptance of Charn Nol's contingent by the area commander. Mark was still suspicious; it had been "just too damn easy," he said.

Nevertheless, he agreed they had to go ahead with the first

step in bringing the three anti-Communist guerrilla groups
into direct physical contact with Charn Nol's. This, as
planned, meant an air drop of new radios, codes, and a small
assortment of medical supplies and ammunition. With secure
radios, the groups could communicate directly with both
Charn Nol and Thailand—securely, and safe from any enemy
direction-finding effort.

Mark and Banchert also hoped this would convince the
others of Charn Nol's actual status—a friend, despite surface
appearances. Since both medical supplies and ammunition
were in very short supply, these should also have a big impact
on the wary groups. A final necessary inclusion was two of
the small URG-4 short-range pocket radios, of which Charn
Nol already had four. These would allow voice communication up to five or six miles over flat terrain, and up to fifteen
ground-to-air. They could also work as beacons, using a push
button, to guide in future flights.

Banchert reported the situation to his boss, who took him
directly to the prime minister. After half an hour of detailed
questioning, Banchert finally got approval for the first flight.

Gary had been down at the PARU base since his last flight.
He had flown every night with PARU crews, practicing for
the intruder missions. One Caribou had been repainted with
Vietnamese colors and tail numbers, and stripped of anything
of Thai origin. Then Banchert's men provided Vietnamese
"litter items" from the store they had collected from recent
refugees—cigarette packs, receipts, matches, and similar
items. Each crew man had a complete set of made-in-Viet-
nam clothing, from the skin out, and carefully forged identification, copied from actual defector or refugee documents.
If the plane should be downed in Cambodian territory, it
would appear to be Vietnamese. In Vietnamese territory, it
would hopefully be attributed to the Cambodians, thanks to
a few items of recent Cambodian origin such as marginal
notes on maps in Cambodian.

General Pranet was eager to go, as were his pilots, whom
Gary pronounced, laconically, "about as ready as they can

be." Then the lean American surprised everyone, especially Mark, by insisting he fly the first mission.

"Look," he told Mark and Banchert at the PARU base, "the first one's the easiest; they won't be expecting it. And it seems like it's also the most important—like we don't want to let those guys think we're amateurs. Right?"

Both Mark and Banchert were relieved. Pranet was over-joyed. He had faith in his own men, but Gary had fifty times their total hours, and their intruder experience was almost nil. So Gary took off in the early evening, feeling much less confident than he appeared.

He followed the normal commercial route, giving the coastline a wide berth. Well offshore, he dropped down to five hundred feet and made his run toward the coast. His navigation was good, and the many-mouthed Mekong was all he needed to compensate for his slight drift. He flew as low as he dared over the swampy delta, between the two middle mouths, then swung right to avoid Viet Long. With this past, and nothing on his radar receiver, he relaxed slightly and searched ahead for the first drop zone, the Hoa Hao. Chert, his copilot, the best of his pupils, spotted it first and blinked the recognition signal. The answer was immediate and correct. Gary slowed, dropped the ramp, and alerted the kickers. Lined up with the T of lights on the ground, he bore in, thumbed the drop signal to Chert, and the first load went.

Nodding at Chert's report the chutes had all opened, he raised the ramp, increased speed, and headed for the second one. Chert again spotted it first. Thanks to the long nights of practice, they repeated the drop procedure flawlessly.

The third one was much harder to find, masked by tall trees; they were on top of it too quickly to drop. Gary swore bitterly, swung to his right, and came back in at ninety degrees to his first approach. It was a smaller target from the side, but he had no choice. Circling to come back would take too much time and pinpoint the location to anyone within hearing. He dropped even lower, reducing the time the chutes could be affected by the wind, and signaled as he saw the first marker light over the treetops. The kickers reported one chute had hit near trees, and the other three had opened over the DZ. Five minutes after the drop, still down low, he poured on power.

"If anybody's checking us down there," he told Chert, "they should figure we'd add power right after we drop. By waiting, we throw them off, and protect the guys on the ground. Sure hope this last one is easier."

It was. Both pilots picked up the signal easily and in plenty of time. The DZ was the old STOL strip Gary had seen on the air photos, so it was easy to get the final four bundles right on it.

They stayed high over Laos, and picked up the RTAF beacon at Ubol before they saw the gleam of the Mekong. As he reached the river, Gary turned the controls over to Chert and activated the special identification signal that would flash on the Thai radar. With Chert flying, they went through three more supply drops to border police units who had been alerted to the "practice exercise." As the tall, muscular Chert made a smooth landing at the base, Gary's muscles refused to relax. He crawled stiffly down the steps to the cargo hatch, grimacing with pain.

Back at the PARU base, Mark gave him a brimming cup of brandy, only slightly diluted with coffee, while Pranet did the same for his former basketball star, Chert.

Banchert had observed Gary's crablike walk and summoned a muscular trooper. While Gary submitted to his expert hands, he listened to the reports from the four groups. Even in terse message form, they were gratifying. As the kickers had reported, they had hung only one half-opened "streamer" in the trees at the Chinese drop zone. But it had been slowed by branches and was still undamaged, though it had taken a long time to get the chute down. All the other chutes had been on or very close to the DZ's.

Back at Pattaya the next afternoon, their satisfaction at the all but perfect mission got a severe jolt. Using a prearranged schedule, Charn Nol had contacted each of the three groups in his area. The shocking results were a mini Tower of Babel.

The Hoa Hao and Cao Dai could make no sense of Charn

Nol's English messages. Their replies, in Vietnamese, made even less sense to him. The only part of the Chinese reply Charn Nol could read was the call sign and signature; it was in Chinese numerical telecodes. Mark squirmed and swore as he realized his mistake. After two days of receiving messages from the three groups, translating them, and relaying them to Charn Nol, then repeating the laborious process the other way, it was obvious the system wouldn't work. The sole bright spot was that the Chinese leader, Colonel Leung, had agreed to meet with Charn Nol. The sects, their suspicions redoubled by the communications foul-up, flatly refused, openly warning the already furious Mark that his Khmer Rouge contacts were almost certainly double agents.

Charn Nol was equally exasperated by the situation but agreed to go ahead with the meeting that had been arranged. It was a very limited success, again due to the language barrier.

Colonel Leung's appearance and manner impressed Charn Nol. Well over six feet, solidly built, the Chinese Special Forces officer dwarfed his three companions and Charn Nol's group. He spoke very rudimentary English, but had brought a tiny, battered Chinese-English dictionary with him. Between that, their maps, and a great deal of pantomine, basic communication was just possible.

Despite the language obstacle, the rugged Chinese and the slim ex–Khmer Rouge were able to agree to an initial small-scale operation by each group. Colonel Leung agreed to raid a small Vietnamese outpost and take at least two or three prisoners. He would bring them to a rendezvous with Charn Nol. Charn Nol, in turn, would raid a target he had already selected—and barely restrained Mun Sin from attacking— killing the Vietnamese during the attack and leaving their bodies to be found by the Khmer Rouge.

His men would also take some of the Khmer Rouge prisoners and hand them over to Colonel Leung to repeat the process on the Vietnamese side. The results of planting enemy bodies on the scene should be mutual accusations between the Cambodians and Vietnamese.

To ensure that both sides understood, Charn Nol radioed Mark his own understanding for relay to the Chinese in their own tongue. Pranee's face paled as she read Charn Nol's message. But Mark gently reminded her of her own suffering at Khmer Rouge hands, and what they had done to Lam In. Still she protested.

"But, Mark, this is cold-blooded murder."

Her balding husband's face tightened, but his tone was gentle. "They're not being tortured, honey. Besides, this is the only way we can be sure each side will blame the other, not our people. If it makes you feel any better, remember the Khmer Rouge prisoners will be some of those teenage devils that are butchering helpless people in the camp every damn day."

The petite woman gave up, but her eyes told Mark she was still silently protesting.

Colonel Leung brought three trussed, gagged North Vietnamese regulars to the rendezvous. Then he surprised and pleased Charn Nol by requesting to accompany him on his raid. Charn Nol interpreted this as a combination gesture of confidence and "Let's see how good your people really are."

His own men, led by the redoubtable Mun Sin, welcomed the chance to show off. Their target was a large camp full of pathetic victims of the Angkha's insensate policy. As usual, the guards were bloodthirsty young teenagers, whom the veterans of Charn Nol's group hated and despised. The early predawn raid was a textbook model. Not a single one of Charn Nol's men was even scratched. Charn Nol himself dispatched the three North Vietnamese and put weapons in their hands before they withdrew. Colonel Leung's respect and approbation were obvious, despite the language barrier.

As planned, Lart Om's group appeared as Mun Sin's men fled. The "rescuers" Lart Om led found thirty-three of the camp garrison dead and another two dozen wounded. They also "found" the three dead Vietnamese. Lart Om brought them to area headquarters to make sure Thom Pan saw them himself. The fat commander was gorging himself, as usual, when Lart Om drove up. His reaction was indifference to the teenagers' casualties, and only slight interest in the bodies of the Vietnamese.

Mun Sin's men escorted four trembling teenage prisoners to a rendezvous with Leung's men that night. They also gave the Chinese two dozen rounds of 122-mm mortar ammunition they had unearthed from one of the dozen caches Charn Nol had located, for a future harassment raid on a large Vietnamese garrison, deeper inside Vietnam.

The success of the initial efforts was heartening, but both Mark and Charn Nol were increasingly frustrated by the obdurate refusal of the sects to meet with Charn Nol. This was increased rather than diminished when both sects reported successful provocation raids on both sides of the border in their areas, using the same tactics. This time, both Radio Phnom Penh and the renamed Ho Chi Minh City—formerly Saigon—Radio angrily denounced each other's "unprovoked atrocities." It also forced Thom Pan to send reinforcements to the south, giving Charn Nol's group an even larger area of responsibility and thus more freedom of action. But the sect problem still remained.

In Pattaya, Mark exhausted a dozen possible solutions on the stubborn sects, who stuck firmly to their belief that Mark was being used to lure them into a Khmer Rouge trap.

In desperation, Mark sounded Banchert out on a ploy he didn't want to try, but believed would work—jumping in himself, literally as a hostage, to guarantee Charn Nol's genuineness. Banchert's immediate reaction was negative.

"Mark, it's crazy. You're too old, and it's far too dangerous. There has to be another way."

"What way, Banchert? Christ, I'm not anxious to jump, believe me, but I know it'll work. Let me at least try it out on them and see the reaction."

With Banchert's grudging approval, Mark radioed his idea. The responses were as Mark had expected, but suggested another American with whom they had worked—because of Mark's age. Both sects were convinced that Mark was still working with CIA, and he had not disabused them of the idea. The fewer who knew Indian Movie was a purely Thai operation, the better; Mark and Banchert also doubted the Vietnamese would support the operation if they knew its real purpose—reducing pressure on the Thais. The northern Cao Dai group offered to secure an abandoned airstrip at Moc Hoa, to allow a plane to land to bring him out, but they doubted they could do so twice.

When Mark sounded out Gary, the reaction was violent. "Are you out of your goddamn mind? You'd bust your ass, or another leg, sure as hell! Forget it."

General Pranet was only slightly less forceful when Mark appeared at the PARU base and asked to make a couple of practice jumps. But after reminding the stocky officer of his own age, a year less, Pranet reluctantly agreed. Mark had been jogging with Pranee on the Pattaya beach since they had been there. At the PARU base, he doubled this, did leg and arm exercises for four days, and stiff, sore in every muscle, "exited an airplane in flight" twice on the fifth day. Despite the others' dire predictions, he made two good landings.

But on the second, he was confronted with a furious ninety-pound wildcat. Pranee had somehow heard about his real purpose in going to the PARU base across the gulf. When she finally calmed down slightly, she delivered her ultimatum: If Mark was going to go ahead with his crazy idea, she was coming with him! While Gary, Banchert, and General Pranet sat on the "sidelines" and cheered her on, Pranee never let up her attack. Finally Gary got into the act.

"Hell, Mark, let her try a jump from the training tower. She can't really hurt herself much. I'll bet just looking down and thinking about it will scare her out of it."

Gary lost the bet. Pranee, with only a few hours of practice falls, made three close to perfect tower jumps in the afternoon, and was starting to climb up again when Mark stopped her, defeated. The next morning she made two real jumps, and begged for more. Light as she was, she drifted down, and on her second jump, made a stand-up landing.

Her battle won, she coyly reminded the men that far from being a burden, her French, which Mark knew both sect leaders spoke but could not read or write, was unquestionably better than Mark's rusty Vietnamese, in spite of his recent brushing up. At this point, Chert, the basketball star turned pilot, attempted to parlay his linguistic ability into joining them. He spoke fluent Cantonese, learned at home and polished by four years of college in Singapore, where he also acquired Mandarin. Banchert reluctantly had to turn him down after a vain appeal to the prime minister. But the flight to drop Mark and Pranee was approved, as was a pickup flight, if Mark reported a landing possible.

The flight was scheduled. Charn Nol also protested at the risk, but accepted Mark's decision. The sects and Colonel Leung were alerted. The two would jump into the Cao Dai DZ closest to Charn Nol's position.

CHAPTER THIRTY-TWO

THE FLIGHT LEFT FROM CHANTABURI WITH CHERT AS co-pilot and Gary as captain. Gary had insisted that if Mark and his equally crazy wife were going to go ahead with "this damn fool idea," he, Gary would "at least see they hit the right DZ." The Chantaburi starting point would reduce the length of the flight and take them over Cambodia most of the way, avoiding the far more efficient Vietnamese radar until the last few minutes. In this Gary was correct; they detected no radar at all as they flew on, well under a thousand feet, once over the Cardamoms.

Gary's navigation, made easier from this angle by the wide, twisting branches of the Mekong, was nearly perfect. The drop to the Hoa Hao went without a hitch. To protect the location, Gary continued east at the same speed for five minutes before swinging about to the north and increasing to normal cruise. This course took them close to Thuy Dong and disaster.

Mark and Pranee were having their chutes given a final check by the PARU kickers when they felt and heard the sudden slam of ground fire that tore through the right wing, ripped the fuselage ten feet behind them, and then the ramp and tail. Encumbered by his chute, Mark forced himself up

254

the steps to the cockpit. Both pilots were fighting to keep the plane in the air.

"Can't hold her," Gary shouted. "Those were 14.7's and 37's. Right engine's had it, and the goddamn ramp's stuck! Bail out the side, Mark, all of you! We can't hold her."

"The DZ, Gary. We're almost there. Look, the signal."

"Jump, damn it; we're going in!"

Mark tried to obey, but his chute hung up as he turned. By the time he got loose, it was too late. The Caribou mushed into the tops of the trees, snapping them off, but also slowing it down. Mark saw Pranee and two kickers—backs to the bulkhead—and spun himself before they slammed into the ground. What was left of the landing gear collapsed. They bounced crazily across the DZ at an oblique angle. Then the left wing dug into the dirt and spun them to a stop.

Mark and Pranee were bounced around, but their main chutes in back and the chest reserves in front protected them. The two kickers beside them against the bulkhead were dazed but unhurt. Mark pushed Pranee and the two PARU out the gaping hole where the door had been, pounded his quick-release, and shed his chutes before trying to look in the cockpit. In the beam of his flashlight, he saw Gary coming down, backward, dragging Chert. He took Chert's feet as other hands also helped. Gary let go and grabbed the fire extinguisher, still in its holder.

"Right engine," Gary yelled. "Better get out. It's still burning."

Mark ignored him and began to crawl back to where he had last seen the other two kickers, struggling to free the jammed ramp. He found them jammed against it, dead. Crawling back, he used his knife to cut the tie-down straps on the cargo pallets and shouted in Vietnamese for help.

Gary's fire extinguisher only checked the burning fuel, but it gave them time to salvage almost half the bundles of cargo before the heat drove them back. Urged on by Gary's shouted warning, "She's gonna blow, keep going!" they were un-touched when the right wing tanks exploded, blowing the wreck into hundreds of pieces. In the flickering light the black-clad Cao Dai guerrillas shouldered the prepacked man-sized bundles of cargo while their leader helped Mark and Gary fashion a rude stretcher for the big co-pilot.

They walked at a fast pace over rough paths for two full hours without stopping. So far, there had been no sign of pursuit. The rear guard, who had dropped off over an hour before, had apparently nothing to do. Both Mark and Gary were puffing hard, but little Pranee might as well have been out for a stroll. She further surprised the two Americans by kidding them about their distress.

Two more long hours on the rough trails brought them to a thickly wooded area. Only a few hundred feet farther, the column halted. The Americans, Pranee, and the stretcher were guided forward to a slanting tunnel. They watched the stretcher ease down, and then followed on hands and knees. After several sharp turns, they emerged into a large, well-lit cavern. As they stood erect, Mark saw his old friend, the Cao Dai leader, Nguyen Chi, with hands outstretched in welcome. As Mark stepped forward, Gary, behind him, exclaimed, "Christ, it's Ho Chi Minh himself!"

The frail, wispy-goateed figure smiled at Gary's outburst, bowed, and spoke an obvious greeting before addressing Mark directly. At Mark's reply he led the way to a smaller room off the main cavern. Chert's legs dangled over the end of a table designed for Vietnamese. He was still conscious. A white-clad team showed the visitors the stitches they had taken over the big Thai's left eye. Mark translated their opinion that his already purple forearm was not broken, just badly bruised. From there, Nguyen Chi led them to another room, where they saw the new radio set up. Mark scribbled a message to Banchert, but before he could begin encoding it, Pranee took it, smiled sweetly, and told him to go on to more important work. Then she gracefully accepted a cup of steaming tea from the operator and thanked him in her musical French. The startled radio operator beamed as he replied with equal fluency. This brought an oath from Mark, and a quick question in Vietnamese. At the answer, Mark threw his hands in the air and shouted.

"I don't believe it! I just don't goddamn well believe it!"

"Don't believe what, Mark?" Gary asked.

"This simple son of a bitch reads and writes French, that's what!"

Two cups of cognac-laced tea later, Mark was still fuming—mostly at himself. When asked by Mark, "Why the hell didn't you say you could read and write French?" the abashed operator's answer had been typically Asian. "Nobody asked me."

CHAPTER THIRTY-THREE

THE NEXT MORNING, CLOSE TO NOON, GARY AND MARK awoke, stiff and sore from their bruises. Pranee, looking smug and pleased with herself, brought them hot tea and bowls of rice soup. It was obvious she was bursting to tell them something, but Mark, still furious at himself and the world, played dumb. Unable to contain herself, his doll-like wife gave in.

"After you two eat, you'd better clean up a bit. We're expecting guests in about an hour."

"Guests?" Gary asked.

"Yes, guests. Charn Nol and some of his men, and also some of the Hoa Hao leaders."

Then she read a message from Banchert congratulating them on their escape and asking what they planned to do next. Did they think a landing could still be attempted? It ended with a reassurance from General Pranet that he still had three planes left, and that Ho Chi Minh City Radio was already gloating about shooting down a *Cambodian* "spy plane."

Mark and Gary exchanged helpless glances. "Have we occupied Phnom Penh, too?" asked Gary, despite his own worry.

Pranee just smiled at them and walked away.

The long-thwarted meeting between Charn Nol and the two sect leaders was all Mark could have hoped for. Both the

Vietnamese liked the "let's you and him fight" approach, for the same reasons Banchert and his government had. If Cambodian and Vietnamese could be provoked into a renewal of their centuries-old antagonism, which French colonial rule had merely interrupted, they would have much less time to spend on the sects. Given respite in this way, the sects could enlarge their former areas of control throughout the delta and gain virtual autonomy.

Charn Nol strengthened his stature by giving the Vietnamese the locations of several old ammunition caches he remembered within their area.

They finished off with a discussion of using fishing boats to bring in ammunition and other vital supplies. As Mark and Charn Nol smiled their thanks to Pranee, whose French was far better than Mark's or Charn Nol's, it was agreed to attempt a trial shipment as soon as Mark got back to Thailand.

It had already been agreed that the unexpected guests, as Nguyen Chi referred to the downed crew, would go north with Charn Nol and wait until things quieted down in the Cao Dai area before attempting the pickup. Meanwhile, a number of provocations would be made well away from the abandoned field at Moc Hoa.

That same night, the crash survivors moved north, mostly by small boats, to Charn Nol's area and a waiting truck. All of them welcomed living aboveground in a real house. The damp, sunless caves had affected them all with instinctive claustrophobia.

The next few days flew by like mere hours. There was no letup in the pace Mark and Charn Nol set. Lart Om and Mun Sin confined their raids to the outer reaches, with considerable success. The sects also stepped up their activities, and the verbal warfare between the two Communist countries intensified. Prodded by a flock of angry orders from Phnom Penh, the lethargic Thom Pan bestirred himself long enough to give Mun Sin carte blanche orders to make reprisal raids where and whenever he could.

Two other major events filled the remaining time. The first was a tragic betrayal of Colonel Leung's highly successful group by his deputy. On their way back from blowing up a key bridge, and all but wiping out a North Vietnamese platoon, his men walked into an ambush. Only fourteen of sixty escaped. But they were quick to revenge themselves.

Led by their huge colonel, they surprised the traitor and his escort, killing them all. Then they made their way over to Charn Nol's area, with only the clothes they wore and their weapons. Colonel Leung was a tragic figure, pleading with Mark and Charn Nol to be given a chance to redeem himself and his unit.

This stunning, unexpected reversal came only three days after the crash survivors got to Charn Nol's area. The previous day, Gary and Dechar had burst in on Mark and the slender Charn Nol with great excitement.

"Mark, Charn, you won't believe this," Gary shouted, with hawk-nosed Dechar grinning broadly beside him. "That goddamn supply depot is just crawling with good stuff, Mark. Tanks, armored personnel carriers, self-propelled artillery, all kinds of ammo, and *beaucoup* drums of gas and diesel. It's a goddamn arsenal."

As Gary paused for breath, Mark laughed. "Okay, okay, Rommel. It's also been sitting out there since April 1975—damn near two years. Hell, it's a bunch of junk."

"Junk, my ass, old buddy. Hear that? That's an M-24."

As Mark, a World War II armored officer, followed Dechar and Gary around the cluttered depot, old lore came to the fore. Though he said nothing, Gary saw the familiar signs: rolling cigar and twirling finger in the hair. When he sprang his final surprise, he knew Mark was hooked.

Like a used-car salesman scenting a close, he led Mark into the tin-roofed, enclosed shop. Gary savored Mark's openmouthed amazement as he stared at three huge Russian T-34 tanks. The clincher was a dozen big wooden cases, half open, containing two new engines, three transmissions, and a flood of carefully weatherproofed spare parts of all kinds.

Mark barely touched the meal Pranee had prepared, while Charn Nol, still puzzled by the two Americans' sudden enthusiasm, asked the usually reserved pilot, "I don't still understand, Khun Gary. How can we use all those tanks and guns?"

"How? Friend Charn, you've been in the boondocks too long. Hell, man, with those babies we can blitzkreig our way across this whole damn country. What have the Khmer Rouge got to stop us? Damn all, from what I know about it. Those beauties are our ticket back home. Right, Mark?"

"Could be, Gary, could be. If we could get enough of them in decent shape . . ."

"But, Mark," Charn Nol asked, "even if they run very well, who can we use for driving, and using the guns—if we need them?"

"No big deal." Gary was pacing the room, unable to sit still as he continued, "Look, we got Dechar and his three men, the two PARU kickers, me and Chert. That's eight right there. You have nine drivers that I know of. Pushing a beat-up deuce-and-a-half all the way from the Thai border is a damn sight harder than driving an M-24 tank with hydromatic transmission.

There's nothing real difficult about those seventy-five-millimeter turret guns. Few hours practice on loading drill is all it takes. Same thing with the armored personnel carriers. Your guys already know machine guns. No problem there."

Charn Nol listened intently to Gary's enthusiastic sales pitch, but turned to Mark, who was poring over a map. "Khun Mark? What about it? Do you think we can really use the tanks and the APC's to help our plan?"

"Just working on that. I got a sneaky sort of idea we just might. First off, though, we've got to find out about some bridges. Tanks and APC's are fine, long as they don't have to swim any rivers. Anything over about a meter is swimming for a tank—unless you've got special snorkel gear, which they don't.

"Look here, all of you. I got this idea just now. Remember that old war movie, *Von Ryan's Express*? Bunch of Allied POW's stole a train in Italy, and made it to Switzerland. Well, if the bridges we need are in one piece, I think we might try using that armor instead of a train. And, even better, if we can hack it the way I'm thinking, it'll get the Viets and Cambodians really going at each other.''

The following afternoon, when Colonel Leung and his men reached Charn Nol's base with their pitiful story, the old supply depot was bustling with activity. After hearing Colonel Leung's tragic news, Mark asked him to go visit the depot—more to try to get Leung's mind off his personal tragedy than anything else. As soon as Leung saw the armored vehicles, his spirits seemed to lift. He poured out a torrent of Chinese, which Chert translated for Mark and Gary.

All of his men were quite familiar with the lumbering APC's, having used them extensively during the last months of the war. So Gary had fifteen new, eager, grim-faced recruits the next day. That evening, Mark received the information he had requested from Colonel Banchert. He plotted it on the overlay he had been laboring over for the past two days, and announced, ''Well, it looks like we can make it. Come over here; look at this.''

For the next quarter hour Mark's audience sat silent, almost spellbound, as he outlined his plan. When he finished there was a multilingual hubbub until Charn Nol spoke for all of them.

''Do you really think this plan can work, Khun Mark? I agree, my men and Leung's can probably learn enough to use the tanks and APC's for small raids; but this? It's at least four hundred kilometers—almost as far as from here to Thailand.''

''Yes, Charn, I do. You see, most people don't realize the amount of pure, unadulterated hell an armored column can raise—especially when it gets rolling behind the lines. People forget what Hitler's blitzkrieg was like! Not to mention what Patton's did to the Germans in France later on in forty-four.

''In our case, the shock effect should be even greater. Unless I'm greatly mistaken, neither the Khmer Rouge nor the Viets are even worrying about an armored attack. And who ever heard of guerrillas using armor? No way are they going to think our column is anything but the other side, pulling a fast one. And we'll do all we can to keep them thinking that way.

''That way I figure it, we'll have them both at each other's throats, and confused as hell, before we've gone a hundred klicks. Put yourself in their shoes for a minute. Old Thom Pan gets a panic report from Mun Sin here. Vietnamese tanks charging through the area from down here—to our south. Then they hit us and shoot up our people here, set fire to the dump, and barrel east across the border—back into Vietnam. With Leung's guys using the radio like hell in Vietnamese plain language all the way, what's he going to think? And report to the Angkha?

"Now, we make a big show of shooting up this side of the border on the way out—nobody there, but the Viets won't know that. Across the river, we head north at Go Dao Ha looking like a Viet task force. At dawn, nobody's going to be very bright-eyed and bushy-tailed. In less than two hours, we'll be back in Cambodia again. From there on we play it pretty much by ear. If our recon team up front finds only a few Khmer Rouge, we smash them up. If we hit a major garrison that looks too tough, we'll change sides, and be a Khmer Rouge column regrouping and fighting a delaying action. In that case, Mun Sin, Lart Om, and your other guys will make Cambodian noises.

"After we get past Snoul, we head for the Mekong and right up it to this road junction, south of Stung Treng. Then east till we hit Virachey and the airfield. The Viet Special Forces will take that—there's only a small garrison—and Pranet will pick us up. It's less than an hour to Thailand from there."

"I see how it might work," Charn Nol said slowly, "but do we have time enough to train all the men?"

"Good question. Gary, what do you figure it'll take?"

Gary thought for a long minute and said, "I'd like to have ten days, at least."

Mark nodded and turned to Charn Nol. "Reckon you and your people can keep on fooling Thom Pan for another ten days, Charn?"

"I think so, Khun Mark. I only worry that if the Angkha send him more men, some will be sent down here. That would be a real problem."

"Well, how about keeping on raising hell in the adjoining areas and leaving your own pretty quiet?"

Charn Nol's doubts diminished, and his confidence in the

plan grew as the work of reconditioning the vehicles, and training their crews, continued with no letup. Mun Sin visited Thom Pan's headquarters every day, reporting only minor "enemy" sorties in his area, and listening in mock anger as the reports of the attacks his men had made were passed on to him. From these, and the reports of other raids by the two sects farther south, it was clear the Vietnamese were getting the blame. The Angkha were very upset, Thom Pan told Mun Sin, and were sending large numbers of reinforcements to the south. Thom Pan was also promised more men, but no date had been given as yet.

This news worried both Charn Nol and Mark when Mun Sin reported it—a week after they had started working on Mark's plan in earnest. The following day, Mun Sin returned with more bad news. The reinforcements, three hundred men, were due two days hence. Despite Mun Sin's protestations, Thom Pan was sending half of them to beef up Mun Sin's command.

As a result, they decided to move up the date of planned operation to the following night. Mark went over their plans again and sent messages to the two sects and the Vietnamese Special Forces group, advancing their own parts in the operation to conform to the new schedule.

The two sect leaders had been given targets that Mark hoped would distract the Vietnamese, and also reduce their ability to pursue his column should the deception fail. The Cao Dai's target was the Vietnamese airfield at Trang Bang—the only one in the area with operational fighters and helicopter gunships. The Hoa Hao would blow the highway bridge east of Go Dao Ha, preventing any pursuit from the major Vietnamese garrison east of the bridge. The big airfield at Tay Ninh, which the column would have to pass, had no operational aircraft. The famous "Black Virgin" Mountain, which dominated the area, was deserted.

Mark had received confirmation of this critically important information from Banchert after the Cao Dai, to whom the mountain was sacred, had initially reported it.

The Special Forces reported equally welcome news about the airfield at Virachey. Half a dozen flyable T-28's and a total garrison of under one hundred, armed mostly with small arms. The Special Forces were maintaining continuing surveillance from the surrounding hills. Their main force was only a day's march away when Mark moved up the operation, so there was no problem at their destination.

The night before they were to start, Gary and Dechar handed Mark a grease-smeared list of the vehicles they had ready. From it, Mark made final dispositions. The column would consist of an advance guard, the main body, and a rear guard. Colonel Leung had insisted that he and his men all be in the advance group. To him Mark assigned one of the M-24 light tanks; one of the Russian T-34's, with its powerful 85-mm gun; an APC; and two jeeps.

Mun Sin would command the rear guard, and have another M-24, the remaining Russian tank, and a jeep. The main body, with Mark in front and Charn Nol in the rear, would contain the four self-propelled 105-mm howitzers, three more APC's, M-24's front and rear for Mark and Charn Nol, and the supply trucks with extra ammunition and fuel. In all, they would have room for the entire strength, nearly three hundred men, even though many would have to ride on the outside of all but the lead M-24.

Communications was the biggest hang-up. Only the M-24 light tanks had radios that worked. Mark doled out the four little URC-4 short-range sets to Colonel Leung, Mun Sin, Charn, and himself. Nar Rang, their fledgling artilleryman, would have to depend on his position directly in front of Charn Nol at the tail of the main body, while Lart Om would ride at the front with Mark. It wasn't a very good setup, Mark knew, but it would have to suffice.

CHAPTER THIRTY-FOUR

JUST BEFORE DARK ON THE NIGHT OF THE BREAKOUT, MUN Sin led two of the light tanks and two APC's across the border into Vietnamese territory. The previous night his men had silently wiped out the small Vietnamese outpost before they could give the alarm. It had been lightly held because the bridge on the Vietnamese side was blown where the road had crossed a major canal.

Mun Sin's tanks and APC's churned up the already poor road along the sloping bank of the canal, to give the impression the tracked vehicles had come ashore there. Then they retraced their route, and at eleven P.M., as scheduled, shot up their now deserted outpost, dropped off the bodies of three of the Vietnamese soldiers killed the previous night, and drove to the Phum Chiphu full tilt.

At three A.M., with the column formed up on the road outside the old supply depot, Mark and Charn Nol made a final check of each vehicle, while Mun Sin and his men placed another four dead Vietnamese in realistic positions.

At four A.M. the prepared demolitions on the little bridge west of town were set off. The tanks in the column each sent five rounds of high-explosive shells into selected targets. This was followed by a full belt from each machine gun. Additional demolition charges were lit as soon as the column had cleared the town. A radio message, which stopped in the middle as if interrupted, gave a fragmentary alert to Thom Pan. "Enemy tanks attacking, many of—"

Colonel Leung's advance guard shot up the deserted outpost at the border very convincingly, and slowed until the main body caught up. Visibility was a bare hundred meters when Colonel Leung's leading M-24 emerged out of the mist and smashed through the wooden black-and-white-striped gate on the Vietnamese side of the border. Clad in tanker helmet, goggles, and a tight-fitting Vietnamese army tunic, the colonel waved a Vietnamese flag and shouted carefully rehearsed phrases. The startled Vietnamese dove to the ditch as the armored vehicles and trucks roared past. Not a shot was fired.

Within minutes, still half-hidden by the combination of roiling dust and mist, the colonel repeated his performance as he plowed through Go Dao Ha, scattering soldiers and civilians alike. At the turnoff to Route 22, several of the inexperienced drivers misjudged the sharp corner and widened it by clipping the corners off the buildings.

Mun Sin had barely completed his report to Mark that he was clear of the town when Leung reported he was crossing a Bailey bridge over a deep canal. Mark had Pranee, now his command radio operator, pass the word to Mun Sin to blow it. Ten minutes later, Mun Sin reported it badly damaged, but not completely down.

They left the next two bridges alone; they were too short, and the streams appeared fordable. The next was an old iron-girder type.

Mark dropped off Sanit, his PARU kicker turned gunner, to make sure Mun Sin did a thorough job. He could handle the gunner job himself, if need be. Dropping the bridge behind them was vital to preventing pursuit.

Colonel Leung reported the bulk of Black Virgin Mountain in sight and slowed down again to allow the column to close up to the ten-meter interval Mark had ordered for running through towns. He wanted no chance of becoming separated where they would be most vulnerable. Then Sanit, sweat running reddish courses down his face, jumped back aboard from

Mun Sin's jeep and reported that both spans had been dropped. No pursuit would be possible from that direction.

Closed up, the column resumed its breakneck pace, scattering pedestrians and the odd vehicle to the ditches. The road didn't go through the heart of the big town but cut across a narrow strip of built-up streets. Here again, the debris from smashed carts and one ancient truck littered the road in the wake of the Chinese colonel's passage. Again Mark sweated in fear of fire from the numerous soldiers they passed, but saw only a few startled hands waving. On the left, as they passed the sprawling airfield, Mark saw a number of planes and at least a dozen Huey gunships. But no sign of activity. Mark hugged Pranee as Mun Sin reported to her that he had cleared the airfield and not a shot had been fired at them.

Mark's relief was short-lived. Only a few minutes after they got through Tay Ninh, Lart Om reported one of their precious fuel trucks had dropped out, and he was checking. Then Mun Sin reported his M-24 refused to go faster than forty KPH. Mark had Pranee tell him to tow the M-24 with his Russian tank until they were past the Bailey bridge he could see ahead of him. Then he told Gary to pull off just past it and wait. Lart Om already had the fuel truck in tow and pulled it off in front of Mark's tank.

A quick look at the truck showed it had torn a hole in the bottom of the crankcase. Mark ordered a hasty refueling and told Colonel Leung to hold up. Gary reported the M-24 engines out of synch; one was pulling the other. It would take about a half hour before the engines were cool enough to work on. Mark gave Mun Sin the M-24 Lart Om had been using. At Gary's suggestion, they decided to keep towing the sick one with the T-34. It had power to spare on level ground.

For the next twenty minutes Mark looked at his watch every thirty seconds, and listened for the sound of airplanes. His men poured fuel into their tanks till they overflowed and manhandled the remaining four 55-gallon drums onto other vehicles. Finally they moved out, and soon caught up with Colonel Leung's advance guard. Another twenty kilometers ahead lay Xom Mat and their reentry into Cambodia.

Halfway to Xom Mat one of the main body APC's threw a track and had to be abandoned. Its crew and riflemen further crowded the already overloaded remaining vehicles. Xom Mat seemed much smaller than Mark had remembered. They were through in minutes. Then Colonel Leung opened up on the unbelieving Khmer Rouge outpost across the border.

Mark heard the crack of the tanks' main armament and the chatter of their machine guns. By the time he got there, the handful of Khmer Rouge were already dead or hiding in the brush.

Ten kilometers inside Cambodia, at Phum Krek, Colonel Leung smashed into the town and was receiving only desultory return fire when the main body entered and quickly took care of the remaining defenders. Colonel Leung went on two kilometers west, to the small airfield, with the remaining APC's. As Pranee encoded a hasty message to Banchert, Mark heard firing from the direction of the airfield. Chert called Leung on the URC-4, then told Mark that resistance was over. Leung was shooting up the airplanes on the runway.

"Christ on a crutch," Mark shouted, "tell him to just run over their tails with his tanks! Don't waste ammunition! We're going to need it all before we get through."

Mark took the opportunity to refuel the remaining vehicles while they waited for Leung to complete his task of crippling all the Cambodian aircraft. Charn, his eyes dancing in a face streaked with rivulets of red where sweat had coursed the mask of dust they all wore, came up to them.

"Good luck, Mark. We found ten drums of diesel and two of gas. There are also two trucks, Gary and Dechar are looking at them now. And even better, the Khmer Rouge had a radio here, a voice one. How about sending them a message to confuse them?"

"Hey, great," Mark agreed. "What do you want to send?"

"I thought to report that a Vietnamese armored force is heading west—toward Kandol and Phum Na. Since we're going north, to Snoul, it may throw them off for a while."

"I'll buy it! I mean, okay, go ahead, Charn."

Colonel Leung led his group back into the town and reported all planes and choppers crippled. "Sorry about the shells, Colonel Mark. I forgot we could just smash them with tanks."

"No sweat. Now, better gas up your vehicles. Chert, I think it might save time if you ride with the Colonel; my Vietnamese isn't all that good. With you up there, I can just talk to you in English, and you pass it on. Okay, Colonel?"

Then Gary and his hawk-beaked shadow, Dechar, came up with more bad news. Another of their trucks was leaking transmission fluid as fast as they could pour it in; a second APC was shot, the radiator apparently plugged up tight. Despite the uncertain condition of the two Khmer Rouge trucks Charn Nol had found, they would have to use them to replace their own casualties.

Half an hour later, with smoke clouds from the four vehicles adding to that from the buildings, they headed east on Route 7 toward the town of Snoul. Mark hoped that when the Khmer Rouge found this out, they would conclude that his rampaging column was going to reenter Vietnam again. By this route, it wouldn't look as if he was going to go any deeper into Cambodia—until he actually reached Snoul and turned west, not east, on Route 13. Route 13 led to the Mekong River's east bank at Kratie, then north to where it intersected with their final turnoff to Route 19, east to the airfield at Virachey.

With the town behind them, the refreshing effects of dunking their heads in buckets of water were soon memories. The dousing of the hot armor, which had streaked the tanks and APC's with odd patterns, also proved only a temporary benefit. The broiling sun soon had the metal too hot to touch with bare skin. Mark was uncomfortably reminded of his early training days on the dusty, sunbaked plains of Fort Hood, Texas.

Here the countryside was different, diked rice paddies instead of featureless dried grass plain, but the remorseless sun was the same. Midway in the column, the frequent rinsings of the cloth he and Pranee used to mask their noses and mouths were an all but futile defense against the roiling red dust. It filmed their teeth with grit, dried the sweat, and cluttered their eyelashes and the corners of their eyes with red sludge. Despite their speed of nearly fifty kilometers, the fine red dust and foul exhaust fumes clung to the column like the cartoon character's "cloud of doom."

In an effort to tear his mind away from the all-pervasive dust and the mind-numbing roaring vibration of his speeding tank, Mark tried to conjure up memories of the lunging armored columns of his wartime days in France and Germany. That had been hot and often dusty, too, but nothing like this. And, he reminded himself grimly, here they were all alone in a hostile country, entirely dependent on their own ability to survive. Nostalgia was useless. The breeze of their passage seemed to have forgotten that evaporation is supposed to cool.

Despite the discomfort, Mark continued to perch, legs dangling over the edge of the hatch, and scan the brassy sky through the dust cloud. Pranee occasionally popped up, head barely above the hot metal of the hatch, but never for long. The dust was winning the battle. It had gradually infiltrated their nostrils, drying the natural mucus, successive waves moving deeper until they caused a sneeze. The involuntary sudden inhalation preceding a sneeze sucked in more dust, deeper into both nose and throat. In a relentless cycle, sneezing caused the eyes to water. The dry, bitter, musty-tasting dust sopped up the tears as they tried to clear the eyeballs and formed crust that almost glued their eyelashes together. Finally Mark gave in and donned the old, cloudy goggles. Before the dust had built up to where it clogged his eyes, they would have reduced his vision; now the scratches on the lenses were barely noticeable.

Despite his worry about attack from the air, and all his vigilance, it was Mun Sin who spotted the planes first. They were propeller-driven A1E's coming from their right rear. Cursing himself, Mark alerted the others on the little URC-4.

"Keep on going; they're Viets. Maybe they'll leave us alone. If they start down, get off the road and spread out."

As Mark was speaking, Sanit, the handsome but boyish PARU kicker, opened the left turret and manned the .50-caliber AA machine gun. Then Pranee pounded Mark's knee to get his attention and shoved the radio at him.

"The planes, Mark. They're calling us, I think."

She was right. To Mark's relief, and amazement, the pilot was asking for targets! Their deception was working! The Vietnamese planes thought the column was their own. Mark held the radio a little away from his mouth, to allow background noise to help disguise his accent.

"Good to have you with us. Targets are airfield and any tanks in Snoul, repeat Snoul. Is anyone following us?"

"Read airfield, tanks, Snoul. Nothing behind you, tank leader."

With that, the lead plane dipped its wings, and the rest followed it ahead and to the left of the column. In minutes Colonel Leung reported the big, heavily armed A1E's were ripping Snoul with bombs and rockets. With the town in sight, the dust-blanketed men in the column came to life as the vehicles closed up. Black smoke clouds rose from the airfield to their right and from the town itself as the Vietnamese A1E's made a final pass, raking the buildings with their machine guns. Then Leung's guns took over. Mark could see the tracers from the turret .50's and .30's arcing toward the first buildings, and the orange and black splashes of the main guns.

Despite the unexpected air support—or, Mark thought grimly, possibly because of it—they met their first serious resistance. The black-clad Khmer Rouge used their machine guns, a pair of rocket launchers, and a mortar on the column with deadly effect. It took all of the main body of riflemen under Lart Om and Charn Nol, plus Mark and Lart Om's M-24's, to wipe out the fanatical defenders. Even though greatly outnumbered and outgunned, they cost precious time—nearly an hour. Mark's men also suffered. Nine riflemen were killed and an equal number wounded, one badly. Leung's M-24 lost its left track and driver from a rocket hit.

While mopping up was still going on, Mark sent another message to Banchert, including the still incredible air support from the Vietnamese. Pranee also decoded an incoming message, which made them both laugh, cracking their dust masks.

DO NOT, REPEAT NOT, UNDERSTAND YOUR ACTIONS, BUT THEY CAUSING MAJOR CRISIS BETWEEN VIETNAM AND CAMBODIA. HAVE REPORTS HEAVY FIGHTING WELL SOUTH OF YOUR LAST POSITION. SPECIAL FORCES READY LAUNCH THEIR ATTACK. KEEP ME ADVISED. BANCHERT.

As Mark doused his head in a bucket of water Gary had brought, the pilot-turned-tank-driver laughed with him. "What did you tell him, Mark?"

"Well, not exactly everything, Gary. I figured what he didn't know, he wouldn't have to lie to his bosses about. I told him we figured we could stir up enough trouble back down in the Parrot's Beak to allow us to make a break for it overland and reach Virachey for evacuation. But I didn't go into any details."

"Like playing Afrika Korps, with you as Rommel? Well, we sure have stirred up a bunch of trouble, from the looks. Those Vietnamese air force jocks have really put the fat in the fire, unless I miss my guess."

"That was a hell of a lucky break, Gary, but now we have to go west. I'm afraid the next planes we see will be Khmer Rouge."

With resistance ended, Mark assembled his sweaty, dusty leaders and told them the gist of Banchert's message. Then he warned them again to keep a sharp lookout for airplanes, particularly to the west. "And remember the air raid drills we practiced. If we disperse off the road fast, we'll make lousy targets. Keep those AA machine guns manned and ready—but don't shoot till I tell you, or you hear me start. Now, let's go see what Kratie looks like!"

Their vigilance went unrewarded until they were less than twenty-five kilometers from the Mekong and the major town of Kratie. En route, they blew two bridges behind them after meeting only ineffectual resistance at each. The short firefights cost them three of Charn Nol's riflemen riding with

Leung's advance party, and two of Leung's men wounded.
But over two dozen Khmer Rouge defenders lay sprawled in
their shattered roadblocks.

These brief interruptions were an almost welcome relief
from the mind- and sense-deadening beat of their engines and
the hostile dust and sun.

Long past the second bridge, the rugged rear-guard leader
gave the first warning. Just as he reported, the road made a
sharp turn, exposing the column to full view of the screaming
F-5 jet fighter paralleling the column a bare five hundred
meters to the right. Mark gulped as his eyes confirmed Mun
Sin's report—the plane was Vietnamese, not Cambodian. On
cue, Vietnamese colors began to wave from every vehicle.
The F-5 was one of six and, apparently satisfied, zoomed
back up as Mark took the radio from Pranee.

"Tank leader, do you read?" came the welcome call in
Vietnamese.

"Flight leader, read you. Target is Kratie, repeat Kratie.
Anything behind us or in front also?"

"Nothing behind you. Will sweep road in front and then
Kratie. Good luck."

Mark watched the sleek fighters with the wingloads of
rockets pull up and ahead. Then the road veered back and
their maddening dust cloud again smothered the column. The
sound of the planes had barely died when Leung reported he
was engaging a roadblock up ahead. By the time Mark came
in sight, Leung's T-34 was pushing the two old trucks that
had blocked the road out of the way.

He had killed eight of the defenders before the others ran,
but he had lost four more killed and three wounded, two with
stomach wounds. As Pranee and Leung's medic dressed the
wounds and administered shots of pain-killing morphine,
Mark and Charn Nol talked.

Both realized that all chance of surprise was gone. The
roadblock gave mute evidence. The F-5's would probably destroy any Khmer Rouge aircraft, but they couldn't eliminate
the rest of Kratie's defensive forces. Despite the need for
haste, Mark asked Charn Nol if he wanted to bury his dead.

"No, Khun Mark, they will forgive us. They wouldn't want to delay us, especially now the enemy is alerted."

"What do you think we should do, Charn? Hit them like we did at Snoul?"

Before Charn Nol could answer, Mark's radio interrupted. It was Chert, relaying more bad news from the bridge Leung's advance group had reached. The two jeeps, waving Cambodian flags, and now filled with Charn Nol's men instead of Leung's had gotten across the bridge, then opened up on the dozen Khmer Rouge on the far side. Too late, they saw another squad hidden in brush along the wide, steep-banked river. One of them had closed the circuit on the demolition charges. One span of the old iron girder bridge was a twisted ruin.

Fifteen minutes later they stood staring at the wreckage. Mark walked to the edge and his heart sank. The twenty-foot span might as well have been two hundred feet! The near bank sloped down at a reasonable angle. Mark could see, from the men testing the depth, that the river was barely three feet deep in the middle of the forty-foot-wide stream. But the far bank was a different matter. Undercut by flood waters, it rose over twenty feet high!

Back on the bank, Leung and Chert gloomily reported possible fords for the vehicles on either up- or downstream sides. Looking up, Mark suddenly tensed as he saw the dusty vehicles. Old memories came to sudden life as he spun and shouted. "Gary, Charn, Mun Sin! Get those goddamn tanks spread out! Everything off the road—fifty meters apart. Start cutting brush. Get them camouflaged."

Furious at himself for forgetting, even momentarily, the prime rule of survival against air attack, Mark ran, sweating and panting, from one vehicle to another. Some could be at least partly hidden in the head-high brush or under trees along the riverbank itself. The others had to use brush. Then Gary picked up the high whine of approaching jets. They sprinted, both puffing hard, to Mark's tank and the radio. Pawing his dripping face with a muddy cloth, Mark picked up the radio.

"Tank leader," the radio crackled, "can we help you?"

Mark pressed the mike button, frustration plain in his reply. "Not unless you've got a goddamn bulldozer. The bridge is blown!"

Then they all gasped as they realized Mark had spoken in English! Mark pounded his fist against the burning-hot side of the tank as they heard the click of the pilot's mike switch, and then an ominous pause before the radio spoke again. "Sorry, old man. We're fresh out of bulldozers. Would you believe a little precision bombing?"

The sweat-stained group looked at each other in incredulous wonder—the answer had been in colloquial English!

Mark gulped, shrugged his shoulders in resignation, and answered, again in English. "Thanks, but no thanks. Appreciate the offer but—"

The pilot interrupted, and they heard, "Sorry, old man, company coming. See you later?"

The F-5's began steeper climbs. Then Gary spotted the reason.

"God Almighty! T-28's. Those jets'll murder them!"

They did. In less than two minutes all six of the old propeller trainers had been turned into pillars of greasy black smoke by the F-5's rockets and guns. Then the English-speaking pilot came back.

"Poor sods. They never seem to learn. Whoever you are, thanks for the target practice, and good luck. Oh, yes, that tank east of the road, by the trees—sticks out something awful."

The still barely half-believing group strained their blood-shot eyes and watched the shining jets disappear. Mark suddenly pounded Gary on the back, startling the rest. "Christ, Gary, he's right! We can blow that damn bank down ourselves!"

Charn Nol's and Mun Sin's grimy faces flashed white teeth as they understood and followed Mark to the APC with the rest of their demolitions hoard.

"Good deal," Mark exclaimed as he lifted the protecting tarp. "Six . . . no, seven cratering charges. Okay, Mun Sin, four should be enough, and about six bags of plastic."

The thirty-pound cratering charges dug jagged holes in the dry clay. Filled with plastic and tamped by dozens of bare feet, the second charge shoved two thirds of the overhanging bank outward—where it collapsed into a rough natural ramp. Twenty minutes later Gary bulled his squat T-34 up the incline, and Dechar's men began rigging a steel tow cable to the first truck.

CHAPTER THIRTY-FIVE

WAIST-DEEP IN THE SHALLOW RIVER, THE BLACK-CLAD MEN swarmed to help rig each of their precious vehicles to the tow cable, frolicking like children in the cooling water. Mark, Charn Nol, and Mun Sin had to settle for pouring buckets over themselves as they leaned over a jeep and discussed their next move.

Mark bent over his map, dripping water that made reddish-brown smears as he mopped at it ineffectually. There was a possible bypass road; no one knew what condition it was in. The map showed it to be a track or trail running through swamp and rice fields for over twenty kilometers before it joined the main road, north of Kratie. Mark jabbed a dirty finger at it and scowled.

"I don't trust the damn thing. Rather take our chances hitting Kratie. Roads are dry, but trails through swamp and paddy . . . barely a month since the rains stopped . . . and it'll be fully dark in a couple of hours—we'd bog ourselves down for sure."

Colonel Leung spoke for the first time. "Colonel Mark, I have an idea, very risky, but it worked here, at the bridge. Send only jeeps and trucks with Commander Charn's men to Kratie. If they come in with their flags waving, like my jeeps, they should make it. Once the Khmer Rouge in Kratie see that they really are Cambodians, that danger will be over."

Mark and the two Cambodians were listening closely as the husky Chinese colonel paused.

"And then?" Mark urged.

"They tell the Khmer Rouge in Kratie that their own tanks are delaying the enemy at this bridge, here, until dark. Try to get them to agree to defend the road into Kratie, to allow our tanks to get farther north, to the bridge here at this river. Kampi, just north of the town."

The Chinese shrugged and smiled apologetically. "I know this means Charn Nol's people taking the risks, which I would prefer for myself, but . . ."

Mun Sin's teeth bared in a wolfish grin. The undemonstrative leader patted the taller man's arm as Chert finished translating.

"I like it. We are also Khmer Rouge in everything but our hearts. Why not? We even have wounded men to prove how well we fought the Vietnamese."

Charn Nol and Mark exchanged glances. Charn Nol answered for both. "It could work! Mun Sin has already fooled Thom Pan, in broad daylight. Now, with everything confused, his chances should be even better. Even if the people in Kratie do get suspicious, it won't be right away. Our men will be ready to fight at all times—they won't."

Mun Sin briefed his men quickly. They decided to make things even more realistic by sending the self-propelled 105's with him—to set up defensive positions just outside the town and fire a few rounds back the way they had come. The rest of the armored vehicles would wait until they received the go-ahead from Mun Sin by radio.

With Mun Sin leading their three jeeps, wounded men in each, the trucks followed a few minutes behind—with Charn Nol and Lart Om. Five minutes later, Nar Rang and his lumbering SP-105's left the others to wait.

While Pranee monitored the radio, Mark, Gary, and Dechar paced nervously until the last afterglow of the sun began to fade. Then they followed, using their headlights to keep from running off the road in the dust cloud they generated.

As agreed, Mark halted the column about three kilometers from Kratie. During their advance, the sound of Nar Rang's guns and the soft whispering of the shells overhead had been reassuring evidence their daring plan was working, so far. Final confirmation came when a jeep, headlights blazing, sped towards them and the radio came to life.

Charn Nol was in the jeep, grinning broadly as he jumped out.

"It is working very well, Khun Mark."

As the lanky ex-basketball star translated to the relieved Chinese, Charn Nol said, "I think it was our wounded men who convinced them at first. The rest went very well. The shooting by Nar Rang was very good, too. There is only one problem, but I had to agree. The Khmer Rouge commander has agreed to slow the 'enemy' down with roadblocks and Molotov cocktails, *if* we leave him one tank and one of Nar Rang's guns. I told him yes. Otherwise, he would insist on going north with us. I'm sorry, Khun Mark."

"No reason to be, Charn. Hell, we would probably have lost a damn sight more if we'd had to try to fight our way through."

"No sweat, Charn," Gary broke in. "Mun Sin's M-24 is on its last legs anyway. Those damn engines are out of synch again. I'll get Dechar to pick the worst of the SP's. We can cram the guys on the others, somehow."

Mark's face relaxed for the first time in hours. "What do we do now, Charn? Just barrel through?"

"I think not too quickly, Khun Mark. My men are preparing a meal—you may have forgotten, but no one has eaten since last night. It will look better this way. Also, we have to refuel anyway."

Half an hour later, Mark was shoveling rice and curry with one hand and holding his map under the jeep headlight with the other when he heard the deep roar and clank of a tank approaching from the town.

To keep inquisitive locals from investigating too closely,

they had parked the armor on the edge of town, facing to the rear. Mark craned to see what was going on. Mun Sin had already driven into town with their gift M-24 and SP. The oncoming tank didn't sound like either. Then he saw why. A long, drooping gun with the distinctive muzzle baffle identified the oncoming tank. It was the 76-mm of an old Sherman M4E8! The high, sloping frontal armor was unforgettable.

In the glare of headlights, Mark saw Pranee standing beside the commander's hatch and what appeared to be a small boy peered from the coaming. Dechar's greasy face was split in a huge grin above the driver's hatch. Mark got the story in dribs from an excited Pranee and Dechar, while the little boy clung to Dechar's hand with both of his.

Pranee had been asked to bring Dechar to the edge of town, to look at the tank Mun Sin's men had spotted parked behind a shed. According to the local garrison, the tank wouldn't start. They had used up a precious battery trying, then given up. The little boy, who spoke, amazingly, English mixed with Cambodian, told them it only needed a new battery.

Dechar soon learned, by sniffing the fuel tank, that this wasn't the only problem. On the sponson, neatly stenciled, he saw, FIGHT POLLUTION—USE UNLEADED GASOLINE. He pointed out the stencil with his flashlight. The weary, grim-faced ex-colonel doubled up in real laughter. Wiping his streaming eyes, Mark was still laughing as Dechar explained.

"The little boy say they fill the tanks with white gas today. They never use for almost a year, but the boy, he take care and keep from rust. He cannot be soldier; his leg is broken and not fixed by doctor, so he limp bad. But they let him take care for the tank. Very clean, Khun Mark, and the engine still good. After I drain out gasoline from tanks and lines, put in diesel, and listen how it runs."

Mark struggled up the steep front and peered inside. His flashlight roved as he confirmed the PARU mechanic's statement. The fresh white paint and spotless metal was in sharp contrast to the hastily half-cleaned interiors of Mark's tanks. Gary had joined them and was in the turret exclaiming at the condition.

"Christ, Mark, this thing's in better shape than any of ours—the goddamn intercom even works. Let's take this baby with us!

"Oh, yeah, here's a present from Mun Sin."

Mark accepted a cool bottle of beer with a happy gasp of surprise.

"Got a whole damn case," Gary added. "Would you believe? How about it, Mark? We take this baby for us?"

Dechar and Gary soon replaced the two .30-caliber machine guns and the .50 AA turret gun that the Khmer Rouge had stripped from the "useless" tank. They had left the full load of 76-mm shells, having no use for them. The little boy went off with Dechar in the jeep to bring back the additional shell crates he had kept in the shed. Charn Nol and Mun Sin joined Gary. While Nar Rang's crews fired a final salvo at the "Vietnamese," they mounted up to leave. Mun Sin reported the local commander was well pleased with the gift armor. "But I will be surprised if they don't blow themselves up when they try to fire the guns. Those children are unbelievably bad. They won't listen to anything—they think they know it all. But never mind, we can go."

As Mark scrambled up the side of the old Sherman, he stopped short when he saw the boy's head sticking out of the right-hand driver's hatch. Reaching down, he swung the little figure up and was putting him down when the child erupted.

"You no good goddamn mothafuka bastah!"

Mark nearly lost his balance as the screaming, weeping figure pounded at him with little fists and kicked with his good leg, mouthing an endless stream of obscenities. Mark set the boy's feet down on the deck as he screamed. "I hope Charlie shoot you ass off, goddamn no-good GI mutha!"

This, plus Gary's and Pranee's entreaties, forced Mark to deposit the little figure back in the assistant driver's seat and mutter, "All right, all right! But he's going to get his own little ass paddled good if I hear any more language like that. Hear me, you?"

"My name Mike," the little boy shouted. "All GI know me. I no fuck up, keep tank very clean. No?"

The tanks followed Mun Sin's jeep through the north edge of Kratie without incident. They arrived at a bridge over Kampi and crossed, before halting to resume their former formations. As soon as they got going again, with Colonel Leung's depleted advance guard beefed up by an APC and additional men from Mun Sin's group, he blew the old bridge and followed. For the next two hours they averaged a steady forty kilometers, tearing through the little river villages before the inhabitants were fully awake. After swinging east again at Kent Prasat, they blew a small bridge over a steepsided stream before Colonel Leung reported he had reached the road junction at Sre Shov, and wanted to try a trick to throw any pursuers off the track.

Mark and Pranee transferred to a jeep and joined the big Chinese colonel at the road junction. The idea was simple. Mark approved it immediately. The road they were on continued east and eventually reached Vietnam. Their route was to the north, just short of Stung Treng, and then east. Leung's idea was to continue east, past their actual route, to a small side road two kilometers ahead, then cut off and rejoin the main north road. After the column passed, they would mine the turnoff area. In the dark, the ruse would cause any pursuers to go past the junction and, following the tracks, turn off into the mines.

From there they continued north another hour, to the edge of the village of Prek Kandie, less than twenty kilometers from the final turnoff onto Route 19. Colonel Leung's group had to slow to a crawl as they negotiated a sharp turn and eased warily over a creaking wooden bridge. The village, like all the other ones they had passed since leaving the river, was deserted. As the big colonel used his flashlight to guide his vehicles across the rickety bridge, his men ripped planks from nearby buildings and laid them across the worn decking to strengthen it, as Mark had taught them. Leung was too engrossed in the work and deafened by the growl of engines to hear the approach of a vehicle from the north.

His alert men were not. The four occupants of the battered Datsun pickup were seized and disarmed before they could fire a shot. Had Leung's column been moving, it would have been much a different story, but they were parked, lights out and engines off, except for the tank crossing the bridge. As a result, the four Khmer Rouge scouts drove right into the arms of Colonel Leung's men.

They were talking freely when Mark and Charn drove up in the Sherman. While their column edged across the hastily reinforced bridge, the prisoners' stories forced a gloomy council.

The Khmer Rouge were not only expecting them at Stung Treng, but also well before! They were busy digging in front of the road junction where Route 19 turned off. The prisoners reported two "big" bulldozers at work digging an antitank ditch, and at least eighteen tanks, including eight or nine big ones—probably Russian T-34's—positioned behind the mound of dirt from the trench. There were also a number of 14.7-mm and 37-mm antiaircraft multiple towed-mount guns in place, manned by "several hundred" soldiers. While Mark doubted the number of soldiers, the armor was more than three times their own strength. The only bit of heartening information was the prisoners' confirmation that the low hills to the right of the road, two or three kilometers short of the enemy position, were as depicted on Mark's stained map. The prisoners also reported the bridge in front of the position was prepared for demolition, but the stream was almost dry and fordable—they had done so on their way south. The low hills, on the part closest to the road, were occupied by an outpost of unknown size and, they had heard, "some big mortars."

Mark swore quietly and fervently as his eyes translated the contour lines depicting the hill mass. The slopes appeared gentle enough for tanks, rising barely two hundred feet from the level of the road and extending several kilometers to the east and north, where Route 19 cut right through them.

That's the only way out, he thought. Just hope the trucks can make it through there without towing. Then he addressed the anxious, waiting group.

"Looks like our only hope is through those hills. If the

prisoners are right, the enemy thinks we're heading for Stung Treng—I hope so. Way I see it, we've got to make them keep thinking we are, while we get most of our people across the hills to Route 19, over here.

"My idea is to make a show at hitting their roadblock head-on, using our tanks and shelling the hell out of them with the SP's. But first the 105's have to hit the outpost and mortars on the near end of the ridge, until the riflemen can clean them out. Then we run all the trucks and APC's across to Route 19. Soon as they get there, the SP's go over and set up to cover our tanks—when they break off and move. Oh, yeah, the first bunch that gets to Route 19 will have to keep going east to that big bridge, secure it, and get it ready to blow it behind us . . . if we get that far.

"It's going to be a real bitchkitty, but I can't see any other way out. Can any of you?"

None could. Mark and the other leaders spent the next hour briefing their men and shuffling the column into the new formation. Colonel Leung packed the captured pickup with his remaining men and one of the prisoners as an unwilling guide. He had insisted on trying this as a possible way to surprise and wipe out the outpost on the hill. The rest of the column followed ten minutes later. All the tanks in front, behind Mark's Sherman, then the three SP's, followed by the APC's and the trucks.

Mark saw the faint loom of the low hills to the right after they rumbled over a small concrete culvert the enemy had curiously left undamaged, even though the almost dry stream would have only delayed the column slightly. He had slid down inside the turret to check his map when Pranee shoved the radio to his ear and Chert reported they had captured the six-man outpost without a shot. Leung had gone after the mortars.

Mark had Gary pull off to the side until the first of the SP's came up. He jumped up with Nar Rang and led them off to the right while Mun Sin continued up the road. Nar Rang's men amazed the worried American with their ability to get their guns lined up and ready for firing on the compass bearing Mark had given them.

Handing the bandy-legged little sergeant his URC-4 radio, Mark again cautioned, "Remember to check those fuse settings. Airbursts first, and until I tell you to change, got it?"

As Mark jumped into the waiting jeep, he heard the slam of tanks guns up ahead. On the road again, he climbed back on the Sherman as Gary gunned it forward. Pranee told him Leung had not only taken the two big 122-mm mortars, but was moving them to a new position where he could turn them on the roadblock. They swung off the road, following the pickup's tire tracks. Mark pounded the turret happily as he saw the wheeled vehicles should have little trouble on the hard, rutted surface.

As he directed Gary off the rough track toward the crest of the brush-covered little hill, he saw the first of the trucks making the climb easily. Then, in front, he saw the stabbing flashes from the enemy tanks at the roadblock, and the orange blobs as his own tank's shells burst, or, too seldom, a red glow as they hit an enemy tank. Using Charn Nol's radio, he told Nar Rang to fire, and watched, binoculars ready, for the first bursts. Over and to the left—a mere hundred yards.

Pranee repeated his correction. "Short, right a hundred. Okay, honey, tell him ten rounds from each gun—that'll give the bastards something to think about!"

It did. So did Leung's big 122's when they joined in only a minute later. The fire from the roadblock slacked to a few scattered rounds from the enemy tanks and occasional wild streams of tracer from a couple of the antiaircraft mounts.

"Okay, Pranee, tell Nar Rang to give them ten rounds of ground bursts, same setting."

Mun Sin broke in to report one of his M-24's blown up by a direct hit and his own T-34 disabled but still firing.

"Get her up the hill, Gary. Time we gave them some help. Easy now . . . Okay, hold it."

In the telescopic sight, Mark picked up one of the only partially dug-in quadruple 14.7's and hit it with his first round of HE. Telling Sanit, the loader, to give him armor-piercing shells, Mark saw his second round throw dirt in front of an M-24 before having Gary back down out of sight and move well to the left. For the next ten minutes, moving after every shot, Mark got solid hits. Low down between the tracks on a T-34. It exploded in a ball of flame. Then another on a T-24 turret, which must have gone completely through, because there was no flame.

Charn Nol breathlessly announced all the trucks had reached the road, and the APC's were directly behind them. Chert also reported Leung and his men had used all their ammunition and were heading for the road and the bridge beyond.

Mark had Nar Rang keep firing with one gun and send the other two across the hill to join the others. Mun Sin had lost an M-24, which left them only one, and the two remaining Russian T-34's. Mark ordered him to pull out and get to Route 19 to cover Mark and the remaining SP.

He and Gary continued to play their deadly game of hide-and-seek, trying to keep the still active enemy from reacting to the outflanking move Mark felt they must suspect, if not already know about. All in the Sherman's turret were gasping and choking from the powder fumes by the time Pranee relayed the message that Nar Rang's two SP's were in position.

"Okay, Pranee," Mark gasped, "tell him ten rounds airburst. Fast as they can. Then ten more half-speed ground bursts. How about Mun Sin?"

Mark jumped, frightened, as he felt a hand on his shoulder, and looked up to see the burly figure peering at him.

"I stay here," the stolid Mun Sin said. "You go ahead."

Reluctantly, Mark nodded and told Gary to back down and head for the road. Mark's feeling the enemy had guessed his maneuver received frightening confirmation as the remaining SP, thirty yards ahead of him, exploded in angry red flames.

Knowing there could be no survivors, Mark directed Gary in a wide detour around the flaming wreck. Reaching the road, they got more bad news. Another truck had given out after nearly reaching the road. Its load of ammunition was quickly loaded into the almost empty tank storage racks.

Pulling into the shelter of an outcrop, Mark sent the still eager Nar Rang down the road to take up a covering position where the road swung down the hill mass and out into the flat country. The trucks and APC's were already across the river by the time he reported he was in position.

Mun Sin had also reached the road, despite a direct hit on the sloping turret, which had gouged a two-inch-deep gash. Mun Sin and his two turret men had been sprayed with bits of metal, and their noses were still oozing blood when they got to the road.

Mun Sin refused to give up his rearmost position as they drove east as fast as they could. Approaching the SP's, Mark pulled off the road and told Nar Rang to get rid of the rounds in the guns by firing them, and pull out. Thirty minutes later, Mark watched several enemy rounds land harmlessly short as the bridge over the clearly unfordable river collapsed into it.

The seemingly tireless Colonel Leung was already halfway up the seventeen-hundred-foot hill mass and nearing the village of Bung Lung, where the road descended to the valley and Virachey Airfield. With him were the remaining M-24 tank, two APC's plus a pair of jeeps—all jam-packed with men. With Mark were the two tough Russian T-34's, two SP's, the remaining APC, and five trucks. After an hour, and almost fifty kilometers of level going on good road, they began climbing along the side of a steep ridge. By the time they reached the top, half the trucks were boiling over and the other vehicles threatening to. Mark halted them. They wearily filled their fuel tanks to lighten the trucks.

They made very good time down the hill and across the little valley. But the next hills were steeper than the first. A quarter of the way up they found one of Leung's APC's with one track off and a dozen men who hadn't been able to squeeze aboard Leung's remaining vehicles. Mark also received a welcome answer to the hasty radio message he had sent Banchert before they attacked.

REPORT POSITION SOONEST. FIGHTING CONTINUING
FROM YOUR AREA NORTH TO SNOUL. FRIENDS RECON

SHOW HEAVY ENEMY FORCES WITH ARMOR SOUTH
STUNG TRENG AT JUNCTION NINETEEN. CAN YOU BY-
PASS?

SPECIAL FORCES REPORT VIRACHEY AIRFIELD SECURE,
BRIDGE USABLE, HEAVY FIGHTING AT FORT AND TOWN.

EVAC PLANES STANDING BY BASE UNIFORM AND XRAY.
BOSS REFUSES FIGHTER SUPPORT.

BANCHERT

Mark felt his stomach churn sickeningly as he reread the
second part about Virachey. They had to get through the town
and past the fort to reach the field! The river was unfordable—certainly for vehicles, probably for men on foot. He
made light of the new threat and sent the rest on while he
tried to contact Colonel Leung. After ten minutes he gave up.
The URC-4 was strictly line of sight; Leung must be masked
by the hills in front. Half an hour later Gary caught up with
the shrunken column.

More trouble. One of the two SP's had thrown a track; all
the trucks were boiling over, despite the chill night. Mark
opened his tattered map. They were about thirteen hundred
feet, and less than three kilometers from Bung Lung. But it
was two-thirty, barely three hours till dawn. Mark's stomach
griped again as he forced the thought of Khmer Rouge planes
from his mind. While Charn Nol, Mun Sin, and Lart Om
packed the men from the SP onto the remaining vehicles,
Mark finally contacted Leung.

Leung had taken the few Khmer Rouge in the Bung Lung
with only two casualties, both serious. He had seen the tracers
down in the valley and was already halfway down. The road
was very bad, he said, but he expected to join the fight in
another twenty minutes.

Mark felt only slightly relieved as they attacked the last
steep incline. Pranee shared his fears; she was the only one
who knew the full contents of Banchert's message.

It was almost two hours before they reached the silent village and found Leung's wounded, with two men guarding
them. From the village, Mark scanned the valley with his

binoculars. After two long minutes he saw no sign of firing. There were a number of fires in the village, but no tracers or exploding shells. Relieved, he turned back and joined the little column. Gary and Pranee were working on Leung's two wounded men. Lart Om was checking the other wounded. With Leung's two new casualties, they now had thirty-six. One of the stomach cases had died, silently, on the long climb.

As he walked among the still-steaming vehicles, Mark was suddenly aware that not only were they in bad shape, the men were as well. Only a few were mechanically going through the motions of topping off fuel tanks or shoving awkward four-hundred-pound full drums off the trucks.

The rest sat or lay on the ground in a semistupor. Mark's sudden concern turned to alarm when he saw Charn Nol, always soft-spoken, slap a man across the mouth, yank him to his feet, and berate him loudly. As the man sullenly began to clean his rifle, Charn Nol moved to the next.

Looking around, Mark saw Mun Sin, Nar Rang, and even the Thai PARU, Dechar, haranguing and shoving at others. Mark caught Charn's arm as he was aiming another blow at an apathetic rifleman.

"Charn, what's happened? I know the men are tired; Christ, we all are. But why now? Hell, don't they know we're barely twenty klicks from the airfield and a fast trip home?"

Charn Nol relaxed suddenly and turned to face the stocky American. "Home, Khun Mark? We have almost a hundred sixty men. Nearly forty are wounded. What can one little airplane do?"

"One airplane? Oh, my sweet Christ! Charn, Banchert has *all* of Pranet's planes, sitting, waiting at Ubol. Plus his own little birds. We *all* go out, wounded first, with room to spare. But first we have to get these zombies down there!"

Mark's last words were lost as Charn Nol turned, cupped his hands, and began shouting in Cambodian. The reaction was immediate. His apparently exhausted men rose from the ground, shouting and waving like children suddenly let out of school early. They surrounded Mark, each trying to grasp his hand or merely touch him, like eager fans mobbing their favorite rock star. Then shouts from Charn Nol and Mun Sin broke up the amazing demonstration, and they finished their assigned tasks as if they had just awakened, instead of having been driving and fighting for over twenty-four hours.

Mark grinned through the tears streaming unheeded down his face as his three ex–Khmer Rouge leaders patted him roughly in turn.

"Goddamn it, you guys," he growled. "How the hell could you think I'd ever run out on you—after all we've been through? I don't care if we have to fight all the way to the bloody border—we all go, or nobody goes!"

CHAPTER THIRTY-SIX

WITH GARY STILL DRIVING THE OLD SHERMAN, MARK LED the way down. Leung hadn't understated the condition of the twisting, narrow road. It was more of a wide trail carved from the steep ridges. Strewn with fallen rocks, it wound around hairpin turns, which Gary had to back and fill to negotiate, with Mark guiding him from behind as he ground the Sherman's gears from first to reverse and back. For all their slow pace and caution, they were sickened as a truck with half their remaining fuel either lost its brakes or slipped out of gear and plunged over the side. Only two men jumped clear. Fourteen rode to their death, hundreds of feet down the ridge.

Finally the road became less steep and the hairpins fewer. Near the bottom, Mark had Mun Sin used their three remaining cratering charges to literally drop a section of hairpin, insuring no possibility of pursuit. Then Mark's stomach tightened again as a sudden outburst of firing came from the area beyond the burning houses. The old French fort was still in enemy hands.

Mark stopped Gary on a small rise about four kilometers from the town. He could see the dim outline of the old fort, and occasional muzzle flashes from the defenders' guns. "Unoccupied, eh?" Mark muttered firmly to himself. "Must be under new management." Then he jumped down and waved Nar Rang and the surviving SP off the road.

"Just aim over the barrel, Nar Rang. Give them airbursts. Slowly, about five or six a minute, as soon as the rest of us get down to the village. When you see Mun Sin and me start with the tank guns, give them ground bursts until we start moving again. Then back to airbursts. Don't want to get hit with our own stuff—the airbursts won't bother the tanks. Not much, anyway."

Mark moved the rest of his ragged force forward to the edge of the town. Screened from the fort by the burning village, he stopped, dismounted, and waved the others to him. From the edge of the village, two figures ran toward them shouting in Vietnamese. Mark peered and then recognized Colonel Leung's medic and his old student, Vietnamese Special Forces Captain Tranh Long.

"Colonel Mark, thank God you got here!"

"Tranh, what's going on?"

The slim figure in the familiar Aussie slouch hat threw his hands high. "Khmer Rouge sent in over a hundred men and two armored cars this morning. We have the field, and what's left of the bridge. Your colonel, the Chinese, was very brave. He knocked out both the armored cars for us."

Mark's stomach had reacted to the past tense. He interrupted, "*Was*, Tranh? What happened?"

"We tried to take the fort, sir. He hit a mine, but kept on firing. The APC hit another one. Most of them got out, because he stayed to cover them. Then the enemy hit his tank with a recoil-less, and it burned. Only this man here, the medic, got out. And we were driven back."

"How many men have you, Tranh?"

"About forty, Colonel. We started with almost one hundred."

Mark and the others turned their heads away from the anguish on the little captain's face. Sixty out of one hundred was too painful to think about. Mark's voice was soft as he gripped the captain's arms. "We'll make goddamn sure they weren't wasted, Tranh."

Then years of command took over. He gave orders quickly.
"We can't waste any time getting fancy. As you can hear,
Nar Rang's giving them airbursts to keep their heads down.
Charn, you and Lart Om take all the riflemen except six for
Mun Sin and me. Go with Captain Tranh around the right
side of the village and wait. Mun Sin and I will go around
the left edge of the houses, hit 'em with everything we've got
until Nar Rang switches to airbursts. Then we'll run right
over the damn fort. As soon as we start shooting, move your
men up. Put the APC in front, but don't fire until you have
to or if you see we can't make it. Got it?"

As his men moved out, Mark gave Pranee a brief message
for Banchert:

ATTACKING FORT 0520 HOURS. SUCCESS UNSURE.
LEAVING PRANEE AND OPERATOR TO SIGNAL RESULTS.

Mark bellowed down Pranee's refusal to leave him, pointing out that if the attack failed, Banchert would have to be
warned or the planes would fly into certain fire from the fort.
Sobbing pitifully, she hugged her big husband and smothered
his dust- and grease-masked face with kisses before he forced
her arms away and followed the sole survivor of Colonel
Leung's fifteen men up into the ancient Sherman.

With Mun Sin fifty yards to his left, Mark guided Gary
into position within plain sight of the fort, less than two thousand meters away. Mun Sin waved from the turret of the
hulking T-34 before he slid down inside. The blast of the
long 85-mm made Mark wince.

Through his gunsight, Mark noted that Nar Rang had
switched from airbursts as his own gun jolted in recoil. With
an oath, he suddenly remembered the little boy. But it was
too late; besides, the bow .30-caliber was spitting a steady
stream in unison with Sanit's turret .50 and his own coaxial
machine gun. After five rounds from each tank, Mark ordered
Gary forward.

At a thousand yards Mark had to search hard for return
fire. The 105's were still making orange splashes over the

fort. At five hundred he jerked Sanit's leg to get him down inside the turret and buttoned up.

Gary gunned the ancient veteran as fast as it would go. On the right were the still-burning hulks of the M-24 and the APC. The tank pitched over a sand-bagged emplacement as one of the 105's burst directly overhead and made their ears ring. Shards of metal clanged off the turret and hull. Mark tried to keep his head jammed tightly against the periscope padding as Gary slammed into and over unseen obstacles. Then Gary slowed, and they were riding smoothly.

Mark peered through his sun-crazed periscope and saw only a final battered tangle of barbed wire in front. Swinging the turret, Mark scanned to the left, saw the bulk of Mun Sin's T-34, and then to his rear the uneven outline of the remains of the old fort. All resistance seemed to have stopped.

Cautiously, Mark raised the heavy hatch cover and, when this drew no fire, opened it fully and stood up, half his body exposed, as he swept the area. Dawn was coming fast. He could already make out the figures of some of Charn Nol's men, as well as Mun Sin's tank. He told Gary to turn back to the fort. He and Sanit in the other hatch watched for any sign of remaining enemy. Off to his left Mark heard a short burst of AK-47 fire that ceased abruptly. Then, as he turned his head back, the Sherman heaved upward! The last thing he felt was a blast of dirt and hot air as he was thrown out of the turret.

Pranee remained with the radioman in the jeep as her husband and the chunky Mun Sin drove toward the firing that still spurted from the fort. She could follow their progress easily by the flash of the tank guns and the streams of angry red tracers that wove threads between the remaining Khmer Rouge defenders and the two tanks. When they were close to the fort itself, and the defender's fire had begun to slacken noticeably, Pranee urged the battered jeep forward over the rough field until she was barely a few hundred feet from the smoking wreck of Colonel Leung's tank. By the time she was past it and the sickening stench of burned flesh, the firing to her front had died to occasional brief flurries of automatic rifle fire. In the faint predawn light, she told the radioman to send the message she had prepared to inform Colonel Banchert that it was now safe to land his evacuation planes across the river on the airfield.

The operator flashed a grin and a thumbs-up signal as he heard the answer. Then there was a heavy crumping explosion. Pranee screamed as she saw the ugly orange blossom right under Mark's tank. Horrified, through the smoke and dust of the explosion she saw a dark blur fall from the turret—Mark!

As she slammed the jeep into gear, Pranee's foot jammed the gas pedal to the floor, and the jeep responded with a convulsive leap that threw the unsuspecting radioman out and to the ground. Pranee never noticed him. She drove the jeep up and through the remains of sandbagged emplacements and dead bodies as if they didn't exist. A bare twenty yards from the silent tank, the jeep struck heavily and stopped, hung up, then stalled out.

Pranee abandoned it and ran, stumbling over debris and tangles of barbed wire, to where Mark lay motionless beside the tank's tread. With shaking hands she felt his chest. Oh, wonderful Buddha! The beat was strong and regular, but her forearm was bloody from touching Mark's face. Pranee lifted her head and eyes to the grayish-pink sky as she murmured a prayer of thanks. Lifting her head to give thanks saved her life. As her glance swept back down, she saw a blurred movement at the front of the tank, to her right. The blur became a man in black, face contorted as he aimed his rifle and pulled the trigger with a convulsive yank. Paralyzed with fear, Pranee's mind refused to grasp the deadly reality until she heard a faint metallic click. The gun was empty!

The tiny click galvanized her into action. As she watched the enemy soldier, who wasted a vital few seconds examining his rifle, Pranee's feverishly searching hands found her husband's sheathed Bowie knife, strapped as always to his calf.

She struggled with mud-caked strap as the Khmer Rouge stopped fumbling with his rifle and started forward, rifle held high to deliver a downward smashing butt stroke. Pranee's

small hands finally wrenched the big knife free. She lurched
to a crouch, knife held in front of her in both hands. She was
moving sideways when the grimacing Khmer Rouge's rifle
and arms were suddenly encumbered by a tiny, screaming,
sobbing, scratching figure. The little boy, whose American
friends had nicknamed him "Mike," forced the Khmer Rouge
to drop his rifle in an effort to protect his face and eyes from
Mike's raking fingers. With his hands raised, Pranee dove
forward instinctively, the big Bowie still held in outstretched
hands.

Had Pranee been a trained knife fighter, she might have
missed. Because she wasn't, she simply dove forward. She
felt only slight resistance as the sharp point sliced through
the cotton shirt, the skin, and then was torn from her grasp
by the shock when it hit bone, and the enemy soldier's body
twisted!

It didn't matter. The soldier's last movement completed the
deadly thrust. Pranee never forgot the look of incredulity,
overlaid by terror, as he slumped and died.

CHAPTER THIRTY-SEVEN

DESPITE SOMBOON'S INSISTENCE THAT COLONEL BANCHERT wanted them to leave immediately in the shiny Twin Beech he had flown in to pick them up, Mark refused to leave until the last of "his" men were loaded. When only Captain Tranh and his unwounded men were left, Mark shook hands and then saluted the tough little Vietnamese.

"You've got all the guts in the world, Tranh—and then some. Sure you won't come out for at least a couple of weeks? We can drop you guys back in again."

"No, Colonel Mark. With your trucks and the jeep, we can make good time back to the mountains. Our fight is only beginning. Just send us supplies and any of my men who wish to come back. Good-bye for now, sir."

Airborne finally, they were all silent, gripped by the mental lethargy that follows the adrenaline depleting stress of combat. Gary, in the right-hand seat, straightened up as he saw the welcome muddy expanse of the Mekong River. Even then he sat and stared wordlessly until ten thousand hours of discipline alerted his overtaxed senses.

"Hey, Somboon! I thought I taught you cross-country navigation better than this. You'll never get to Ubol on this course."

Somboon squirmed uneasily and averted his glance from

his former instructor as he said, "We're not going to Ubol, Khun Gary. My orders are to fly all of you directly to Takli."

"Takli?" Both Mark and Gary spoke together.

"Yes, Colonel Mark. Takli."

Despite their physical and mental fatigue, both men came suddenly alert, as did Pranee and Charn Nol. Sitting beside Somboon, Gary saw from his former student's expression that an inner conflict was raging. He and Mark waited for the explanation, which came in a sudden torrent.

"Colonel Mark, Khun Gary. Things are very bad! I only know a little, but everything has changed—down in Bangkok."

"Changed, Somboon? How?" Mark asked gently.

"I don't understand it myself, Colonel Mark. After you started coming north, I think something happened that made the prime minister and the National Security Council people angry—or maybe afraid. Anyway, I know General Pranet and Colonel Banchert were very upset and worried. That was late last night, when we were waiting to hear if you would make it to the airfield.

"It was a little after midnight when all of us pilots were told there was a new plan. We were all to fly from where we picked you up directly to Takli, and then stand by."

Again, Mark and Gary sounded like a duet as they exclaimed, "What the hell . . . ?" and exchanged puzzled glances.

"That's all I know—what I just told you." Somboon's features mirrored his personal anguish and worry as he turned his head.

The others were silent for a long time, each trying to flog an already overtaxed brain into finding some logical explanation. After twenty minutes of silence, Somboon suddenly sat upright and, with his left hand, fished out a bottle of Hennessy brandy as he apologized.

"I forgot; General Pranet told me to give this to you."

The fiery brandy made them all feel a little better, but even its stimulus was no help in finding an answer to the unknown change of plan and what had caused it. They were still silently mulling it over as Somboon greased the little Beech onto the runway at Takli and taxied to the former CIA parking area, where an ambulance and a jeep were parked.

Their concern was deepened when they saw only the short, muscular figure of the paratroop general sitting in the jeep. With only a muttered greeting and a warm hand clasp, General Pranet hurried them into the ambulance and then followed it to the weatherbeaten little dispensary. Inside, he refused to discuss anything until Mark's and Charn Nol's wounds, and Gary's ankle, had been treated. The two police doctors and their nurses put a dozen stitches in Mark's head and restrapped his lame shoulder, which they said had probably been dislocated.

Charn Nol's muscular forearm and bicep were cleaned and sewed up where bullets had plowed furrows. While one doctor strapped Gary's ankle, which a quick X ray showed only sprained, not broken, the other doctor examined Pranee and the still-sleeping Mike. His frail body had collapsed into a deep sleep in Mark's lap before the Beech had even taken off.

Impatiently, the four agreed to take quick baths and change into clean clothes from their suitcases, which ominously were waiting for them inside the small ward.

Mark and Gary were fuming in frustration. Pranee and Charn Nol were less demonstratively impatient when General Pranet finally reappeared. The mingled anger and inner worry his face reflected carried over to his voice as he spoke in short, spitting phrases.

"I am very ashamed of my people, Colonel Mark, all of them! They are like rabbits. But I can do nothing. Believe me, I have tried every possible way."

The tough little general waved off Mark's and Gary's questions as he continued. "Look, somehow, I don't know how, both the Chinese and the Vietnamese ambassadors have found out about Indian Movie. Both Banchert and I are sick about it, because we feel it must have come from one, or maybe even two, Communist agents in either his group or mine. It doesn't matter now. The damage is done.

"Early this morning, both the Communist ambassadors

woke up the prime minister and accused him of using Indian Movie to stir up trouble between their countries. The Chinese were speaking for the Cambodians, because we have no relations with those scum. They were very angry, and they made many threats—I don't know exactly what, but they were very bad.

"They had hardly left when the American ambassador appeared. He was also furious. He threatened to stop all American aid to Thailand. It seems the two Communist ambassadors had talked to him first. They accused the CIA of being behind Indian Movie. Of course, neither he nor the CIA had even heard of it."

General Pranet's hurried words brought understanding, painful understanding, to his four listeners. Indian Movie had been betrayed. The desperate battles . . . the dozens of dead and wounded who had sacrificed in vain. Reading their faces, Pranet continued in a soft, apologetic tone.

"Don't blame yourselves, my good friends. The fault is not with you or with what you did. Indian movie *was* a good operation. And you carried it out perfectly. But—"

"Christ on a crutch, Pranet," Mark burst out. "No wonder there's so much fuss. Goddamn it all! I don't blame the prime minister for being pissed. What a mess!" Then he straightened. "Okay, Indian Movie is blown wide open and skyhigh. Now what? Where's Banchert?"

For the first time ever, Mark saw fear in Pranet's face. He held his finger to his lips, and checking to make sure no one else was within hearing, he whispered. "You will meet him very soon. But first listen to me. I have been ordered to hold you under arrest until the CID people come to take charge. But I will not do what I have been ordered! Not if they kill me. I lied to the CID. I told them you would be taken to Korat with the others. Don't worry, they will not be bothered by the CID. They are only *pu noi*, little people.

But you four, and I guess the little boy—you want to take him with you? All right, he is a child; I will take care. I have your passports, Mark and Gary, and Thai ones for Pranee and Charn Nol, all stamped with exit visas." Pranet's face broke into a brief smile as he said, "My old friend Banchert is very thorough, and his men—except for the traitors—are loyal. A C-123 is parked outside on the strip. It is full of my men. They are going to Satun, to relieve others at the border garrison. The plane will not land at Satun until after it lands you in Alor Star, just across the Malaysian border. We go there often, so there will be no trouble with the authorities. They all know me well. You just tell them you are going on vacation and my plane gave you a free ride, to save you money. Now you must go quickly, before the CID learn you are here."

Inside the high-tailed C-123, the blue-clad paratroopers greeted Mark, Mike in his arms, with wide grins. As the tail ramp lifted, all four waved to Pranet until it closed, and the big plane began lumbering out to the runway.

They were halfway down the runway when a figure in the uniform of a Thai Air Force Air Police corporal, sitting across from them, removed an oversize pair of sunglasses, smiled, and waved. All four stared in surprise as they recognized Colonel Banchert in the unfamiliar uniform.

Glancing around him quickly, Banchert put his finger to his lips imploringly. The four exchanged quick glances and ignored Banchert for the remainder of the long flight.

They lost sight of him at the small Customs and Immigration shack at Alor Star, where their passports were cursorily examined and quickly stamped. As they were waved through customs by a smiling official, Mark saw the Thai colonel, now wearing dungarees and a vividly patterned sport shirt, waiting outside. Still wordlessly, but without his former cautious attitude, Banchert strolled the few yards to the little Malaysian Airways passenger terminal. Inside, he opened a flight bag, after carefully placing his other baggage, a good-sized, well-traveled attaché case, between his legs. With a tight smile, he withdrew a sheaf of airplane tickets and handed them to Mark.

"You see, my teacher, your old pupil remembered your excellent advice to always have a contingency plan. Here are round-the-world tickets from Kuala Lumpur, plus one-way from here to KL. You can probably get a refund for the little boy's; I got an extra adult ticket—just in case?''

Mark accepted the tickets with a formal palms-joined Thai wai of thanks, which the others emulated.

''Things must have really come unglued, Banchert. How come?'' Mark asked.

The trim colonel's face darkened in sudden anger as he replied. ''Communist penetrations. There is one, probably two of my men, who have sold out to the Chinese or the Vietnamese. I am shamed by them. I forgot another of your lessons, my teacher—never grow overconfident about security. I did. This is the price.''

EPILOGUE

My fictional story ends in the late spring of 1978, just before the rainy season. Relations between Cambodia (renamed Kampuchea) and Vietnam were already strained then. During the 1978 monsoon, the Khmer Rouge (according to Thai intelligence reports) drew increasing numbers of soldiers from the Thai border, to reinforce their eastern border with Vietnam. Each country engaged in small-scale border intrusions and vitriolic public accusations—this despite the supposed common bonds of Communism.

By December 1978, as the new dry season began, border clashes grew in size and intensity. Then, on Christmas Day, the Vietnamese launched an all-out invasion. Tough North Vietnamese regular troops, well supported by armor and artillery and covered by a blanket of fighter-bombers, used a cosmetic National Liberation Front composed of Cambodian exiles as a weak cover for their assault.

The results were worthy of a Rommel or Guderian—within a mere twelve days the Vietnamese army occupied eighty percent of Cambodia! The few Khmer Rouge leaders, the Angkha Leou, who weren't killed fled the country.

While the Khmer Rouge's patrons, the Chinese, wrung their hands in angry frustration, the Vietnamese regime's new allies, the Soviets, chortled. But the remaining free countries in Southeast Asia braced themselves in fear they might be next.

If there *was* a Thai operation along the lines of my fictional Indian Movie, it succeeded too well! Preoccupation with their eastern border certainly did remove much of the Khmer Rouge pressure on the Thais. But by what might be called "over-achieving," Thailand has gone from the frying pan of the Khmer Rouge maniacs to the fire of the Soviet-backed Vietnamese. Worse, they are being overwhelmed by the massive numbers of refugees who continue to escape their new masters, and the pockets of jungle controlled by Khmer Rouge.

Tragic little Cambodia is now, for the third time, a battleground. But this time for the pawns of the two huge Communist superpowers, China and Russia. China's brief, inconclusive 1979 invasion of North Vietnam, and her present heavy support to *anyone* fighting the Vietnamese, are balanced by massive Russian support to their puppet, Vietnam.

In a sense, Thailand, on purpose or accidentally, is again in a "King Mongut" posture—while the Chinese and Soviet "proxies" fight each other next door. But they are paying the price in unexpected ways—the costs of feeding, housing, and controlling their six hundred thousand or more refugees are enormous. Worse, the fighting constantly threatens to spill over into their country.

ABOUT THE AUTHOR

HUGH MCCAFFREY'S FATHER WAS A COLONEL IN THE U.S. army, a fact that early cemented his interest in the military. After graduation from LaSalle Military Academy, he attended Harvard University, where he ran cross-country.

During World War II he served as a sergeant in the Pacific before being nominated by the men in his company for officer training. After graduating from the "Benning School for Boys," he served as an infantry officer in the Pacific Theater for 122 days, where he was twice decorated.

Following service in the Korean War, Hugh McCaffrey went on special assignment to Thailand, remaining 22 years and learning to speak Thai fluently. There he became a Buddhist and raised four daughters. An avid sailor, Hugh raced his own boat against the King of Thailand at Pataya.

After the death of his first wife, Hugh married Kitti Ping Yung and lived in Hawaii, where he worked as a computer programmer.